THE RELUCTANT ASSASSIN SERIES BOOKS 4-5

FAHRENHEIT KUWAIT / TARGET: NEW YORK

LEE JACKSON

Severn River
PUBLISHING

Severn River Publishing
www.SevernRiverBooks.com

This is a work of fiction. Names, characters, businesses, places, events and incidents are either the products of the author's imagination or used in a fictitious manner. Any resemblance to actual persons, living or dead, or actual events is purely coincidental.

ISBN: 978-1-64875-800-3 (Paperback)

ALSO BY LEE JACKSON

The Reluctant Assassin Series

The Reluctant Assassin

Rasputin's Legacy

Vortex: Berlin

Fahrenheit Kuwait

Target: New York

The After Dunkirk Series

After Dunkirk

Eagles Over Britain

Turning the Storm

The Giant Awakens

Riding the Tempest

Driving the Wave

Never miss a new release! Sign up to receive exclusive updates from author Lee Jackson.

severnriverbooks.com/authors/lee-jackson

FAHRENHEIT KUWAIT

To my wonderful family.
We've always been there for each other.

MAJOR CHARACTERS

Code Name Atcho: aka Eduardo Xiquez
Klaus aka Sahab Kadyrov: Chechen Terrorist
Sofia Stahl: Atcho's Wife
Burly Retired: CIA Officer
Tony Collins: Investigative Reporter
Ivan Chekov: Former Soviet KGB Officer
Rafael: Cuban Freedom Fighter
Major Joe Horton: US Army Intelligence Officer
Kadir: *Hawaladar* in Berlin
Hassan: *Hawaladar* in Libya
Yousef: *Hawaladar* in Riyadh
Detective Berger: Berlin Police Force
Gerhardt: German Federal Intelligence
Dr. Burakgazi: Orthopedic Surgeon in Berlin

PROLOGUE

Berlin, November 9, 1989

Dawn burst over Berlin, turning the skies a flaming red. Tony Collins, investigative reporter for the *Washington Herald,* had remained all night at his position on the border at Checkpoint Charlie watching a human drama unfold.

In a thrilling reversal of policy that had existed in East Germany since the end of World War II and had been enforced at the point of machine guns, the Berlin Wall had opened for all East and West Germans, allowing them to cross freely to the opposite side of the Wall. Effectively, the border between East and West Germany had been erased.

All night, Collins had stood at Checkpoint Charlie with his cameraman, interviewing East and West Berliners as they crossed both ways to greet long unseen family members and friends. He watched people as they wept over the joy of familial intimacy after so many decades of forced separation; and as they grieved the lost time and wasted lives of departed souls, the result of a cruel dictatorship, now vanquished.

Collins broadcast his live reports to a breathless world. The crowds that came by him were buoyant and friendly. Some people did not care to be interviewed but the overwhelming majority, when they saw him with his cameraman and the bright lights, at least waved and called to him, and many stopped to share their newfound freedom with a worldwide audience.

One man passed by whom at first, Collins barely noticed. He was of medium height, wore a thickly padded jacket, and his dark hair was unkempt. He made a beeline toward Collins and his cameraman, and as he passed, he called to them. "Thank you. Thank you, America. I love America. I am going to America."

Collins beamed and waved back. "Would you like to speak to the camera?" The man grinned to decline and kept walking. Collins watched him go, wondering what life the man had come from and what life he would lead now. He was alone, and the reporter watched him until he disappeared into the crowd, noting that nothing about the man distinguished him from any other East German intending to stay in the West, except he carried two duffle bags, one slung over each shoulder. *Maybe his life's possessions.*

When Collins turned back to the east side of the city, another man briefly caught his attention because he avoided not just the camera, but the lights themselves. He was nondescript except that he looked in remarkable physical shape, and he walked rapidly compared to the rest of the crowd. However, his facial expression showed an attempt to hide extreme pain. He shot Collins a look of contempt but as he did so, his pain seemed to surge, because he stopped and set down a suitcase he had carried in his left hand. Now oblivious to Collins' observation, he reached into his jacket with his good hand and tended to his right shoulder, which seemed to be heavily bandaged. Then he picked up the suitcase again, recommenced his trek, and disappeared into the crowd.

Collins sighed. *Another new beginning.*

1

Berlin, November 10, 1989—The morning after the Wall fell.

Klaus hurried through the crowds of celebrating Berliners, away from the news reporter and his cameraman at Checkpoint Charlie. The notion that the term "East Berliners" was no longer accurate did not escape him. Now, they were simply "Berliners."

People danced in the middle of what had been, only yesterday, the kill zone. For the umpteenth time, Klaus stopped among the masses and set his suitcase down. Gingerly, he looked inside his jacket at his shattered shoulder. He had managed to apply a home remedy coagulant to stop the bleeding and had wrapped a rough bandage around it and secured it under his arm. Nevertheless, blood seeped through. If he did not get medical attention soon, not only would his appearance be noticed, but infection would set in.

He set his jaw against the pain, picked up his bag, and started out again. He walked at a fast pace not only because that was his nature, but also because of the need to see a doctor. Furthermore, he carried a precious cargo in his luggage and expected that bad people would soon be looking for him, if they were not already.

He was almost unmindful of the merriment around him. He jostled anyone who slowed his progress, but he was careful to keep hidden the pistol he carried in his belt.

People turned to look at him, a fearsome sight. He was medium height, with a day's growth of whiskers. His surly glance warned away anyone who showed curiosity or was hesitant or obstinate about moving out of his way. He knew where he wanted to go and needed to pass only a few more streets before he made his turn.

Then ahead, the figure of a particular man caught his attention. The man blended with the crowd and was unremarkable except for two duffle bags he carried, one on each shoulder.

Pain forgotten, Klaus' pulse raced. He stepped up his pace and closed the distance, his eyes locked on the bags, examining them. Certain that they were the specific ones he knew about, he slowed his pace to stay near the man. The ache in his shoulder increased again. He ignored it and trudged on.

The sun moved high in the sky. Klaus had been up for thirty-six hours with little to eat. Besides his badly wounded shoulder, the suitcase had become a dead weight. He had intended to go straight to an apartment where supporters lived on the west side of Berlin, but having seen those two duffle bags, he pursued, determined not to let them out of his sight until he could retrieve them.

The man who carried them continued walking until the crowd had thinned at its extremities. Then he looked around as though searching for something. He was in a residential section of the former West Berlin that mixed with some light commerce, including *gasthauses,* the German version of bed-and-breakfasts. He selected one that appeared clean and tidy. He did not seem to be familiar with the place, because he stood outside studying it, and even turned and observed two others in close proximity.

Klaus watched him, and when the man walked through the front entrance, Klaus found a side access. It was locked. Klaus had little time to think or improvise, so he took the quickest action he could—he broke one of the windowpanes in the door. Reaching inside, he found the knob on the deadbolt, turned it, and let himself in. He was in a short, empty hall. At the other end, it turned into a long, dark corridor leading off to his right. On his left was a set of stairs, obviously set against the back wall of the building.

From down the hall, he heard the murmur of voices at the reception desk. Then briefly, he saw his quarry head toward him and turn slightly to his right. Moments later, the man climbed another set of wooden stairs at the front of the building.

Klaus turned and slipped up the back stairs, careful to make as little noise as possible. He paused so he could observe over the top step. He did not worry about being seen. The stairwell was dark.

Still carrying the duffle bags, the other man moved down the hall and stopped in front of a door. He inserted a key into the lock and entered.

Klaus flew up the remaining stairs and down the corridor to the man's room. Before the door closed, he crashed through with his good shoulder. Using his suitcase as a battering ram, he thrust it into his quarry's startled face. The man fell back. Klaus shoved a foot behind his ankle, dropping him backwards to the floor. The man landed on the duffle bags still hanging from his back.

Klaus kicked hard into his victim's kidneys. When the man doubled up in pain, Klaus let go of the suitcase, kicked his head, and continued kicking until there was no movement. Then he grabbed a pillow from the bed and threw it across the beaten face. He drew his pistol and pushed the barrel deep into the pillow next to the man's temple. When he pulled the trigger, only a muffled explosion sounded. The body lay in a pool of blood.

Quickly, gingerly, Klaus pulled the duffle bags from under the limp body. Blood had spilled onto them. The agony in Klaus' own injured shoulder suddenly became almost overwhelming, and he sat heavily at the end of the bed, his breath coming in short gasps. Perspiration streamed from his forehead and neck and down into his shirt. Some seeped into his wound, with stinging salt adding to excruciating pain. *Can't stop.*

He dragged the duffle bags to a sink in the room and cleaned off the blood. Then he did the same with his boots. When finished, he set both duffle bags at the end of the bed, sat down again, and opened them. He peered inside. *So, that's what five million dollars in cash looks like.*

Klaus struggled with the two duffle bags and his suitcase through the side streets of Berlin to Little Istanbul, a Muslim area in former West Berlin. The pain in his right shoulder was excruciating, but he staved off anyone showing curiosity with a fierce look, backed by showing his pistol. Blood caked over his shoulder and right arm added to the effect.

He went to an apartment building and descended a set of stairs to the basement. Ignoring pain, he searched in the dark confines until he found a well-hidden niche that could accommodate the duffle bags and his suitcase. Before leaving them, he opened one of the bags and pulled out four bound stacks of cash. He put two in each of his jacket pockets. Then he staggered upstairs to the apartment.

When he stumbled in, he found several men sitting cross-legged in a circle on the floor drinking mint tea. Seeing his condition, several jumped to their feet and helped him to a bed in another room. Soft Turkish music played.

Klaus collapsed on the bed. "Turn off the music," he gasped. He pulled two one-hundred-dollar bills from his pockets. "Get some pain medicine." He handed the money to one of them. "I can't go to a hospital. Find a nurse or doctor who will come here."

Mercifully, he swooned, and when he awoke, at least a day had gone by. A man and a woman sat at the end of the bed. He recognized neither of them.

"I am Abdul Kareem," the man introduced himself. "This is my sister Zohra. She is a nurse." He spoke gravely. "You need major treatment, or you will lose that arm."

Klaus stirred, barely comprehending. His shoulder throbbed, and he saw through bleary eyes that it had been heavily bandaged. He tried to pull his mind from a fog but felt incapable of coherent thought.

"The bones in your shoulder were destroyed," Abdul told him. "You should be moved to a hospital."

"No," he gasped. He fell unconscious again.

Two weeks later, Klaus managed to stay awake longer than a few minutes at a time. He became aware that he had been bathed and his shoulder cleaned and dressed regularly. His clothes had been washed, and his money neatly stacked in a drawer with an accounting of how it had been spent, mostly for medicine.

———

A month passed. Klaus was on his feet and moving about. The pain subsided but became excruciating if he bumped his arm or tried to move it. When not bound in a tight sling, the limb hung limply at his side.

While he convalesced, he nursed hatred for all things Western, particularly the man responsible for his shoulder wound—a man called Atcho. Atcho had also killed his brother.

As mental acuity returned, Klaus wanted to know about news events. "Did the Wall open permanently?"

His hosts assured him that it had. "People go back and forth freely every day. East Germans are moving into West Germany by the thousands. The entire East German government leadership resigned the day after the Wall opened. Helmut Kohl, the West German chancellor, is negotiating with the interim East German government to reunite the country."

Klaus did not know how to assess that piece of news. Before the Wall came down, preserving it had seemed to be of paramount importance as a means to maintain alliances, control the population, and have a ready supply of oppressed people for East German leaders and their Soviet masters to manipulate to their advantage. However, with five million dollars and a whole new world for Klaus to move around in—not to mention a nuclear bomb at his disposal—the possibilities seemed endless. *Allah will be very happy with me.*

But first things first. He had to heal and recover strength. He would need identification for Western countries. Finally, he had to secure his money in a way that it could be moved easily. *I need a good* hawala. When all that was done, he could worry about undergoing surgery.

Klaus felt comfortable moving about Berlin's underworld. Despite the changing status of the two halves of Berlin, the city remained a hotbed of espionage, and with that came active black-market services. He knew only too well what they were, how to get them, and the dangers they presented. In his weakened state, those dangers were magnified as surely as vultures hovered around a dying carcass. He knew how to handle that as well. He kept his pistol within easy reach.

When he felt strong enough, Klaus sought out a reliable *hawala,* a service that moved money instantaneously anywhere in the world. The system was ancient and relied on trust. A *hawala* at each end of the transaction kept immense amounts of cash handy and hired effective security. To cross one was to die a slow and painful death. Conversely, for a *hawala* to cheat a client invited the end of the business and a violent end to its service providers.

When a client needed to send money, he would go to a local *hawala,* where he would pay the sum required to cover the transaction costs added to the amount to be sent. A phone call to a *hawala* near the cash recipient completed the transaction. The client there immediately received cash. The *hawaladars,* the people operating the *hawalas,* settled between themselves.

The system allowed for untraceable movements of cash, perfect for Klaus' purposes. To contact one, he turned to the Berlin Mosque on Brienner Strazze. The mosque had been in place since 1923 and served a large congregation. Klaus had begun attending sermons, making quiet inroads, and taking pains to become acquainted with the imam.

After a couple of months, when the feeling of familiarity had settled in, Klaus gradually enhanced the quality of his clothes and appearance to be perceived as a businessman. When he felt confident in his associations, he went into the basement of the apartment building and pulled a large sum of money from one of his duffle bags, made his way to the mosque and delivered a generous contribution.

He and the imam drank tea together. They spoke on various subjects. At a propitious moment, Klaus told the imam, "I'm prospering in the West. I want to expand my business to other countries. Will you please recommend the best *hawaladar* and make introductions?"

When that arrangement was complete, and Klaus had delivered his cash into the safe hands of a *hawaladar* named Kadir, he made another contribution to the mosque. This time he asked the imam to recommend a surgeon in Berlin whose practice included shoulder replacement. "The doctor must be Muslim. I don't want infidel hands on my body. But he must also be competent."

The imam promised to find the best surgeon meeting those criteria. Meanwhile, Klaus sought out less savory elements of the mosque, those familiar with illicit activity in Berlin, particularly high-quality forgery. Within weeks, he purchased stolen and superbly altered passports and drivers' licenses complete with associated credit cards—the documents he needed to travel smoothly around the world with only normal scrutiny. They were attributable to multiple aliases.

A few days later, the imam called. "I set you up for an appointment with the best Islamic orthopedic surgeon in Berlin, Dr. Burakgazi. He's expecting your call."

2

Austin, Texas, January 1991—Fourteen months after the Wall fell.

"Not only no, but hell no! I won't stand for it. You've done enough."
Sofia's eyes blazed, and Atcho knew that now was not the time to discuss
the matter further. He did not have much more to tell her anyway and
knew her sense of duty would compel her to accept what must be—but
later. He leaned across the table, picked up her hand, and kissed it.

They were in a restaurant in downtown Austin. It was a quaint niche
in an old historic building with a downstairs foyer and an upstairs dining
area that doubled as a quiet bar with warm Texas chic. Since making the
move from Washington, DC, it had become a favorite spot. It's location
and price tab made it a good place for privacy, and its atmosphere and
great food made it desirable. Atcho had chosen it for this conversation to
prepare her for forthcoming news which, at the moment, was only a
hunch.

Sofia's reaction was expected. Her hunch matched Atcho's.

They finished their meal. Atcho rose to his feet. "I have to go to that
meeting. I'll be home in time for dinner."

Sofia stared at him distantly, and then nodded. "I'll be there," she
said, and added softly, "maybe I'll have news of my own."

A cold January wind blew through the streets as Atcho walked to his car. Thirty minutes later, he entered a secure conference room on the manufacturing compound of the company he had purchased nearly two years earlier. It was situated in a flat area a mile behind the cliffs of Mt. Bonnell, near Lake Austin in the Hill Country surrounding Texas' capital city.

A big man with a balding head stood to greet Atcho. He wore a serious expression that broke into a wide smile.

Atcho extended his hand. "Burly, how good to see you."

Burly ignored the hand and wrapped his arms around Atcho in a bear hug. "You can greet others with a handshake," he said. "We've been in too many scrapes together."

Atcho stepped back and looked up into the big, friendly face. "Yeah, and apparently you're here to get me into another one. Sofia is already steamed."

Burly shook his head sadly. "I'm surprised she doesn't hate me. You know I love her." He walked across to a buffet and poured himself a cup of coffee. Then he looked around the room. "I hate to think that every time I come to town or speak with you, she thinks I'm recruiting you into a black op." He leaned over the long conference table to scrutinize a piece of Texas bronze sculpture—a cowboy on a bucking bronco. "This sums up your life." He chuckled. "Maybe you could tell me about your company." He gazed around the room again. "These are impressive digs you've got here."

Atcho poured his own coffee. "There's not much to tell beyond what you already know. Our product is classified top secret because of the alloys and manufacturing methods we use, and it's of strategic importance to national security. The defense department is our customer. We don't sell to commercial companies except as they need our product to fill their government contracts. The protocols for distribution are tight. We don't let anyone come on this complex without a high security clearance."

"I know. Your people put me through the wringer to get in."

"We won't even meet with vendors here. If they want to pitch us or conduct contract admin stuff, we meet them off-campus."

"Do you still have just two products?"

"We have some projects in R&D, but nothing to be released anytime soon. I'm looking to expand into consumer goods, but the power source is still our primary product, and we're working round the clock to keep up with demand. The NUKEX has limited use. There just aren't that many suitcase nuclear bombs to disarm. The only units we sell are stored by various government agencies for 'what if' scenarios. Hope to God no one else ever has to use one."

Burly's eyebrows arched. "That was some incredible stuff you and Sofia pulled off in Siberia, disarming that one." He looked around the conference room again, taking in the rich rosewood paneling on the walls and the various pieces of distinctly Western paintings that adorned them. "You've adapted to Texas well." He chuckled. "You got your Stetson, Justins, and denims yet?"

Atcho smiled. "A Western shirt too, for when we go to the rodeo. Sofia tells me I look great in them—for a Cuban." His voice took on an edge. "We like it here. We're not anxious to leave."

"I know." Burly pulled out a chair and sat down at the table. "You're the chairman? That's impressive."

Atcho took a seat across from him. "Don't get too impressed. I know enough to be dangerous. I got this company because I made a better offer than the other suitors." He shrugged. "The founders were ready to expand out of start-up mode and needed second round financing. We were ready to leave DC."

"Your ties to the defense department didn't hurt. You open a lot of doors."

"And you just made my point," Atcho rejoined. "I'm not a techie. I barely understand the rudiments of what we do. I sold off a lot of my real estate holdings in DC to acquire controlling interest and buy our house here. I paid a premium to outbid the others trying to buy the company, and I happily agreed to limitations on how I could affect decisions. Frankly, the concerns and remedies the founders had on that score impressed me. I'm happy to let them run the business and keep me in the loop. We recruited some business operations and marketing expertise." He grinned slightly. "Maybe some of the smarts of the whole crew will rub off into my feeble brain."

"Then if you were away for an extended time, that wouldn't interrupt operations?"

Atcho sucked in his breath and locked his eyes on Burly's. "Sofia was right. When she heard you were not staying for dinner, she told me you were bringing me another mission. With the short heads-up, I thought so too. This isn't a social visit."

"Guilty." Burly stood to refill his coffee cup.

"They brought you out of CIA retirement. Again. To be my case officer. Again."

"The powers that be know you like to work with your own team."

Atcho shoved his chair back. He leaned over, rested his elbows on his knees, and brought one hand to his forehead. After a minute, he looked up at his big friend, still standing by the buffet. "Do you know that Sofia and I are trying to have a baby?"

Burly's face lit up. "That's great—"

Atcho cut him off. "I won't make her a black ops widow, and I don't have many summers left to pull off the baby-making achievement." He dropped his head again to stare at the floor. "If Sofia wasn't twelve years younger than me, we wouldn't have a chance. But it's late in the day even for her."

Burly contemplated Atcho, his face grave. "I'm sorry. You know I wouldn't have come if—"

"I know, I know," Atcho interrupted with a wave of his hand. "I'm the only guy on the planet who can pull it off. Whatever 'it' is."

Burly re-took his seat. He leaned across the table. "Atcho."

Atcho did not move except to drop his hand from his face and interlace his fingers between his knees. He remained silent.

"Atcho, please look at me."

Atcho raised his head, his eyes weary.

"Do you trust me?"

Atcho nodded somberly. "You know I do. You don't even have to ask."

"Then believe me when I tell you. You really are the only guy to get this done."

Atcho held Burly's steady gaze. "All right, give it to me. Tell me what's going on."

Burly took a deep breath. "Klaus surfaced. He's on the move."

3

Five months earlier, August 2, 1990—Nine months after the Berlin Wall opened.

Klaus waited outside his apartment building for a boy he had often seen there. He was a serious young man, diligent about religious studies. Although pleasant and respected among his peers, he rarely participated in their street games, preferring to sit nearby reading time-worn books. He and Klaus had crossed paths a few times and had engaged in light conversation.

On this day, the boy had crossed the street on return from school. "Onur," Klaus called. The young man waved and approached Klaus.

After greetings, Klaus put his good arm around Onur's shoulders. "I have a very important task and I need your help."

"Of course," Onur replied. "Tell me what you need. I will do my best."

Earlier that morning, Klaus had taken the suitcase from its hiding place and dusted it off. It set by his knee. "This is a very special piece of equipment," he said. "It's a highly sophisticated camera, but as you can see, it's camouflaged." Onur's eyes scrutinized the suitcase as Klaus spoke.

"I need pictures of a particular building in Berlin, but I can't take them myself. My face is too well-known. I need for you to do it for me.

I've seen that you are responsible and reliable. I want you to perform this task for me."

Klaus watched Onur closely while he spoke. He saw the boy's expression change from curiosity to veiled caution to being pleased as Klaus complimented him.

"What do you want me to do?"

"It's very simple. The technical aspects are set up. All you have to do is carry this suitcase to anywhere along the sidewalk on the opposite side of the street from the American Embassy. Stop and open it facing the embassy for no more than five seconds. Close it and bring it back to me."

Caution bordering on suspicion returned to Onur's face. "Please tell me you don't want me to blow myself up like the *intifada* martyrs in Palestine," he joked, but his laugh was uneasy. "I hope to be an imam."

"No, no," Klaus assured him. "If I intended you to be a martyr, I would have to tell you that, and you would have to do it willingly. My efforts are aimed at *jihad*."

He paused and looked around as if checking for anyone who might be listening. "We have someone inside the embassy who needs to pass on a piece of intelligence but can't get out to give it to us. It's time sensitive. That camera will take a high-density photo of the front of the embassy. We'll be able to magnify it enough to read the document. It'll be posted in one of the windows."

Onur was obviously impressed, but not convinced. "What if I'm caught?"

"Caught doing what? Carrying a suitcase with a camera? Lots of people take pictures of the embassy. If you do this, I'll pay you one thousand dollars."

Onur's eyes widened with surprise, but then showed concern. "I'll be happy to do it, but I should not be rewarded for helping you in the cause of Islam."

Klaus smiled. "You're a great Muslim already, Onur. Your generosity should be rewarded. When you get back, I'll donate a thousand dollars to the mosque in your name and pay you one thousand dollars. Maybe your mother needs a new stove?" He thrust a one-hundred-dollar bill at the boy. "Take a taxi. You can be there and back within an hour."

Onur stared at the money. He took it and the suitcase.

Klaus gave him final guidance and watched him disappear down the street. Then he went to wait in the basement of the apartment building. *Fortunately, the embassy is two miles away. The blast area is only a mile wide.*

Onur returned an hour later. Klaus was thrilled. *The anti-tamper mechanism on the bomb didn't work! Allah is truly guiding me.* He felt fierce humility.

True to his word, Klaus paid Onur and made the donation to the mosque. At Onur's insistence, he met with the boy's parents and explained the great service their son had provided. "He's a good boy," Onur's mother said proudly.

The next day, Klaus visited the old *Stasi* building in the former East Berlin. The headquarters of the former East German secret police had fallen into disrepair since he had last seen it. That had been the night the Wall fell.

The lobby was the scene of the gunfight that had damaged his shoulder. The building was all but empty now, protected by a few policemen and staffed by civilian volunteers who helped people search archives for records of atrocities committed against them, their friends, and relatives.

Seven stories high and several blocks long, this edifice had been built specifically to inflict cruelty in order to intimidate East Germans into uncomplaining submission. It housed the offices where the master plans for constructing the Wall and the eight-hundred-mile fortified border and their kill zones were hatched. It was where orders went out to imprison and torture hundreds of thousands of men, women, and children over the course of the *Stasi's* forty-four-year life. The building had also housed the most horrific of all prisons in East Germany.

When Klaus had escaped from the firefight last November, he had held tight to the suitcase bomb he had retrieved. He had stopped only long enough to grab some discarded cloths and stuff them around his shoulder to stop the bleeding. Otherwise, he stayed with the crowds as they joined the million-strong East Berliners moving toward Checkpoint Charlie and other crossing points.

Five days later, a mob of angry citizens invaded the *Stasi* headquarters. They had overturned furniture and equipment, emptied file cabinets onto the floor, and vandalized the building in expressions of revulsion for the organization and the officers who had brutalized their lives for decades.

Fortunately, cooler heads had prevailed. The vandalism stopped for practical reasons: the East German government, including the *Stasi*, had been meticulous record-keepers. The files at the *Stasi* headquarters held evidence that could convict the previous tormentors and lead to sentencing them.

Seeing the building again felt surreal to Klaus. Ghosts of memories played on his mind as he stepped over debris and entered the foyer. No one had cleaned the mess of that night. Bloodstains remained on the floor. They had to be his own or those of his dead fellow conspirator, Borya Yermolov. Across the foyer was a hall from which shots had been fired that took Klaus down. And there was the spot where he had last seen his nemesis, Atcho. Klaus' nostrils flared at the recollection.

A volunteer lounged near the main entrance. Klaus approached and pulled an identification card from his jacket pocket. "I'm an inspector from the International Atomic Energy Agency, the IAEA," he said. "I'm sure you've heard of it."

"Yes. How can I help?"

They spoke in broken English. "We want to ensure that all records pertaining to nuclear research and anyone involved in it are secure. That information should not make its way to the general public."

"I don't know how much of that you'll find here."

"Probably not much. My job is tying up loose ends, making sure nothing leaks out that shouldn't. I heard that a few people were imprisoned here who had been educated as nuclear engineers. Where should I look to see if those records still exist?"

"That won't be easy. Looters destroyed a lot." The volunteer pointed to a file cabinet. "You could start there. East Germany didn't have its own nuclear program, but good students were allowed to pursue studies and received degrees in Moscow. Some of them worked there too. Files in that cabinet could point you in the right direction."

Klaus spent several days at the headquarters, searching through records, combing through a huge number that had been thrown in piles on the floor. At one point, to satisfy an insatiable curiosity, he climbed to the top floor—the elevators no longer worked—and visited the office of the former director of the *Stasi*, Johann Baumann.

The director had disappeared that night. His role in a conspiracy to prevent the Wall's collapse had been to arrest the upper echelon of East German leadership. Whether deliberately or by inability, he had failed. History was sealed. Klaus had heard rumors that Baumann had escaped to Argentina.

Strangely, the director's office was as Klaus had last seen it. The looters had not come this far. A television on which Klaus had watched the announcement of the new policy that opened the Wall still set on a table near the desk, covered with dust. Klaus recalled cloistering around the screen with Yermolov and Baumann while the momentous pronouncement was made. So much had been set in motion as a result.

He looked behind the desk at the spot where he had placed the duffle bags with the five million dollars in them. He had set them there to make room for three suitcase bombs on the desk. *How did that man in the street get those bags?* He dismissed the thought. *Doesn't matter now.*

He recalled having jerked the bomb maker, Veniamin Krivkov, by the collar, forcing him to walk Klaus through the arming process for the bombs for a fifth time. *None of the bombs detonated. Veniamin must have done something to all three of them.* He went back to his search on the floors below.

Finally, on the third day, he found what he was looking for, a file containing the names of five men whose educations had been in nuclear engineering. The files were thorough and contained the addresses where each man had lived at the time of arrest.

Klaus hurried from the headquarters. He felt rejuvenated. Over the next two days, he visited each address. One of the men had died. A bitter family told of his cruel treatment while in the *Stasi* prison that caused his death.

Three of the men had moved, and quick conversations with neighbors revealed that they had migrated into the Western world.

The fifth man appeared an improbable subject at first. He was old with no remaining ambition beyond sitting on his porch and watching life go by. However, he was pleased to engage in conversation.

Klaus presented himself as a researcher with the IAEA and set aside his usually abrasive personality to turn on the charm. He learned much about the nuclear engineer that could be useful.

The man, Rayner, had worked in Hitler's nuclear program for a short while in his youth, before the war ended. Because of his reputation among peers of being exceptionally bright, he had been coerced to work in the nuclear program of the Soviet Union. He had spent years on teams in nuclear arms facilities designing more and more destructive weapons.

On retirement, Rayner had been allowed to return to his home in East Berlin. He had been arrested by the *Stasi* for complaining about food prices. His tenure at *Stasi* headquarters had been brief and benign, but in that short duration, he had seen and heard the agony of other prisoners in the prison cells. Because of his stature with the Soviets, Rayner had only been required to sign a confession. He was sent to a short re-education course and released.

Klaus took his time getting to know Rayner. He learned his favorite foods and drinks and brought some with him on subsequent visits. Then one morning, he brought with him his suitcase bomb. "I'm hoping you can help satisfy my curiosity," he told the old man. He opened the case. "Would you give me your opinion of this?"

Rayner opened it. Inside, he saw a metal plate with etching diagonally across its surface. Two small handles indicated that the plate could be removed. Rayner's eyes narrowed. "Where did you get this?"

"As I told you, I work for the IAEA. I was doing research at the *Stasi* headquarters, and came across it. I was hoping you could help me identify what it is."

Rayner had already lifted out the metal plate and scrutinized the components. A tube placed diagonally from the lower left of the case to the top right matched the orientation of the etching on the plate. "This indicates the proper positioning of components," he muttered. He studied each component. "Do you mind if I open them?"

Klaus assented. Rayner disappeared inside his house. He reappeared a few minutes later with a small tool kit and began tinkering. He first removed tiny screws from the tube and opened it. His eyes registered shock at what he saw, but he said nothing. He left his seat to go inside the house again. When he returned, he brought with him a small instrument. He unfastened a port at the top end of the tube and held a probe next to it. An audible clicking noise sounded. Rayner arched his eyebrows and closed the port quickly but remained silent. Then, he unsealed what appeared to be a timing device and a miniature data entry keyboard and screen.

Finally, he raised his head and faced Klaus. "My friend," he said gravely, "you have here a nuclear bomb, complete with plutonium. It was designed to be detonated either by a timer or remotely. But there is something strange about the wiring."

Klaus did his best to act shocked. "I had an idea it might be a bomb, but I had no clue it might be nuclear."

"Where did you find it?"

"In the office of the director of the *Stasi*. What's wrong with the wiring?"

"This is a real bomb, but do you see this heavy wire running between the components?" Klaus nodded. Rayner continued. "That should be the line conducting current from the battery to the individual parts, including the trigger mechanism. But look at this smaller wire." He pointed it out. "It comes directly out of the battery, and this little piece steps down the current so that the data entry screens and test diodes receive sufficient electricity for them to show the components as active when they are not.

"Whoever made this wanted it to appear that it would detonate when, as a matter of fact, it can't." He studied the bomb further. "If he had wanted it to explode, he would have connected this main line here and here and here... The small line then serves no purpose. Beyond that, arming the bomb is straightforward. See, there is even a remote connection. The operator would enter the frequency or set the timer here."

Klaus' heart took a leap. The modifications Rayner had indicated were not difficult. "Is there a fail-safe mechanism?"

Rayner scoffed. "There is a semblance of a fail-safe system, but all it did really was light up a test diode. Whoever built this bomb wanted it *not* to go off." He went back over it one more time. "The engineer knew what he was doing. The electronic components are off-the-shelf, and the structural ones are easy to fabricate. I'm sure the only difficult part of building this was acquiring the plutonium. Even the trigger mechanism is simple. In truth, this is an elegant design."

Klaus' spirits were high when he returned to his apartment that afternoon. He lay wide awake that night thinking of the potential. He foresaw the need to chance a trip to the Soviet Union. His risk was daunting. He was a wanted man there, having deserted the KGB. If caught, he would be summarily executed.

In the early morning hours of the next day, August 2, Klaus watched TV, mesmerized by the news that Saddam Hussein had invaded Kuwait. Live video showed heat mirages floating up from the desert floor and Iraqi tanks charging across the common border, seizing Kuwait's oil fields and continuing their advance on Kuwait City.

On hearing the news, Klaus called the orthopedic surgeon, Dr. Burakgazi. "Set a date for my surgery."

4

Austin, Texas, January 1991—In the evening after Atcho's lunch with Sofia, and after the meeting with Burly.

Atcho drove up the long, landscaped driveway to his Spanish colonial home with stucco walls and a red-tile roof, set among massive oak trees on the bluffs of Mt. Bonnell above the Colorado River. This was a far cry from the plain town house he had inhabited in the DC area before marrying Sofia, and far above his needs. But its elegance and beauty reflected the wife he adored. He could well afford it and had enjoyed watching Sofia decorate, enhancing a Western-ranch flair with her own impeccable style.

After the Siberia mission a little over a year ago, she had been happy to retire from the US State Department where she had been a senior intelligence supervisor. For much of her career, the job had been a cover for her employment with the CIA as a field operator. Over the years, bad guys had perceived her femininity as weakness. They learned the hard way about the effectiveness of an upward blow to the chin by the heel of her open hand, or the lethality of her legs, developed from years of ballet converted into black belts in several martial arts. Some had missed the chance to regret being at the wrong end of her marksmanship. They were dead.

She met Atcho at the door and embraced him. "I'm glad you're home." The lights were turned down, and soft music played. Atcho noticed. She took him by the hand and led him through the living room to a set of stairs.

When Atcho had constructed the house, he had directed the contractor to excavate into the limestone and include a good-sized basement, a rarity in Austin because of the expense. When completed, the room had been comfortably furnished as a lounge with a large home entertainment center at the far end, and it had been sound-proofed. He had created his own secure location where he and Sofia could be assured of privacy when speaking. They even swept the base-ment periodically for listening devices. They had learned from experience.

As they descended into the lounge, Atcho saw that Sofia had taken care to continue the romantic atmosphere with soft lights and music, and a low table with *hors d'oeuvres*. A wine bottle rested in a bucket of ice, but oddly, with only one crystal glass.

Sofia sat on a sofa and pulled Atcho to sit close to her. Then she poured wine into the glass and handed it to him. "Tell me about your visit with Burly."

Atcho took a sip. "Aren't you having any?"

"No. I wasn't feeling great today, especially after our conversation at lunch. So, tell me about Burly."

Atcho studied her face. "You've been feeling off-balance for several days. Are you all right?"

Sofia rubbed her eyes. "Just a little under the weather. Are you going to tell me about Burly or not?"

Atcho frowned and hesitated. "It's like you thought. Burly's visit was official, not social." He took a deep breath. "Klaus surfaced."

Sofia sat up straight, realization on her face. "They want you to go after him."

Atcho nodded slowly. "I don't see that I have a choice."

"You're not buying into that again." Sofia's eyes burned with anger. "You're not a CIA operator, you've never been one, but they keep convincing you that you're the only person on earth who can go into these impossible situations to save mankind." She stood abruptly. "Let someone else do it for a change."

She looked at her husband, hurt and concern in her eyes. She saw a man with classical Latin good looks. Silver lined his dark brown hair, but his daily exercise regimen kept him in superb physical shape. He was a man toughened by combat, years of imprisonment, and impossible undercover field operations normally undertaken by intelligence professionals. His West Point education and training at Ranger and Airborne schools had prepared him for much, but his covert operator skills had been developed on the job, and much of the time, going solo. Whenever she looked at him, she saw a man who had suffered excruciating circumstances and never surrendered his courtesy, humility, or great heart. "They have no right to come to you again."

Atcho stood and took her in his arms. "Darling, it'll be okay. I'll be okay." He nudged her gently until they both sat down again. "You said you might have some news of your own."

Sofia was momentarily bewildered. "What?" Her eyes gained a stoic, faraway quality, but she waved her hand dismissively. "Oh, it was nothing. The garden club nominated me for an award. They like what we've done with the house. That's all." Her eyes met his. "Why are you the only one who can do this mission?"

Atcho took a deep breath and exhaled. "Burly gave two reasons. He pointed out that I'm one of the few people in Western intelligence circles to have seen Klaus and interacted with him."

"I saw him," Sofia interjected defiantly. "I was there when that bastard kidnapped my husband, remember? I'll never forget his face. I gave a description to that German detective's sketch artist."

"Yes, you were there, and you acted brilliantly. But I was with Klaus for a while. I know his mannerisms, his voice, and the way he walks and talks."

"So do I." Sofia was obstinate. "Ya take in a lot under that kind of stimulation, especially when you're trained."

Atcho continued. "The other reason: Klaus has that nuclear bomb."

Sofia contemplated quietly. Then she sighed. "We've known all that. No one's put on much of a search for Klaus since the Berlin Wall came down. That's not why you'll go on this fool's errand which, as I pointed out, I could do—or someone else could."

"That's right. Klaus was wounded badly in East Berlin, but we don't know which part of his body was hit. For all we knew, he died. If not, he must have taken a few months to recuperate, but did he stay in the East or go west? We don't know. Over the last week or so, listening surveillance picked up calls mentioning 'Berlin,' 'suitcase,' 'nuclear,' and 'bomb.'"

"And you think they refer to him."

"That's sketchy, I know. His name wasn't mentioned. 'Klaus' is an alias, so we wouldn't hear his real name. Anyway, when those four words are used in bad-guy chatter over the course of days with increasing frequency, it's a good guess they mean Klaus, whatever his name is. The trouble is, we haven't isolated a location, or even a region. He could be anywhere in the world."

Sofia leaned into him and wrapped her arms around his neck. She drew her face close to his. "But why are you taking the job? There are plenty of others who could go after him."

Atcho blew out his breath again. "To Klaus, it's personal. I killed his brother, Etzel. Because of that, Klaus threatened me in Berlin, and he'll never give up. He's a danger to our home, our friends and neighbors—you. He could plant that bomb near our house and incinerate everything within a square mile. The radioactive fallout alone could turn Austin into a ghost town."

Sofia listened intently, her instincts piqued by years of experience in the intelligence community. "Okay, I get all that, but something isn't adding up." She pulled away to gather her thoughts. "If Klaus were coming after you for revenge," she said slowly, "he would do it quietly. He was in the KGB and was part of both coup attempts against Gorbachev. When the second one failed, he deserted and went underground. If he makes noise now, he risks alerting the KGB and putting the Soviets on his trail. Come to think of it, why hasn't that happened already?"

Atcho shrugged. "Because our intelligence is better?"

Sofia looked skeptical. "Demonstrated by what?" She shook her head. "Something else is going on." She thought in silence. "We know he's a Chechen Muslim who hates the US as much as he hates the Soviets."

Atcho noticed a change in Sofia's demeanor. Gone were notions of an evening of romance. She now thought professionally, tactically. "We're pretty sure he never exploded the bomb. That would have been hard to hide, and besides, he'd look to inflict massive destruction. So, if he still has the bomb, and it's intact, the fail-safe mechanism must still be engaged. At least that's what he would think.

"Veniamin, the bomb maker, wanted to get away from the conspiracy and protect his family. He was coerced to make the bomb. He said he wired it to look like it was active when the arming mechanisms were set, but that neither the timer nor the remote control would detonate it for real. Klaus never knew that, and besides he never had the remote. That maniacal general who led the plot kept it under his personal control, until you killed him." She drummed her fingers against her chin and went on.

"As far as Klaus knew, he had a bomb ready to detonate remotely or by a timer, and he could neither set it off nor open up the suitcase to shut it down."

Atcho listened closely. Sofia's insights had been widely respected at both the state department and the CIA. He was the beneficiary of a keen analytical mind at work.

Sofia ruminated out loud again. "What else could he be thinking?" She leaned her forehead into her palm. "He's been involved in at least two big conspiracies, one to depose Gorbachev and one to stop the Berlin Wall from opening, so he's a guy who participates in big-picture projects. Atcho, tell me his background again."

Atcho sat back to reflect. "Well, he's Chechen, and his real name is Sahab Kadyrov. 'Klaus' was his alias for the conspiracy in East Berlin after he deserted from the KGB. It's the name US intelligence first came to know him by. For operational simplicity, it's still the name used to identify him. When we hear the name 'Sahab,' we link it to Klaus."

"Got it," Sofia interrupted, "and Chechens hate the Soviets. The oldest known tribe of Caucasians comes from that region, and Chechnya has been under Russian rule for centuries. They resent that, and most of the population converted to the Sunni Islamic religion as passive resistance. Persia and Russia fought for centuries, with Persia supporting

Chechnya. That aligns modern-day Persia—now Iran—with Chechnya, even though Iran is mostly Shia. Chechens were inspired by the takeover of the US Embassy in Tehran in 1979. First chance, Chechnya will buck the Soviets.

"That means a target in the Soviet Union is possible. If that's the case, that's a Soviet problem, and you don't need to be involved. Go on."

"Klaus had a network already established in Berlin that got him back and forth between the two halves of the city through the tunnels under the Wall."

"Okay, so he had support. Any idea where it came from?"

"If I had to guess, I'd say he developed contact with Turkish immigrants in West Berlin. He's Muslim, they're Muslim. Turks came to West Germany for work after the war. Germany was short of men because of wartime casualties. So, Turks helped rebuild the country, but are resentful of their poor treatment there. I'd put my money on them."

"That makes sense. If his network is still active, he could strike a target in Berlin to disrupt reunification, but I don't see what he'd get out of that. East and West Germany are about to formally reunite. They've got a long way to go to complete the process, but I don't see how Klaus or his cause benefits by targeting there."

Atcho shrugged. "He could be acting as a mercenary. That's what he did for Yermolov." He searched his memory. "I overheard a conversation he had before the firefight where I killed Etzel. Klaus said that the *jihad* might come sooner than anyone thought."

Sofia looked at him sharply. "That's right, he's a *jihadist*. That puts another whole spin on things."

"I don't know his beliefs. I know what I overheard. He wasn't motivated by money. When he abducted me, he demanded a bomb, not money. He wanted the nuke for his own use, and he got it. I don't know what his agenda was."

"Well that begs the question about funding. He had to have had medical costs for his wounds, and he had to live somewhere. Come to think of it, he couldn't meander around the world carrying that bomb. He would have to stash it somewhere until he was ready to use it. So, how is he paying for all of that?"

Atcho stood and stretched, frustration showing on his face. "I don't know, but your last thought brings up another question. How would he fix the bomb so it could be reactivated? Veniamin told us the fail-safe was a fake. The bomb would have to be rewired in order to be detonated. Klaus would have to find someone who could do that.

"The US put Veniamin and his family under protection in a secret location, so Klaus would have to find another nuclear engineer. Before that, he'd have to figure out that the fail-safe was a fake. As far as he knew, if he opened the suitcase, he'd blow himself up. How would he find out that the fail-safe wouldn't work?"

Sofia absorbed Atcho's musings. "I don't know. If we still lived in DC, his coming after you at home might make sense. He could get personal revenge and hit a strategic target at the same time. Austin doesn't offer that, and Berlin isn't a target that forwards *jihad* objectives, at least not now. Being a *jihadist*, Klaus would strike in the Middle East. You know what's going on there now."

Atcho nodded glumly. "Operation Desert Shield and the Kuwait-Iraq war. Sorting out whether he would support Kuwait or Iraq is murky. Since he's Chechen, he's probably Sunni.

"Saddam Hussein and his ruling Ba'athist Party are Sunni. Then again, Chechnya has that centuries-old history with Iran, which is Shia. When you add in that Iraq and Iran just fought a seven-year war to a stalemate, the peace between them is tenuous at best. He could throw final victory either way in that war, depending on whatever outcome he wants. And that could dictate his target. He could become a potent force in the region."

"My head is about to explode," Sofia said, burying her face in her hands. "Going back to how Klaus could reactivate the bomb. If he could do that, then he might also be able to replicate it, as many times as he wants. Talk about becoming a potent force."

Atcho mulled implications without expression before he spoke. "He'd be limited by how much plutonium he could get. I'm sure the Soviets tightened up security on their nuclear stockpiles after the episode in Berlin."

"Don't count on it. Anyway, where does all this leave us?"

"With more questions than answers. I've got to head to DC tomorrow to try to figure it all out and what to do about it."

Agitation showed on Sofia's face. "Burly must have some preliminary thoughts, or he wouldn't have come all the way here to see you. What does he want you to do?"

Atcho stared at her, obviously reluctant to speak.

Sofia's nostrils flared, her eyes widened. "Don't do this to me, Atcho. You know I can find out, so tell me now." Her voice took on an insistent note. "What is Burly planning?"

Atcho thrust his hands in his pockets and stared at the floor. "All right," he said slowly, "but you're retired. Stay out of it."

"Just tell me. Whatever it is, I'd rather hear it from you. I'll decide what I will or won't do."

Atcho sighed. "Okay. But I don't want to come home to an empty house because you got in the way of Klaus' bullet or his bomb trying to save me."

Sofia stared back at him expectantly. "Tell me."

Atcho leaned against the wall, looking strained. "They want me to draw Klaus out, so they can locate him. I'm the bait."

5

Five months earlier, August 2, 1990—The day Saddam Hussein invaded
Kuwait. Nine months after the Berlin Wall opened.

The orthopedic surgeon, Dr. Burakgazi, advised Klaus that the
soonest he could operate was in early November. Klaus was happy for the
timing. It left him three months to acquire more plutonium.

In the days after leaving Rayner's house for the last time, Klaus had
carefully reopened and rewired the bomb as the nuclear engineer had
indicated. When completed, he had been chagrinned at how simply
Veniamin's ruse had fooled him.

Now all the component tests worked, and Klaus felt comfortable to
arm and disarm the bomb at will. He even acquired a new remote control
and entered the frequency. The bomb was ready to be placed when he
decided on a target.

He opened an account with cash at a bank, rented a large safety
deposit box, and secured the bomb there. Then he made travel arrangements to Paris. Before leaving, he paid a visit to Kadir and worked out
instructions for moving money into traditional banking accounts from
remote locations. Finally, he purchased a worn briefcase from a special
dealer. It contained a hidden compartment. In it he secured a large
amount of cash and the documents needed to support several aliases.

In Paris, Klaus rented a car and drove north to a village at the base of a forested hill. He knew the area well. At the top of the hill was a cluster of cabins. It was there he had first met Yermolov. The rogue Soviet general had been supported with money, cars, and shelter by a splinter group of Russian Orthodox Church members who still revered Rasputin.

Near the base of the hill and in the village was a tavern. Although normally a strict adherent to Islamic proscriptions against the consumption of alcohol, Klaus had no problem with imbibing when doing so furthered the aims of Islam. He entered the tavern and took a seat at the bar.

"Hello, friend," he said to the bartender. "Remember me?"

The bartender peered at him and broke into a smile. "It's been a while. What brings you back?"

"Business, I'm afraid. You know how that goes." They both arched their eyebrows and nodded in mutual understanding.

They spoke in broken English. Klaus ordered a drink. "I enjoyed my stay here. Can you believe that was two years ago?" He shook his head. "I came up to visit now while I had some free time. Does that group of Rasputin people still come in here?"

The bartender smiled benevolently. "They do, and they still bring that awful fish soup." The both laughed. He referred to a special concoction that had been passed through generations of Rasputin followers. Many regarded it as sacred as holy water. "A few members wander in and out most nights. Some should be here shortly."

An hour later, Klaus sat with several of the Rasputin followers at the back of the tavern. Curious about what had happened to the conspiracy to overthrow Gorbachev, they were happy to see Klaus. He did his own probing before responding. "I suppose you heard about what happened with Veniamin?"

No, they told him in hushed tones. All they knew was that the entire family had disappeared, their property sold.

"General Yermolov protects him," Klaus lied to them, their expressions incredulous. "Other people tried to coerce him into making bombs for them." His audience collectively shook their heads in disgusted indignation.

"What happened to the plan for the coup in Moscow? Didn't it work?"

In the dim light, Klaus looked into their faces sadly. "We were betrayed."

Silence. Then one person interjected. "A news reporter came here a few weeks after General Yermolov and your group left. He stayed around for a month and spoke with Veniamin. I was there when they met. The last question the journalist asked was where Veniamin got the plutonium. The reporter was here again looking for Veniamin a few days before the Berlin Wall came down. That's been over a year ago."

Klaus felt the hackles on his neck rise. He fought down a sudden rush of anger. "What did Veniamin tell him? Do you remember the reporter's name?"

"Tony Collins. He writes for the *Washington Herald*. Veniamin wouldn't tell him where he got the plutonium."

Klaus felt simultaneously relieved and in shock but kept his outward expressions in check. He threw his head back and laughed. "Ah yes. Tony Collins. We know him well. A good man, but it's also good that Veniamin didn't say anything. Let me tell you something." He gestured for them to bring their heads close together. "General Yermolov wants to try again."

He sat back with a deliberately smug look and watched the mixed expressions of excitement and concern. He leaned forward again. "The nuclear fuel degraded and needs to be replaced. Yermolov sent me to get more, but I don't know how to contact the arms merchant who sold it to us."

He watched closely for reaction. The faces looking back at him wore bewildered expressions. "Couldn't Veniamin come, or tell you how to meet his contact?"

Klaus sighed. "You'd think so, but Yermolov promised him a vacation in the Swiss Alps with no phone for a month. He's there now with his family. We just learned about the problem with the plutonium, and we're about to launch the new plan. We can't wait for Veniamin to get back. Do any of you know where to locate that contact?"

The men exchanged glances between themselves, and once again shook their heads in unison. "We never knew where Veniamin got the materials," someone replied. "We led Yermolov to Veniamin in the first

place, but then we knew nothing more about how it all came together."
They sat looking doe-eyed. After a couple more hours of small talk, Klaus
bade the group farewell and returned to Paris.

He had reached a dead end. Although disappointed, he lost only a
day and still had three months to complete this stage of his plans. The
positive aspect was that, regardless of success in finding more plutonium
immediately, he already had a fully operational bomb which he could
replicate—and he called his own shots.

Klaus contemplated his next destination with trepidation. Moscow. He
had been there many times and knew his way around, but his brother
Etzel had always been with him. This time he was alone and a wanted
man. Aside from having deserted the KGB, he had little doubt that his
part in Yermolov's coup attempt was known at the highest levels.

To conceal his real identity, he wore body and stomach padding to
look overweight and hide his trim physique. He let his beard grow and
trimmed it neatly. He walked with a slumping gait, and he tied his bad
arm beneath his business suit jacket.

On deplaning at Sheremetyevo International Airport in Moscow, he
presented a Soviet passport showing he was from Chechnya. The advantage of entering as a Soviet citizen was that he would not be trailed by a
"minder," a government official assigned to follow around and report the
movements of foreign visitors.

He walked through the airport noting a changed atmosphere from
any he had perceived in the country before. Unfamiliar nervous energy
seemed to pervade. People still walked like they were oppressed, but
Klaus sensed furtiveness. They looked about with interest until they were
observed doing so, and then quickly reverted to expected depressed
behavior. The demeanor reminded him of people in East Berlin in the
days before they coalesced into the huge crowds that made the Wall a
relic of history.

That's it. He felt sudden excitement rising. *I told Etzel that East*

Germany would fall, and it did, and that the Soviet Union was on its last legs. I feel it.

As he walked through the concourse, he reviewed the historic events of the past few years. Soviet troops had been forced out of Afghanistan. Poland had seized its independence much like the East German regime had been vanquished—by the force of its citizens. Czechoslovakia and Hungary had been early in securing greater autonomy, although with less drama. They had now sealed their independence from the Soviet Union. All three Baltic states appeared to be on the verge of gaining their liberty, within months. Demand for greater national self-rule permeated through every country of the Soviet empire, including those in the Islamic sphere of influence.

Klaus stopped walking with a stunning realization: The Soviet Union was already unraveling. He looked up at the massive ceiling in the terminal, seeing past it into the heavens. *I told you, Etzel. I told you that the Soviet Union would fall. You and I will stamp our mark on the rise of* jihad. *It's started, and we're the proof.*

Klaus moved into the underworld of Moscow with skill. He understood criminals, their habitats, common practices, how to identify the hierarchy and make contact, and how to limit his risk of bodily harm. Within a week, he started negotiations to acquire plutonium.

The first part of the transaction required establishing credibility that the black-market merchant could deliver. Next came confirming that the product was genuine and could be delivered at the desired level of quality and quantity. Finally came the trickiest part: agreement on price and terms, including time, place, and delivery method.

Klaus hoped to find the man who had provided nuclear material to Veniamin for Yermolov. Since he had no clue of the man's identity or location, he thought that possibility to be an idle hope. If he could find the merchant though, the advantage would be dealing with a known entity who had already delivered reliably.

He moved about carefully, purchased a pistol with ammunition from street thugs, and stayed in places where he could rest while assured of minimal to no government attention. As he gained confidence in his knowledge of "who's who" in capabilities and the pecking order of those he met, he let drop among specific people that he wished to purchase a small quantity of plutonium. He also dropped Yermolov's name.

Moving about the city, he found it remarkable that his initial sense of a population anticipating imminent, cataclysmic change became reinforced. As he had witnessed in East Berlin, people rapidly shed their fear of authority. He mentioned his impressions to a few select people.

One man in particular, Rostislav, spoke brashly. "The Soviet Union is history," he said with such finality that Klaus could only stare. He had no response.

"Look," Rostislav continued, "Ronald Reagan mounted an arms race that all but bankrupted us. We lost the space race years ago. Gorbachev's *glasnost* and *perestroika* not only urge people to speak their minds openly, but they also encourage national governments of Soviet republics and satellites to push for greater self-rule. Those countries demand independence. Look what happened in Germany, Poland, Hungary..." He ran down the list. "Mark my words. Within a year, the Soviet Union will be finished." He smirked. "That will create enormous opportunity for our 'profession.'"

As he spoke, Klaus studied him. Despite his rough appearance, Rostislav was educated, stayed up-to-date with current events, and thought deeply. Klaus weighed his risks and informed him in greater detail of his wishes. "I'd like to find the man who dealt with Yermolov. He's already performed, more than once."

Rostislav scrutinized Klaus. "I might be able to find him. Only a few people can deliver plutonium, and I have contacts in that specialty." He chuckled at his use of the last word. "First, I need to know that whatever you do with it won't happen in Moscow. I don't want to be anywhere near the explosion."

"I'm Chechen. That should tell you something."

Rostislav eyed him and nodded slowly. "You'll hit either a Soviet target in your own region or somewhere else that helps Islam." He inhaled and leaned back in his chair. "I'll see what I can do. How much is it worth to you? I'll expect to be paid for trying and for delivery. The more you pay, the higher the priority."

"How do you want to be paid?"

"In American dollars. I have a Swiss bank account."

They negotiated for several hours and reached an agreement. Rostislav would put highest priority on the project for a month, for which he would receive twenty thousand dollars, deposited immediately by wire transfer to his bank. When Rostislav delivered, Klaus would transmit an equal amount. The identity of the merchant would be confirmed by correctly detailing the last three transactions the arms merchant had conducted with Yermolov, including where and to whom the product was delivered. Final payment to Rostislav was due regardless of whether or not the merchant supplied more plutonium.

At the end of the third week, Klaus began to feel anxious, but Rostislav contacted him, and they met again. "I've found him. Here is the confirmation information." He handed Klaus a single sheet of paper.

With rising excitement calmed by deliberate skepticism, Klaus read down the sheet. "That's him. What's next?"

"I'll put you in direct contact, but it'll cost you ten thousand dollars more." He shrugged. "The man made me pay him to give you that sheet of paper."

Klaus sat back in his chair. "I'll arrange it."

A month later, Klaus waited outside of Veniamin's former weekend home, a repurposed barn north of Paris on a secluded plot of land carved out of a defunct farm. It had been the site of the last plutonium delivery to Veniamin. Half of the million-dollar price had already been transmitted. Today, on receipt of the nuclear material, Klaus would deliver the balance in cash, made possible by Kadir through a cooperating *hawala* in Paris.

While waiting, Klaus reviewed his financial position. After paying for forged travel documents, the money remitted to Rostislav, the plutonium transaction, and his normal living and travel expenses, he had more than three million six hundred thousand dollars remaining. *After delivery, I'll have enough material to make four more bombs. Crossing into Germany with it is not difficult.* He felt an immense sense of satisfaction.

He heard a crunch of gravel and looked up to see a sedan approaching. The exchange of cash for plutonium took a matter of minutes, and then Klaus was on his way back to Berlin.

He spent the next month engaging several machine shops, each one replicating four copies of an individual component of his bomb. In the same time frame, he arranged for illicit cross-border private flights to various countries, to be flown with twenty-four-hour notice. He also rented a small workshop in a secure area of Berlin.

When the machine shops had completed their work, he checked to ensure that each new component had been produced to his exacting specifications. Satisfied, he took the various pieces to his workshop and there, careful to assemble and wire exactly as the original had been done, he built four more bombs embedded in identical suitcases. He tested and retested each one until satisfied that they were fully functional. *Now for my shoulder surgery.*

6

Washington, DC, January 1991 – Five months after Hussein invaded Kuwait, fourteen months after the Berlin Wall fell. Two days after Burly visited Atcho in Austin.

"Sofia wants to come here, to DC," Atcho said. "She agreed to stay out of the field if she could be on your team as an analyst. She won't go rogue that way."

He and Burly were in a secure room in the Executive Annex across the street from the White House. Atcho had flown in the night before.

"I anticipated that," Burly replied. His voice was flat and deliberate. "Look, I love Sofia. You know that. We're great friends. Having her here as an analyst would be terrific, but I can't have her going off half-cocked to interfere in the mission."

Atcho's temper flared. He held it down. "Slow down, buddy. We're talking about my wife. She's been effective for the CIA and the state department. I just told you that she volunteered to be an analyst and stay out of the field."

"Got it. But she has a blind spot when it comes to you. That's normal, and that's why we don't let people participate who have a personal stake in a mission. In Berlin, you were the target and she had to stick to her task, or a much larger catastrophe might have taken place. But a year earlier, when you went to Paris and Siberia, she went indie on us. We can't have that happening here."

Atcho controlled his anger while still communicating dissatisfaction. "She ferreted out critical information for you and got that NUKEX to me in the field. Both of those actions saved the mission, and she risked her life to get it done."

"She risked her life because she didn't want you in the field alone and unsupported." Burly's voice matched Atcho's tone.

"She saved my life, the rest of the team's, and the mission."

Burly heaved a sigh. "I know. Sofia's incredible. I didn't stick around to see her in Austin because that wasn't the time or place to have this conversation. We could use her experience and analytical skills. She has specific knowledge related to this mission. So, I'll be pleased to have her on the team here, in this office, but there's a caveat." He paused to be sure Atcho was listening. "If she tries even once to go off the reservation, we'll isolate her from the mission and detain her until you come home. She'd be in a comfortable place, but she wouldn't have freedom of movement. There's no negotiation on that. I'm not trying to be mean. I want to be sure everyone knows the boundaries. She has to accept the condition in writing."

Atcho quelled his anger. "Do you want to tell her, or should I?"

"Why don't you tell her that I'm open to the idea, and that she should fly here to discuss it with me. I'll take it from there."

"I'll tell her, but she won't like that you're attaching conditions."

A knock on the door interrupted the discussion. When it opened, a medium-sized man with a balding head, horn-rimmed glasses, and a wrinkled overcoat poked his head in the door. "Am I in the right place?"

"Come in," Burly's voice boomed across the room. "You found us." To Atcho, he said quietly, "Relay my message to Sofia."

He and Atcho stood to greet Tony Collins, the investigative reporter. Collins thanked the young man who had escorted him from the security desk in the foyer.

"Great to see you," Atcho said, extending his hand. "I never got to thank you in person for what you did in Berlin. You had a critical role in pulling that off."

Collins shook his hand and waved off the compliment. "I did my job." He shook Burly's hand. "What's up? You guys are usually trying to shoo me away."

Burly laughed. "How could you say that? We've always treated you like a kissin' cousin." His face became serious. "We're on a short fuse. Everything we talk about this morning is off the record. None of it's for publication. Agreed?"

Collins was taken aback and perplexed. "Then why did you invite me here?"

Burly gestured toward a small, round conference table, and the three sat down. "There's specific help that you can provide, if you'll do it. We'll fill you in. If you're OK with the conditions, you'll get first access to any story that *can* be printed."

Collins sighed. "Let's go."

Over the next hour, Burly and Atcho briefed Collins. Atcho included the informal analysis he had done with Sofia two nights ago. "Much of this I already knew," Collins said when they had finished, "but a lot I didn't. That part about chatter coming over the bad guy net is new. Are you sure it's Klaus?"

Burly shook his head. "No. We have people chasing down other possibilities. The pertinent chatter is on phone lines in Islamic areas, and we're hearing it everywhere there are radical Muslims. We'd key in on 'nuclear' and 'bomb' anyway. Thrown in with 'Berlin' and 'suitcase' in the context of what went down with the Wall, that's what perked our ears up, and points to Klaus."

He rose and walked to his desk. "Atcho, after I spoke with you in Austin, I remembered that Sofia had also seen Klaus the morning you were kidnapped. I contacted Detective Berger in Berlin, the one who worked with us on the case. He faxed over some sketches that their artist did from Sofia's description." He took some papers from his desk and brought them back to the table.

Atcho studied them. "That's a good likeness." He passed them to Collins. "We should get them widely distributed."

Collins took the sketches and gasped. "I saw this man. I reported from Checkpoint Charlie all that night at the Wall. I remember him because he was the only person I saw who scowled. He carried a suitcase and seemed to be in a great deal of pain. He stopped to check his shoulder."

Burly went behind his desk and brought back a piece of luggage. "The bastard was wounded, but we didn't know which part of his body was hit or how bad. If he's the guy, now we know one of his shoulders got ripped." He placed the suitcase on the table. "Did his bag look like this one?"

Collins stared at the suitcase. "It looked *exactly* like that. The guy I saw nursed his right shoulder. He wasn't limping. In fact, he walked faster than the rest of the crowd. I might have footage of him on video. He avoided the camera, but we might have caught him before he became aware of it. We were already past dawn, so the camera lights might not have made much of a difference. I'll look. If it's anything, I'll bring in the video."

"Great. That's news we weren't expecting today. Each case had a nuclear bomb. The second one is behind my desk. Atcho saw Klaus leave *Stasi* headquarters with the third one. We removed the plutonium from the two here. They're inert."

"There's more," Atcho interjected. "Klaus is right-handed. That's his shooting arm. He might be less of a threat up close and personal. On the other hand, he'd fight like a cornered jackal.

"While we're brainstorming, we might want to look at the surveillance video for that night from outside the US Embassy in East Berlin. Klaus parked the *Stasi* car across from the main entrance there. That was the target. One of the suitcases was in the trunk. We might find clear video of him there.

"Another element is that Veniamin spent the most time with Klaus. Remember that Klaus drove him to Berlin from the border at Helmstedt – Marienborn. They were together for several hours. He might have insights."

"Good thinking," Burly said. "Veniamin is coming here tomorrow. I want him to dissect one of those bags and show me what it would take to reengineer it to work. Klaus seems to want to stay alive. I think he must still have his bomb and has either made it operational or believes he can. If not, we wouldn't be hearing all the noise that points to him." He paused. "I want to know how hard it would be to get inside the suitcase when you think that opening it would explode it."

"I've been thinking about that for a couple of days, and it wouldn't be hard," Atcho said, his tone grim. Burly and Collins shifted questioning, somber eyes to him. "Given his mentality, all he'd have to do is take a kid out in the desert and promise him ten bucks to wait long enough for Klaus to get out of the blast area and away from fallout. When the kid opened the suitcase and it didn't detonate, he'd bring it back. For that matter, Klaus wouldn't have to go to the desert. He could do it in the heart of Berlin, which was the original target anyway. If it went off, at least he'd have killed a lot of infidels. If it didn't, he has a bomb that's safe to open and rewire. Has anyone heard of an unidentified nuclear blast anywhere?"

The other two men's faces were grim masks. Collins was first to break the silence. "Tell me why you asked me here."

7

The morning after Atcho met with Burly and Collins in DC, Sofia woke up with a start at the house in Austin. A wave of nausea washed over her. She took deep breaths and turned her thoughts to Atcho. *This can't be happening again. They always send him in alone.* Another wave of nausea hit. She edged out of bed and staggered to the kitchen.

There, she poured cereal into a bowl, sat down at the table and ate it dry. While munching, she reflected on her conversation with Atcho last night. He had relayed Burly's comments about her participation as an analyst. Anger welled. *Who the hell does Burly think he is? I offered to help. He wants to handcuff me.*

Half an hour later and despite her pique, she felt better and went back to her room and dressed. Then she took the stairs down into the basement lounge and crossed to the home entertainment center. She reached around to the backside near the floor and pushed a button. The entertainment center swung out, revealing a door into a room as large as the lounge. It lit up automatically and was arranged neatly with a fully stocked gun rack over shelves of ammunition. Next to them were stacks of packaged food and bottled water. One narrow, shuttered window at floor level was built into an alcove on the river side.

Sofia walked to the opposite end of the room to a cabinet built into a bare limestone wall. She opened it to reveal a safe and punched in the combination. Moments later, she removed a box. Opening it, she glanced through various passports, drivers' licenses, and credit cards arranged in packets with corresponding aliases. Then she thumbed through several stacks of cash. Keeping out what she needed, she returned the rest to the box, replaced it in the safe, closed it, and retraced her steps.Four hours later, a very different-looking Sofia boarded an international flight in Houston bound for Berlin, the reservation booked under one of her aliases. When she arrived, she checked into a *gasthaus* and paid with cash. Then she made her way to Little Istanbul, a section of the city largely inhabited by Turks. She sought out thrift shops and stores catering to them, made a few purchases and returned to the *gasthaus*. When next she emerged, she looked like a Turkish woman, covered from head to toe in layered clothing. Only part of her face and hands remained uncovered.

Burly and Atcho met back in the office at the Executive Annex in Washington about the time that Sofia dabbled at her dry cereal in Austin. "What did she say about my caveats?" Burly asked.

"She wasn't happy. She said to send whatever document you want her to sign. She'd think about it."

Burly shot Atcho a piercing glance but said nothing. *She's buying time.*

A knock on the door interrupted his thought. An old man entered. He was thin and stooped and wore wire-rimmed glasses. He cast a wary glance about the room. Behind him, his security escort left, closing the door quietly.

"Dr. Krivkov," Burly greeted, advancing toward him, palm extended. "I'm glad you agreed to come." After shaking hands, he turned to present Atcho. "I'm not sure you ever had a chance to meet Eduardo Xiquez while we were in Berlin. We call him Atcho." He chuckled. "There's a long story about his war-hero father named Arturo. His American Army buddies couldn't pronounce his name correctly, so it morphed to Atcho. That became Eduardo's code name at the Bay of Pigs invasion, and it stuck."

While Burly spoke, the old man peered at Atcho, studying his face. "I know about you," he said. He used formal vocabulary in a French accent tinged with Ukrainian. "The general was very concerned about you. He was afraid you would get in the way of his plans. You did. You know, he was my cousin?" He smiled. "Please, call me Veniamin."

Atcho reacted coolly to Veniamin's greeting.

The old man sensed his reserve. "I'm afraid I helped cause a bit of trouble," he said. "Yermolov threatened my family. He said he would kill all of us if I didn't build three bombs and bring them to Berlin."

Atcho's expression softened. "No apologies needed. I've been in your shoes. The way you wired those bombs to neutralize them was brilliant. You risked your life to do it. Your family members' too."

Veniamin removed his glasses and wiped them with a cloth he pulled from inside his jacket. His eyes misted. "Well, my family is safe, thanks to all of you." He looked around to include Burly. "What can I do for you now? By the way, you can trace back the origin of the plutonium. I never knew where it came from. A man would show up and deliver it, and that was that. But nuclear materials leave a signature that you can use forensically to find out its source."

Burly nodded. "We know where it came from. I'm not at liberty to say."

They moved to the small conference table. "We need two things," Burly began. "First, tell us your impressions of Klaus. He's active. Maybe with the bomb."

Before Burly could continue, Veniamin's head jerked upright. His eyes became wide and rounded. He looked at Atcho. "Oh, Klaus hates you. His face became terrifying whenever your name was mentioned. You could see the fire coming out of his eyes. He told Yermolov that he would plant that third bomb under your bed in DC. He might have been kidding, but you never know with a man like that."

He sighed. "He's highly intelligent, speaks several languages, and is physically very fit. He can easily be underestimated because he can present himself as a thug or as an educated person within seconds, and he knows how to dress the part.

"Most of the time I saw him, he was the thug, so I think that is his natural state. But, when I first met him, he dressed and acted like a *Stasi* officer. He did it so easily that no one questioned him. That's how he got me through Immigration and Customs into East Germany. He assumed authority, and nobody dared question him. Yermolov said that Klaus had been recruited and trained by the Soviet special forces, the *Spetsnaz*. He is very dangerous."

Now Burly's eyes were wide. He whistled as he leaned back in his chair and looked up at the ceiling. "*Spetsnaz*, huh? I didn't know that. We'd better get word into the field about what we're up against." He glanced at Veniamin. "Those are great insights."

Atcho's eyes narrowed, but he did not speak.

"One thing about Klaus that might be useful," Veniamin continued, "he does not want to know *why* things work. He just wants to know *how* to make them work. He gets impatient with technical explanations."

"That's good to know," Burly interjected. "The other thing to discuss, Veniamin, is the bomb." He set one of the suitcases on the table. "How could it be rewired to make it work?" He read Veniamin's horror on seeing the suitcase and added, "Don't worry. We opened it under controlled conditions. The plutonium has been removed. The Atomic Energy Commission has it under lock and key. We know that Klaus has one of the bombs, but we don't know if he's figured out that the fail-safe system is fake. If he has, he'll want to rewire it. I need to know how that's done. Knowing that might help identify who could do it."

"It is simple," Veniamin said, "but if done wrong, the system would either not work, or it could kill the person making the changes."

Burly opened the suitcase on the table. Over the next three hours, Veniamin unsealed the bomb, disconnected and separated its components, and showed how he had wired it.

"One question," Burly said when the old engineer had finished. "How hard would it be to replicate your bombs?"

Veniamin leaned back in thought. "Not hard. The difficulty was designing it. A good technician could reverse engineer what I did. As long as he understands the wiring and has the materials, it could be done. I did it. The first bomb took months because I had to design it. The other three I did in a few hours. Of course, the materials were delivered cut to my specifications. Then it was a matter of assembly."

They broke for lunch. When they returned, Burly checked with other members of his staff, and took Atcho aside. "Have you heard from Sofia? I sent the fax to an FBI field office. I couldn't send it in the clear. A special agent went out to deliver it. Sofia didn't answer the phone, and when the agent arrived at the house, no one was home."

"I wouldn't worry," Atcho replied. "She keeps herself busy with the garden club and other activities, but I don't know the schedule. She's always shopping for things to decorate the house. She has one of those new cellular phones, but coverage is spotty in Austin because of the hills. Here's the number." He wrote it down on a slip of paper and handed it to Burly. "If I get to her first, I'll let her know to call you."

Veniamin re-entered the office. A few minutes later, Collins appeared. The two men greeted each other warmly. "I knew you would be here," Collins said. "I hoped I would see you." He turned to Burly. "I have the video we talked about yesterday. I spotted the man we think is Klaus."

"Let's see it." Burly took a cartridge from Collins and slipped it into a machine connected to a television monitor. The four men gathered around to watch. Having been filmed by a professional news cameraman, the images were crisp and clear.

Collins took the remote from Burly and manipulated the video to a particular point. "He first appears way back here," Collins said, and pointed out a figure far back in the crowd pouring through Checkpoint Charlie the night the Wall fell. "You see from his face that he's in a great deal of pain. Then as he gets closer to the gate, right here," he pointed the figure out again, "he becomes aware of the cameras, and tries to make a wide detour. The crowd was channeled through the border crossing there, so he couldn't escape the camera completely. Next, the view is good enough that we see he carries a suitcase, and it looks like the ones we have here." He paused the video. "And right here is the clearest shot we have of him."

Frozen on the screen was the face of a man with unkempt dark hair and a day's growth of beard. His face ducked away such that his right cheek was in shadows, but his eyes looked out of their corners, directly into the camera. They showed pain and insolence, and they burned with hatred between curled lips and a furrowed forehead.

"That's him!" Veniamin exclaimed. "That's Klaus. That's his face, those are the clothes he was wearing, and that was one of my suitcases."

"That's the man who abducted me," Atcho remarked.

"Zoom in," Burly said.

Collins complied.

"That's definitely him," Atcho affirmed. Veniamin agreed.

"All right," Burly said. "That face looks like the sketches Detective Berger sent us. I'll get this enhanced and forwarded to all stations. We should have the surveillance videos from the embassy here later this evening. They might have a better view from the front." He turned to Collins. "Great work."

Collins thanked him, and then addressed Atcho. "Any idea where you'll start and when you'll go?"

Atcho nodded. "Berlin is the last place he was seen. He can't be carrying that suitcase across borders. I don't think he'd flash his *Stasi* ID around. The headquarters was sacked by mobs a few days after the Wall opened. Lots of *Stasi* officers went to ground, and others hopped across the border that night and later.

"Add in that Klaus needed medical attention. How would he have paid for it? He deserted the KGB, Yermolov could no longer support him, the *Stasi* disintegrated, and he had to live somewhere. He couldn't go around bragging that he had a nuclear bomb. Plenty of people would be happy to take it from him. So, who's funding him?"

"I don't know if this helps," Veniamin interjected. "While I was still in the *Stasi* director's office, another man in the conspiracy came in. His name was Ranulf. He brought two duffle bags. He said there were five million dollars in them. His role in the conspiracy was to get the money. He told Yermolov he had bribed and threatened every East German official he could to collect it. Three million of it was supposed to pay me for the bombs, and the other two was to be divided among the other conspirators. When I escaped, those bags were still in the office, and so was Klaus."

The other three men stared at him. "I never asked for payment," Veniamin added quickly. "I built the bombs because of the threats to my family. Yermolov had ideas of using me for other things in the future. He thought the money would keep me happy."

"Relax," Atcho told him softly and grasped his shoulder. "You're fine with us."

"You know," Collins muttered, thinking out loud. "I saw a man carrying two duffle bags that night. He called to me, telling me he loved America and that he was coming to America. He came through a few minutes before Klaus did. I got that on film. He shows up in an earlier segment. If he and Klaus met up after crossing through Checkpoint Charlie, that might explain how Klaus supports himself. Five million dollars would take them a long way."

He manipulated the remote until he found the footage. They watched, mesmerized at the cheering crowd of celebrating East Germans moving across the screen. Then, a man passed by waving and smiling. "Thank you, America," he shouted.

Collins paused the video. The man stood in profile, his face turned to the camera. Clearly visible was a duffle bag slung over the man's left shoulder.

"Is that one of the bags?" Burly asked.

Veniamin stepped closer to the screen and squinted through his glasses. "I cannot be certain, but it appears to be the right size and color. I cannot see from this angle if he has another one on the other shoulder."

"That's good enough," Burly said. "I'll get this picture enhanced, enlarged, and send it and Klaus' photo to Detective Berger. Who knows what might turn up?"

The four men stood silently around the monitor studying the photo, absorbing it in the context of the events that led to the footage. Then they took their seats at the conference table again.

Collins spoke first. "Getting back to my earlier question, Atcho, is Berlin definitely the starting point?"

"It is. I'll fly over tomorrow. My appointments are set up."

"My first articles will be ready to go. They'll hit the wires as soon as Burly tells me, so they'll have wide distribution in large newspapers everywhere. They'll be placed prominently and will be printed in the major languages. If Klaus pays attention, he'll see them. Or someone close to him will. Good luck to you."

Late that night, Burly called Atcho. "I'm not trying to be an alarmist, buddy, but I've had people calling Sofia regularly. Not a peep heard back."

"I know," Atcho replied, his voice betraying his anxiety. "She called me a little while ago. I don't know where she is, and she won't tell me. She's flown the coop."

8

While Atcho and Burly discussed Sofia's whereabouts, daybreak was three hours away in Berlin. Nevertheless, Sofia lay wide awake in bed. Setting aside the wave of nausea that hit her when her eyes flickered open, she felt regretful over her conversation with Atcho a couple of hours earlier. She had expected his frustration, and he delivered in Atcho-style, most of it controlled.

She had called to let him know that she was still among the living and to apologize for leaving with no notice. "Burly will not control what I do," she said stiffly. "You're going to need help in the field. No one's more qualified for that than me."

"Where are you?"

Sofia hesitated. "Darling, you know I'm not going to tell you," she purred. "Why ask?"

After a short silence, Atcho replied, "I thought I'd give it a shot. You could've had a mental lapse. What are you going to do?"

"I'm not sure yet. Watch, listen, learn. I'll pick up a thread and follow it. When I find out something useful, I'll let you know. How will I reach you? Can you tell me on an open line?"

Atcho laughed, his tone ironic. "I'll be highly visible. Intentionally. I'm leaving for Berlin tomorrow."

Sofia's breath caught. *Berlin seemed to me the logical place to start. I guess they thought so too.* "Why there?"

"We found video showing Klaus coming through Checkpoint Charlie. Now we know that his right shoulder was wounded. Someone had to have treated him."

"Where will you stay?"

"I'll be at the primary location for the US Embassy at the Chancery in old East Berlin. We'll see where it leads from there." Germany was still in the midst of reunification, and the US along with other countries struggled with combining their embassies in Bonn with the consulates in Berlin. "Walking around in areas where a year ago I could get shot by government officers just for being there will feel strange. Once news of my presence is out, I imagine someone might site me in their crosshairs." He laughed. "That'll restore some sense of familiarity."

"Don't even joke about that. I want you back in one piece."

"Ditto, lady. I'm being nice, but I'm not happy that you went indie again. I'm a husband now, your husband, and I don't need to worry about where you are and what danger you're in." His voice grew heated. "I'm still hoping to have a family with you. If you don't get yourself killed first."

Neither spoke for a full minute. "I'm sorry," Sofia said at last. "I'm just tired of seeing you go into these situations and having to drum up your own support. I know what I'm doing. I can help."

"Well the difference this time is that I'm getting lots of support, and you're out there alone."

"And it's going to stay that way," Sofia retorted. "I can take care of myself. I'm not going back to DC so Burly can dictate to me. I'm most effective in the field."

Atcho sighed audibly into the phone. "All right. There's no changing your mind. One piece of good news, Major Horton is being assigned to help me. I requested him."

Sofia chuckled. "Is he still in Berlin? That *is* good news. He knows his way around, he speaks the language, and he's a fighter—when he's not cracking jokes. He's a good man to have at your back. I feel a little better now."

"Good. Now will you go home?"

"No." Frustration hung in the air, palpable through the phone. "How did your day go in DC? Did you learn anything useful?"

"Not much. We knew Klaus was wounded. He either got surgery, or he kissed that arm goodbye. That's about it."

———

Two hours later, Sofia got out of bed in the dark and fumbled in her suitcase. She found a pack of crackers she had picked up at the airport and nibbled down a few. When she lay back down, the wave of nausea gradually passed. She fell asleep.

When she awoke four hours later, the sun was already high in the sky. She dressed in Turkish garb and set out for Little Istanbul. Turkish immigrants had shaped the area toward their own culture. At the edge of the area, she looked for tearooms and cafés where customers had settled in for morning conversation.

Little Istanbul was run-down compared to most of West Berlin. Colorful graffiti adorned the walls on narrow streets. Women dressed similarly to Sofia scurried in twos and threes or in the company of a man, a family member. Along the sidewalks, chairs had been set outside of the eateries interspersed among various shops. Melodies of Turkey played amid the aroma of mint tea.

She entered a café and immediately noticed everyone staring. All were male. The proprietor, a portly man with an apron, hurried from behind the counter. He yelled at her in Turkish, waving his hands in the air. "You can't be in here, whore. Get out!"

Sofia stood her ground. "Are all German Turks so rude?" she retorted in perfectly accented Arabic. "I'm here from Kuwait while the war is going on. All I want is breakfast, and if I can't eat here, maybe you can show a stranger the courtesy of pointing out where I *can* eat." She was on thin ice, and she knew it. If this man felt insulted, her life could be in jeopardy. She counted on the fact that she was in Berlin, not Turkey.

The proprietor diverted his eyes from her face, looking past her, still angry. "Where is your husband, or a male member of your family?"

Sofia pulled her cell phone from the folds of her clothing. "He's a prince of the royal family, and he'll be on his way. In Kuwait, it is permitted for a woman to go about alone for short errands. I was looking for a place for breakfast and then I'll call him like a good wife should."

The proprietor showed his uneasiness as the men around him mumbled between themselves. "You still should not be in here," he grumbled. He started toward the front of his café, waving his hand for her to follow. "Go down to the next street and then turn that way." He demonstrated with his left hand. "Go another distance and then you'll see a *Kemasil* restaurant on this side of the street." He gestured with his right hand. "I shouldn't help you like this, but that's where it is. They let women in there alone. Don't come back here. This is a respectable establishment."

Sofia thanked him and started off. She knew *Kemasil* was a more secular practice of Islam. In the melting pot of Islamic culture that Germany had hosted over centuries and accentuated in Berlin, *Kemasil* was a fairly recent Islamic splinter group. Its practitioners prospered better and were more educated than most of their Islamic brethren. Professional women were not uncommon among them. Sofia knew that the *Kemasil* philosophy had separated Islam from politics under Ataturk, a revolutionary leader who transformed Turkey into a democratic republic in the early twentieth century. For governing purposes, Islam had been removed there.

She found the establishment. It was off the street, and comparatively upscale. Before entering, she went into the ladies' room of an adjoining office building and changed her appearance by removing the scarf over her head and the outer layer of the robes wrapped around her. She stuffed them into a plastic net-bag she took from her purse. When she presented herself at the door of the restaurant, she appeared in more Western attire, although still having the distinctive flavor of Islamic culture.

She ordered a breakfast of Turkish breads, meats, and cheeses, and requested a copy of the *International Herald Tribune*. She scanned the headlines and articles. At the top of the news, Saddam Hussein, the dictator of Iraq for decades, still ruled Kuwait with an iron hand. Reports of his troops' looting and raping were widespread.

Sofia knew the history. Saddam had long maintained that Kuwait rightfully belonged to Iraq as another province. The royal family in Kuwait had ceded defense and foreign policy to the British near the beginning of the twentieth century, and the country had regained its independence in 1961. Over the intervening years, Kuwait had grown its petroleum industry, and had become a wealthy country.

According to an article, a major section of Kuwait's oil fields bordered those of Iraq's Ramallah. Hussein accused Kuwait of slant-drilling and siphoning petroleum from Ramallah. He demanded ten billion dollars in reparations. When Kuwait paid only nine billion, Hussein used the underpayment as a pretext to annex Kuwait and invaded. US President George H. W. Bush pledged military support and organized a coalition of thirty-three nations to expel Iraq from Kuwait. Full combat operations by the US and its coalition were imminent.

Sofia shook her head. *What a world.* She scanned other articles. Then her attention riveted on an article in the center of the front page, below the fold.

US Ambassador and Berlin Mayor to Welcome US Businessman

Ambassador McCay and Mayor Schneider will welcome Eduardo Xiquez to Berlin today for discussions regarding potentially opening a manufacturing plant in the city. Xiquez is a minor celebrity in the United States, having been honored by former President Ronald Reagan in a State of the Union Address. Reagan introduced him to the nation as "Atcho," his code-name during his days of fighting Castro in Cuba. He is the chairman of Advance Power Source Technologies, a Texas-based company that manufactures an alternative to batteries. His units are reported to be lighter, more efficient, and more cost-effective. The United States' defense industry is a major customer. The technology to produce the power source is highly classified. Many hurdles exist to locating a plant in Berlin. US NATO allies are anxious to apply the product in their equipment. Having such a facility located in central Europe would accelerate availability and shipping time at a lower price. Xiquez is expected to tour various places in Berlin for the next three days. He might extend his European trip to visit sites in other NATO countries. Experts say that the power source is a game-changer in war fighting because of its much lighter weight and greater reliability, crucial to smooth communications and targeting systems. In particular, the technology is better able to deal with extreme temperatures as will be experienced in upcoming combat operations in Kuwait.

Her heart in her mouth, Sofia read and re-read the article. *Talk about exposing Atcho!* She was suddenly furious with Burly for recruiting him, with Atcho for accepting the mission, and with Tony Collins for providing so much key information. *If Klaus intends to hit Atcho at home, now he knows where to look. We'll need heavy duty security for the rest of our lives. In Berlin, Atcho's a sitting duck.*

She forced herself to moderate her breathing and calm down. *It's done. Focus on helping.* She put the paper down and observed her surroundings. *Where would Klaus get medical attention?* She called the waiter over. "My family is staying in the city temporarily, and my husband needs a doctor. Can you ask the owner or manager if he would come speak with me to recommend one?"

"My father is the owner," the young man said. "I can send you to our family physician. Let me get the address." He left and came back with a note. Sofia read it aloud for correctness and a few minutes later, she left.

She found the doctor's office. The room was crowded with patients wearing various versions of Middle-Eastern garb. "I'm looking for specialized treatment for my husband," she told the young woman at the front desk. "He was wounded in Kuwait, and his shoulder needs reconstructing. Does the doctor here do that kind of treatment?"

The answer was no, but the attendant gave her a list of Turkish surgeons who might specialize in reconstructive surgery. Sofia moved about Little Istanbul, modifying her appearance as she went, to blend in with the surrounding population. She stopped in several of the surgeons' offices on the list, asking the same question in each one. "Has the doctor performed reconstruction on a shoulder demolished by a gunshot wound?"

Her quest took most of the day. Before entering each office, she took a quick glance at the patients in the waiting room, and then found somewhere to modify her appearance to reflect them as much as possible. Then, she waited patiently for her turn to speak to the attendant at the front desk. As the day wore on, she embellished her story and her emotional expression, morphing into a sympathetic figure suffering from the war in Kuwait with a terribly wounded husband. She emphasized that she preferred an Islamic surgeon because she did not want an infidel touching him.

That evening, having struck out, she sat in her room to reassess. *What if all Klaus did was stop his bleeding and close the wound without reconstructing the shoulder? If so, any doctor could have treated him—or first-aid could have been applied by anyone with a bit of competence. That would complicate the search.*

She pushed the thought from her mind. *Stay on this thread until it's exhausted. There can't be many surgeons who've done that type of procedure.*

The second day yielded no better results. Exhausted from walking the streets for two days, she flopped on her bed, turned on the television, and roamed to a news station. Then she sat up in bed abruptly and stared at the screen.

In clear relief, the US ambassador stood in the office of the mayor of Berlin. They beamed at the cameras as they shook hands with a man standing between them. Then the cameras zoomed in for a close-up of all three. The caption at the bottom of the screen read, "Berlin Welcomes Atcho."

9

Klaus groaned as Dr. Burakgazi pressed on his right shoulder. "It's still painful."

"The surgery was successful though. You've made a lot of progress since November—that's only been a little over two months. I'm encouraged that you're getting your strength back. That will increase with physical therapy. Shoulder replacement surgery is not easy, but it is common these days. You should have come to us as soon as you injured it."

Klaus shrugged. "And I should've been born rich. I didn't know about you then. I wasn't high enough in the Communist Party. If the Wall hadn't come down, I wouldn't have known about this treatment."

Dr. Burakgazi prodded Klaus' shoulder again. "Let's check the range of motion. Be patient, keep working your muscles regularly but not too much. You'll return to near normal use." While speaking, he lifted Klaus' arm and moved it gently through circular motions. "You're healing well. Thank Allah for his mercies."

He cleared his throat and stepped back, clearly changing the subject. "Listen, there is a lady from Kuwait staying in Berlin. Her husband was wounded in Kuwait and he needs shoulder surgery. A colleague called me about her today. He wanted to know if he should refer her to me. He told the woman about your surgery and that I was the premier Muslim surgeon in Berlin in this specialty. She requested to speak with you so that she could explain to her husband what to expect. She told my friend that she has gone to all the Muslim surgeons she could find in Berlin. She will only go to an infidel doctor as a last resort."

"Sounds like a good Muslim woman. Why hasn't she come to you yet?"

Burakgazi shrugged. "I understand she's working from a list. She's visiting doctors' offices personally. My name must be near the bottom. After my colleague's recommendation, she'll be here tomorrow or the next day. Her husband must be highly ranked to travel to Berlin to get the care he needs."

"If she stops in, and you think it makes sense, I don't mind meeting with her."

Burakgazi completed his examination. Klaus put his shirt back on. He started to leave but stopped at the door. "Doctor, what do you think of this war in Kuwait? Which side do you support?"

Burakgazi sighed. "That's a tough one. You're Sunni, aren't you?" Klaus nodded. "So am I," the doctor continued. "Kuwait is mainly Sunni, and so is Saddam Hussein and his party. But most of Iraq is Shia. Iran is Shia, and this whole mess was caused when Iraq invaded Iran in 1980 and started that bloody war. At the end of it, Saddam owed billions in loans from Saudi Arabia and Kuwait. He was furious when they refused to forgive the debt.

"You know he also claimed that Kuwait belonged to Iraq as a province. I've looked at the history. Saddam had no claim on Kuwait, but by making that nine-billion-dollar payment, Kuwait all but admitted that it stole Iraq's oil. And don't forget that Kuwait had been underselling OPEC pricing. Saddam claimed that cost him billions."

"He has a point about who owns Kuwait," Klaus responded. "Way back when, Kuwait was part of Iraq's Basra Province."

"Well, like you said, way back when, before the British created Iraq with lines on a map, and before the royal family in Kuwait ceded foreign policy to the British."

Klaus nodded. "As you say, it's a mess." He sighed. "Let me ask the question a different way. How would Islam be best served? By Kuwait winning or by Iraq winning?"

The surgeon peered at him closely. "I'm not sure. I'm a doctor and took an oath to do no harm. Saddam is a monster. He treats his people in ways that hurt to think about. I've met some of his victims. One soldier was taken to prison because a member of the secret police on the street overheard him complaining that the price of tea was so high. At the time, Saddam could not afford to pay the army. They tortured that soldier, and one day they forced him to watch dead prisoners being pushed through a meat grinder." He stopped talking as unwelcome visions of the horror invaded his mind.

Klaus studied his face. "The Kuwaitis are no angels either. And don't forget that the US supported Iraq against Iran. They only did it to weaken Iran. Before that, the Soviet Union supported Iraq."

"True. And not long ago, Kuwait's people were a poor tribe in the desert. Now they are drunk with oil riches. Kuwaitis don't work—they import foreign labor and have servants for everything. But that's not the same as torturing people."

Klaus weighed the doctor's comment. "I see that." He contemplated a moment. "Getting back to my question, take it from another angle. How is the infidel most harmed, by Iraq winning, or by Kuwait winning?"

Burakgazi took a seat on his stool next to the examining table. He shook his head slowly. "I really don't know. I suppose if Saddam wins, he can continue to shake his fist at the West. That would deprive the West of an ally in the region."

"A traitorous ally," Klaus muttered scornfully. "Saddam has the fourth largest army in the world. President Bush won't commit ground troops. He's afraid of another Vietnam, and the American people have no stomach for another prolonged war. All this buildup is just a show of force.

"Bush gave Saddam a five-day ultimatum to leave or face combat. Like the lion of the desert that he is, Saddam stayed. You'll see, in a few more weeks, the US will withdraw, and Iraq will still own Kuwait."

"I'm not so sure," Burakgazi said doubtfully. "Bush is a combat veteran, and look what he did in Panama last year. He's been very careful in how he's built up forces in Saudi Arabia to fight Saddam."

Klaus mulled. "Iraq needs a game-changer," he muttered.

"A game-changer? What do you mean?"

"Never mind, I was thinking out loud."

"Well," Burakgazi continued, "if Iraq keeps Kuwait, Saddam will own one-fifth of the world's oil supply and threaten Saudi Arabia. The US will never allow that."

"Saudi Arabia," Klaus growled, his voice thick with disdain. "They defile Islam by selling out to infidels for oil riches and letting them put military bases on the sacred Arabian Peninsula. If Allah wills it, and I pray that he does, Saddam will win this fight in Kuwait, and then roll over the top of Saudi Arabia." He started for the door again. "Thank you for a very interesting discussion, Doctor." He left, calling back over his shoulder. "Let me know about that woman, when she wants to meet."

10

That same day, Atcho arrived in Berlin. He did not care for the spotlight. He had endured it once before under coercion when Ronald Reagan honored him at the State of the Union Address, but he shunned publicity as much as he could. Therefore, when he descended onto the tarmac from a private jet in the general aviation section of the Berlin Tegel "Otto Lilienthal" Airport, he steeled himself to appear relaxed and affable. He knew that an official welcoming delegation would greet him, but when US Ambassador McCay showed up with a gaggle of reporters and television crews, the effort to be gracious was more than he had expected.

McCay escorted him to a waiting limousine and whisked him to the main embassy compound. "You understand that you're getting royal treatment," McCay told him. "Ordinarily, an ambassador wouldn't come to greet a businessman at the airport. But I understand that raising your visibility for a classified purpose is the intent, with German cooperation. I'm happy to help."

"Thanks for your courtesy."

"I read up on your company, so I know it's *bona fide* and impressive. Are you really considering opening a plant here?"

Atcho smiled blandly. "Our hands are full, servicing the markets we have. But who knows? We might do it someday if sufficient demand is there, and the timing and finance came together."

McCay nodded. "Well, the articles covering your arrival and the stated reason were published this morning in major newspapers in multiple languages. You'll have a long interview tomorrow morning on the US Armed Forces Network, and you'll have at least one televised interview each day for three days. Those will be more like informal press updates. All of those interviews will be shared on German television multiple times a day. By the second or third day, everyone in Berlin should know your name and face." He shook his head. "That's probably not an enviable position. I hope we can keep you safe and that your risk is worth it."

Atcho was touched by the ambassador's humanity. "Thank you, sir. I appreciate your concern."

"There'll be a reception in your honor this evening, and Mayor Schneider will be there. That's to be consistent with the attention you're getting. The real show starts tomorrow morning with the interview. Between now and the reception tonight, relax and enjoy yourself. The next few days are not likely to be fun."

They arrived at the embassy. Self-important assistants bustled about, opening doors and taking his bags. A few reporters jammed microphones in his direction and yelled questions. Atcho waved at them with a smile he did not feel and followed the ambassador through the main door. Another group of attendants waited inside. Then, he caught sight of a man who made him smile for real.

At the end of the hall, a US Army major in a dress-blue uniform stood with a huge grin on his face. When his eyes met Atcho's, he pulled his face into a serious expression and moved his eyes from side to side as if checking to see if anyone was observing him.

Atcho knew the major could not care less. "Major Joe Horton," he exclaimed in a command voice, and held out his hand. "Why are you all dressed up?"

"It's about time you got here, sir," the major responded. "I've been standing here waiting for at least," he looked at his watch, "two minutes." He broke into a grin again. "Good to see you, Atcho. As for this monkey suit, I got to escort you to that *soirée*." He intoned the last word with a dose of sarcasm in a heavy Texas accent, and then turned to the ambassador. "I got him from here, sir, unless you have something else right now."

McCay shook his head, clearly amused at the interplay. "Nothing now. I'll see you both at the reception."

Atcho thanked McCay and followed Horton from the foyer. "Let's get someplace where we can talk," Horton said. "How's the little lady?"

"Independent as ever," Atcho replied. "I'll tell you more when we're in a secure location."

"You mean we gotta talk quietly about what she's doing too?" He looked up at the ceiling as if pleading for sanity. "What have you got yourself into this time, Atcho? When they said you needed my help, I said hell no, I won't go 'cuz I like living." He led Atcho through a door into a conference room. "We're good here. This place is secure."

They sat across from each other at the table. Atcho studied his friend's face. He had not changed in any way that Atcho could detect. "I see that you have at least three more wrinkles under your eyes."

"Yes sir," Horton replied stone-faced. "That's from laughing so hard about your screwups last time you were here." His face broke into its characteristic grin. "Now are you going to fill me in, or are we going to sit and gab all day?"

To Atcho, Horton was a one-of-a-kind, a maverick, a stocky Texan who was proud to be one and enjoyed exaggerating the accent. He had entered military service in the enlisted ranks, fought in the swamps of Vietnam as a foot soldier, traveled that country on loan to the CIA for special missions, and advised the Montagnard tribes in Vietnam's central highlands. He could be singularly irreverent and respectful at the same time, an aspect that sometimes bewildered his superiors. But he was the man they wanted at their side in a firefight.

Two years ago, he had been assigned as a team leader to the Berlin Brigade's Flag Tours, special intelligence assets that roamed East Berlin. Ostensibly, they enforced the travel and accessibility rights accorded by the Four Powers Treaty that governed post-WWII Berlin. In reality, all such teams gathered intelligence. In effect, they were legal spies.

Horton had rescued Atcho out of East Berlin at a time when they both could have been shot, before the Wall came down. At Atcho's request, Horton had been assigned to assist in a mission that led in part to opening the Wall. With his tenacity, experience, and knowledge of Berlin and the German language, there was no one Atcho would rather have backing him.

"Sofia was thrilled that you're working with me. I don't know how she'd feel about your still calling her 'little lady.' She might smack you."

Horton's eyes grew wide. "Well then don't tell her. I sure as hell don't want her coming after me."

The truth was that Sofia loved Horton. She had seen him bring out a rare side of Atcho that could relax, laugh, and even crack jokes.

Horton had met Sofia and Atcho in Berlin. He knew Sofia's capabilities from personal experience.

"Where's Miss Sofia now?" he inquired.

"We don't know." Atcho related what had transpired between Sofia and Burly. He went into detail about Klaus and the lone nuclear bomb still outside of the control of authorities. He also recounted what they'd learned from the videos.

"I'm here to draw Klaus into the open," Atcho concluded.

Horton listened intently. "So that's why all the special attention," he said. "I wondered, 'cuz you sure didn't earn it." He broke into his wide grin. "Would you do me a favor, sir? Would you and Sofia invite me over for dinner sometime? Just a nice dinner with no excitement." He chuckled. "I could use the peace and quiet."

Atcho laughed. "You're welcome any time, Joe."

Horton looked at him through squinted eyes. "Be sure to have a fresh bottle of cognac." He pronounced it "cony-ak." "I like my cognac." He leaned back, spread his legs apart, and interlocked his fingers behind his head. "I got read in on the plan this morning, and I gave my guys a warning order. They're ready. It's a little easier moving around in Berlin now. We can use civilian cars instead of those olive-drab sedans we had, and we don't have to wear uniforms.

"We'll shadow everywhere you go. We'll augment the normal security that surrounds the ambassador and the mayor. We'll be invisible, but, and this is a big but, when you're not with him or the mayor, you won't have their security." He grinned. "Then it'll just be me and my guys. As far as anybody watching will know, you'll be traveling solo. That'll leave you exposed."

"That's the idea."

Joe scrunched his mouth and shrugged. "OK, it's your neck."

"That's what you told me going into *Stasi* headquarters last year."

"You mean that night you almost got me killed?" He rubbed his left thigh. "Ooh, that wound still smarts sometimes. You made me screw up my perfect score on the PT test. Any idea where Sofia is?"

Atcho nodded. "She's a logical thinker. She'll come to the same conclusion we did, that Klaus is probably still in Berlin, or that he'll come to Berlin when he knows that I'm here."

Horton nodded. "He was sore at you for killing his brother. He won't let that go."

"You're the guy that shot out his shoulder. You'd think he'd be mad at you too."

"He never saw me."

"Anyway, back to Sofia, my guess is she came here operating as a free agent."

"Makes sense. I'll have my guys keep an eye out for her. If we spot her, I'll tell them not to engage, but to call for reinforcements." His eyes twinkled. "All we got here is the Berlin Brigade. Do ya think that'll be enough?"

Atcho smiled. "If you spot her, let me know. I expect to hear from her soon."

"All right. What do *we* do next?"

"Not much. Sit tight and go through the motions the next couple of days until something breaks loose."

The reception that evening was uneventful, with no more nor less news coverage than would have been present at any black-tie gala attended by public officials. Atcho mingled awkwardly and forced himself to stand his ground when he saw cameras aimed his direction. Fortunately, he had no press inquiries to deal with that evening.

The next morning, he sat with Ambassador McCay and Mayor Schneider for the AFN interview. When it was over, McCay and Schneider returned to normal duties while a few business leaders hosted Atcho on tours of potential sites for the proposed manufacturing facility.

Late that afternoon, Atcho and Horton reconvened in another secure room of the embassy, this one set up to address their specific needs. "We saw nothing unusual," Horton reported. "I hope those business types don't get wind that this is all for show. They'll be all over you like bees on honey, only their stingers'll be more like claws. They went all out to impress you."

"I know, and they're already offering incentives. Wouldn't that be crazy if real business comes out of this?"

11

The next morning, Klaus walked into a barbershop in Little Istanbul. Dr. Burakgazi had called late the evening before.

"The lady we spoke about yesterday came in after you left. Her name is Ranim Kuti. She's very concerned that her husband has gone too long without surgery. She said she could come tomorrow afternoon, if you can be here."

Klaus had agreed. He came to the barbershop to ensure he made himself presentable. A number of customers were ahead of him. He picked up an Arabic language newspaper and scanned the top headline.

The article reported on the Iraq-Kuwait war. Iraq had consolidated its control of Kuwait, but pockets of resistance still existed. Saddam's troops had been merciless in quelling opposition. Even when Kuwaitis submitted, whether soldier or civilian, they were treated with the cruelest humiliations and tortures. Homes were confiscated, wives and daughters raped and taken for slaves, and household goods looted to be carted off to Iraq or sold. Thousands of people were executed.

In retaliation, the world community, including much of the Arab region, sided with Kuwait in condemning Saddam. For his part, the strongman ruler remained pugnacious, maintaining his right to annex Kuwait, take its oil, and be unrepentant.

The article went on to report that US military staging in the region was reaching critical mass. Combat operations to oust Saddam were imminent.

Klaus read the piece with interest but without emotional attachment to either side. He had never tortured anyone but had done his share of killing, and he saw an element of reason in Saddam's argument—if Kuwait had indeed stolen Iraq's oil, then they should be made to pay. *The price seems high, but if Kuwait had paid the money, this war could have been avoided.*

He looked up from reading to check on the progress of those ahead of him. Several customers still had to be served, so he scanned further down the page. He found an article just below the fold titled, "US Ambassador and Berlin Mayor to Welcome US Businessman Xiquez." He started reading, and then his eyes grew large as they locked in on the word, "Atcho." Fury welled inside him. He took several deep breaths and started reading the article again from the beginning. When he had finished, he looked wildly about, ripped out the article and stuffed it in his pocket. He got up to leave but paused to check the date of the newspaper. It was published the day before. *Atcho is already here.*

Klaus left the barbershop and hurried back to the apartment. He turned on the television and tuned in to one of the news stations—and then another, and another... In frustration, he turned to the US Armed Forces Network. Usually the reception was weak because it was intended to serve those areas where US military members and their dependents lived. It broadcast on a low power transmitter, but sometimes the signal extended beyond intended limits.

Today, the channel was clear, and there onscreen, sitting in a discussion with Mayor Schneider, US Ambassador McCay, and a moderator, was Atcho himself. Klaus stared in disbelief and sucked in his breath. Shaking with anger, he reached over and turned up the volume.

"...but it's a fairly new technology," Atcho was saying. "I was fortunate to become acquainted with the company as it emerged from infancy. I'm pleased to help it grow."

"It seems you've done a good job," the moderator interjected. "I've heard the technology described as a game-changer on the battlefield. Is that true?"

Atcho appeared to choose his words carefully. "I don't want to over-state, but our units should have a positive effect. When you think of the weather extremes that our forces will meet in Kuwait if fighting extends into summer months, a power source that continues to operate reliably in those temperatures might make the difference in securing a military objective.

"Interchangeability between multiple pieces of equipment means that fewer spare units must be carried. Add the weight savings resulting from a lighter source and the increased range might be enough to tip the scales in a battle, not to mention operational cost savings.

"Then throw in fewer communications or computer breakdowns from overheat or battery expiration. That translates into better intelli-gence collection, analysis, and decision making. It means more heavy munitions delivered on target. Yeah, we think our little piece of tech-nology can make a difference."

Mayor Schneider sat quietly listening to the discussion. "You're talking over my head," he said in English with a Germanic accent. "I'm not a military man. I don't understand military discussions. But I do understand commerce and jobs, and as you know we are working hard to absorb our cousins from the former East Germany. I know that the Pentagon is enthusiastic about your product, and our European defense industry shows great interest. How many jobs do you think could be generated if you were to install a plant here?"

"Let me take Mr. Xiquez off the hot seat," the ambassador broke in. "By the way, Americans fondly call him Atcho."

"We don't know the answer to your question, but that's why Atcho is here. As chairman of his company, he'll be meeting with various defense officials to assess the demand. He'll also tour sites where manufacturing assets exist. He'll see vacant properties for building new facilities. We think the project could be good for Germany, Berlin, the US, and our allies."

"That sounds great," the moderator interjected. "I hope you'll keep us informed of your progress."

The interview continued. Klaus snapped off the television. He sat staring at the blank screen for an indefinite time, livid, shaking. He breathed in short gasps. Every ounce of anger and hatred he had known on that fateful night when he found his brother Etzel's limp body surged through him. He left the apartment to take a walk, and to think.

For the next two hours, Klaus roamed the streets. His mind was too numb to conduct any deliberate thought but gradually his pace slowed, and his mind calmed. *Impulsiveness kills.* He stopped in a café to rest. While drinking tea, he decided to take a day to absorb the implications of Atcho's arrival back in Berlin.

He glanced at his watch, remembering he had promised Dr. Burakgazi that he would come by to speak with Ranim Kuti. That was in twenty minutes. He paid his bill and hurried to keep the appointment.

Sofia sat in a crowded tearoom situated where she could observe the approaches to Dr. Burakgazi's office. She dressed in the garb of moderately fundamental sects of the Muslim religion. Her face was partially covered.

Pedestrian traffic was fairly thick, so keeping effective watch over everyone who entered the building was difficult. She finally gave up the effort, left the café, and hurried to Burakgazi's office. On arrival, instead of checking in at the reception desk, she sat among the waiting patients, looking as obscure as possible.

She had been there twenty minutes when a man entered. Before approaching the receptionist's desk, he surveyed the room.

Sofia's heart beat faster. She felt her palms moisten. She averted her eyes, but she had already taken a quick glance at him. He was the right height and build for Klaus, but he was dressed in a business suit and his hair and beard were trimmed. Nevertheless, she was sure it was him.

Klaus' eyes passed over her and the other patients in the room. Then he announced himself to the secretary. "Oh yes," the young woman said, "the doctor is expecting you." She stood and gestured for Klaus to follow.

As soon as he disappeared into the inner offices, Sofia hurried back to the tearoom. She asked to use the phone, called the doctor's receptionist, and made apologies for not being able to keep the appointment. She gave no reason.

She waited. Five minutes later, she saw Klaus leave the office building. He looked angry and walked at a swift pace. She followed at a safe distance.

Klaus seethed. Not only had he read the news and seen the television report about Atcho's arrival in Berlin and suffered through all the bad memories and feelings that they conjured up, but he had also been stood up for a meeting that he had agreed to as a courtesy. *I even cleaned up for it.* Most infuriating about the broken appointment was that he had gone to Burakgazi's office out of respect for a Muslim fighter. In Klaus' mind, the wounded man was on the wrong side of the fight, but he was a Muslim who had placed himself in harm's way for what he believed was right.

He reached the street, paused to check his surroundings, and started walking in the direction of his apartment complex at his normal fast pace. He passed a tearoom close to the office building and on a quick look inside, he noticed a woman whom he had seen a few minutes ago in the doctor's reception room.

The apartment was a good mile away. At the moment, all Klaus wanted was to get to a quiet place where he could lie down and think.

As was his habit, he stopped to look into shop windows or admire elements of the city as he continued toward his destination. When he did, he routinely looked back in the direction he had come. This time, he saw a woman stopped in front of a store viewing items in the window. Her headdress was similar to the lady's in the doctor's office and the tearoom, but he could not be certain she was the same person. The woman he had seen had been sitting both times. He abruptly retraced his steps.

Sofia watched Klaus pass in front of the tearoom. She waited a few moments and then followed from a healthy distance. She noticed he was alert and practiced at watching for surveillance, glancing into shops and stores, and sweeping his vision into the street, along the opposite sidewalk, and back again. He stopped in front of a shop.

Sofia halted too, in front of a women's apparel boutique. She stepped close to the display window and stared at the array of shoes, handbags, and accessories. From the corner of her eye, she saw Klaus walking again —toward her. Keeping a nonchalant demeanor, she entered the store. It was small and longer than it was wide. Sofia headed to the rear.

A door blocked passage into the storage area. She tried the handle. It was locked. She looked back to the front. A tall, round freestanding rack of scarves and other accessories set near the front counter to the right of the entry, about ten feet inside the door.

Sofia moved next to the display so that it blocked the view of her from the door. Just as she did, she heard a bell announcing someone's entry. Her heart raced. She moved farther around the rack. A woman emerged from the other side examining merchandise. Sofia breathed a sigh of relief.

The door at the rear opened. An officious-looking woman entered. She walked directly up to Sofia. "Did you need something? I saw you on our surveillance monitor. You tried the door into our storage area."

"Ah yes," Sofia said, a cold tone in her voice. She spoke in deliberately broken English with an Arabic accent. She reached into her purse and pulled out an official-looking ID with Arabic writing. "I'm here from the mosque to do a quick check to see that the clothing you sell meets the standards required for Muslim women. I won't bother your customers in the front but take me into the back and let me check the inventory."

The manager looked at her in alarm. "Of course, we always try to accommodate our Muslim customers. What would you like to see?" She headed toward the back of the store. Sofia followed her.

When they entered the storage area, Sofia closed the door behind them and headed to an outside exit at the back of the building. Without saying a word, she slipped through, leaving the store manager looking bewildered. Finding herself in an alley, Sofia paralleled the street in the same direction she had been going when Klaus saw her.

The passage was long and dark, casting gloom along its length. Sofia stopped in the deepest shadows long enough to rip off her full-length skirt and loose upper body covering. Underneath, she wore fashionably torn denims and a heavy sweater. She exchanged her high heels for a pair of flats pulled from her purse. Then, she removed her head covering, tied her hair into a quick bun with another scarf, and put a pair of sunglasses over her eyes. She pulled a light bag from her purse, jammed the items in, and threw it over her shoulder. The transformation took all of two minutes. Then she hurried to the end of the alley.

Making her way back onto the street, she crossed to the opposite side and headed back toward the store, watching the area to its front. She spotted Klaus under a tree, ostensibly reading a newspaper. She sat on a bench in the shade well back from the edge of the street, where she could observe without being easily seen.

Ten minutes passed. Klaus entered the store. He remained only a few minutes before re-emerging. He looked about and proceeded in his previous direction.

Sofia followed, ensuring that something was always between them that would inhibit his view of her. Whenever his head turned too far toward the street, she paused. Fortunately, a large number of people walked in the same direction.

Klaus took a side street. Sofia maintained her direction of travel, but as she crossed the intersection crowded with other pedestrians, she took a quick glance the way Klaus had gone. It led into Little Istanbul. Klaus stood against the wall a few yards down the street, lighting a cigarette while facing her direction.

Sofia kept walking. Whether or not Klaus spotted her again, she could only guess. She went to the next intersection, turned right, and doubled back to where she had last seen Klaus. He was no longer there.

Klaus was angry with himself. *Was that woman really following me?* He had no idea. Her departure from the doctor's office and being in the tearoom close by seemed questionable. *Maybe she just went to get a drink while she waited.* He was not even sure she was the same woman he had seen in front of the dress shop. *And where did she go?* He had gone inside and queried the girl behind the counter. The clerk had seen the woman he described, but simply remarked, "She left," without offering further comment. When Klaus pressed, the girl merely shrugged her shoulders.

Admittedly, Klaus had become engrossed in an article while conducting surveillance. *Did I miss her?* On turning off the main street, he lit a cigarette. His real reason for pausing was to observe pedestrians crossing the street. Several unaccompanied women went by. None resembled the woman he had seen.

As he trudged back to the apartment, he thought through the events of the day, acknowledging that he might be allowing unmerited anxiety to take hold. *Can't do that.*

He had been thinking overtime about what to do with his bombs and had considered several alternatives. One in particular had developed. The more he thought about it, the better he liked it. Since his entry into West Berlin with the great crowds, he had worked alone. He lived in an apartment with others, but he had never divulged his secrets, and insofar as he could tell, none had been discovered.

The truth was, although his cohabitants respected him, they feared him. They knew his capabilities. They saw him in action the night his brother was killed.

The men had been generous in providing shelter. They had arranged for the nurse to care for him during his convalescence. But Klaus recalled that Etzel had once admonished, "They won't do us much good in a real fight." Klaus had to agree. They had demonstrated that in the firefight with Atcho.

The thought of Atcho set off another round of anger. *And that Ranim Kuti woman wasted my time.*

After Klaus' initial frustration wore off, he sat back in his apartment to think. He was not a believer in coincidence. One that seemed to have occurred was the almost simultaneous acquisition of his nuclear material and Atcho's appearance in Berlin.

He tried to think through how the two events could be linked. He knew about electronic surveillance, and he had made phone calls—many phone calls—but his calls had been mundane conversations about his shoulder, and inquiries about the type of medical treatments available. He had steered clear of keywords that surveillance would zero in on, like "bomb" or "nuclear."

The trips to France and Moscow had required telephonic discussions to make reservations and move money. The last sum he had moved had been very large, totaling over a million dollars. *That could have tripped something.*

A thought flashed through his mind. The plutonium. For a month, the arms dealer in Moscow, Rostislav, had worked to supply Klaus with the nuclear material he would need. *Could Western electronic surveillance have picked up Rostislav's conversations?*

He thought that possible, but how did that relate to Atcho? Certainly, the CIA knew he hated Atcho and why, and that Klaus had escaped with a suitcase bomb in his possession. If they knew about his shoulder injury, they could surmise he had to stay in the vicinity of Berlin for medical treatment. In any event, crossing borders with a nuclear bomb carried unique difficulties. *But they don't know that I got out of East Berlin with five million dollars.*

He suddenly sat upright. *Are they using Atcho to catch me? Could that whole story about his investments in Berlin be made up to get me to go after him? If they get me, they get the bomb.*

He let the idea settle into the back of his mind and took a break from thinking. He changed into gym clothes and left the apartment.

An hour later, sweaty and physically spent, he walked back. He was pleased with the healing in his shoulder. He could now force his full range of motion, although with some pain, and he managed a degree of weights. The agony in doing so was still considerable but improving rapidly. *I'll get back to full strength.*

As he walked, his thoughts returned to Atcho and the irrationality of coincidences. His mind went to the morning he abducted Atcho from the Mövenpick Hotel. He remembered Atcho's wife's calm face as she watched her husband forced into the hall to disappear.

Klaus stopped in mid-stride. Atcho's wife. She was CIA. Yermolov had said so. In the Siberian operation, she had helped Atcho. That had frustrated Yermolov immensely.

He hurried back to his apartment and placed a call to Kadir. They met an hour later. Klaus brought with him the article announcing Atcho's visit to Berlin.

The *hawaladar* read it carefully. "I saw the reports on television. What do you want from me?"

"Do you have resources to find out if that's a real company? I want photographs of Atcho. He was born in Cuba but he's an American citizen. I need photos of his wife too."

Kadir turned to his telephone. He punched in numbers, spoke a few moments, read aloud from the article in Arabic, repeated himself a few times, and finally hung up. "It's done," he said, turning to Klaus. "We'll have answers within twenty-four hours."

Before going to bed that evening, Sofia called Atcho at the embassy. "Sofia?" he said on answering. He had to keep his emotions in check. For all the professional distance they maintained when working, he loved her more than life and missed her. He was confident she felt the same way. "Where are you?"

"Don't ask. I've located your guy, or at least his general vicinity. If you put some surveillance out there with his picture, you should be able to pick him up. He looks the same, except that he keeps a cleaner look, keeps his hair and beard trimmed, and he wears a business suit." She gave him the information.

"Are you sure it's him?"

"One hundred percent. By the way, his doctor's name is Burakgazi. He replaced Klaus' shoulder." She gave him the surgeon's address.

"Great work. Why don't you come in now?"

Sofia remained silent a moment. "I love you, darling," she said with a note of melancholy, "but I think I'll stay loose."

When Atcho hung up, he relayed Sofia's information to Horton. "I'll be damned," the major exclaimed, "that is one wildcat you got. No wonder you keep taking vacations in Berlin." He laughed at his own joke. "All right, we're on it. We'll get field guys into that section of town. That's Little Istanbul. We'll put someone observing the doctor's office too. Maybe we'll close this Klaus clown before he gets up a full head of steam."

Across town, Sofia stood alone in a phone booth, fighting down deep emotion. Her mind went back to when she had first met Atcho. He had been gaunt and dirty, newly released from Castro's dungeons in Cuba, yet he carried such nobility of spirit that Sofia was immediately drawn to him.

She shook off the feeling. *If I go in, they'll detain me.* She composed herself and headed back to her *gasthaus*.

12

Early the next day, while Atcho toured more facilities shadowed by Horton and his teams, Sofia once again moved through Little Istanbul in frequently changed disguises. To be even less noticeable, she moved with disorganized groups of people going in the same direction. She started near the point where she had last seen Klaus. However, by the end of the day, she had gained no new information.

At lunchtime, Atcho called Burly in DC. He passed along what Sofia had related about spotting Klaus. "She really is amazing," Burly remarked. "I wish she wouldn't go off on her own like that, but I have no basis to stop her now that she's a private citizen." He changed subjects. "I heard back from Detective Berger on the Berlin police force."

"Anything good?"

"I sent him the photos of Klaus and the other guy that Collins saw coming through Checkpoint Charlie. Berger says that they had a positive ID on the unknown man. He was murdered in his hotel room the same night the Wall opened up. They traced him through *Stasi* records. He was some type of contract special operator—off the books."

"Any sign of the duffle bags?"

"No. I developed a working hypothesis. Klaus saw those bags in the *Stasi* director's office. He knew what was in them. Both he and the murder victim went through Checkpoint Charlie at nearly the same time. Klaus must have seen the duffle bags and followed the guy. If true, Klaus got them and the five million dollars."

Atcho exhaled slowly. "Then we know how he's living, getting medical treatment, and paying for supplies. He basically has unlimited mobility."

"Yep. We'll go forward on that assumption."

"OK. Horton has people staking out the doctor's office. Berger might want to do the same thing. We don't want to crowd up the place, but he might have his own informants he could use in there."

"It's worth a shot." They hung up.

In the early afternoon, Klaus visited Kadir. "What have you learned?"

The *hawaladar* reached below his desk and brought out a folder. "This man Atcho is real, and so is his company. He does business with the US government—the Pentagon." He handed over the folder. "Here are details about the corporation."

"And his wife?"

"She retired last year from the US State Department. A photo of her is in the file. They moved to Austin, Texas after her retirement."

"Do we know where she is?"

Kadir shook his head. "We didn't send anyone to her house. We could do that if you want, but surveillance is expensive and might take several days."

Klaus opened the folder. A photo of Sofia was on top. He recognized her from their brief encounter the morning he abducted Atcho. He shook his head. "No need. I have another idea."

He left and went to the mosque. "Peace be upon you," he greeted the imam. "I want to make another contribution to the mosque."

The imam smiled deferentially. "And upon you, peace. Thank you. Is there anything we can do for you?" When Klaus feigned reluctance, the imam urged him. "Please, speak. Tell me what is on your mind."

"Islam is always under attack by the infidel. Everywhere that Muslims go to live and raise our families, these evildoers want to drive us away.

They are resentful that we walk in righteousness, and they resist our attempts to encourage them to revere Allah."

"That's true. We must protect the only true way of life. What is your concern?"

"Times are troubling. The infidel pits brother against brother. In Kuwait, Muslims fight Muslims. The Great Satan America supported Saddam Hussein in the war against Iran. A million were killed on both sides. Now, it supports Kuwait against Iraq. I fear they will keep inciting wars that kill our people, with no cost in life to themselves. Worse, I think they will provoke war in places where we are not fighting now."

The imam listened carefully. "Do you mean here? We have a long history in Germany."

"I know, and I don't want to raise alarm unnecessarily. As you know, I came from the East." The imam nodded. "I was an intelligence officer with the KGB," Klaus continued, "trained by the *Spetsnaz*." The imam looked impressed. "I keep contact with former comrades. They tell me that a known spy and provocateur was spotted in our community."

The imam arched his eyebrows. "To what purpose?"

"I don't know. But I thought that in the interest of keeping our people safe, I should let you know." He pulled out Sofia's photo. "I think letting people know about her would be good. They can watch for her. Do you have any idea how to accomplish that?"

The imam thought a moment. "I could have copies of her photo printed and circulated. Maybe someone will recognize her."

"Great idea. If you like, I'll print up a thousand copies and bring them back to you. Then you can distribute them."

"If we see her, what should we do?"

Klaus appeared to think the matter over, but he already knew his answer. "Detain her and notify me. I'll work with German intelligence on the matter."

Disconcerted, the imam nevertheless assented. After delivering the copies, Klaus returned to the apartment to study the rest of Atcho's file.

His dilemma was whether to take action against Atcho now or wait. *If he's bait, he'll be surrounded by security, most of it hidden.* He raised his injured arm and rotated it in a full circle. Nearly three months had passed since his surgery. The arm gained strength daily. Dexterity had returned to his fingers. He could fire a pistol.

The other part of his dilemma was that he had the means to make a huge difference to cure injustice in the Middle East, to strike for Islam. The moment of his greatest opportunity approached. He could not afford to be distracted.

He read Atcho's file. In the process, he gained grudging respect for the man. Atcho had done some fighting, suffered injustice, and rose above circumstances to become a highly successful businessman—*yet he still went into the field as an operator.*

That last part was not in the file, but Klaus knew it from personal experience. Hatred boiled again. *He's an infidel, opposes Islam, and he killed my brother.*

He read deeper into the file. It included articles from when Atcho and Sofia had moved into a Mt. Bonnell home overlooking Lake Austin, a part of the Colorado River running through the Texas' capital. It even mentioned that Sofia had joined the Yellow Rose Garden Club of Mt. Bonnell. The members had been so pleased to have her that they honored her with a reception.

As Klaus read, the germ of an idea formed. He smiled. *You can wait, Atcho. And so can Austin.* He went to the phone and called Kadir. "Start the surveillance."

The next morning, Sofia trekked again to Little Istanbul. She had left the *gasthaus* later than usual. Her nausea had taken longer to subside, but she felt fine now. She entered the enclave using her usual tactics to be invisible in a crowd.

She had been there only a little while when she noticed people moving away from her. They joined in clusters where they stared and pointed her out to each other.

Unease descended. Without changing stride or appearing to notice, she retraced her steps. Women moved to the sides of the street. Men filled the center. Sofia pushed through them, but when she was within twenty feet of the main street bordering Little Istanbul, five burly men blocked her.

She looked to her rear. Behind her, a crowd had formed. She faced the front. In a swift motion, she tore off her outer garments, remaining in denims and a sweatshirt. She wore running shoes. The cold January wind bit through to the bone. Setting her jaw, she headed toward the center of the line of men. She walked deliberately, her eyes meeting those of the biggest one.

She came within arm's length. Her eyes showed intent to break past him. The man reached for her. She crouched low and came up hard, the full force of her legs transmitted through her arm. The cup of her hand thrust into the man's chin, slamming his lower jaw against his upper teeth. Simultaneously, she jammed her ankle behind his. When he started falling backwards, she shoved her shoulder into his midsection. He hit the street surface hard. She drove her foot into his head, pounding it on the pavement. He lay still.

The man's companions barely had time to react. The two on either side looked down at their unconscious comrade. They moved to block her.

Sofia breathed deep. She backed up, seeking another exit. The men glared. Once again, she chose the biggest one. This time she ran toward him. When she was within a few feet, she leaped into the air and brought her trailing foot forward to kick squarely in the middle of his face. He went down and did not move.

Behind her, the crowd muttered and jeered intermittently. Her mind worked furiously. *I can't lose this fight. My life is not the only one at stake.*

She sized up her remaining opposition. From behind, she heard footsteps approaching. Something slammed down on her shoulder, the pain piercing. She whirled and kicked upward into a man's groin. He howled and backed away.

She whirled again. Three men remained blocking her path. She ducked her head and ran toward the center of the line. At the last moment, she diverted to her left, rotated in a complete circle, kicked her leg high, and brought it crashing into the jaw of the man at the left end. He fell into his companions. All three tumbled like dominoes.

Sofia did not stop. She ran past her would-be assailants and kept running. Turning at the intersection, she increased her speed, taking to the center of the street and dodging cars until she was well inside the general population. Then she slowed to a walk. As soon as her breathing returned to normal, she hailed a cab and returned to her *gasthaus*. She changed her appearance, paid her bill, and ducked out the back exit.

Forty-five minutes later, Sofia checked into a major hotel. As soon as she was alone in her room, she placed a call to Atcho at the embassy. The operator put her call through to the ambassador's secretary.

"Atcho is out touring with some developers," the secretary told her.

"This is his wife. It's an emergency."

Minutes passed amid electronic noises. "I'm trying to reach him," the secretary said. "Please don't hang up."

Then the big, friendly voice of Joe Horton came on the line. "Hello, Little Lady. It's sure good to talk to you…"

"I don't have time for BS, Joe. Put Atcho on."

All playfulness dropped from Horton's voice. "Got it, but I can't get to Atcho immediately. Give me a couple of minutes."

"Fine. Have him call asap. Here's the number."

Sofia paced the room. She tried relaxing on the bed. No relief.

Atcho called within five minutes. "What's wrong?"

"Call Burly," Sofia said without niceties. "Tell him I've been ID'd. I still intend to be part of this, and I'll work with him, but on my terms. No restrictions. I'll stay on the reservation. It's a take it or leave it deal. I need a fast decision. I'll wait ten minutes." Feeling a wave of nausea, she hung up, rushed to the toilet, and wretched.

Atcho called back within ten minutes. "It's done. Burly agreed."

"You'll have to come get me. I might have a tail." She told him where she was. She heard muffled voices over the phone, and then Atcho came back on the line.

"I'm twenty minutes away. Joe has people closer to you. They'll be there in ten minutes. They'll bring you to the embassy. I'll meet you there."

When Atcho hung up, he felt an unusual amount of worry. Sofia did not panic. Ever. Yet panic sounded in her voice. Her insistence on what amounted to an extraction mission puzzled him.

He and Joe rode together back to the embassy. Joe knew better than to disrupt the somber atmosphere. When they reached the compound, Sofia had already been let into his room at the guesthouse. He entered and found her lying across the bed, weeping. He rushed to her, took her by the shoulders, and held her.

Sofia rose to a sitting position. She clung to him, sobbing quietly into his chest. Atcho wrapped his arms around her. "Darling, what's wrong? What happened? This isn't like you."

When Sofia's sobs subsided, she wiped the tears from her eyes. "I'm so angry with myself." She brought herself under control. "All right." She took a deep breath. "I'm OK. I was attacked. In Little Istanbul." Suddenly, the tears brimmed again, and she sobbed once more into his chest. "I could have lost the baby."

Atcho sat back and stared, hardly believing his ears. "You what? What baby?"

Sofia pulled his face close to hers. "Our baby. I'm pregnant." She stared into his eyes, seeing that he still did not comprehend. Then the tears started again. "I found out that day that Burly came to Austin. I was going to tell you that night... But... but..." She gasped for air as more tears rolled. "I was irresponsible to come over and go into the field. That was so, so stupid. If anything's happened to the baby, I'll never forgive myself." More tears rolled.

Atcho listened, but hardly heard. He gazed at her stomach and then back into her eyes. "A baby? A baby? We're going to have a baby?" He felt overwhelmed with mixed emotion. "We have to get you to a doctor. Make sure everything's all right." He threw his arms around her and held her close.

Horton hurried into the infirmary. Atcho sat in the waiting room.

"How is she?"

"She's fine. She took a hard blow to her shoulder, but she came out all right. From what I could pick up, a mob attacked her. She took down six of them and got away. She feels terrible about endangering the baby.

"I knew something was different when she called. She's always been so 'I can handle myself,' and suddenly she wants to be extracted from a safe place?" He looked over to find Horton gaping at him.

"Did you say baby? Did I hear you say something about a baby?" Horton's eyes were genuinely wide open. "And she took down six guys?"

Atcho nodded. "The doctor's checking now to see how the baby is doing."

Horton's face morphed to one of mock seriousness, his eyes narrowed. "Well, have you punched her in the stomach any time recently?"

Atcho smiled and shook his head. "No."

"Did she get punched in the stomach today?"

"No."

"Well then sir, you just need to stop worrying about it 'cause it's just like my momma used to say..." He looked up at the ceiling as if searching for words. "Ah hell, I cain't remember what my momma used to say." He grinned. "But it was good, and you should follow her advice." His forehead furrowed. "I think she would say that the baby's going to be just fine."

Atcho grasped Horton's shoulder. "I'm glad you're here."

"Who, me?" He looked around and ducked his head close to Atcho's as if to tell him something in confidence. "Truth is, I'm out of cognac, so I came over hoping I could bum a few bucks to go get some."

They both laughed hard. Atcho could not believe how much better he felt. The door into the treatment room opened, and the doctor came out. Atcho looked up, anxiously searching his face. The doctor smiled. "Everything's looking good. You can go in and see her now."

Klaus fumed. "How could they let her get away?" He was alone but expressing his anger out loud, incredulous about the story of the fracas.

Many people had identified the woman as the one in the photo. Klaus was sure he would not have another such opportunity.

He sat down to clear his mind and think. *The odds are against me in Berlin. I need to even them up.*

Late in the evening, he made two calls. The first was to order a taxi. "It needs a large trunk. I have at least five suitcases." He gave the address of his workshop and set a pickup time for late the next evening.

The second call was to the no-questions-asked air service he had engaged with twenty-four-hour notice. "I need a flight out tomorrow at this time. I'll tell you the destination when I see you."

13

Atcho and Sofia entered the office set aside for their mission. They found Horton watching television intently. The view focused on a close-up of a slew of jet fighters taking off into the skies, one after another, until they disappeared into a field of blue.

"All hell broke loose," Horton announced. "It's D-Day!" He spoke with animation, excitement tinging his voice. "We started air combat operations against Saddam this morning. A 101st Airborne Division task force sent in four Apache attack helicopters under radar. They hit ammunition depots and fuel dumps with forty Hellfire missiles. Then they knocked out air defense guns with a couple hundred rockets carrying flechette rounds. They finished off with a huge number of thirty-millimeter rounds." He looked up at Atcho. "They're saying it was one hundred percent destruction. The Apaches flew back low level. They cut an air path twenty miles wide. On their way out, the pilots watched four hundred fast-movers fly in over their heads."

Atcho had to chuckle at Horton's enthusiasm, while reminding himself that he was watching a fight to the death for many, on live TV.

"That Shephard guy really knows his stuff," Horton said.

"Who's Shephard?"

"A buddy of mine. He ran the 101st tactical operations center last night." He smirked. "That's called a TOC, for you civilians." He turned abruptly from the television to Sofia. "Oh, forgive my manners. Are you feeling better today, ma'am?"

"Yes Joe. Sorry I was so short with you yesterday." She smiled and touched his arm. "I'm ready to get to work."

"Quite understandable. Nothing more to say. Me too—about getting to work." He started toward the conference table. "Oh, and congratulations. I don't know if I'm supposed to say anything about the—you know." He rolled his eyes toward the floor and put on his best sheepish expression.

Atcho and Sofia chuckled. "It's OK, Joe," Atcho remarked. "Let's get to work."

"You got it, boss. Burly should be calling in any moment for a status."

"Joe," Atcho fired back, "since when did I become 'boss'?"

The phone rang. "Sorry, sir." He grinned. "You don't like that either. I forgot." He flipped a switch on the speakerphone. "Is that you, Burly? I got you on speaker. We're all here."

Burly congratulated Atcho and Sofia on the baby and then got down to business. "I want to go over everything and get a handle on where we are right now. Obviously, Sofia, you presented a threat to someone. A good guess is, that 'someone' is Klaus."

"I think so too. I saw him in the doctor's office. He saw me when I followed him. I don't know how he managed to get so many people looking for me so fast though."

"I know how that happened," Horton interjected. "Last night, while these two lovebirds were consoling each other, I sent some of my guys out to talk with informants in Little Istanbul. It's like I was tellin' Atcho earlier, someone distributed a huge number of copies of Sofia's photo there. I don't know where they got the original, but instructions to the residents were that if someone saw her, to hold her and report to the imam at the mosque. Rumor has it that German intelligence was involved."

Sofia and Atcho looked at him, startled. Burly cleared his throat. "All right. It looks like we smoked Klaus out, but he went after the wrong target. He must have seen the news reports about Atcho though, so now he knows that both of you are in Berlin and he can figure out that Sofia was searching for him—and why. Atcho, he's either going to come after you soon, or he'll stay quiet until you leave."

"Sir, if I may," Horton cut in. "We have sources in the mosque. We can use them to find out where Klaus hangs his hat. I'm friendly with German intel too. I can check on that rumor about their alleged cooperation."

"Good idea. Set it up. What else?"

"Dr. Burakgazi definitely did the surgical work on Klaus' shoulder," Sofia said. "Collins told you he saw both Klaus and that guy with the duffle bags come through Checkpoint Charlie. Veniamin identified the duffle bags. Shouldn't that be enough for Detective Berger to question Burakgazi regarding the murder investigation? We have photos of Klaus. The doctor might know where he lives too, or he might have picked up on some other useful information."

"Good thinking. I'll run it by Berger. Maybe y'all should get together with him. By the way, I heard from him this morning. Seems that some upstanding citizens in Little Istanbul filed a complaint about a crazed she-devil who beat up some of their people yesterday. Sofia, did you really take down six big men?"

Sofia smiled. "Four. Two went down under the weight of one of their buddies when I shoved him."

Burly chuckled. "The way I heard it, you shoved him with your left foot to the side of his face. OK, next topic. Any theory on what Klaus' target might be—for his bomb?"

Atcho, Sofia, and Horton exchanged glances. "Yermolov wanted him to hit a target in Chechnya," Atcho said after a prolonged silence, "to help destabilize the Soviet Union. I don't see that being something he'd want to do now. The idea was to detonate a bomb there in conjunction with one here in Berlin, but that was overcome by the Wall coming down. I guess he could still strike here, but I don't see any benefit to him."

"We're pretty sure he got that five million dollars," Burly said. "Any chance he'd just forget the terrorism racket and disappear to enjoy his money?"

"I don't think so," Atcho replied. "If that were the case, he would have hidden from view when Sofia came on the scene. He came after her. Besides, he won't leave me alone until one of us is dead." As he made the last statement, he glanced at his two colleagues. Horton raised his eyes to the ceiling. Sofia remained expressionless.

"Does anyone think he might try to get in the middle of what's going on in Kuwait?" Burly asked.

"God help us if that happens," Sofia said softly. "Our job will be much more difficult." She looked across at Atcho and held her emotions in check. "Much more dangerous."

Burly spoke after an extended pause. "Let's put first things first. Atcho, you keep doing your tours with the business types. Horton, he'll still need your security. Go ahead and get your guys talking to German intel. Sofia, follow up as we discussed with the mosque and the doctor. I'll call ahead to Berger to give him a heads-up." He started to say goodbye, and then added, "And Sofia, use your resources. Please don't go out on your own again, for any reason. I'm asking as a friend who cares about you and your new family member."

Klaus could not believe what he saw on the television screen. Scene after scene of fighter jets taking off from land bases around the Persian Gulf and aircraft carriers. Their missions: first to destroy Iraq's radar and surface-to-air missile sites, thus blinding Saddam Hussein to the intentions and actions of the US coalition arrayed against him. Immediately following, massive strikes bombarded assets critical to Iraqi communications, command and control, and logistics. He watched, dumbfounded and dismayed at the dizzying numbers of fighter-bombers pounding Saddam's forces.

Despite himself, he found the videos of pinpoint precision munitions fascinating. One report even showed the first guided missile to strike its target in Iraq—it entered through the side door of an Iraqi hangar and blew the aircraft protected inside into a huge ball of fire and dust.

The air attack seemed to come from all directions. He could almost hear the whistle and roar of incoming munitions, feel the thunder of explosions shaking the ground and the fall of reinforced concrete as massive buildings caved, crushing everything inside. The technology he saw performed beyond belief, one bomb striking within the city of Baghdad into the center of Iraq's air operations command, and descending through its spine, demolishing the building and destroying the Iraq air command system.

The range of air combat assets awed Klaus. F-111s and Marine F/A-18 Hornet fighter-bombers flew anti-radar missions and hit bunkers and bridges with precision GBU laser-guided bombs directed by their Pave Tack pods. F-16s and Saudi F15E Strike Eagles flew joint missions with the fabled A-10 Warthogs, the titanium-encased close-air support jets with their cluster bombs and 30-mm multi-barrel cannons attacking Saddam's vaunted Revolutionary Guard tank formations with impunity, raining down destruction. Even Vietnam-era A-7E Corsair IIs flew Wild Weasel missions against radars and SAM launchers.

The British flew their Tornado GR1s in low to take out the short tarmacs from hardened hangars to main runways, thus incapacitating Saddam's air force while his jet fighters and bombers remained encased in what became their tombs. The news reporter on Klaus' TV screen emphasized the danger of the attack, and Klaus felt a bit mollified to learn that five British airmen lost their lives in completing their missions.

French pilots flew their Jaguars and Mirage 2000s equipped with laser-guided AS30L missiles. Even the Kuwaiti air force entered the fray, flying their Skyhawks against Iraqi targets within their homeland to soften the occupying forces there.

As Klaus watched, his fury grew, seeing that missions flew from six US aircraft carriers, attacking from unpredictable directions, and from Arab countries arrayed around the Persian Gulf. "Traitors," he railed. "Cowards."

His dismay mounted as he witnessed Iraq's response—all but nonexistent. He watched, further disheartened by videos of Iraqi MiG29s, the finest Soviet fighter ever built, running from engagement, failing to employ the impressive armaments and capabilities of the aircraft, and rapidly succumbing to the attacking force. ""They go up to get shot down," he muttered.

Meanwhile, AV-8B Harrier II jump-jets established close-in support bases near the front with improvised runways, while flying missions into Kuwait to further soften up Iraqi positions. Watching the reports, Klaus' anger peaked when a pilot returning from a bombing mission over Baghdad was met by reporters as he climbed down from his aircraft. They pummeled him with questions.

The pilot was young, looking healthy, and not even tired. He seemed shy and carried an air of humility. "There are not enough wows and gollies to describe all that stuff—the anti-aircraft fire coming up at us. Hard to dive into, but we got the job done. And now I have to eat breakfast and get ready for the next mission."

Klaus stood, fuming. "That son-of-a-bitch. We'll teach you a lesson."

All morning he watched and listened for reports from which to seize hope. He turned to other channels, including those with sympathy for Saddam Hussein's side of the fight. They only showed expressions of anger over the progress of the war.

Some accounts were taken in neighborhoods in Little Istanbul where Kuwaiti expats waited out the conflict. Those people smiled and laughed. Some demonstrated for the camera that they were already packing to go home.

Early in the afternoon, Klaus walked into Kadir's offices. They conferred for a while about how and where to move his money, and afterward, he returned to his apartment to weigh alternatives. His only remaining question: *Where can I do the most damage?*

With intelligence services closing in on him in Berlin, he had to leave. Vengeance against Atcho would have to wait. All the countries in the Arab League had sided against Saddam, except Libya and Sudan. The Palestinian Liberation Organization also supported Saddam, but Klaus regarded Palestine as a place with little use aside from keeping hostilities with Israel alive. That was good for business. From his experience, that was the way most Arab countries viewed Palestine.

The idea of allying with either Sudan or Libya brought little comfort.

He knew scant about the former, and the latter was led by a madman, a clown, Muammar Gaddafi. Many Arabs liked to listen to him speak for the comedy value. He made pronouncements, and at one time, he had been feared in the world. However, after Ronald Reagan bombed his tent in the desert while Gaddafi was in it, he changed his tune, or at least his actions. He gave up nuclear ambitions and settled down to be a compliant little dictator who sought pleasure only from the torture of his own people and left the rest of the world alone. Europeans and Americans who lived in Libya touted the country's safety and security.

With his money and bombs, Klaus lived within the irony of having resources which, if revealed to others, would make him a target. Without them, he had freedom to move at will, but would have no resources with which to travel, and no bombs to further Islam.

He was not personally familiar with the countries around the Persian Gulf, but he had spent time speaking with the imam, mosque members, and immigrants from each country such that he had a working knowledge of them. He had even gone to a library and studied maps of eastern Mediterranean and Persian Gulf countries to understand relative proximity and their geodynamics.

Late in the afternoon, he visited Kadir again, this time to confirm plans. Then he took a taxi to his shop to retrieve his five suitcases. An hour later, he climbed aboard a small private jet.

"Where are we going?" the pilot asked.

"Riyadh," Klaus replied. "Saudi Arabia."

"I can't fly there directly and keep you undetected," the pilot replied.

"Do what you have to do but get me there as quickly as you can." Klaus' choice carried huge risks, but for him, it made sense. The petroleum-producing behemoth occupied most of the Arabian Peninsula and was a friend to the US, at least on the surface. Yet, many fundamentalist Islamists of various sects worked behind the scenes to promote their own objectives. The country had grown wealthy on oil revenues and followed an aggressive schedule of infrastructure development. As a result, Klaus' needs to secure his suitcases and establish a means of moving money were readily met there. Kadir had arranged introductions to contacts in the "Kingdom."

Saudi Arabia had two other advantages that determined Klaus' decision. The first was its proximity to Iraq, Kuwait, and the war. The second was that a major target for one of his bombs currently resided in Saudi Arabia—US and coalition forces spread along the border with Kuwait and Iraq.

He felt a surge of excitement as the small jet took to the air. "Keep looking for me in Berlin, Atcho," he smirked. "Your day will come."

14

At the end of the second day of Desert Shield, Atcho found that he had to resist the urge to stay glued to almost constant televised news reports of the war. He could scarcely believe the rapid progress.

He had just returned to the embassy in Berlin from yet another tour of facilities, this time in France. He had begun to feel guilty over the deception. Executives representing companies eager to bring his product to market in Europe spent a lot of money on him. Touring Berlin in limousines and stopping for lunch was one thing, but to be flown in a corporate jet to a central location in France and then toured by helicopter to potential facilities so that he could be back in Berlin by nightfall was another. The trip to France had been done for appearances to placate NATO allies. Other countries pressed to be included.

That evening, the three of them, Atcho, Sofia, and Horton, gathered in their office at the conference table to compare notes. They called Burly to include him in the discussion. "Things have been quiet the last two days," Atcho began. "How long can we keep up this pretense? We're likely to wear out our welcome with the business sector soon."

"I know," Burly agreed. "Has anyone turned up anything at all?"

"If Klaus is doing anything," Sofia interjected, "he's being very quiet.

No visits back to the doctor or the mosque. We even located the gym where he works out, but he hasn't been there either."

"I met with Detective Berger today. He's going to quiz Dr. Burakgazi about the murder. He'll do it discreetly."

"I got something on that," Horton cut in. "I contacted people in German intel. The rumor about them looking for Sofia is BS. They think it was planted to get people in Little Istanbul thinking that detaining her was okay.

"The other thing is that our informants in the mosque said that the photos were circulated by the imam himself. They don't know where he got them, but he had men distribute them with the story that German intelligence was looking for Sofia."

"Klaus had to be behind that," Atcho added, "and when the effort failed, he went to ground. He'd figure that my being here is a setup, and he wasn't going to play ball."

"Hey," Horton cut in, his eyes twinkling. "You just used a gringo expression."

"I've been hanging around you way too much." Atcho smiled wryly, deep in thought. "Where would Klaus keep his money? How would he move it?"

"Good thought," Burly said. "Where are you going with it?"

"Well, he can't keep the cash in the duffle bags forever, and he's done some expensive things, like getting his shoulder rebuilt. How did he move his money?"

"He'd use a *hawala*," Horton answered.

"A what?"

Horton explained the workings of a *hawala*. "They have to be honest. They're trusted for other things besides just moving money. They forward documents, arrange introductions... Really, they can provide almost any service off the record."

"He's right," Sofia said. "I've never encountered them, but I know about them. Burly probably does too."

"Yep," Burly agreed. "The doctor could have taken cash, but if Klaus is going to do much traveling or buying big ticket items, he'll have to have a way of securing the funds and circulating them. At some point, he'll have to move some of it into the traditional banking system."

"Time for Detective Berger to bust some chops," Horton chimed in. "With that kind of dough, if Klaus is using a *hawala*, he could already be socializing in higher circles—if you catch my meaning. Klaus might have tricked the imam, but he was still involved. If Berger doesn't want to get tough, leave it to me. I'll get the job done."

Atcho smiled. "I'm sure you could."

"Let's do this," Burly said. "Atcho, at your press brief tomorrow evening, announce that you'll take the next day off. Say you're going to take a day or two to analyze the merits of what you've already seen. That'll relieve pressure from abusing the business community.

"Sofia, get to Berger. Run by him everything we've discussed. I'll talk with him to impress on him that we need to know whatever the doctor and the imam know.

"Major Horton keep your informants active and see if they turn up anything. If Berger doesn't come through, we'll turn you loose. Germany might be unified, but we still hold Four Powers Agreement authority there."

"Geez, sir." Horton chuckled. "Are we going formal now? The name's Joe. And you're right. I can still do secret squirrel stuff here."

"Got it, Joe. Is everyone on board with that?"

Horton slapped his hand down on the table with a loud smack. "We're on it, sir, like—well, you pick your own metaphor. I mean simile."

15

The next day, Sofia contacted Atcho in the field around noon. "Get back here as soon as you can."

"Are you all right?" he asked, alarmed.

"I'm fine, but we've heard from Detective Berger. He has information that's critical. He'll join us here with a guy from German intel."

Two hours later, Atcho, Sofia, Horton, Berger, and the German intelligence officer met in the conference room and dialed in Burly. After greetings, Berger introduced his colleague. He spoke with a slight Germanic accent but with excellent use of English. "This is Gerhardt of the *Bundesnachrichtendienst.* You know it as our Federal Intelligence Service, and we just call it the BND. Gerhardt's been following a case we think is the same one you've been investigating, and it might be linked to the murder we talked about. He'll fill you in."

Gerhardt spoke with an almost identical accent in stilted English. "We are familiar with this man, Klaus. He spent days at the *Stasi* headquarters several months ago. He claimed to be with the IAEA and said he was searching for anyone who has ever been involved in a nuclear program. There would not be many people like that, but he was interested to the point of raising questions about why he would be so diligent. One of our volunteers contacted the IAEA and was told there was no such person in the organization. So, our offices were called in.

"I am afraid several days passed before the report was seen and acted on. By that time, Klaus had disappeared. However, we were able to reconstruct his search. He marked five names in the records. Of those, three moved out of East Berlin to somewhere else. One of the five died, and one lives on the east side of Berlin. His name is Rayner.

"One of our officers visited Rayner and showed him Klaus' photo. Rayner positively identified Klaus, who visited him several times."

"Tremendous work," Burly exclaimed. "Does Rayner know where to find him?"

"Unfortunately, no," Gerhardt replied. "Klaus represented himself as a researcher for the IAEA and wanted Rayner's professional opinion of the contents of a suitcase. Klaus said he'd found it in the office of the *Stasi* director."

While Gerhardt was still talking, Burly groaned audibly through the speaker. Atcho, Sofia, and Horton exchanged glances. "That ain't a good thing," Horton broke in.

"No," Gerhardt said. He related the rest of Rayner's conversation with Klaus, that the suitcase contained a viable nuclear bomb. It had to be rewired to detonate. It contained plutonium and had no real fail-safe. "Here's the worst part. Rayner showed Klaus how the wiring had to be redone, and," he paused, arching his eyebrows, "Rayner confirmed to Klaus that the design was simple enough that it could be replicated. He could copy it as many times as he had resources to do so."

The room became deathly quiet.

"Rayner is a retired nuclear engineer," Gerhardt continued. "He lives alone and enjoyed the conversation. He thought he was helping the IAEA. He told us that most of the parts could be made in a machine shop. The rest, the electronic items and the battery, were off the shelf. That leaves getting the plutonium."

Again, the room descended into silence. Horton broke it with lathered Texas twang. "I got two points to make. I want y'all to remember that I'm just a country boy and don't know much, but that ain't one of my points.

"I think we got this Klaus guy figured out. We know he's got money, he's got a bomb, he has the smarts to rewire it, and he knows he can make more—if he can get the nuclear stuff to make them go boom. If he's still messing with the one he's got, he's thinking about targets. We need to figure out what the most likely ones are.

"The second thing is that he usually sticks close to the mosque. His contacts come through there. I think he's after *jihad*—he ain't basking in the Bahamas. He's figuring out where he believes he can do the most good for Islam.

"The other thing is, how's he going to get more nuclear material and how's he going to pay for it? I mean, how's he going to locate the stuff and what's his mechanism for moving payment? I'd bet that holy guy in the mosque knows who his *hawaladar* is."

He paused with his finger under his chin as if in thought. "Huh, I guess that was three more things. Oh well, one more won't hurt." He grinned. "As I recall, we're having these meetings because of chatter about nuclear stuff in Berlin. My guess is that if we take another gander at those conversations and press Dr. Burakgazi and the imam, we're likely to get some answers."

He paused again, this time, his face deadly serious. "We ain't got much time. Klaus had months to get the plutonium. The chatter was heavy, but it's died down, and we ain't heard nothing from him in two days. He's on his way to do whatever he's doing, and," he gestured at Atcho, "no offense, but you're second fiddle as his target right now."

To Atcho, the atmosphere felt like the silence before a thunderclap. He scraped his chair and leaned forward. "Joe, you hit the nail on the head," he said slowly. He looked at the others in the room. "What are the next steps?"

"For starters," Burly intoned over the speaker, "Atcho, drop the site tours. We'll make that scenario quietly go away. We need to pick up the pace. Detective Berger and Gerhardt, can the two of you do whatever it takes in Germany to pull in the doctor and the imam and find out what they know?"

"We've already taken steps," Berger responded. "A murder was committed. Both men could be material witnesses. We'll be interrogating them before the day is out."

"Good. Joe, I'll make phone calls to put you in touch with the specific signal intelligence people who picked up the chatter. Going through all of that will be grunt work, but it has to be done. In particular, we need to know where the noise originated."

"We also picked it up," Gerhardt cut in. "I'll put our analysts in touch to work with yours."

The group reconvened the next day in a larger room at Berlin Brigade headquarters, joined by a mixed group of American and German signal intelligence analysts poring over transcripts of telephone conversations. Some listened intently to replay devices.

"What do we have?" Burly asked, joining by phone.

"We interrogated both the doctor and the imam overnight," Berger replied. "Burakgazi was cooperative. He's a nice man who takes his doctor's oath seriously. When we showed him the photo of Klaus, he immediately identified him as a patient. He confirmed having repaired Klaus' shoulder. He said Klaus had almost fully recovered and had concentrated the last couple of months on regaining strength. The doctor hasn't seen him since a few days ago when Klaus came to meet a woman named Ranim Kuti. Her husband needed similar surgery and she wanted to talk to him about it. She never showed up."

Atcho, Sofia, and Horton exchanged glances. They volunteered no explanation.

"One interesting comment that Burakgazi made was that Klaus was very interested in the war in Kuwait. He wanted to know which side the doctor would support. They had light discussion about it. Klaus asked whether supporting Iraq or Kuwait offered the greatest ability to harm infidels."

To Atcho, the air seemed suddenly charged with electricity. He sat bolt upright. "That makes sense," he said. "He could potentially throw the war one way or the other. If he has more than one bomb, he could explode them where the main coalition forces are deployed. That's his best shot at waging *jihad.*"

"Not so fast, hotdog," Horton replied. "Sorry to throw a damp towel on that thought. The last time we sighted Klaus was the day before Desert Shield started. That was coincidental. At the time, no one knew it would start the next day. Right now, Saddam's forces are hunkered down and praying to make it back home."

"You might both be right," Sofia interjected. "We need to think about what's over there that Klaus could get to. If he could hit the US somehow to breathe new life into Saddam's ambitions, that's the best way he could help his notions of Islam. If that's where he's going, he would have specific targets in mind."

"Agreed," Burly said, "but how would Klaus deliver a bomb in Kuwait? Getting into the war zone isn't easy. Let's not get so focused on Kuwait that we ignore other possibilities."

"Excuse me, let me brief you on the imam," Gerhardt interrupted in his formal manner. "That might give more perspective. We jointly questioned him with Detective Berger. The imam was not so cooperative, although he thought he was helping BND by circulating Miss Sofia's photo. That is what Klaus told him. That is why the people in Little Istanbul tried to detain her.

"We had to exert considerable pressure on him, but he finally admitted to having introduced Klaus to a *hawaladar,* a man named Kadir. We questioned Kadir as well but getting information was difficult. His business relies on confidentiality. At first, he refused to speak with us, but when we pointed out that we could tell the public he cooperated with the police and the BND, he became much more helpful.

"He conceded that Klaus had deposited nearly five million dollars with him. Klaus ordered reports and photos of Atcho and Sofia through him. He procured the photo of Sofia that was circulated in Little Istanbul. He said two other things of note. Klaus transferred half a million dollars into a regular bank account and wire-transferred it to a bank in Switzerland. Swiss authorities have so far not cooperated in tracking down who owns that account. Klaus also arranged to pick up the same amount in American dollars in Paris."

"That's got to be payment for more plutonium," Sofia breathed.

"Anything else?" Burly asked.

"Yes, one more thing," Gerhardt replied. "Klaus asked Kadir to make introductions to another *hawaladar* in Tripoli, Libya. He transferred all his money there."

16

Klaus watched the news with frustration. More than a week had passed since the US had launched its air attack against Saddam, and from his perspective, the war was not going well. He had flown out of Berlin the evening of D-Day, his chartered Lear taking him to Heraklion on the isle of Crete. His only reason for that destination was that it was away from Berlin and no pursuer could use logical rationale to trace him there.

He had picked the island at random. When he said that his destination was Riyadh, the pilot pointed out that his aircraft would have to refuel. The distance was out of range without a stop and getting into the Kingdom was difficult because of the war. He offered several alternatives, Crete among them. While in flight, Klaus decided to stay for at least a day to think carefully without the pressure of evading authorities.

The pilot was familiar with procedures and personnel at the airport in Heraklion. A few dollars slipped in the right places allowed Klaus' five suitcases through customs without difficulty. Then, while the pilot flew out, Klaus found a small hotel and spent the next day catching up on sleep.

When he rose early in the afternoon the next day, he acquired maps of the Mediterranean and Middle-Eastern countries. He spent that evening studying them and researching alternative routes into Riyadh and the areas near the coalition forces.

Although a Muslim, Klaus knew little about the geography of the Middle East. Most of his life had been oriented around Chechnya and its subjugation by the godless Soviet Union. Therefore, he had always looked to the northwest. Kuwait, his area of current interest, lay fourteen hundred miles due south of his homeland and fifteen hundred miles southeast of Crete.

He took a break and went to dinner. He had not determined the next leg of his route or a timetable. In spite of his mission, the beauty of Heraklion and the charm of its streets captured him. *Chechen life could be like this, if we could break Soviet chains.*

He was not surprised at the loose attire of people in the streets. He had become accustomed to similar dress in Berlin after the Wall fell. He tolerated the clothing and otherwise enjoyed the friendliness of people and welcomed a chance to rest his mind. *Maybe I'll stay a few days.*

Night descended. Klaus found a quiet restaurant with a pleasant aroma. He took the opportunity to eat and catch up on news from a television on the wall. Despite the agreeable setting, anger surged as he watched nonstop reports of continued US and coalition bombing of Iraq. The young pilots nonchalantly describing their heroics to gaggles of reporters more eager than litters of puppies galled him. The endless footage of laser-guided munitions blowing targets into dust with pinpoint precision fed his fury.

Still, Klaus found life in Crete's sun to be invigorating. His shoulder continued to heal and gain strength and mobility. He decided to stay until he was back to full health. He had entered the country under an unused alias, so he was not concerned about detection.

After a few days, he set a regimen of working out and running along the beach early in the mornings, eating lunch at favorite restaurants, enjoying the seawater for most of the afternoon, and watching the news in the evenings. The latter activity he limited to as much as he could take before once more becoming infuriated.

Frustration pervaded the group as its members met yet again at Berlin Brigade headquarters. Klaus seemed to have vanished. A week had passed, and the last sign anyone had of him was Kadir's statement that Klaus had moved his money to Tripoli. They had checked all the commercial flights going anywhere, in particular to Libya, but nothing turned up. Operatives in the country detected no trace of him. Chatter regarding "Berlin," "suitcase," "nuclear," and "bomb" had died.

The business community grudgingly accepted Atcho's explanation that the US Commerce Department had held up licensing for export of his company's technology. Invitations to social functions fell to a trickle, a factor that Atcho welcomed.

Detective Berger pressed hard enough on the imam that he learned where Klaus had lived, but the apartment had been vacated. When shown Klaus' photo, few neighbors admitted to having ever seen him and divulged that several men had lived in the apartment. The few who spoke of seeing Klaus would not acknowledge knowing any of the other men or where they had gone. No one hinted at the source of Klaus' money. When asked about Sofia's photo, most claimed no knowledge of it. Those who admitted seeing it said it had come from the imam in an effort to help the BND catch a terrorist.

Gerhardt, the BND officer, had no better luck. Neither Rayner nor the doctor had any more information to add to their statements, and nothing new had come in from signal intelligence. No one from the US side had any new insights.

"Let's go over everything again," Burly's disembodied voice said over the speaker when all were assembled. "We know he has money, that he spent a million dollars in the same place. We know he was here in Berlin, that his shoulder has been repaired and he was mending well. What else?"

"He figured out that the original bomb had no fail-safe on it," Horton kicked in, "and Rayner showed him how to rewire it."

"We assume he bought more plutonium to make more bombs," Sofia added, "but that's pure speculation. What's the going price for plutonium on the black market anyway? Anyone know?" Sofia looked around the room at blank stares. "Here's a thought," she continued. "If he were going to make more bombs, he would need to have some parts of them fabricated. How about if we get Rayner to give us a sketch of the bomb and any component part he remembers. If we went around to the machine shops, we might find one or more that made those parts for him."

Detective Berger stood. "I'll make the phone call. Our detectives will be combing the shops today."

"Tell them to put a burn on," Atcho said. "If Klaus left Berlin, he's on his way to his targets." Berger nodded and left the room. "If Klaus acquired more plutonium," Atcho went on, "he only had a few sources that could provide it. India, France, and Pakistan wouldn't sell it to him, and neither would the US or the Brits. He might try China or North Korea, but then he has the problem of delivery. That leaves the Soviet Union, which is where we believe Yermolov got the original nuclear material. They've been lax on securing their stockpiles." He edged closer to the speakerphone. "Burly, do we have assets in Moscow or elsewhere in the Soviet Union to run that down? Maybe it's time to go to the president and get him to have a conversation with Gorbachev. Once we have that answer, we might be able to stop speculating about whether or not he has more bombs."

"We can do that," Burly responded, "but even if we find that out, we still don't know where he is or where he's going. Somewhere, he left a trail."

As he spoke, Berger returned and took his seat.

"How about this?" Horton cut in. "We've been looking at this guy like he's a foot soldier. We've checked commercial flights, train stations, car rentals, blah, blah, blah. But he's operating in a new class. He's got millions to throw around and no one to answer to. If you were a rich man and needed to get out of town fast, how would you go?" He switched his attention to Berger. "Are there any private jet charter services that operate on the fringe of the law?"

"Good thought," Berger said. "To borrow an American expression, I'm on it." He rose to leave again. "We'll take his photo to every charter service, big or small, and find out where every flight went in the last month."

"You work that end," Gerhardt told Berger. "I'll contact the LBA and get their records for the same time period." He also rose to leave. "That's the *Luftfahrt-Bundesamt*," he explained to the others, "the German equivalent of the FAA."

"Bring the hammer down," Horton called after him. "The fox is sniffin' out the coop, if you get my drift." He did not smile.

"All right," Burly said. "What are Klaus' possible targets? He'll want the most bang for his buck, and it'll be a target that in his mind, forwards Islam."

"The most obvious one right now is Kuwait," Sofia replied, "but getting into any of the war zone countries is difficult. Air surveillance is tight, there are checkpoints along all roads, and travel documents to get in and out of there are checked and double-checked."

"We've got a BOLO with his photo at all major commands in Saudi Arabia and the countries in the war zone, down to troop level," Burly interjected. "Getting in there would be particularly tough for him."

"So where else could he go?" Sofia asked.

"Pretty much anywhere," Atcho muttered.

The room descended again into silence. Gerhardt returned. "I spoke with the managing director of the LBA. He promised a list of all chartered flights originating in Germany for the last thirty days. I'll have it within an hour." Atcho filled him in on the current discussion about potential targets.

"If Kuwait is his target, he's likely to be frustrated when the war ends faster than he expected," Gerhardt observed. "The US and coalition air campaign is the greatest in history. It's obliterating Saddam's war-fighting capability. He's threatening to set the oilfields on fire. What other targets should we be considering?"

Burly sighed audibly over the phone. "You all tussle with that. I'm going to see the national security adviser. I'll recommend that the president call Gorbachev immediately about where that plutonium could have originated."

17

Heraklion, Crete, January 22, 1991

Klaus viewed the news channels in astounded silence. They reported that Saddam Hussein had just set fire to the Al-Wafra oil wells in southern Kuwait and the oil storage facilities at the Shuaiba and Mina Abdullah refineries. The Iraqi dictator threatened to set ablaze wells along the coast to frustrate amphibious landings.

Klaus watched, enthralled, and flipped through channels until he found one that reported in a language he understood, English. It reported the US reaction to the fires. He had not heard of the expert being interviewed, but the lettering at the bottom identified him as "Dr. Carl Sagan, Professor at Cornell University."

The professor said that if carried far enough, the smoke from the burning oilfields could disrupt agriculture across South Asia and darken skies around the world. "You need only a very small lowering of average temperatures in the Northern Hemisphere to have serious consequences for agriculture."

The report went on to state that other experts thought hundreds of wells would have to be set on fire to cause such a cataclysmic global event. Sagan agreed. However, UCLA scientist Richard Turco compared the potential for disaster to the 1815 explosion of the Tambora volcano in

Indonesia. It spewed sufficient ash and debris into the skies to make 1816 the "year without summer" in the United States. It caused crop failures in other parts of the world.

The segment of the report ended with Turco stating that even with hundreds of oil wells burning, the climatic disruptions would not reach to the level of a "nuclear winter" as Sagan described to Congress. "So far," the journalist said, "only a few wells are burning in Kuwait, and even if Saddam set them all on fire, a much greater force would be required to bring about that nightmarish scenario."

Klaus listened, mesmerized. He felt simultaneously elated and humbled, as though the report had been placed to speak directly to him —as if it manifestly directed him to his mission. Saddam Hussein had created the opportunity to effect devastation across the globe to further Islam, *and I have the means.* His eyes burned with purpose. *I can rain death and destruction on infidels the world over a thousand times worse than what they brought on the people of Islam.*

Early the next morning in Berlin, Atcho *et al* met again in the secure offices at Berlin Brigade headquarters. The air bristled with electricity as information was shared.

Burly led off over the speaker from his office in DC. "The president is furious that Saddam lit those oil-well fires. If the lunatic dictator does more of that, he could spark a widespread ecological disaster.

"Regarding the plutonium, the president spoke with Gorbachev— reluctantly because the information we provided is scant, not confirmed, and the Soviet Union is a big place. But he asked the general secretary if it were possible that a small amount of plutonium could have escaped to the black market and been delivered in France during this past summer. Gorbachev agreed to investigate. He's not anxious for loose bombs to go off around the world either."

"I have news," Gerhardt broke in. He controlled his excitement with difficulty. "Our analysts went over the list of flights originating out of Germany provided by the LBA. We concentrated on those departing one of the airports around Berlin. We found one which we handed off to Detective Berger." He turned to Berger. "Tell them."

"A flight originated in Berlin and flew to the Greek island of Crete and returned. We spoke with the pilot. He was evasive at first, but as Major Horton so colorfully put it, we brought the hammer down. There was one passenger on the flight and the pilot positively identified him as Klaus. He had five identical suitcases and a small overnight bag. The passport was issued to an alias. Most important is that when Klaus arrived to get on the aircraft, he wanted to go to Riyadh, Saudi Arabia. Crete was supposed to be a refueling stop, but on the way down, Klaus decided to terminate the flight there."

Gerhardt continued where Berger left off. "Greece is part of NATO. We cut through those established communication lines and found the hotel Klaus stayed in. He's there now. We already sent a team to question the lady who checked him in. She said that he kept to himself, was not unpleasant, and seemed to have in mind to stay a few weeks."

"Can we take him?" Atcho interrupted.

Gerhardt shook his head. "The European Union isn't formed yet," he said with an air of frustration. "We have a few protocols to get through. Our foreign office is working with the Greeks. Your state department was notified through formal channels, and it's helping to expedite."

Horton shook his head. "Bureaucrats," he scoffed. "By the time they get through we'll have celebrated the next New Year and the one after that—and this Klaus clown will have skied out to who knows where." He shook his head in disgust. "Send me down. I'll bring him back tonight."

"You know you can't do that," Burly intoned.

"I know," Horton sighed. "We know where he is, and we can't get him." He stood and paced across the room. "If he finds out we're on to him, he'll disappear, go deep, and we'll never catch him."

The room descended into silence. Then Atcho broke it. "I'll go," he announced. "Get me on a plane and I'll have him by breakfast."

"No!" Sofia's eyes blazed. "You can't go. Our baby needs his father."

"You can't go anyway," Burly's disembodied voice said. "You're currently on the CIA payroll and I'm your boss. Get another idea."

Atcho stood. He stared across at Sofia. "Our baby needs a safe world to grow up in," he said softly but firmly, "and I can get this done." Then he shifted his view to the speakerphone. "Burly, if all that's in my way is that lousy CIA contract, I quit. I'll pay my own way." He turned to Gerhardt. "Give me the details."

Driven by his newfound purpose, Klaus barely slept. He ate little, and he altered his routine. Instead of working out, taking a long lunch, and lounging on the beach, he sat glued to the television screen, watching reports as they came in.

His fury at infidels grew. He had allowed his beard to grow and when he went out that night for dinner, he viewed the local populace and tourists with disdain—women in scanty dresses and deliberately provocative outfits, their faces laden with makeup, their cleavage on exhibit beneath skin-tight mini-skirts.

Men leered. Raucous music filled the air.

Klaus seethed. *When Islam is victorious, women will dress properly, and men will be educated to keep them in their places.*

He suddenly felt a burn to get to Riyadh. The next morning, he checked with local charter services but found none that could or would take him all the way there. The best he could find was one that could get him as far as Cyprus. That flight would not depart until the next morning, and upon arrival, he would still be nine hundred miles short of his destination.

He could almost feel the war rolling past him. He decided to go to the airport to find a better flight.

18

On arrival at the Heraklion airport in Crete the next day, Atcho instructed the pilot of his chartered jet to wait for him. Then he hopped a cab to Klaus' hotel. The afternoon sun had sunk low in the sky. He hurried up the few steps at the entrance and approached the desk clerk.

"I'm supposed to meet a friend staying in this hotel." He produced a photo of Klaus. "Have you seen him today?"

"A friend?" The woman eyed him suspiciously. "And you present a photo instead of asking for him by name?" She sniffed. "Yesterday, two government agents were here asking about him. What's he done?"

Atcho shrugged dismissively. "I don't know that he's done anything. I'm supposed to meet him here, but for security reasons he's traveling incognito."

The clerk looked amused. "It doesn't matter anyway. You missed him. He checked out early this morning."

Dismayed, Atcho tightened his fists involuntarily. "Did he say where he was going?"

"No. He took a taxi. A good guess is that he went to the airport."

Atcho put in a call to Horton in Berlin. "Get someone to check all commercial flights out of here since this morning. I'm going back to the airport to check chartered flights."

Klaus barely contained his vexation. The sun had just slid behind the horizon, and he had been at the terminal all day trying to arrange a better flight out of Crete. Finding himself unable to reserve a seat on a commercial flight to anywhere near the war zone, he had returned to the general aviation terminal and sought out private flights. A major obstacle was moving his luggage past customs inspectors. Frustrated, he called Kadir, his *hawaladar* in Berlin.

"I'll get you a plane, but it will be expensive, and you'll have to negotiate where the pilot will take you. Most pilots won't go anywhere near Kuwait."

"I must get into this war. Please help me."

Kadir was silent a moment. "All right. This is what I suggest."

Klaus listened.

When Kadir finished speaking, Klaus thought a moment, and then assented.

"Good," Kadir said. "I'll call Hassan."

When Atcho arrived at the airport, he found a bank of phones and called Horton. "There's no record of him on commercial flights," the major said, "but he probably switched IDs again. We went ahead and checked on chartered flights too. No sign of him there either, but there's an unscheduled aircraft prepping in one of the hangars. It's a private jet with a long range. One of the air traffic controllers noticed it on the way in for his shift. The pilot hasn't filed a flight plan yet though."

"That's a shot in the dark, but I'll take what I can get."

"Get to the general aviation terminal. We'll have someone take you out to the hangar. We got a few bureaucrats off their butts. They moved things along a bit. By the time you get there, we should have backup for you, but the best we can do right now is detain him. If it's him, he'll fight like a cornered tomcat. Don't do any gung-ho crap."

Atcho grunted and hung up. He hurried outside, hailed a cab, and instructed the driver to take him to the general aviation terminal. His muscles tensed. Klaus' face appeared in his mind's eye, angry, determined, seeking revenge.

The taxi turned onto the concrete apron in front of a row of private hangars. Airplanes of all types and sizes sat in the parking area. Some hangars were open, their lights on against waning daylight. Atcho scrutinized them all, looking for a jet with an active crew preparing their aircraft for flight.

They passed hangar after hangar, and then Atcho saw a Challenger 601-3AER parked in an open bay with ground-crew members moving about it, apparently preparing it for flight. The aircraft was a new business jet model by Bombardier, already known in aviation circles for its reliability, performance, and luxury. From Atcho's perspective, it also offered other critical factors: a range which could be extended with spare tanks and a cruising speed at near Mach-1. Klaus could get anywhere he wanted to go within thirty-five hundred miles and get there fast.

Atcho directed the taxi driver to slow down so he could better observe the plane. As he did, his heart leaped and then felt like it had stuck in his throat. A conveyor belt had been attached to the cargo hold. Five identical suitcases glided up the belt. They were also identical to the one Veniamin had dissected in Burly's offices.

At the bottom of the conveyor belt, a man stood observing the progress of the suitcases into the jet's interior. Even at this distance, his features were unmistakable: Klaus.

"Drive into those shadows," Atcho ordered the driver, indicating a dark place behind a row of planes that blocked the view from the hangar. Heedless of Horton's admonition to wait for backup, he tossed a one-hundred-dollar bill on the seat. "Keep the change. Slow down but don't stop. I'm going to roll out while you're still moving. Then you're done. Thanks."

Startled, the driver glanced over his shoulder. Then a devilish expression crossed his face. He chuckled and nodded.

Klaus breathed a sigh of relief as he watched his precious cargo finally placed on the conveyor belt to carry it into the cargo hold. He suddenly grasped the previously unrecognized stress of transporting them from one place to another across international boundaries. The officials who had accepted bribes to bring his suitcases into Crete were only too pleased to help move them out again—for a generous price.

The pilot of this magnificent plane spoke little. He had flown in from an unknown origin, providing coded recognition signals establishing his connection to Kadir. A short phone conversation to the *hawaladar* confirmed that forty thousand dollars had transferred to the pilot's account. Klaus would be his only passenger.

As Klaus observed his bombs ascend, he absentmindedly watched traffic in front of the hangar while the engines of his chartered jet idled. He was mesmerized by the variety of aircraft and the array of equipment required to keep them serviceable. He had known no such bounty of resources inside the Soviet Union.

His attention was drawn to a taxi driving along the apron toward the general aviation terminal. He directed his attention back to his suitcases, but then noticed in his peripheral vision that the taxi slowed down perceptibly. He shifted his attention to it and watched as it then speeded up and turned behind a row of airplanes into shadows. Once there, he lost track of it, but watched a point where he calculated that the taxi must re-emerge. It did, but its rear door had swung wide open.

Klaus' anxiety took a jump. "Finish it up," he yelled to the conveyor operator. "We have to go." He ran to the front landing gear where the co-pilot inspected the front tires. "Can we get out of here?" he demanded, masking the vicious emotion overcoming him.

Startled, the co-pilot looked up at him. "We're ready as soon as the cargo door is closed. I was just double-checking these tires. They're new." He peered at Klaus and gestured toward the rear of the plane. "They're pulling the conveyor away now. I'll let the captain know."

Klaus watched him climb into the plane and then turned back toward the parking area. At first, he saw nothing out of the ordinary. Then he spied a shadowy figure slip between airplanes.

Klaus mounted the stairs and stood in the door while keeping an eye along the line of aircraft. Suddenly, a man leaped into the light, heading directly toward Klaus' plane in a dead run.

"We're ready, sir," a voice behind him said. A flight attendant stood there. "If you'll take your seat, I'll close this up."

After rolling out of the taxi, Atcho moved in a crouch to the front of the line of planes, obscured by shadows. By the time he had a clear view, the conveyor belt had been backed away from the plane. Klaus stood near the front landing gear with another man in a pilot's uniform. The two conversed briefly, then they both moved to the stairway.

Atcho watched Klaus scrutinize the parking area while the co-pilot climbed into the jet. Then Klaus followed, but he paused at the top of the stairs and once again stared into the shadows cast by the row of planes where Atcho hid.

Atcho leaped from the darkness into the brilliant airfield lights. He ran hard, arms pumping, legs extended in long, powerful strides. He had closed only a quarter of the distance when Klaus entered the aircraft and the door closed. Nevertheless, with no weapon and no plan, Atcho pushed his body to extremes.

Too late. The jet lurched into motion coming straight toward him, gaining speed.

Atcho called on all his reserves, his lungs heaving, sweat streaming from his face.

The plane turned right, and suddenly sirens blared and cars raced across the tarmac toward him. The plane continued on as a bevy of security cars surrounded Atcho. He tried to dodge past them, but six security guards jumped from their seats and tackled him, bringing him to the ground on his stomach.

In despair, Atcho craned his neck to look up at the jet as it glided by.

Klaus could not hear the sirens of the police cars, but he saw them as the plane made its turn. He watched them surround the man running across the tarmac. Then a host of security guards tackled the man. Fascinated, Klaus stared, seeing the man lift his head to watch the plane roll past him. He recognized the face. *Atcho!*

19

Atcho walked disconsolately with Sofia toward the conference room at Berlin Brigade headquarters. He had arrived early that morning, having started his return trip immediately after his close encounter with Klaus.

"If I'd had just one more minute," he said. "Or a gun."

Sofia stopped dead in her tracks. "You didn't have your gun?"

"There was no time to arrange a permit or to smuggle one in. I had to go with what I had."

"What if he'd had a gun?"

"I figured he had the same problem."

Sofia shook her head. "So, he can smuggle five nuclear bombs in and out of the country, but he can't get in a peashooter?"

Atcho looked sheepish. He shook off the comment.

They entered the conference room and took their seats. "I blew that one," Atcho said as he sat down. "Do we at least know where they went?"

"Libya," Burly's intoned over the speaker. "The pilot filed his flight plan after takeoff. That plane is fast. Klaus was in-country before we could activate any operatives there. Besides, the pilot called an in-flight emergency and diverted to an airfield outside of Tripoli. Being in Libya, he had no problem establishing a legitimate purpose. Klaus is now among friends."

"Libya," Atcho groaned. "From there, he could go anywhere, and he transferred all his money to Tripoli." He scooched his chair back and stood abruptly. "What next? Where do we go from here?"

Sofia glanced at him. She recognized his extreme frustration. "A better question is, where does *he* go from *there*?"

20

"It's been a month since you got back from Crete, Atcho," Burly said over the speaker from DC, "and not a peep from Klaus."

Atcho looked around at the big conference room the group had used since they combined the team of US and German intel analysts. It looked desolate. The analysts were gone, and so was the clatter of busy people at work over keyboards, monitors, and electronic communications devices.

"The chatter on Klaus has gone to zero," Sofia interjected. "Berger's back to his regular activities, and the BND pulled Gerhardt and his team out yesterday. Right now, it's just me, Atcho, and Joe."

"My boss cut my involvement way down," Horton interjected. "I'm free to go whole hog again when we got something. Meanwhile, he wants me back doing my regular job." He snickered. "Maybe one day he'll clue me in on what that is." He looked around furtively. "Don't tell him I said that. I need the paycheck."

"How's the war going?" Atcho asked. "What's the news reporting stateside?"

"Saddam keeps igniting more oil-well fires," Burly replied. "General Schwarzkopf must be planning to launch ground combat soon. Saddam's battle formations and infrastructure have been decimated but I'm sure the Iraqi Republican Guard still has plenty of fight left. I thought Klaus

might take sides to influence the outcome of the war, but his opportunities are running out. And still no sign of him. Maybe he's waiting for
ground combat."

"Well he's startin' to annoy me," Horton said. The corners of his eyes
crinkled with a grin. "There's a war on, and I'm not in it? That's just not
natural."

"He *is* going to Kuwait," Atcho announced flatly, "and he's not after
military formations." Sofia and Horton turned questioning eyes to him.

"When I watched the news this morning," Atcho said, "the channel
re-ran an interview with Carl Sagan. In one segment, Sagan said that for
the fires in Kuwait to have a significant effect on world climate, hundreds
of oil wells would have to be ignited.

"When Sagan first made that statement, Saddam had lit maybe ten oil
wells and storage facilities. That started on January 22, right after Desert
Shield kicked off and when Saddam knew he had lost his battle against
the Saudis in Khafji.

"At last count, Iraq has ignited over seven hundred oil wells." He
paused, reflecting. "Can you imagine the effect of dropping a nuclear
bomb, or multiple bombs in the middle of those fires? Think nuclear
winter. There's no action Klaus could take to equal that." Sofia and
Horton stared at him. Burly's speaker remained silent. Before anyone
could speak, Atcho added, "That's where Klaus is going. Kuwait." He
paused. "That's where I'm going."

Sofia gasped, her eyes wide with uncharacteristic fear. Then, Horton
slowly stood. He advanced toward Atcho and stopped when their faces
were only inches away. They looked at each other, eyeball to eyeball.
"Now you listen to me, sir," he said, his voice full of indignation. "You ain't
going nowhere." His eyes bulged, and he crossed his arms. "Without me."
A grin spread across his face.

"Hold your horses," Burly called over the speaker. "Neither of you is
cleared into the war zone. Atcho, we let you play lone ranger on your
foray into Crete, but going into Kuwait or even Saudi Arabia is different.
The military owns that ground right now, and Stormin' Norman wouldn't
appreciate a freelance agent rummaging around in his backyard while
he's running a war."

Atcho pushed his chair back and stood, his arms folded, staring at the speaker. "We can't sit around in Berlin doing nothing."

"I agree," Burly said, "and you might be right about what Klaus' aims to do. But if you're going to be effective, you'll need Schwarzkopf's cooperation. If he's even heard of this situation, it's no more than a blip on his horizon, and you'll need to be cleared to get into the war zone. That'll take a few days. Sit tight. I'll work things on this end."

The room was quiet after Burly hung up. Atcho leaned on tightly curled fists over the table. Sofia kept her eyes on his face, reading his agitation.

Horton broke the silence. "You know what my momma used to say during situations like this?"

Atcho lifted his head with hooded eyes and a slight smirk.

Horton laughed. "Hell, my momma never saw a situation even close to this. But somewheres along the way, I did learn the best way to keep things in perspective." He paused for dramatic effect. "It's time for cognac. That's co-nee-yak!" Then he glanced at Sofia. "Oh, sorry, ma'am. You cain't partake. We'll get you some warm milk." He laughed at his own joke. Sofia ignored him, her eyes still glaring at Atcho.

21

Saudi Arabia, February 24, 1991

The rotary blades of a Blackhawk helicopter whirred over Tony Collins' head. He sat in the middle seat behind the cockpit. From that vantage, he watched the pilot and co-pilot prepare for liftoff. Through the windscreen he had a panoramic view of what lay ahead. For the moment, that included only more Blackhawks waiting on the tarmac, rotors spinning. The doors were slid back and locked open. The deafening roar of their engines permeated the ground. The vibration traveled through the frame of the helicopter and coursed through Collins' body. He reached up to check his helmet.

Two gunners perched over their machine guns on each side of the aircraft. They checked and rechecked the functionality of their equipment. Their combat gear, including Nomex gloves and huge helmets with room for earphones, covered them completely. Dark sun visors obscured their eyes. They had painted the lower parts of their face masks to look like the jaws of human skulls, giving them an otherworldly appearance.

A large man climbed into the seat on Collins' right, and three soldiers on each side perched in the door, their legs dangling over the edge. They sat grim-faced, their weapons pointed at the ground. The large man put on a set of earphones, checked his commo, and nudged Collins. "Can you hear me?"

Collins nodded. Despite the intercom, yelling was required over the clamor of competing noises.

"Good. I'm Major General Alsip. I run this outfit. I know who you are. Glad to have you aboard. You can ask me anything. I'll answer what I can. Same with my staff and soldiers. But stay out of my way, stay out of their way, and if you so much as breathe information that compromises our mission or could get my soldiers killed, you'll be out of here so fast you'll think you never left stateside. Is that understood? I don't want to see any maps drawn in the sand for TV cameras."

"Got it," Collins yelled back. By "this outfit," he knew the general referred to the 101st Airborne (Air Assault) Division, the storied military unit that fought to so many victories in both World Wars and in Vietnam.

"Good." The general whirled one hand over his head, his index finger pointing up. The co-pilot, who had been watching diagonally across from the front, nodded to the pilot. Collins heard voices over the intercom. Moments later, the pitch in the engine gained deep-throated intensity, and the Blackhawk vibrated more stridently. Then it lifted to hover in the cold February air, made wet by smoke from oil-well fires.

On his left and right, against a black sky, other helicopters floated upwards as if choreographed, and then held steady in formation three feet off the ground. He took a deep breath. *Desert Sabre has begun.*

He found the names of operations confusing. Only this morning he had come to realize that Desert Sabre referred to the direct attack on Iraq's forces in Kuwait. It was a subset of the larger operation, Desert Storm, which encompassed the entire combat operations against Saddam Hussein's army in Kuwait, and inside Iraq.

Atcho and Sofia entered the conference room in the embassy where, once again, Horton sat absorbed by the television. The view focused on the wheels and tracks of an armored personnel carrier and then panned out to show that it was one among a vast number of military vehicles spread out and speeding over a desert panorama. Black smoke marred the sky.

"We started our counterattack against Saddam in Kuwait," Horton announced.

The three stood mesmerized by the unfolding scene. "That Stormin' Norman Schwarzkopf, he's a tricky fella," Horton continued, beaming. "His air war destroyed Saddam's air force, so the Iraqis couldn't see what we was doin'. He kept an amphibious force offshore to make them think we was goin' to do an assault from the sea. Meanwhile, he got the Marines set to charge straight up toward Kuwait City."

Horton warmed to his narrative. "While the Marines and the amphibious force were sitting there to the east, ol' Stormin' moved the Brits, the French, and a major US Army unit to the west. This morning, he called the signal to snap the football. The Marines charged up the center while those units on the left swept wide to come in deep on the flank. Saddam had his army concentrated in front of our amphibious force, and it's still just settin' in place." He relished the telling. "Just like a Hail Mary."

Watching the news from his lodgings in Libya, Klaus fumed. Large numbers of men, some in military uniform, others in civilian clothes, walked toward the news camera, their arms raised in the air, to join a larger group already sitting cross-legged on the ground.

To the left and right in the field of view, American soldiers with rifles guarded them while others patted down newcomers for hidden weapons. The journalist broadcasting the report identified the location as being inside Iraq and the men on the ground as surrendered Iraqi soldiers. The prisoners looked meek, beaten, even obsequious before their captors.

"These men say they don't know why Saddam invaded Kuwait," the journalist reported, "or why they were sent here. They tell us they are glad that for them, the war is over."

More reports showed footage of demolished Iraqi tanks with live ammunition still stored in their burned-out hulls. News video showed highways with mile upon mile of destroyed vehicles of every description piled together on both sides of a desert road. Smiling American soldiers posed for the camera. They waved US flags as their troop carriers drove by one fire after another shooting flames from blasted-out rubble.

Klaus grabbed the phone and dialed a number. While he waited for it to be answered, he glanced outside his window. The crystal blue of the Mediterranean Sea sparkled at the bottom of steep cliffs. At their base, the salt water sprayed as massive waves crashed against boulders.

Defensive walls outlined the compound that housed him. Men with machine guns protected the front gate and manned spaced-apart positions. The room that Klaus occupied was comfortable, but sparsely furnished.

A man's voice answered the third ring. "Hello?'

"Hassan, this is Klaus. It's time for me to go."

"How is your shoulder?"

"It's sometimes painful, but I have most of my strength and can move it almost normally." He laughed. "I can shoot with it. What else is important?"

"I'll send a car to bring you to my house."

Hassan was the *hawaladar* in Tripoli Kadir had recommended. He had secreted Klaus in an ancient fortress outside of Tripoli and sworn the security team to silence.

"The war is moving fast, and Saddam will lose," Klaus told Hassan on arrival at the *hawaladar's* house. "That should embarrass every Muslim. Our Saudi and Kuwait brothers betrayed us to the infidels. They win against Saddam only with the help of the Great Satan. Get me there."

Hassan was a tall thin man in a straight, plain robe. He wore no beard. His hair, although unkempt, was cut short, and he spoke little. When Klaus had finished speaking, he nodded. "I made a few phone calls. We should have you on your way soon, if Allah wills it."

Klaus felt an immediate lessening of tensions. Being in a faithful Islamic country with Muslims who understood *jihad* was truly a blessing. He rested in Hassan's house for a few hours that afternoon, and then the two met in the early evening.

"It's set up," the *hawaladar* said. "There is a chartered jet flying to

Riyadh in Saudi Arabia the day after tomorrow. You won't be the only passenger, but no one knows your mission. The pilot is taking you because I asked, and the flight will cost you nothing. It was already scheduled. Arrangements to get your luggage through customs is done. When you arrive, you'll be met by a man with a car. The driver will drop you at the home of the *hawaladar* in Riyadh. That's the best way to get there undetected, and you should arrive, if Allah is willing, by noon the next day." He gave Klaus written details.

When Klaus finally settled into his seat on the flight two days later, he felt contentment he had not known in years. He was among Muslims. His shoulder gained strength and mobility every day. His remaining funds amounted to three and a half million dollars, and the way was paved for him into Saudi Arabia. Most importantly, he had his bombs secured in the aircraft's cargo hold. *Allah truly chose me as his instrument for* jihad. He slept, aware that when he arrived in Riyadh, the war would be in its fourth day.

22

Collins had never experienced such highs and lows or been as exhausted as he was during his four days covering Desert Storm. General Schwarzkopf's strategy at first seemed to him extravagant. The 101st Airborne (Air Assault) Division swung wide and north to strike Iraqi forces from the left flank. The 82nd Airborne Division maneuvered at the left in a parallel trajectory. The French did the same to the north, and the Brits to the south. Marines on the right flank cut straight up into Kuwait City.

From Collins' perspective, the strategy initially appeared to him simple on paper but unnecessarily complex in action. The enemy was to the front, and Schwarzkopf's main force swept past it on the left side in a wide, risky maneuver through the desert. The chance of major units bogging down in the sand seemed high.

As he gained deeper understanding and watched the strategy play out, Collins' view changed. He grasped the fundamental elegance of it. At its core, the plan's success relied on the skill and endurance of the soldiers on the ground, the quality and reliability of their equipment, the judgement and tenacity of their leadership, and the ability to resupply. But it was the application of better intelligence, technological superiority, and the ability to put soldiers where they needed to be at critical moments that made the strategy viable. In effect, Schwarzkopf pinned Saddam's main force in place and pounded it from the left and rear.

Collins first observed from the air, and then rode with troops in their tanks and armored personnel carriers as units pushed toward their objectives. Their war machines stirred up the desert into billowing, gritty clouds. The sand, driven by wind that bit through clothing, lodged tiny grains in the seams of sweat-drenched uniforms, rubbing the skin of soldiers and Marines raw.

The wind and the sporadic crackle of small-arms fire jarred him. The incessant cacophony of far-off artillery booms, the *thwump thwump thwump* of Apache attack helicopters and roar of Warthog strafing runs, and overhead bombers dropping thunderous munitions seared his nerves, allowing not a single moment of quiet.

Amid controlled chaos, a new omnipresent element spread over the battlefield: the stench of burning oil wells. It permeated the air and everything it touched, like a wet cloud of burning rubber with a pinch of human flatulence. It filled nostrils, adding to the misery the fighting force endured for a chance at victory. And still the soldiers slogged on in the cold February wind.

Collins watched them, unabashed in his respect for their courage and tenacity. He saw the army of Iraq collapse before their onslaught, Saddam's wretched fighters walking, even running to be captured and removed from the devastation wreaked on them by superior forces. They came in with anxious faces, arms held high, and when ordered to sit cross-legged, they complied as docile as lambs.

The few hours Collins slept were in a dug-out trench in the sand. He ate rations seeded with sand. When he managed to grab scarce water, it came with a complement of grit. Everywhere sand, sand, sand, and the stench of oilfield fires in cold, wet gusts.

He took pains to get close to soldiers, recording their heroics when bullets flew, when vehicles broke down, when communications failed. He visited medics' tents where those bloodied and maimed received emergency care. He attended field ceremonies of the fallen. He grieved with their comrades.

Then suddenly, the war was over. After one hundred hours of fighting, the US president called a halt to combat operations. The Allies had chased the remains of Saddam's vaunted Republican Guard over the Kuwaiti border and into the southern Iraqi province of Basra. Kuwait had been liberated.

Collins could scarcely comprehend that an event so momentous, so violent, had ended so abruptly. His communication with his home office had been sporadic and scant. The sense of euphoria at sharing victory felt tainted by the inability to adequately show what had been achieved by the sacrifices of the few going into harm's way for the benefit of so many.

When fighting stopped, Collins caught a flight with General Alsip back to division headquarters. On the way, he eyed the immense black plumes emanating from the oil-well fires, so that the aircraft diverted around them. He was too tired to do anything other than take notice.

They arrived back at the airfield near the headquarters. A Humvee met them and drove them to the building. "That was one hell of a war, General," Collins observed. That was all his worn-out mind could manage.

Alsip nodded, obviously weary. "It's not really over."

Startled, Collins wrinkled his forehead in confusion. "What do you mean?"

"You've been out on the battlefield, away from the news." Alsip chuckled at the irony. His face shifted to serious. "The big discussion now is whether to stop in Basra or continue on to take Baghdad. The thought is to make sure that Saddam never has the chance to cause havoc like this again. The president is against the idea because we might outrun our supply lines. Baghdad is eight hundred miles north. Some allies are balking, saying they signed on only to expel Iraq from Kuwait. Pursuing that beaten army would be a slaughter, not a war. Hard to justify killing thousands to punish for the sins of one man. If we keep going, we'll break the alliance. Our intelligence is telling us that he's likely to be dealt with by his own internal forces anyway."

Alsip took a breath, his face grim. "That's not the worst of it though. You know Saddam set fire to Kuwait's oilfield."

Collins nodded.

"That's over seven hundred wells burning out of control. The environmental impact and economic cost are already staggering, and we don't know how long it'll take to put them out." He regarded Collins, the sockets of the reporter's eyes sunk deep between his weathered cheeks and craggy brow. "Where are you headed now?"

"I need to get to a hotel where I can file my reports. I'll catch a ride."

"Come on inside my office. My adjutant knows where most of the reporters are holed up. It's in Dhahran. We'll get you there."

23

A white Mercedes sedan swept at high speed over the desert highway east of Riyadh. Klaus sat alone in the back seat. Fatigue had worn off some of the good feeling he had enjoyed on his flight out of Tripoli. Still, he relished a snug sensation, something rare to him. For most of his life, he had been vulnerable. Even when active with the KGB, he had the sense of having to watch what he said and be alert for hostility toward anyone coming out of Chechnya. The Soviet system being what it was, the ordinary habit of its citizens was to be wary of everyone and to speak openly to no one.

The driver was good-natured, even exuberant. He had obviously been chosen for his competence. "You impressed some powerful people," he called back to Klaus. "You and my employer share the same *hawaladar*. My instructions are to deliver you safely to his house outside of Riyadh. He only accepts clients that come with high recommendations."

"Who's your employer?"

"I cannot say, but my instructions were to get you and your luggage into the country with no record. That is my specialty. Sit back and relax. We'll be there soon."

Klaus' new *hawaladar, Yousef,* met him at the front door. He was a rotund man who nevertheless moved about with energy. He wore a *farwah,* a traditional Saudi dark robe worn in winter weather. On his head was a *shemagh,* the traditional red-and-white headdress held in place by a sturdy black cord. His house was palatial.

"I'm taking an extraordinary risk," he, said. "My clients usually do not stay at my house. I don't typically extend the kind of help you are receiving."

"Why are you doing it? Saudi Arabia is on the side of the Americans."

A flash of anger crossed Yousef's face. "Not everyone in the Kingdom is happy about that. The fact that infidels defile our land is an abomination against Islam. That will not stand, I promise you."

They sat on sumptuous sofas in a courtyard surrounded by reflecting pools and palms under an open sky. The soft burble of fountains soothed Klaus' travel fatigue. He had never witnessed such opulence, astounded that everything he saw belonged to a single man. Coming from a communist society, the concept challenged his comprehension.

While they spoke, a boy carrying a brass tray with fragrant servings of tea and fruit approached. He set them on a low table at Yousef's side, poured two cups, and withdrew silently.

"Back to your question," Yousef resumed, "I understand you are an amazing fighter with impressive resources who paid his own way to join the *jihad.*" He picked up some papers from the table. "You're a former KGB officer, trained by the *Spetsnaz.* When there was an East Germany, you dealt directly with the director of the *Stasi.* You organized our brethren in West Berlin to carry out *jihad.* You opened up old tunnels built by the Nazis under the city, and you and your brother killed eight *Stasi* officers in one night. An infidel murdered your brother and you seek revenge. You were wounded in that firefight, and the Turkish doctor Burakgazi repaired your shoulder. You set aside personal emotion until after a greater task is accomplished, and you carry five suitcases with you that can alter the balance of power worldwide." He set the papers down and gazed at Klaus. "Is that enough?"

Astonished, Klaus nodded involuntarily. "How could you know all of that?"

Yousef smiled ambiguously. "You wouldn't be here if I didn't know those things. How did you contact the Turks in West Berlin before the Wall fell?"

"I found an unsealed entrance to the tunnels. It was covered over in a bombed-out ruin from the last Great War. No one had paid attention to it. I worked my way through."

"But you didn't get lost."

Klaus shrugged. "I took several balls of string with me. I tied off the end of one of them at the entrance. When I came to the end of it, I tied it to the end of the next string and kept repeating. I followed the flow of air. There wasn't much, but it was enough."

"And when you got to the other side in West Berlin, you found your way to a mosque?"

Klaus nodded. "That's where I recruited people who helped me."

"And there's your answer. The imam would not have helped you without talking with those men first. You had to tell them your background and intentions for them to follow you. The imam would not have introduced you to Kadir without exceptional reason. I know Kadir. We do business together. We're both in import/export, gold and jewelry exchanges, car rentals in several major cities, and other cash businesses around the world. He introduced you to Hassan, the *hawaladar* in Tripoli?"

Klaus nodded. Yousef shrugged. "There you have it. When you asked for the introduction, you gave permission to pass along all that was known about you. Hassan and I also carry out routine commercial dealings. We both do business with Kadir, most of it through Dubai. There is hardly any banking scrutiny there. You brought Kadir five million dollars in cash?"

Klaus nodded again, scarcely believing that so much about him had been pieced together.

"Turning that much money into legitimate assets is no easy task," Yousef went on. "Kadir did it like an artist. Your funds are safe and already transferred among transactions in our businesses where we take cash and make regular large deposits in banks. You can have any amount or all of your cash whenever you wish. If you like, I'll invest it for you. You have roughly three and a half million dollars remaining?"

Travel fatigue fogged Klaus' mind. He only nodded while finishing his tea. Yousef studied his face. "You're tired. I wanted to give you assurance that your money is in good hands, and you are among friends."

He stood, and when he did, a servant appeared. Yousef instructed him to show Klaus to the guest quarters. "We'll talk more when you are rested. Meanwhile, if you need or want anything, please ask."

Minutes later, Klaus fell asleep on a luxurious bed in an enormous bedroom. Set neatly side by side at the foot of the bed were his five identical suitcases.

When Klaus awoke the next morning, he felt fresh and enlivened. He found his clothes washed and folded on a chair near his bed. After showering and dressing, he walked out of his room onto a wide walkway bordered by a grand balustrade overlooking the courtyard. A male servant approached him.

"Please come. I will take you to breakfast. Yousef will meet your there."

Yousef arrived five minutes after Klaus sat down. "Ah, it's good to see you rested. You slept for fifteen hours. You must have needed it."

They ate while they talked. "You said yesterday that you could invest my money?" Klaus inquired.

"I can arrange that, but it can be complex. We'll talk more about that. I'd like to know what your plans are. You went through one and a half million dollars quickly, and I'm curious about those five suitcases."

Klaus remained quiet. He munched on a variety of dates and pastries while he contemplated.

Yousef read his thoughts. "Let me show you something." He looked back over his shoulder and gestured. Two servants pushed a cloth-covered cart up next to him. Yousef pulled back the cover to reveal stacks of cash, denominated in dollars. He turned to Klaus. "This is yours. It's all there. Count it if you like. You may keep it or leave it with me. Take your time until you are comfortable with your decision."

Klaus sat back grasping the sides of the breakfast table. "I don't know what to say. You've been good to me. I've fought my whole life. Even when I left Berlin, German intelligence and the CIA were after me. They're probably hunting me now."

Yousef scoffed. "The CIA. Any enemy of theirs is a friend of mine. You are a Muslim brother, a warrior. We need more like you." He glanced at the cart, the bills packed in neat stacks. "If you'd like to take your money now, the driver will take you to Riyadh and help you settle in anywhere you choose. If you prefer, I can have it deposited for you. It's been laundered. It's yours. Or, you can stay here, leave it with me as we discussed, and we can talk. The money is always available to you."

Klaus sipped his tea. "While I decide, tell me about the progress of the war."

Yousef grimaced. "Not good. President Bush ended combat operations a few hours ago. Saddam's representative will sign a cease-fire tomorrow." He shrugged. "You should have come a few weeks earlier, when all the coalition forces were concentrated a hundred miles south of Kuwait below what the Americans called Tapline Road. Targets then were thick. A warrior like you could have wreaked havoc, and maybe Saddam would still have Kuwait." He looked beyond the veranda across the desert, disconsolate. "Now the war is over, and we are left with these oil-well fires."

Klaus' mouth formed a crooked grin. "I couldn't get here then. My shoulder was still healing from surgery, and I had to make sure I could move my money and—" he looked around, checking to see if he could be overheard, "—and my luggage." He drew his face closer to Yousef's. "Besides, the war is not over," he hissed. "I could have taken out most of the coalition forces, that's a fact. Allah put in my hands the ability to strike at the whole infidel world."

Kadir stared in disbelief.

Klaus explained, and as he spoke, Yousef's eyes grew wider and wider. He ordered the cart of money moved back to his vault and invited Klaus for a stroll through the compound. They talked for hours, sometimes sitting, sometimes walking through the stately halls of the palace or ambling through the gardens and palm groves.

At one point, Yousef asked, "Can I see inside the suitcases?"

Klaus hesitated, and then consented. They returned to his room. He opened the first bag.

Seeing the etching on the metal plate, Yousef brought his hand to his face. Klaus lifted the plate, exposing the bomb's components. Disbelieving wonder imprinted on Yousef's countenance. He alternated glinting eyes between Klaus and the bomb.

"They were designed by a retired nuclear engineer from the French weapons program," Klaus informed him. He summarized how he had come by the bomb in Berlin and how Rayner had checked it out. He paused. "I've studied satellite photos of the smoke from Kuwait. The winds blow it away from Saudi Arabia. We get some along the eastern border, but compared to the rest of the region, we're getting very little." His expression became solemn. "The Kingdom is truly sacred ground."

Yousef pulled his corpulent frame to stand in front of Klaus and grasp his shoulder. "You are a blessing from Allah. The day of his vengeance is near." A look of righteous determination crossed his face. "Tell me what you need, and we will provide it. You will pay nothing. We have friends who will gladly contribute to see this great victory." He strolled out of Klaus' room to the balustrade and looked across the courtyard to the desert beyond. Klaus joined him.

"Saudi Arabia and Islam will soon take its rightful place in this world," Yousef said. "What can we do for you right now?"

Klaus took a moment to think. "First, I'll leave the money with you. I know you'll take good care of it." Yousef nodded. "Next, I need the full story of the war in Kuwait. Newspapers only tell part of it. There must be a hotel where foreign reporters stay. Can your driver take me there? I want to listen in the lobby and bar—talk with reporters. With the fighting stopped, they should be making their way home. They'll be trading war stories."

"There's a hotel where war correspondents have come and gone for months, in Dhahran. Some reporters were stranded there while the fighting took place. You might get a sense of the battlefield there. The drive usually takes four hours, but the army has the highway locked down tight. With all the checkpoints along the way, six to seven hours is more realistic. We'll take you." He paused as a thought struck. "You'll have to leave your luggage here. They won't get through those checkpoints."

Klaus jerked his head up. "Will they be safe here?"

Yousef drew back, startled at the inference. Then he smiled and wrapped a heavy arm across Klaus' shoulder. "My brother, I am a *hawal-adar*. My word guarantees their safety. They will be here when we return."

24

Tony Collins surveyed the International Hotel in Dhahran. It was a spectacular glass building, reflecting the modern architecture that had overtaken much of the oil-rich Arab countries around the Persian Gulf. With evening falling fast, the neon signage in Arabic calligraphy flickered. Collins picked up his bags and headed through the main entrance.

General Alsip's adjutant had called ahead and made a reservation, so checking in took little time. Within a few minutes, Collins was in his room contacting Tom Jakes, his editor at the *Washington Herald* in DC.

"Hi Tom. Sorry to have been out of touch." He ran down his activities of the last four days.

"You must be exhausted. I don't see any scoops on your list, but don't sweat it. The tele-journalists got those. We're glad you're safe. A few in-depth articles with your analysis will go far."

"Thanks, I'll fax them from here." They spoke a while longer and signed off.

Despite feeling relieved, Collins finished the call emotionally spent. He had never been in an active war zone. The scenes he'd witnessed moved him. The gallantry of soldiers and Marines juxtaposed against the savagery of combat left him with a sober sense that would stay with him. The cries of the wounded heard up close; seeing their blood spilled on the ground with missing limbs—and the impersonal black body bags making their way to the rear—they haunted him.

He heard that the US had taken less than three hundred casualties. Estimates of Iraqi casualties conservatively topped twenty-five thousand. Knowing those numbers did not assuage his raw nerves. He desperately wanted a strong drink.

Feeling the walls closing in, Collins made his way to the restaurant off the lobby. News media personalities and their crews packed it. He recognized some of them. Most looked as exhausted as he. He spotted a few he considered friends and sat down, glad for the company and the distraction. From habit, he sat close to the wall in a dimly lit corner where he could observe without being easily spotted.

He ordered dinner with the rest of his colleagues. A subdued atmosphere hung in the air. A few pockets of boisterous people regaled their exploits. Being that they were in Saudi Arabia, no alcohol was served.

Absently, Collins glanced into the lobby. A rotund man wearing Saudi *farwah and shemagh* began checking in. Next to him was a man in a business suit. His manner projected quiet confidence backed by superb physical conditioning.

Something about the second man seemed familiar. Collins looked closer. The man had deep-set eyes, a light complexion—in a flash, Collins' mind took him back to the night in Berlin when thousands of people had trudged by—including the only man who scowled and carried a suitcase and stopped to nurse his right shoulder. Klaus!

Yousef and Klaus finished checking in and strolled toward the restaurant. Collins leaned into his dark corner.

―――――――――

Klaus entered the restaurant ahead of Yousef. He paused momentarily to take stock of those inside. Dim candles flickered on the patrons' faces. Nothing seemed out of the ordinary, except that one man leaned into the shadows.

Klaus took his seat with Yousef, positioning himself to observe the entrance. He picked up his menu, feigning absorbed scrutiny. Soon, the man in the shadows made his way out of the restaurant. Klaus did not get a clear view of him.

Several minutes later, Yousef's driver entered. "Someone in the parking lot looked over the car," he told them in a whisper.

"Did he see you?"

"No. I stayed out of sight. He wrote something down and left."

Klaus turned to Yousef. "I'll check it out." To the driver he said, "I'll meet you in the parking lot."

A few minutes after the driver departed, Klaus excused himself. He stopped at the front desk, had a low-tone conversation with the desk clerk, and delivered several high-denomination dollar bills. Two minutes later, he stood in front of Collins' room.

"This president knows how to make a statement," Sofia said. She sat in the big empty conference room with Atcho and Burly at Berlin Brigade headquarters. "Stopping hostilities exactly on the one hundredth hour? I sure would not want to have been the last casualty."

"We need to stick to business," Burly replied on the speaker. "Atcho, you and Horton are both cleared to enter the war zone. You'll fly out to Riyadh tomorrow. You'll get full cooperation from US military forces. Do you know where you want to start?"

"We'll figure that out when we get on the ground," Atcho replied.

"Sofia, what will you do now?" Burly asked.

"I'll come there to Washington and work with you," she said. "I want to stay in the loop and see this mission through."

"Let me know your travel arrangements. Hold on a second—" The line went quiet a moment, then Burly came back on. "I have a call coming in from Tony Collins. He says it's urgent. I'm patching it through, so you can all hear it." A few electronic tones sounded, and then the reporter's voice.

"I'm in Dhahran, along the Saudi border with Kuwait," Collins said without greeting. He sounded hoarse, strained. "I covered the war." His voice took on added urgency. "I just saw Klaus downstairs in my hotel."

For a moment, no one spoke. "Did you hear me?" Collins repeated. "Klaus is here in Kuwait."

"We heard you," Atcho broke in. "Are you sure it's him?"

"Positive. He's cleaned up and wears a business suit, but that's the man I saw at Checkpoint Charlie with the suitcase and the wounded shoulder."

"Did he see you?"

"I don't think so. I managed to move out of his line of sight before he entered the restaurant. He was reading the menu when I left. I called as soon as I got back to my room."

"Good job. Get out of there. He's got to know you helped us last year, and that was your byline on those articles we planted in Berlin. If he sees you, he might come after you."

"I thought of that. Listen, I went to the parking lot before I called, and I think I found their car. Klaus' companion looks like a rich Saudi. Most of the hotel guests are reporters. They don't have cars. There was only one Mercedes. Here's the license number." He read it to them. "I'll fax it so that you have the Arabic figures too."

Suddenly Collins heard loud pounding on his door. It was clearly audible over the speakerphone.

"Collins, get out of there."

Collins responded, his voice melancholy, resigned. "It might already be too late."

Burly and the group in Berlin heard a crashing noise, two ballistic spits of bullets splitting the air, a thud, and then quiet. A moment later, another voice came over the line. "Are you there, Atcho?" Silence, then the sound of breathing. "You're too late. You can't stop what is already in motion. You killed my brother. I got your friend. I'll get your wife. Then I'll come for you. But before then, the world will see the might and justice of Islam." Click.

Atcho, Sofia, and Horton stared numbly at each other. "Oh God," Burly muttered, then he was quiet. After a moment, he said gruffly, "I'll call back." He hung up.

When Klaus rejoined Yousef after fifteen minutes, he took his seat and picked up the menu. "Things are under control," he said amiably.

They spent the evening in light conversation. Klaus made a point to circulate among the reporters in the restaurant and lounge, get their impressions of the war, and glean information.

The next morning, they left early for the return trip to Riyadh. When they were far north of Dhahran on a desolate stretch of the road, Klaus asked the driver to pull over. Yousef shot a questioning glance but did not object.

When they stopped, Klaus and the driver walked to the rear of the car. They pulled Collins' body out of the trunk and dumped it on the side of the road. Yousef watched through the back window.

"I had to clean up a detail," Klaus told him on climbing back into the car. "He was a reporter that recognized me. He was the man checking out the car last night."

They drove a distance in silence. Klaus studied Yousef. Finally, he said, "You haven't been this close to violence before."

Yousef nodded. "You see things on television and in the newspapers. It's not the same as seeing it in actuality." He sighed. "I'll be all right."

Klaus smiled. "You take care of the money and support. I'll handle the blood work." He described what had transpired the night before. "We need to step up the schedule."

"Did you learn anything from the other reporters last night?"

Klaus grinned. "Not a lot we didn't already know, but there was one significant piece of information. The wells will take months to close down—to put out the fires."

"Then why does the schedule need to speed up?"

"Because the CIA knows I'm here. They'll guess why, and they'll be after me." He put his hands behind his head and leaned back, enjoying the moment. "This could be the start of a beautiful partnership."

25

"Breaking news." Atcho stopped packing and stared at the television screen. "This just in. The body of Tony Collins, well-known investigative reporter for the *Washington Herald*, was discovered this morning along a highway leading out of Dhahran, Saudi Arabia. His fans will recall the all-night reporting marathon he did from Checkpoint Charlie in Berlin sixteen months ago when the Wall came down."

Across the room in the guest quarters of the US Embassy in Berlin, Sofia stopped what she was doing to watch the report. Her eyes brimmed. "He didn't deserve that," she whispered. "He was a good man. He had a family."

She remembered what a nuisance Collins had been while he pursued her and Atcho through Europe and even to Moscow on their mission to end the conspiracy against Gorbachev. Last year, he had produced key evidence showing a plot existed to use a nuclear device to stop the Berlin Wall from opening. He had won a warm place in hers and Atcho's hearts, a cherished friend.

"Klaus wanted the body to be found," Atcho muttered. Sofia cast him a questioning glance. "Look at where they found Collins. On a highway. It might have light traffic, but anyone traveling there couldn't miss it. He wanted us to see the report."

They held each other for several minutes. "Evil exists," Atcho said after a while. "It's why we do what we do." He returned to packing.

Sofia wiped her eyes. "I wish I could go with you."

"Not this time. We have our jobs to do, and right now," he took her in his arms and caressed her stomach, "your job is to keep that baby safe. You should go to your parents' house."

"No," Sofia said firmly. "You think Klaus can't find out where they live? I won't let him destroy our lives. I'm going home to Austin. If he comes there, he'll find a lot more than he bargained for."

Atcho studied her. "I thought you were going to DC to work with Burly."

"I changed my mind. If I can't be with you, I want to be at home."

Atcho nodded. "All right. Horton will meet me at the front of the embassy in a few minutes. Let's make that phone call."

He picked up the receiver and dialed a number. A familiar voice answered. Atcho turned on the speaker so that Sofia could participate. "Ivan, it's great to hear your voice. I won't be able to speak long. Sofia is here with me. She'll explain in more detail when she gets home."

"Understood I just heard the news about Tony Collins. He was a good man."

"Yes, he was, and that's partly why we're calling. I can't say much on an open line, but our house needs protecting. Highest level of security. You know what to do."

"Consider it done. Send your flight information, Sofia. I'll pick you up at the airport." They hung up.

Ivan Chekov was a defected KGB officer living in Texas, and now an American citizen. He and Atcho had worked together three times before on covert operations. On the second one, Ivan pressured Gorbachev personally to approve his family's immigration to the United States. Ronald Reagan had rewarded Ivan's effort with expedited citizenship.

Being an avid reader of Louis L'Amour novels, the Russian had become enamored with the American West. As a result, after his defection, he settled in Montana. However, when Atcho bought the company in Austin, he lured Ivan to Texas.

Because of his past associations with the KGB, Ivan could never receive a security clearance. For that reason, Atcho could not hire him directly into the company. However, he helped Ivan establish a corporate security services firm and hired it for his security needs. Ivan used the latest technology and methods.

"I'm so glad we have him," Sofia said.

Atcho picked up his bag. Together they headed toward the front of the embassy. "I feel good knowing he'll keep an eye on the homestead."

"You mean keep an eye on me."

"I'm glad he'll keep an eye out *for* you." Atcho smiled. "I know you can take care of yourself."

Horton waited for them at the entrance. His normal upbeat attitude was subdued, but he still smiled. "Get your goodbyes said. We've got to go."

Atcho turned to Sofia. She flung her arms around his neck. "Please come home safe," she whispered.

"Don't worry, Miss Sofia," Horton called from the side. "I won't let him do any Lone Ranger crap. If you keep our rear secure, I'll make sure he gets back in one piece."

Sofia smiled back her tears. She hugged Horton. "Make sure you get home too. You've got a wife and a son."

Horton squeezed her. "All right, but don't you go getting mushy on me." He stepped back and wiped his eyes with the sides of both fists, like a child. His face dropped into mock misery and his voice lilted. "I think I'm gonna cry."

Sofia punched his shoulder and pointed a finger in his face. "I'm serious. You better both come home, or I'll make you pay."

Horton looked from his shoulder to her face. "Cain't let that happen." He grinned.

She hugged him again.

26

Ivan met Sofia at the Robert Mueller Municipal Airport when she landed in Austin. He reminded her of a lethal version of the comedian Bob Newhart, medium height, balding head, but always physically fit and deadly serious. She remembered him standing erect, waving to joyous East Berliners through Checkpoint Charlie as though he had final authority in allowing the Wall to be breached.

Sofia said very little when Ivan picked her up. She remained quiet in the car.

"I don't want to alarm you," Ivan said after a while. "It's good that you and Atcho called. Your house is under surveillance."

Sofia did not respond, and when Ivan checked to see if she had heard, she seemed preoccupied. She asked no questions and offered no conversation. They wound through Austin's scenic hill country and turned onto Mt. Bonnell Road.

When they reached the house, Ivan entered each room to clear it. Sofia meandered in a daze to the veranda and looked over the limestone cliffs to the Colorado River below. When he had finished his security checks, Ivan sauntered next to her.

"This place is so beautiful," Sofia said. "Atcho and I fell in love with it the moment we saw it." She shifted her view to the road running on the opposite side of the river. "The tranquility here can't stay this way forever. Austin is growing fast and coming our way. More development will take place on this side of the lake."

Ivan was concerned. *She's rambling. Unusual for her.* "Sofia, are you all right?"

Sofia turned her back to him and put her hands to her face. Her shoulders began to shake. She wept softly, wiping away tears before they escaped.

"Sofia, what's wrong?"

"I'm sorry." She gulped. "I feel so bad about Collins—and I'm going to have a baby. I've never been so scared."

Astonished, Ivan could only say, "Is that a bad thing? The baby? Can I say congratulations?"

Sofia remained in place without turning. After a moment, she replied. "Look at those cars on the road over there." She gestured across the river. "The people in them live normal, happy lives. You and I and Atcho and others, we're always dealing with evil.

"I want this baby so much, but I'm scared to bring it into this life. And now with Collins dead and Atcho still..." Tears ran freely. "...and I can't help him."

Despair broke her voice. "I've never felt helpless before." She caught herself after a few moments and wiped her face with her hands. "I'm sorry. How are Lara and Kirill?"

Ivan put an arm over her shoulder. "They're well. Kirill is a star on his soccer team. Lara enjoys the culture of Austin." He laughed quietly. "And I'm getting to see the Western sites I used to read about in Louis L'Amour's books."

He watched the traffic across the river. "I grew up in a totalitarian state. Atcho saw Cuba turned into one. To most people in this country, places like that aren't real. They're the stuff of novels and spy movies. They don't believe life can be so bad anywhere. The Europeans forgot in three generations how cruel and sadistic things were under the Nazis. They haven't stopped to think that most people in the world are ruled by dictators. The West lives freely because of people who go into dark places and do what needs to be done, like you and Atcho."

"And you," Sofia said, patting him on his arm, "you go into those dark places. I don't want that for my kid."

"Better your child is equipped to deal with danger than go blithely through life while evil creeps up from behind. That's what happens to most people. We know evil exists because we've dealt with it." He squeezed her shoulders. "Your child will be fine because of how his parents prepare." He tried to lighten the mood. "You know, the feminist movement would probably not like your attitude. Worrying about family before career and choosing to have a child and put him or her first?" He shook his head. "Heresy."

"The feminist movement can go to hell," Sofia replied flatly. "On their best days, I'll be more feminine than any of them, and on my worst day I'll kick their butts." She gazed out over the river, her expression becoming resolute. "Thank you, my friend. Enough melancholy. Tell me about who's watching our house."

Ivan pointed at a maroon Crown Victoria parked around a curve on the way to Atcho's company headquarters to pick up Sofia's car in Austin. "Those are a couple of the men watching your house," he told her. "I don't know who they are, but there are at least three separate teams. The other two are at different vantage points."

"Did you augment our security?"

"We're monitoring your surveillance system remotely from our offices, and we have three men staking out the house. They're not as visible as these clowns. We also notified the sheriff's office through Atcho's company that you were coming home and had received threats. The deputies do drive-bys. When you get back to your house after picking up your car, we'll see how they react."

"Sounds like a plan, but they must have seen us when you drove me home."

"I'm sure they did. That could be good. If they intend on doing something bad, they might be slowed down knowing you've got friends at your back. I could have taken you straight to the office, but you looked like you were ready to see your own house and could use a friend hanging around for a while."

Sofia nodded her appreciation.

They arrived at the company office. "Keep your gun loaded," Ivan said before Sofia exited his car. "Use your remote to open the garage, and don't get out of the car until it's closed. No use giving a sniper a clear shot."

Sofia shot him an amused look. "I know what to do, Ivan. This won't be the first time I've thrown a lariat."

"I know. I just don't want to forget a detail."

An hour later, Sofia entered the safe-room in her house without incident. "I'm in," she called to Ivan over the phone.

"The watchers are still in position. We saw them talking on their radios when you arrived."

"What do I do now, sit tight? I can't stay cooped up here for long."

Ivan chuckled. "When you're at the point of pulling your hair out, give us a call, and you can leave the same way you came in. We'll watch out for you. If you have an emergency, we'll pick you up by boat at the bottom of the bluff. Meanwhile, feel free to move about the house. If we see movement, we'll call and be ready to pounce."

"Great." Sofia's voice was laden with sarcasm. "This is going to be fun."

"Oh, and Sofia." Ivan chuckled again. "You can turn off the internal surveillance."

Sofia spun around in her seat. She made a face at a pinhole over the entry and waved. Then she flipped a switch.

"OK," Ivan said. "All the internal cameras are off."

———

Kadir spoke with Klaus over the phone from Berlin. "I've heard from the surveillance company we hired in Austin. Ms. Sofia is back in her house."

"That's good to know," Klaus growled. "Don't do anything now. Keep one man watching her and let me know if she's leaving town. I'll be there in a few days."

27

A Blackhawk helicopter settled on the helipad outside the Ministry of Defense building in Riyadh, Saudi Arabia. Atcho and Horton stepped down from its open doors into the warm prop wash beneath the strumming rotors. A soldier met them where a surprisingly cool desert wind overtook the chopper's down thrust. He pointed to a door on the side of the building where an Army captain in camouflaged fatigues stood to one side and beckoned them. They walked briskly toward him, ducking their heads to one side to let their Kevlar helmets break the wind and absorb stinging sand.

The captain saluted Horton and held the door open for them. "The general is expecting you," he said when they were inside and could talk without shouting. He introduced himself. "I'll take you to him."

He stopped at a security desk, signed them in, and acquired visitors passes for them. Then he led off at a fast pace through a maze of hallways and offices. "Things have been a bit hectic here," he said as they hurried through the beehive of activity all around them. "Combat operations terminated, but now with those oil-well fires..." He shook his head.

He turned into a massive room divided up by cubicles with officers busily typing into computers or reading their monitors or conferring with each other. The captain led past them to a row of offices at the far end.

The door to one of them in the middle stood open. He knocked and stepped inside. "General, they're here."

"Bring them in," an enthusiastic voice called out. When they entered, a youngish man in battle-dress rounded his desk and approached them, his hand extended. He carried a slight build, dark hair with the first signs of gray, and he exuded energy despite sunken eyes attesting to days in the desert. Atcho noticed a single star at chest level on his blouse.

"Hi. I'm Jason Forrester. I'm read in on the situation but could use a briefing on the nitty-gritty. General Schwarzkopf is tied up at the moment but detailed me to support your mission. Sounds serious."

After introductions, he gestured them to chairs in front of his desk. As he returned to his seat, he peered at Horton. "Your legend precedes you, Major. Don't try any of that Texas dumb-guy stuff on me." He grinned slightly.

Horton glanced at Atcho, his eyes wide and round. He said nothing.

"I've been briefed about you too, Atcho," Forrester continued. "Now, down to business. General Schwarzkopf got a call from the chairman of the joint chiefs. I'm supposed to do everything I can to help you. I work in his operations section."

"Have you spoken with General Alsip?" Atcho asked.

Forrester's face clouded, and he nodded. "I'm sorry to hear about Tony Collins. I hear he was a close friend of yours."

Atcho nodded, a lump forming in his throat. "We worked together a few times. He set a standard for reporting that few in the profession approach."

"Alsip had only good things to say about him. In particular, he appreciated the way he loved and respected soldiers. He got down in the sand with them."

"Did Alsip know anything about this terrorist we're chasing—Klaus?" Atcho said.

Forrester shook his head. "Collins flew with Alsip at the outset of ground combat, and Alsip got him to Dhahran on cease-fire. They didn't get a lot of chance to chitchat."

"Collins gave us a license plate number that he thought connected to

Klaus. We ran it up but haven't heard anything back. Do you have anything on it?"

The general shook his head. "Not that I've heard, but I just came in the loop. I'm still in the dark on a lot of it. I hear the FBI is sending a couple of guys to investigate with the Saudi police."

"Can you get us to that hotel in Dhahran?" Horton cut in.

"I'll get a crew to fly you down there," Forrester replied. "What are you going to do?"

"Look around. See if we can pick up anything useful. It's a starting point."

They conferred for an hour and then left for their flight to Dhahran. As they made their way back through the maze of offices, Horton elbowed Atcho. "Geez, sir. I'm a legend."

Amused, Atcho shook his head. "Get over it. What do you expect to find at that hotel? We don't have much time. Klaus is way ahead of us, and Saudi Arabia is three times the size of Texas."

Horton circled in front of Atcho, his hands on his hips. "You think I don't know that? But guess what. This country has a lot of sand. That narrows things down a bit."

"We still don't know where he is."

"Well that's what we're trying to find out. Geez, Atcho. Who's the legend around here anyhow?"

———————

Another Blackhawk waited for Atcho and Horton at the helipad. On arrival in Dhahran, a military sedan drove them to the hotel. Horton instructed the driver to wait for them.

Inside, they asked for the manager. Immediately, Horton struck up a conversation in fluent Arabic. He saw Atcho stare at him in amazement.

Horton caught Atcho's reaction. "What? I was stationed in this country for three years. I had to communicate."

Atcho chuckled and turned to observe the foyer, decked out in Saudi opulence. He saw nothing of particular note, but when he turned back to listen to Horton and the manager, he noticed one of the clerks lurking behind the office door.

As they climbed the stairs to the third floor and entered the hall where Collins had stayed, Atcho related to Horton what he had seen. "We'll need to talk to him," Horton said. "The FBI ain't been here yet. The manager said they're supposed to arrive this evening with Saudi police detectives."

The door to Collins' room was shattered. A piece of yellow tape had been hung across the entrance. When they entered, the atmosphere was cold, gloomy, with signs of Collins' last movements. The bedspread was wrinkled. A shirt hung on the corner of a chair. His suitcase sat next to a shallow closet. Shaving cream and a razor were set on a glass shelf below a mirror. Splatters of blood marred the walls.

"I can feel him," Atcho said. "I hear his last words over that phone." He pointed. Then he picked up a piece of paper balled up in the corner next to the bed stand. He smoothed it out and studied it. "Joe, what was the license number we got from Collins?"

Horton reached inside his jacket for a small notebook. He thumbed through it and read the numbers to Atcho.

"He was one digit off," Atcho said. "That could be why the Saudi authorities haven't found the owner yet."

"Or it could be that someone doesn't want to find him," Horton said. "They got computers in this country. They could have figured out if one digit was wrong. Not everyone in official Saudi Arabia loves us, not even on the police force. We'll check the register downstairs and see what we find." He copied the numbers down. Atcho balled up the paper and tossed it back in the corner for the FBI to find.

They spoke again with the manager at the front desk. "Your boy back there listened to our conversation," Horton told him. "I want to talk to him."

The manager at first refused, but Horton pressed him. At one point, Horton's face grew red and he spoke in a terse voice. He pulled out his military ID and shoved it in the man's face. Atcho understood none of what was said.

The manager stepped to the office door and called out angrily. A moment later, the clerk appeared. He looked both shamefaced and scared. He had a slight build and could not be more than seventeen years old. His boss yelled at him in Arabic.

The clerk crossed to the computer and typed into it, ran his finger down the screen, and pointed.

"We got a name and address, and we got a correct license plate," Horton said flatly as they climbed back into the Army sedan. "Let's get back to General Forrester with this. He can send this up the totem pole and put pressure on authorities to run it down better than we can."

28

"I need an airplane," Klaus told Yousef. "I need to see the oilfields."

"That is a difficult request," Yousef replied. "The US and Saudi Arabia have the airspace locked down. Flying in there will be dangerous. I have a friend near the border who is a pilot and flies his own plane. We'll see what he thinks. Crews are already organizing to put out the fires. They'll be on site within six days."

Klaus agreed. "I'm not a pilot, but I know enough to be careful about the turbulence from those fires too. The thermals above them must be terrible. I've seen videos from the ground. I'm looking for huge wells with plumes going straight up."

"Do you plan to drop all five bombs on one well, or put each one on a different site?"

Klaus cast him a sideways glance. "It's only going to be four bombs. I have another target already selected for the fifth one."

Yousef studied him silently for a few minutes. "There's a saying. 'Revenge is best served cold.'"

"I've been patient," Klaus snapped. Then he took a deep breath. "I haven't decided yet about putting the bombs together or keeping them separate. Together is much simpler. All I have to do is put them on the same frequency from the remote control.

"If I go after separate wells, there's a greater probability of something going wrong with one of them, or worse, I get stuck in the blast area. I have no desire to be a martyr, at least not yet."

"Of course not," Yousef replied, his face expressing horror at the idea. "You are much too valuable to lose. You know how to do things, get places, and you're not afraid to act. The *jihad* needs a thousand more like you." He paused, drumming his fingers on the table. "There is a man in Riyadh. His family owns the largest construction company in the country. He is disgusted that the royal family allowed the US to base its troops and war planes on the Saudi Arabia Peninsula. He's been so vocal that the government is likely to expel him from the country. His driver brought you to my house when you arrived in Riyadh. Have you heard of Usama bin Laden?"

Klaus pursed his mouth. "I'm not familiar with the name."

Kadir shrugged. "You will be." He thought a moment. "My pilot friend has a Mooney. He brags that it is built for speed and maneuverability. It should be able to handle the turbulence. He's a good pilot." He laughed. "He'll charge me a lot of money because he'll whine about how dangerous it is to fly into the smoke with all the air defenses, and I'm sure the plane will come back looking very different than when it goes out."

"I can pay."

Yousef shook his head and raised his palms to protest. "You are the warrior risking your life. When you succeed, you'll further *jihad* more than anyone in recent memory. Save your wealth for your old age."

Klaus and Bandar, the pilot, took off shortly after dawn broke the next morning. They flew close to the ground at full throttle until a veil of dark moisture coated the windshield. Then they climbed steeply until breaking into bright sunlight. Even for someone as battle hardened as Klaus, the view of the fires from above was ghastly.

Shroud-like pollution hung over Kuwait City. They flew east above the cloud until it stretched as far as the eye could see in any direction.

"Can you descend back into it?"

"I'll take the plane down until either the turbulence is too much, or the oxygen is too thin for the engine—or us."

Wisps of smoke slid over the windscreen. The plane bumped through the increasing blackness until the sun was a dull orb in the sky. An unearthly roar seared through the light metal airframe louder than the combined noise of the engine and the wind. It shook the small plane. Then the wet stench of burnt oil spread through the cabin, causing Klaus and the pilot to gag. Ahead of them, an orange plume reached into the black sky, clutching at them.

Bandar maneuvered the aircraft around the updraft of hot air that must be immediately above the flame. When the plane banked, a dark panorama stretched out below. Towers of flame burst from the ground like demons dancing on blackened desert sand.

Klaus glanced at Bandar. He had blanched, gripping the yoke and starting into a steady climb. "Time to go home," he said when they broke back into sunlight.

Klaus nodded. He looked back at the wing on his side of the airplane. It had turned black, with only rivets showing intermittent splashes of the original white paint.

Later, while meeting with Yousef, Klaus still coughed out the effects of smoke over a parched throat. "This is going to be more difficult than we thought, but I have a couple of ideas."

"Whatever you do," Yousef replied, "it should be done within the next five days. After that, security around the oilfields will be extremely tight."

"I know. Can you get me in on the ground?"

―――――――

"Can you get me in on the ground?" Atcho asked General Forrester. "I need to see what the conditions are at the wells and how difficult it will be for Klaus to get close to one of them. I want to get into Klaus' head, see what he sees—figure out what he'll do." Forrester nodded. "We'll fly you down to 1st Marine Division headquarters. That's their sector. Someone there will drive you into the oilfields. I'll arrange it. Be ready to leave in an hour. We'll have special clothing and equipment for you. I'll get the CG

there to assign one action officer each from their intelligence and operations sections. I'd suggest you work out of there for anything you want to
do in the oilfields."

On landing, a Marine pulled in front of them in a civilian pickup. He
wore yellow coveralls, a safety helmet, and gloves. A pair of goggles
stretched over the front of his helmet. He jumped from the truck. "I've got
these Sunday-best duds for y'all." He lowered the back of the pickup,
revealing two boxes. "We just got these in. They're rushing them here for
the cleanup crews."

They drove through abandoned battlefields on the way to the wells.
Massive numbers of scorched cars and trucks lined the roads where days
and weeks ago terrified refugees fled the onslaught of the Iraqi army.
Spread out in the sands, burned-out hulks of battle tanks, personnel
carriers, field artillery guns, rocket launchers, and all manner of war
machinery lay strewn about, relics of the folly of misplaced ambition. In
one charred vehicle, the upright corpse of the driver testified to the
horror of the flames. The black ashes of his hands clawed at the windshield, his blackened brow stretched in terror. His burnt-out eyes still
stared into a cauldron and his lips parted over carbonized teeth in a
silent, eternal scream.

No one spoke as the trio drove past the carnage. The ground turned
black beneath them as they approached the wells. Above them, the sky
darkened. The combined roar drowned any other sound. Ahead, gigantic
flames, separated by indiscernible distance as far as they could see, shot
hundreds of feet into the air, their unearthly glows shedding the only
light other than vehicle headlamps. Around some wells, oil had spread
and ignited, creating ground fires on desert sand.

Some of the plumes burnt straight up, perpendicular to the ground.
Others angled to one side. "Watch those sidewinders," the driver yelled.
"If we get downwind of those flames, the heat and fumes could kill us real
quick. And the winds change constantly."

As they drove by individual wells, they saw melted steel casings and
equipment strewn about. Unignited oil streamed into the air and fell to
the ground, collecting in low areas to form lakes of black oil, needing
only a lighted match to convert them into yet more hellfires on earth.

They drove back as they had come, in silence. The profoundness of what they had seen bore down to the cores of their spirits.

Later that evening, Atcho tried to tell Sofia about the experience over the phone. He found he could not. "Words to describe what I saw don't exist." He felt drained of energy in mind and body. "If Klaus succeeds," he said, "he'll touch every part of Earth."

Sofia could not think of a reply that fit the moment. "I love you," she whispered.

They hung up. Atcho sat alone in his room on the edge of his bed. He sank his head in his hands. "How did this land on me?" He tried to put his sense of overwhelm out of his mind, but it persisted. He slept little that night, torn by nightmares of the world wrapped in billowing flames, the faces of those he loved emerging in agonized, burning images. He woke up in a cold sweat.

Early the next morning, he met Horton for coffee in the mess hall. The major's drawn expression indicated he had encountered an equally disturbed night. "I tried to explain to my wife what I saw yesterday," he said. "I couldn't."

"Me too," Atcho replied. "Any ideas on how we stop this guy?"

Horton sighed and shook his head. "I wish I did, but I'm clean out of ideas. First we got to find him."

"I'm guessing we have about four days," Atcho said. "The cleanup was announced, and security is already tightening around the wells. By the time work starts, the area will be sealed off."

They walked to the headquarters offices and entered a conference room for the Marine commanding general's morning briefing. Atcho was astounded at the number of people in attendance. The primary staff officers sat on three sides of a massive table that abutted a large screen on one end.

A colonel approached them and introduced himself. "Y'all don't need to be here," he said. "I'm the general's chief-of-staff. This will be a long meeting covering lots of subjects that won't interest you. I'm fully read in on the situation, and so are our intelligence and operations officers. They've each designated a senior subordinate to assist you, and you have the full assets of the division to help. The CG asked me to say that you have unimpeded access to him. If our staff can't help, go to him directly. The staff is advised of that, and I'll help any way I can." He focused his attention on Horton and then switched it to Atcho. "The major knows the ropes."

The colonel directed them to a specific room where two lieutenant-colonels met them. After introductions, they sat down at a conference table.

"We've been out there on the oilfields," Jones, the intelligence officer, opened the discussion. "We know what it's like. We'll tell you what we know, what's being done. You can fill in the gaps."

"One thing to let you know," Green, the operations officer, broke in, "a couple of days ago, a private plane flew into the area. It was spotted flying high, but then it descended into the smoke. A couple of fighter jets scrambled, but their orbit was wide. We had a couple of helicopters on standby, but we lost the plane in the smoke. It popped out high again a while later but beat feet back into Saudi airspace and flew low into an area with lots of hills. That pilot knows his turf. We don't know where they landed. We never saw the tail numbers. The aircraft was white when it went into the smoke. It came out pitch black."

Atcho regarded them grim-faced. "Hills? In Saudi Arabia."

Green grinned. "People are always surprised when they hear that. They have green hills too, with vegetation. Lots of them."

"All right. Any word on the license number?"

"The car belongs to a Saudi businessman," Jones replied. "Yousef Al-Zahrani. He's known to have ties to Usama bin Laden, an up-and-coming terrorist." He pulled two photographs from a file folder, one each of Yousef and Klaus. "We showed these to the clerk at the hotel. He positively identified both men as guests who stayed in the hotel that night."

"Let's go get 'em," Horton exclaimed. "What are we waiting for?"

Green grimaced. "It's not that easy. Yousef is a *hawaladar*. Do you know what that is?" Atcho and Horton nodded. "Then you know he has high-level contacts, including on the police force. Being in the hotel that night wasn't against the law, and we can't prove that Yousef's car transported Collins' body."

"Don't the Saudis know that Kuwait is a furnace?" Atcho asked, aghast. He noticed Horton regarding the two officers with a look of skepticism. "Don't they know that a weapon like the ones Klaus has can destroy beyond anything ever seen?"

Jones sighed. "They know it, but they don't necessarily believe this man Klaus has any nuclear weapons." He paused. "If you see things from their view, it sounds outlandish." He indicated himself and Green with a flick of his thumb. "We're here because we're assigned. We believe you believe the threat, but it's a lot to swallow."

Atcho glanced at Horton. The major's face had turned scarlet. His eyes bulged. "Sirs," he said through gritted teeth, "the fact that the Kuwaiti oilfields are on fire is a lot to swallow. No one in his right mind would do such a thing, right? But take a good long look out that window?" He walked over, jerked a curtain aside, and pointed. He took a deep breath. "We're guessing we have four days to stop this turd Klaus." He held up a hand with four fingers extended. "Count 'em. One, two, three, four. That's it."

He put his hands on his hips, still glaring. "Suppose we're right about Klaus. Do you want to be here when five nuclear bombs ignite all the oil in that field?" He pointed again, toward the darkened sky. "I came from Berlin by order of my commanding general to help Atcho chase this guy down and put him six feet under. Do you think the general would send me here if this wasn't a credible threat?"

His jaw jutted toward Jones and Green in a pugnacious stance. "If you don't believe us, that's fine. But since you're assigned, I suggest you shake off your battle fatigue or whatever is muddlin' your brains. If we're right, more than your careers could be at stake." He stared them down a moment, and then relaxed. Dropping his hands to his sides, he grinned. "Respectfully, of course."

Jones and Green were visibly shaken at the onslaught. As Horton had spoken, their expressions morphed from shock, to disbelief, to reluctant acceptance. Green looked at Jones, "Makes sense." He turned back to Atcho and Horton. "What do we do?"

Horton chuckled. "We was hoping you'd have some ideas."

"That was one hell of a scolding you gave those guys," Atcho told Horton when they were alone.

"Yeah, well, I had to get their attention. They were about to blow us off with courtesy."

"What now?"

"Their general will want to hear from them. I think we scared them enough that they'll give him a good picture. I think we'll get more priority now."

"Good. I talked to Burly a few minutes ago. He's set up support in Riyadh with the CIA. They've coordinated with Saudi intelligence to put surveillance on Yousef."

"Have they spotted him?"

"Yeah, but if Klaus was with him a few nights ago, he's not there now."

"What about that airplane?"

"That's a mystery. There are quite a few small airports along that eastern strip of Saudi Arabia. That plane could have taken off from any of them, or even an unmarked strip. When it came out of the cloud, it got down to the ground and out of sight fast."

Horton blew air threw pursed lips. Exasperation replaced his normal humor. "What do we do now? Sit and wait until someone puts up a sign pointing the way?"

Atcho felt his partner's discontent. "What are the alternatives for putting the bomb on target? He had to be thinking about an air drop, but there are several obstacles. How would he pinpoint the location? If the bomb goes directly into one of the wells, the trigger mechanism would melt before it activated. If it drops to the side of one, the force of landing could jar the mechanics and have the same effect, neutralize the trigger."

"What about if he dropped it with a parachute and used one of those barometric devices to self-detonate when it reaches a certain altitude?"

"That's a thought, but he'd better have a very fast plane. He's not the type to be a martyr, and the air defenses will be looking for him. Besides, the barometric pressure inside those smoke clouds must be irregular, so he couldn't be sure that it would go off at the right altitude."

"At least he'd get an airburst."

"One that would take him with it. Keep thinking."

29

Atcho and Horton sat at a table in a conference room at Alsip's division headquarters. "I'm stumped," Horton grumbled. "How in hell are we going to find this guy and stop him?"

Atcho rubbed tired eyes and took a sip of coffee. "I don't know. The Saudis aren't helping much and General Alsip, good guy that he is, took a little jogging to get him to believe this could really happen. He's looking for us to come up with a plan."

"I know." Horton mulled. "Have you heard from Sofia?"

"She's at home. She and Ivan have coordinated. There was a surveillance team of three watching her when she arrived, but that's been cut to one. She's taking precautions but comes and goes normally. Ivan's men are watching the watchers."

"That's good, I guess." Horton heaved a sigh. "This is frustrating. You'd think two Texas boys could figure out how to corral one scrawny terrorist." He caught Atcho's glance, his eyes twinkling over a slow grin. "You are a Texas boy now, right?"

"Right. Let's go over what we know again."

"Again?" Horton stretched his legs out, linked his hands behind his head and stared at the ceiling in a parody of boredom. "What happened with Jones and Green? I thought they were supposed to help us."

"They are helping. Right now—" Atcho stopped in mid-sentence. His head turned to stare out the window at the smoke-blackened sky. "Joe, you are brilliant."

Perplexed, Horton squinted at Atcho. "I know. What did I come up with this time?"

Atcho was still lost in thought. He moved closer to the window and looked outside at the soldiers, contractors, and their equipment moving past on their individual tasks. "Get Jones and Green back in here."

General Alsip leaned back in his chair and studied the screen. "Am I understanding that you want us to do an information operation and step up security now? We're still pulling maintenance on our machinery. Information operations take a while to get approved, and they are usually squelched."

"Yes, sir," Green said, "but we're talking about a nuclear bomb and—"

"I know what we're talking about," Alsip growled, "and the president believes the threat too. We should evacuate this area." He plopped his forearms on the table in frustration. "But if we do that, we'll cause panic and create another target that could blow up at any minute."

An orderly entered and handed the general a note. He read it and directed his attention to Atcho and Horton. "This thing's been elevated. You're going to see General Schwarzkopf. I'll call ahead and fill him in on what I know about your plan."

"Good lord, what are you dragging me into?" Horton grumbled as they walked to the airfield. "You know I kept my career alive by keeping a low profile. You got me going in front of the most colorful general since MacArthur." His eyes bulged. "They say he's got a hot temper. He's likely to get mad at me 'cuz some people hereabouts think I might be a legend." He smirked when Atcho rolled his eyes. "He might not like competition."

"He's a master of information operations," Atcho retorted. "He knows how to handle the press, and there's no one else here who can order the assets we need."

Horton thought about that. "Still, you're messing with my career. Do you know how low the odds are of my getting promoted again? You just took them to zero."

Atcho smacked his lips. "I know that keeps you awake at night."

"It might. I'm a sensitive guy."

They flew via Blackhawk to meet with Schwarzkopf, expecting to go to his headquarters far back at the Saudi foreign ministry in Riyadh. Atcho was surprised when the aircraft settled in a remote part of the desert inside Kuwait under the shroud of black clouds.

"This ain't a shock," Horton told him when the helicopter parked near two other almost identical choppers, and the engine had wound down sufficiently so that they could talk. "He leads from the front."

Schwarzkopf met them a few yards from the Blackhawk. He was a barrel of a man and towered over Atcho and Horton. When they shook hands, his palm swallowed theirs. "Sorry to meet you out here in the middle of nowhere," he said, "but we're on short timelines. I spoke with the chairman of the joint chiefs this morning. He had been briefed by a guy you call Burly. The president believes the threat is credible, so we got our marching orders. General Alsip gave me the outlines of your concept. Let's go over the details. Quickly." They entered a small compound. He gestured around. "This is what's left of an OP we had out here. There's a tent set up where we can get out of the wind and talk."

As they walked through the sand, Schwarzkopf peered at the major. "Aren't you Joe Horton?"

"Yes sir, that's me."

"Hmm. Thought so. I heard about you."

Horton sucked in his cheeks while shooting a wide-eyed glance at Atcho. "I hope some of it was good, General."

"I heard about you," came the reply in a noncommittal tone.

They reached the tent. It was large enough for a small group to stand in. At one end, a map-board of Kuwait stood propped against the canvas wall. A colonel stood in front of the map, studying it. "This is my aide,"

Schwarzkopf said without further introductions. "Now, tell me what you got."

They talked for less than an hour. Atcho explained his concept.

"I think we can handle that without cutting into existing plans," the general told Atcho. "We'd be accelerating some of them, and what you need is more of a show than actual force." He turned to the aide. "Colonel, can you fill in the blanks, get them to ops and make sure the frag goes out tonight? I want this executed tomorrow morning. In fact, if we can get ready in time, the first reports could go out tonight."

"You got it, sir."

Schwarzkopf turned to Atcho. "I'm sending you down to the Marine headquarters. Your operation will be in their sector, so that's where it should be run."

"Can we get Lieutenant-colonels Jones and Green to go down with us?" Horton cut in. "They're already up to speed. We won't have to educate a new set of people."

Schwarzkopf gave him a hard look, and then nodded. "I'll get Alsip to send them down there. Anything else, Major?"

Horton's eyes widened, and he exaggerated standing at attention. His characteristic grin played at the corners of his mouth. "No, General. That ought to do it."

The small group started back toward the helicopters. "I need to commune with nature a minute," Horton said, "if you catch my meaning." He headed into the desert.

"I'm glad I got a chance to meet you, Atcho," the general said as Horton disappeared over a low sand dune. "Always good to talk to a fellow alum. I know your background. I saw you that night that Reagan talked about you in Congress."

Atcho shook off the compliment. "That's nice of you to say." They both scanned the horizon. The black cloud hovered above them. To the west, the sky was clear blue. "That was one hell of a war, General. The devastation is hard to grasp."

They talked for a couple of minutes, and then saw Horton heading back their way. "Do you really know Horton?" Atcho asked.

Schwarzkopf chuckled. "He's known all over the Army. He did some things in combat that were impressive, one might even say heroic. He has a couple of Silver Stars and Purple Hearts and a few other medals, but he's really famous for ragging on everyone. Anyone who can't take it and dish it back will be in for a rough time."

Atcho chuckled. "Had you met him before today?"

"I've never laid eyes on him. I shoved BS his way before he started in on me. Being a general, all I had to do was look at him and tell him I'd heard about him. I'm sure he'll tell you his opinion about that later."

He glanced toward Horton still making his way back. "I heard about the chewing out he gave Jones and Green over in Alsip's outfit. Horton got that ball rolling. Then I heard from the joint chiefs' chairman, who heard from the president." Schwarzkopf touched Atcho on the shoulder. "Don't tell the major I said any of that stuff about him." He chuckled. "His head's too big already. But in a firefight, that's who you want by your side. And he's not really a braggart. He has the warmest heart you'll ever meet. That's his other reputation."

Atcho took a long look at Schwarzkopf. *And you're a leader who values compassion in a fighter.*

Klaus sat on a low couch on a terrace looking to the east. He had arrived at Bandar's house the night before after a long, circuitous route through the desert on the back of a camel with a band of Bedouins. "You cannot get stopped at the checkpoints with those suitcases," Yousef had insisted. "Do you want to trust someone else to bring them to you at Bandar's?"

Klaus had admitted that he did not care for the idea.

"Then this is the way to keep control of your luggage and have it where you need it. Bedouins wander all over the desert. They avoid commonly used roads and don't recognize international boundaries. No one bothers them."

Reluctantly, Klaus had agreed, and had thus spent a day and a half atop the wave-like motion of a "ship of the desert," his bombs carefully slung on the back of the beast.

Bandar's house sat below the crest of a hill with an uninterrupted view for miles. In the distance, the black cloud over Kuwait hung dark and expanding, but above him the sky was clear. He had spoken with Yousef by phone on arrival.

"This is for your information and nothing to worry about," Yousef told him. "I heard through friends in the police that the Americans inquired about my car being in Dhahran. The FBI is there investigating the death of Collins. Someone must have checked out my house by now. You're safe where you are. Bandar is a good host and knows the country."

"And he's a great pilot," Klaus agreed. "He took us in and out of the oilfields through those clouds with no problem. He had a pressure steamer waiting when we landed to wash the oil off right away. The plane shows no sign of being there."

They hung up. Klaus turned on the television to the English-language channel of Al Jazeera to catch up on news. The screen opened to a split picture of the newscaster and the fires raging in Kuwait. Then it switched to a view of General Schwarzkopf on a stage, speaking at a press briefing. Klaus turned up the volume.

"We're happy with our progress," the general said, addressing the reporters. "Recovery from combat operations is proceeding faster than expected. Because of the way our plan succeeded, we sealed off the battle area and kept the fighting contained mainly in the area of the oilfields and south to Kuwait City. The French did a marvelous job of sealing our left flank, and the 101st Air Assault Division reinforced their mission. Those oilfields are dangerous. We don't want people wandering in, so we're already putting a tight perimeter around the whole country."

Klaus picked up the phone and dialed Yousef's number. "Are you watching Schwarzkopf's press briefing?"

"I will turn it on. Call me when it's finished."

The general was still talking when Klaus turned his attention back to the TV. "...air operations are proceeding nicely. We're sealing off air traffic anywhere close to Kuwait until the wells are extinguished. Putting out the fires could take years."

He shuffled some papers before he spoke again. "A private aircraft flew into the airspace a couple of days ago. We figure some idiot sightseers wanted to take a look. They gambled with their lives—we'd have been within our rights to shoot them down.

"We'll keep AWACS on station and deal forcibly with anyone headed that way from fifty miles out. They won't get close. Fortunately, Saudi Arabia and the surrounding countries are cooperating to establish a no-fly zone. We're not asking permission on the Iraq side. We're pretty sure Saddam will have no objection—at least he won't say so."

Klaus scowled at the light laughter from the press audience.

"How will the cleanup crews get in and out?" a reporter asked. "They're already starting to arrive."

"They've been assigned staging areas. On arrival they'll be briefed. We expect that our most difficult area to control access will be south of Kuwait City. The level of traffic is a lot higher there. Managing crowds is more difficult."

"Do you expect Saddam loyalists to try to hit the oilfields again while they're still on fire?"

Schwarzkopf furrowed his brow. "Good question. We don't expect it so much as allow that it could happen. We'll take precautionary measures, and of course instruct crews to report anyone coming on site they don't recognize."

The general continued through the briefing. Klaus listened closely, and then called Yousef. "What are AWACs?"

"They're airplanes the Americans use to watch air traffic out for a distance of two hundred and fifty miles. They also direct coalition fighter aircraft around the battlefield. Schwarzkopf is saying the US will intercept unauthorized aircraft that come within fifty miles of Kuwait."

"After I flew with Bandar the other day, I wasn't crazy about that alternative anyway," Klaus groused. "Too much uncertainty. The US is tightening the perimeter. We'll look for a weak spot, but we need to move soon. Security is only going to get harder to penetrate."

"I understood from what the general said that the toughest place to control access is down by Kuwait City. I'll send a man through there early in the morning to see if we can find a gap inside Kuwait."

"All right. Your man should look for a work crew and pretend to be part of it. He'll need to steal a work uniform and pass, and a pickup that looks like it belongs there."

They spoke a while longer to coordinate details and hung up. Klaus walked through the house to the guest room and pulled out the five suitcases. He set each one of them on the bed, opened them, and ran them through their test procedures. Then he carried them out the front door and loaded them into the trunk of a nondescript small car. Within an hour, he had joined the flow of traffic heading toward Kuwait City.

30

"How will we know we're corralling the right guy?" Horton squinted his eyes as he asked the question and shook a crooked finger at Atcho. "See, you didn't think I'd catch on to my brilliant idea, but when I listened to Stormin' Norman in his press conference, I knew what I had in mind—a couple of Texas boys corralling one scrawny terrorist." He grinned. "So, how're we going to pull that off?"

Atcho laughed. "I've got to hand it to you, Joe, you have a unique way of keeping spirits up." He walked over to a map showing Kuwait and large sections of the surrounding countries. "Klaus won't get another opportunity like this. He'll want the biggest boom he can muster. He'll put them in the middle of the oil fires."

"What if he doesn't?"

"That's fine. We're looking for an individual displaying certain behavior."

Horton looked skeptical. "You're not goin' all social scientist on me, are you?"

Atcho laughed. "Hardly, but bad guys doing bad things act predictably. Klaus'll try to blend in, look like everyone else. He'll have to drive across a big chunk of Kuwait to get to the oilfields. He could drop the bombs in any of the debris clusters, but he's no longer a wild-eyed mercenary working for someone else. He's well-funded, and you can tell by the way he left Germany and entered Saudi Arabia undetected, that he's become deliberative. He hooked up right away with influential people with even more money. I'd bet that was him in that airplane the other day, doing a little scouting.

"Anyway, he'll be mission focused. He won't see or hear things going on around him. He'll avoid contact with other people and drive deep into the oilfield."

"And you're going to leave a path open for him. Do you think that's smart? I mean we're talking about a nuclear bomb."

"Which he can set off anywhere at any time. I see this as our only opportunity to nail him. The crews will form a cordon to guide him to where we want him. It won't look like a cordon to him. People will be scattered about, but if he makes a turn we don't want him to make, he'll find his way blocked by crew doing their normal jobs. People who are supposed to be there won't be bothered by the unusual activity and will continue what they're doing. The guy we're looking for will avoid engaging with crew and military members and will keep going in the direction we want him to go. It'll be the only way open to him. Army observers will report things up as they happen."

Horton blew out a puff of air over pursed lips and shook his head. "I don't know. This looks like one helluva long shot to me. Aren't you worried he might get mad, clock out, and take all of us with him?"

"That could happen, but Klaus likes to live. Besides, he won't want to depart this earth until he knows I'm six feet under. But, if you've got a better plan, let's hear it."

Horton ignored the last comment. "Are we using jammers?"

Atcho nodded. "He won't be able to detonate by remote. He's figured that out by now. He'll plan on using the timers and getting out fast to a safe distance before they blow. I think he'll head back to Riyadh. Ironically, if he succeeds with the blast, that might be one of the safest places in the world to be for a while."

"Yep. The winds will blow the fallout the other way. Any of it Riyadh sees will have checked out the lights in Paris before it gets there."

"I have the report from Jamshed," Yousef told Klaus. "He's the man we sent through the security checkpoint this morning. He drove along the entire southern border of Kuwait, and security is tight. The probability of infiltrating through there is small. There is separate security to cross the border. Once inside Kuwait, there is another checkpoint to get onto the special road leading to the wells."

"What special road? I've been studying the maps. There is no special road."

"The army engineers are building one. Well, they're scraping one out over the desert—really just flattening out the sand and reinforcing the subsurface where needed. It's for contractor traffic coming through Saudi Arabia. It goes around Kuwait City on the west side from south to north. The report I saw on TV said the road was to make securing the oilfields easier and to keep heavy equipment traffic out of the city."

"How is security north of the checkpoint?"

"Tight. Jamshed said that security was also tight at the checkpoint, but if you go through with credentials when traffic is heavy, you should not have a problem. He went back and forth several times with a stolen badge. He said that by his last trip, the guards had begun to know him and waved him through."

Klaus took in the information. His brow creased as he considered it. Then his eyes glittered. "I'm bothered that he got through so easily with a stolen badge. Why wouldn't the guards have checked it against a list of stolen or lost badges?"

Yousef chuckled. "I pick good people. He went to a clinic where contractors are already gathering. The fumes in the air are making people sick. He took the badge from a man who was sent to his quarters for several days of recuperation. It probably won't be missed until the man goes back to work."

"I want to talk to Jamshed personally," Klaus said. "Tonight. I need the details of what he saw. I can't get caught, not at the gate or anywhere else. I'm moving to Khafji, south of the Saudi-Kuwait border. Tell Jamshed to meet me there."

"All's quiet on the home front," Sofia told Atcho when he called. "I've managed to reacquaint with my garden club. I've been out to lunch a few times and to the stores. Ivan keeps me well covered. We can both see our surveillance zones outside our house on the monitors. How's Joe?"

"Must you ask?" Atcho chuckled. "He keeps things light."

"I'm glad he's there with you. He brings out a side of you I hadn't seen before—someone who relaxes and laughs, even when things are rough. I like that.

"On another subject, I've been following the news. The videos from the oilfields are horrendous. Are there any estimates of how long it'll take to close down the wells?"

Atcho sighed. "I've heard everything from five to ten years."

"So, Klaus could conceivably wait a while."

"He could. I'm not sure he has that kind of patience. Let's get onto a better topic. How's our baby?"

Sofia smiled. "I felt a kick this morning."

In his room at headquarters, Atcho stretched out on the cot where he rested. His head dropped on the pillow. He smiled. "Girl or boy?"

"Which do you want?"

"I don't know. Maybe a boy so that I can have help handling you."

"Ha, ha. I want a healthy child. That's all."

"Me, too."

They were silent a moment. "Please come home safe," Sofia murmured.

"I will. This will be over soon."

31

"We've got movement." The disembodied voice came through clearly on the speaker over the crackle of radio static. In an office set up as the operations room for what had been dubbed "Operation Take-Down," Atcho sat up, alert. "One man in a white pickup just came through the checkpoint," the voice on the radio speaker continued. "The license plate number is not on the list of approved vehicles, but he had credentials."

"Roger," a Marine sergeant replied. "Tracking. Out."

Atcho looked at his watch. It showed four thirty in the morning. "How many is that?" he asked the sergeant.

"The third one tonight. The other two went to legitimate destinations. Our Marines on the ground checked them out. Other members of the crew vouched for them."

Lieutenant-colonel Green poured a cup of coffee. He ambled over between Atcho and the sergeant. "Didn't the contractors get the general's order to keep vehicles out that were not already listed?"

"They did," the sergeant replied, "but you know how it goes. Some didn't get the word, others ignored it." He shifted his eyes to Atcho, looked him up and down, and grinned. "You know how civilians are."

"Get some rest," Green told Atcho. "As soon as we have someone to tail, we'll wake you up and get you out there."

Atcho consented, went into a darkened room next door, and stretched out on a cot. Across from him on another cot, Horton was already asleep.

Atcho rested fitfully, alternately awakened by Horton's snoring, by throat-catching thoughts of a cooing baby in Sofia's arms, and by having that pleasant dream interrupted by nightmares of a flaming mushroom cloud blotting out the sky.

Four hours later, he awoke with a start. Horton was gone. Atcho found him in the ops room holding forth with the sergeant on duty. He had one hand in his pocket, one holding a coffee cup, and a big grin on his face. "I was just telling this Marine how me and your wife saved Berlin, but he don't believe me. You tell him."

Atcho shook his head. "Don't believe anything the major says," he admonished the soldier. "You're better off that way. Even the general knows…"

"did you hear what the general said about me the other day?" Horton interrupted. He turned to the Marine. "Stormin' Norman himself said he'd heard about me. Do you believe that?" He turned back to Atcho, a concerned look plastered on his face. "Do you suppose that's a good thing or a bad thing?"

Atcho laughed through an interrupted yawn. "I don't know, but he shut you up faster than anyone I've seen." He turned to the sergeant. "Did any more unlisted license plates come through?"

"Yes, sir." The sergeant looked at his notes. "Ten total, so far. That's not a bad number for an operation as big as this cleanup is going to be. Word must be getting out, because fewer are coming through. We only had one come in during the last two hours, and that was during rush hour."

"Where's Lieutenant-colonel Green?"

"He went to get something to eat. He'll be back in a few minutes."

"Is our chopper still on standby?"

"Yes sir. You've got highest priority after the CG. Once you call, it will be less than ten minutes before you're picked up."

Atcho looked around the room. It was almost bare except for the sparse furniture and equipment needed to run Operation Take-Down.

The plywood walls of the temporary building had been in place long enough that desert dust had embedded in the grain.

"Major Horton, do you have any nuggets of wisdom?"

Horton glared at him, stupefied. "Nuggets of wisdom? You know me. I got truckloads of wisdom. What do you want to know about?"

Atcho grunted. "I should've known better than to ask. What do we do now?"

Horton's expression turned deadpan. "We're doing it. We wait."

Morning turned to afternoon, which passed into evening with no activity. At dusk, Atcho stood outside the operations office and stared into the distance at the omnipresent black cloud that still seemed to grow. As darkness crept in, the orange glow from hundreds of wells became visible on the horizon. *The dance of demons.*

Shortly before midnight, Atcho rested again. He tried to force himself to sleep, but it did not come easy. A feeling of dread came over him. *Did I guess wrong?* A competing thought gnawed at the other side of his consciousness. *If Klaus wants to hit the wells before the crews start shutting them down, he'll make his move today.*

At four a.m., Atcho got up and went to check in the ops room. "Still nothing?"

The young Marine sergeant on duty was one Atcho had not seen before. "Nothing, sir," he replied. "We had five trucks with unlisted plates go through in the last two hours. We're still waiting for final reports on them."

"Isn't that a high number? I thought they were dwindling down."

The sergeant checked his notes. "Yes, sir. The number does seem to have jumped. From early afternoon until two hours ago, we only had one truck go through with unlisted plates, and his crew vouched for him."

"Do we have eyes on those five trucks?"

"Yes, sir." The sergeant's eyes betrayed a jump in tension. "The observation posts reported in as the trucks went by. So far, they've stayed on the main road heading north. But they're not traveling together. They're spread behind each other and separated by miles."

Atcho stood in the middle of the room, deep in thought, his eyes half-closed as he assessed the situation. Then he turned to the sergeant. "Get that chopper over here." He strode to the wall between the ops office and where Horton still slept and pounded on it. "Major Horton, get in here." He pounded again. Seconds later, Horton burst into the room, half-dressed.

"Get me into the tactical operations center," Atcho said. "I need to see the satellite screen."

Lieutenant-colonel Green hurried into the office. "What's going on?"

"Klaus is inside the oilfield perimeter. I'm sure of it. Get me into the TOC. I need to see that screen."

Green glanced at Horton with a questioning look.

"He's got the clearances, sir," Horton replied to the unspoken question. "We need to see where those trucks are going. There are five of them."

Green turned to Atcho. "No disrespect sir, but the satellites won't do you any good. The smoke obscures everything."

"I need to know where on the map those trucks are."

Green spun around. "Sergeant," he ordered, "you've got two minutes to roust Lieutenant-colonel Jones and the rest of the support crew for Operation Take-Down. I'll wait until you get back. Go." He turned to Atcho. "The chopper will be here shortly after he gets back. When the support crew arrives, we'll have them query the observation posts for the location of those five vehicles, and radio the coordinates to us. We'll be in the air by then."

"Are you sure everyone knows what to watch for?" Atcho called across the intercom to Green. Horton sat silently behind Atcho.

"They're looking for a man delivering some type of object," Green replied. "He'll be unknown to the crew, wherever he stops. He won't want to engage in conversation. He could stop near a well, an oil lake, or a debris cluster and carry the object out and set it down. No one is to try to stop him. Just observe and report. Fast."

"Roger."

The Blackhawk flew close to the ground, below the ever-present black cloud that hung in the sky. When Atcho last traveled through the area, the landscape was an empty wasteland, dark, with no other living creature in sight. Now, it was still a wasteland, but populated with people and equipment. The area under the cloud was illuminated by thousands of ghostly lights dimmed by the fog of dirty vapor emanating from the wells.

And the demons still dance. Atcho stared out the window at the vast expanse of desert with its oil-blackened sand and tall jets of glowing flame under billowing smoke. *Can it ever be put out?* He looked ahead through the windshield. Discernible from the air were two parallel lines of loosely separated vehicles and equipment with their individual lights stretching toward the oilfields.

"Sir," Green called over the intercom. "All five vehicles in question are ahead of us. The closest one is roughly ten miles ahead."

"All right. Hang back. Let them reach whatever their destinations are."

"We just got a report from one of the observation posts. One of the trucks tried to turn off. When he found his way blocked, he stopped the truck. He's just sitting in it." He paused, listening to his headset. "Hey. He's getting out."

"Get a couple of guys over to look inside the truck."

They waited while the Blackhawk closed the distance in the eerie orange glow against the black sky and the combined sound of engines and the unearthly roar of burning wells. "The truck is clear. Nothing in it."

"One down. Have your guys take the man into custody."

Green gave him a thumbs-up. "We've got another one going down. Pretty much the same way. The driver is sitting in the truck." He held up a finger. "Two more have pulled to a stop."

The pilot jinxed the Blackhawk through the turbulent air while avoiding flying too close to any wells. The corridor of vehicles below led deep into the oilfield. At one juncture, they had blocked the road.

Green pointed down. "That's where they're holding the first guy. We're coming up on the second one ahead. He's clear now too." He put his hand to his ear. "OK. The fifth truck has stopped. It's near one of the largest fires in the field. The guy is getting out. He's carrying a box."

"Tell the observers to stay back and appear not to notice him. Take the others into custody."

Green nodded. A few moments later, he raised a finger again. "Fifth man walked to a debris cluster. He set the box on the ground and returned to the truck. He's reversing direction."

"Cut him off and detain him," Atcho called. "Keep his hands secure." His heartbeat surged. "Pilot, get us to that location ASAP."

"Roger."

The nose of the Blackhawk dipped as the pilot nudged the cyclic forward and pulled power. Within moments, the nose leveled out as the aircraft reached full speed and zipped through the dark sky.

Soon, Green pointed. "There."

Atcho stared through the windshield. Ahead of them, a tower of flame at least five feet across jetted into the air. A lone, melted derrick stood to one side. Across the road, a cluster of nondescript debris spread across a wide area. A few yards beyond that, a low area in the desert collected oil runoff and formed a lake. *The perfect site to plant the bombs.* He pushed the thought from his mind.

The aircraft landed. Atcho stepped onto black, spongy sand. The heat from the flames hit, searing through his clothes. He fought against the wind generated by the churning fire's suction of air and circled in front of the helicopter. He met Green and Horton on the other side. The three stooped and hurried from under the whirring blades.

"What's going on with the prisoner?" Atcho yelled through the roar.

"They've got him, but he isn't saying anything."

"Right. Send the man from the observation post over here."

A few minutes later, a clench-jawed young Marine presented himself. "Did you see where he put that box?" Atcho asked.

"I said it's a box because I didn't know what else to call it. It had an odd shape. In this light, I couldn't make it out very well. He took it over this way." He led off.

The three men followed across the road to the clutter of debris. Up close, the area did not seem so large, just a collection of rubble at the side of the road. A few feet in, a cube-shaped object stood out in the shadows. "That's it," the Marine said. "It looks like several suitcases bound together."

Atcho's adrenaline surged. Despite seeing what he had expected to see, the reality of the nuclear bomb up close and ready to blast against the backdrop of the towering flame and a rolling black sky took his breath away. "Wait here," he told the others, and started into the field.

A heavy hand grabbed Atcho's shoulder. He whirled to see Horton's face grinning into his own. "You cain't go in there, sir," he said. "That's my job."

Atcho started to protest.

"Sir, this is still a military operation, and you're a civilian. If I have to pull rank on you, I will. For all you know, that bomb has been booby-trapped. It could be set up to kill anyone tampering with it without setting off the bomb."

Atcho stared.

"Are you a demolitions expert?" Horton continued. Without waiting for a response, he went on. "Well I am. I taught the Montagnards in Vietnam how to set booby traps. My MOS as an enlisted man was in explosive ordinance disposal. I'm what they call an EOD specialist. Now if you'll step aside, I'll do my job." He started into the debris field.

"Don't you need a special suit?" Atcho called after him.

Without turning, Horton shook his head and waved him off with both hands.

Atcho turned to Green. "Doesn't he need a special suit?"

"It's in the helicopter. He asked me to bring it."

"So, you knew he was EOD?"

"He told us. It's why we didn't bring one with us."

"Why isn't he putting the suit on?"

"I'd say he thinks he might not have time."

Atcho's mind raced. "Fine. Is that piece of equipment I requested here?"

"It's about ten minutes back. We pre-positioned it halfway up the road. It started following when we flew over it."

"I'll need to talk with the operator before he does anything." Atcho turned back anxiously to the debris field.

Horton circled the bomb, scrutinizing it and the ground around it with a flashlight. He took deliberate steps and then lowered himself flat on the ground and inched toward the suitcases. He reached along his leg, pulled out a long, flat piece of wood, and slid it under the bomb. Then he felt along its underside gently.

He repeated his motion on each of the other three sides. At one point, he pressed into the sand, pulled on a long wire, and stuffed it into his pocket. Finally, he stood up, waved an all-clear, picked up the suitcases in both arms, and walked toward Atcho.

"The guy who set the booby trap on this thing was an amateur," he gasped through staggered breaths. Perspiration ran down his face. "If it had gone off, it might have scared someone and cut a finger, but that's about all. Looks like it was meant to buy time." He set the suitcases down next to his leg. They had been strapped together.

Horton put his mouth close to Atcho's ear. "I thought you said there were five of them. Where's the fifth?"

Atcho stared at the bundle. His jaw set in a grim line. "Let's deal with what we've got. We'll go after the other one when we're done."

Green tapped Atcho on the shoulder and pointed. The lights of a huge machine approached, the sound of its engine deafened by the roar of flames and wind. The apparatus looked like a mutated earth mover. Instead of a bucket, two pincer-like arms extended out the front.

Green caught the operator's eye, guided him into position, and signaled him to halt.

Atcho climbed into the cockpit. Despite an air conditioner running at full blast, the heat of the cauldron was almost unrelenting. The driver streamed sweat. His face was coated in black oil, the whites of his eyes setting in sharp contrast against the blackness. Only the red edges of his eyelids showed any color.

When Atcho closed the door, the outside roar abated a bit. "What's your name?"

"Bob."

Atcho shook his hand. "Do you know why you're here?"

Bob grinned slightly and seesawed his hand, the international standard for, "Maybe."

Atcho shot him back a smile he did not feel. "Do you see that object down there next to the major's leg?" The man nodded. "I need you to put it in that fire." He pointed to the giant flame in front of them. "Can you do that?"

A look of caution crossed Bob's face. "I can, but what is it?"

Atcho stared into Bob's eyes. "It's a bomb, and it's probably on a timer. If you can't do it, then you need to tell me how to operate this machine. We need to make decisions now."

Bob stared at the suitcases and then at the fire. He turned back to Atcho. His face had gone slack. Even the edges of his eyelids had drained of blood and were now a pasty white. He swallowed hard. "Won't that set off the bomb?"

"No. The heat will melt the trigger mechanism."

"Are you sure?"

Atcho looked around. A crowd of crew members and Marines had formed behind them. In front of them, Horton and Green watched.

"It should work. Melting the trigger worked before." He took a deep breath. "Look, before you decide, there's something else you should know. That's a nuclear bomb. Well, in reality, it's four of them strapped together."

Bob stared in silence. Against the darkness outside, he looked like two floating, disbelieving eyes on a black silhouette. "That's four nuclear bombs, and you want me to put them in that fire?" He took a deep breath and let it out slowly.

"Bob, listen to me. They're on a timer. Neither of us has time to get out of the blast area. The only way to stop it now is to disable the trigger mechanisms. If we open the bombs, their fail-safe systems will activate to set them off. We can destroy the triggers by melting them. Without the shock they produce at precise points, the bombs can't detonate. Putting them in the fire is our only chance."

Bob sat in silence.

Atcho could not tell if he were in shock or just thinking. "Let me do it," Atcho called. "No one will blame you. We dropped this on you with short notice."

Bob still said nothing, staring to his front. Atcho started to clamber over to the driver's seat. "Let's switch places."

Bob snapped out of his trance. "No. I'll do it."

"You'll what? Are you sure?"

"I'll do it." He turned his eyes to Atcho. "Have you ever operated one of these machines?"

Atcho shook his head without speaking.

"If you do it wrong, we're all going to die, right?"

Atcho nodded. "Probably."

"So, my best chance of living is to do it myself. This is a very precise machine. It's used to cap runaway oil-well fires. I can't teach you in one minute how to operate it. How much time do I have?"

"We don't know. The bomb was placed out here thirty minutes ago. The guy who planted it is under guard a few hundred yards from here. He's not the martyr type. He'd want to get at least to Riyadh. So, relax, take your time, and do it right the first time."

Bob nodded. He turned to Atcho again, the whites of his eyes still floating in darkness. He glanced at the group of Marines and workers standing back, watching. "Those are my friends," he said. "I have a family." His voice broke. "I need to see them again."

Atcho reached across and grasped his shoulder. "Do what I tell you, and we'll all get out of this, and you'll see your wife and kids." An image of Sofia with a baby floated across his mind. The tenor of his voice changed. "Now, listen to me. Pick up the bombs so that the far end of their bottoms goes into the fire first. I'll position them in the pincers.

"Don't rush. Inch into the flame. The pincers will act as a shield for the near side of the bombs until the triggers are melted. When you see the ends of the suitcases burnt up, drop the rest of them into the fire."

"The bottoms of the far ends go in first?"

"Yes."

"Okay, I'm ready." His eyes looked straight ahead. Then, as Atcho started to clamber out of the cockpit, he turned. "One thing," he said, those floating eyes staring at Atcho. "Don't ever ask me for another favor."

His white teeth showed in the dark. They shaped into a grin. He reached over and slapped Atcho's shoulder. "On second thought, you owe me a beer." He faced straight ahead again. "I got this."

Moments later, Atcho kneeled on the ground and set the strapped-together suitcases between the pincers. Their ends jutted out a quarter of the way beyond the giant fingers.

Atcho stepped back. He signaled Bob. The ground shook. The roar of wind and flame still muffled the great engine. The arms lifted, the pincers extended, the black smoke roiled overhead. The mammoth machine began its slow roll toward the fire.

Inch by inch, it crept forward. Watching, Atcho sensed a fracturing between a single moment and eternity. Horton stepped next to him, at a loss for words.

The machine rolled on, its pincers fully extended. The gap between them and the flame narrowed to yards, then feet, then inches. Even before reaching the fire, the corners of the suitcases began to smolder. The iron beast slowed even more. Its deadly cargo edged into the fire and burst into flame. Farther and farther, the bomb moved into the inferno, the steel pincers turning red hot. Then suddenly they separated, and the remaining parts dropped into the flames.

Despite the continuous roar, a deafening quiet seemed to have descended. For a moment, no one moved. Then Atcho felt a strong hand clap him on the back. He turned to see Horton's signature grin as he threw his arms around Atcho's chest and lifted him into the air. If he cheered, Atcho could not hear it for the omnipresent roar. Next to them, Green jumped up and down, his fists raised over his head in unabashed joy. Beyond them, some among the crowd of oilfield workers raised their arms in expressions of a job well done, but nothing celebratory. *They don't know what just happened.*

When Horton set him back down, Atcho turned to look at the pincer machine. It moved in reverse now, at greater speed than it had approached the fire. When it reached a safe distance, it stopped. Bob clambered down. He reached the ground and leaned against the machine to steady his wobbly legs.

Atcho headed in his direction. Bob saw him coming. He took a cloth from a pocket and wiped the oil from his face as best he could. He kept wiping as he stumbled toward Atcho. When they met, Bob almost fell to the ground. Atcho caught him and stood him up.

"I want you to see my face and remember it," Bob croaked. "You're going to get me my beer."

Atcho threw his arms around Bob in a bearhug. "How could I ever forget those eyes?"

32

"Where is that son-of-a-bitch?" Atcho demanded. His hands tightened into fists.

Horton chuckled. "I didn't know you knew how to use those descriptors." He snickered. "See how my vocabulary is expanding from hanging around with you?" He laughed again. "Descriptors," he repeated. "Descrip-tors. I like that word."

"I save my cussing for special occasions. It's more effective that way. Where's Klaus?"

"The MPs took him back to the rear. They'll hold him." They rode in the back seat of a pickup headed south, back to headquarters.

"Why did Green fly off with the helicopter?" Atcho asked.

"He got a call from the boss. The big boss, ol' Stormin'. He said the mission was accomplished, and Alsip needed Green." Horton chortled. "We ain't important no more."

"But the mission isn't accomplished," Atcho said. "Klaus had five bombs. We only saw four of them. Where's the fifth?"

Horton pursed his lips. "I was the guy who raised the question, remember?"

They urged the driver to greater speed. Two hours later, they arrived at the Military Police station at Marine headquarters. Atcho jumped from the pickup and rushed inside. Horton followed.

"Where are the prisoners?" he demanded without ceremony. Startled, the desk sergeant looked up at him. "Sir–" Before he could say another word, Horton intervened.

It's all right," he said. "Those men that were brought in from the oilfields a little while ago. Where are they being held?"

The sergeant still eyed Atcho. "They're at the back in a holding cell. I'll have to get clearance to let you see them."

Horton stared at him, stone faced. "Get it," he said. "Here. Radio out to this call sign." He handed over a piece of paper with writing on it.

The sergeant snapped to attention, focused on Horton. "Sir, that's General Schwarz—"

"I know whose call sign it is, Sergeant," Horton interrupted, "an' I ain't got a lot of time or patience. Get the general on the horn or get us back to see those detainees."

"Do you need to speak with them? I mean actually talk?"

"No, we just need to see them."

"I can have them brought into the interrogation room. You can see them through the window. They'll be heavily guarded."

Horton leaned against the wall. He blew out a long breath of air. "Whatever works."

Ten minutes later, Atcho and Horton peered through a small window at five men backed against a wall. Their wrists were handcuffed behind their backs and two armed guards stood across the room.

Atcho whirled from the window. "Get me to a secure phone," he told the sergeant. "Fast."

"Burly," he said when the call had gone through. "We stopped the bombs in Kuwait. We caught the men driving the trucks."

"Good. I'll inform the White Hou–"

"We didn't get Klaus."

"What?"

"We didn't get Klaus. He didn't drive any of the trucks. And he placed only four bombs. He's loose, and he still has one."

33

Klaus had picked his observation post well. He occupied the highest suite in Riyadh with an unobstructed view looking east. From there, he could remain in relative safety and see the massive black shroud hanging at the edge of the horizon. In the living room, he had three televisions arrayed next to each other receiving different newscasts. *The best is yet to come.*

He looked at his watch. *Five minutes.*

Ten minutes later, nothing out of the ordinary had come across the news. No breaking stories, and no change to the black cloud on the horizon. He called Yousef. "I was right. They set a trap. It should have gone up five minutes ago."

"How many did you use?"

"Just one. I included it in case they were foolish enough to open the suitcases. At least we'd have got the effect of one detonation. The others were filled with enough rocks to approximate the weight of the real one."

"Where did you hide the others?"

"It's best you don't know. I'm not disappointed. Experts estimate that five to ten years will be needed to put out the fires. We have lots of time. Meanwhile, I have an errand to run. I'll need your help. Get your police friends to set up a meeting for you and me. I'll explain then."

"They're back up to three people watching me," Sofia told Atcho. "They keep a safe distance, but they follow me when I go out. Ivan beefed up the security force."

"Good idea. Meanwhile, you should sleep in the safe-room."

"I already do that. We have a guy upstairs at night. He comes in from the river in the evening. We bring him in when the bad guys have their shift change. They're pretty predictable."

"The climb from the river has to be at least two hundred feet. Thank them for me."

"I will. Anything you can tell me?"

"Only that I'm still on the job. How's our baby?"

"Kicking. He doesn't like me to sleep."

"He?"

"He, she. I'll take whatever we get. Let me tell you, if not for our little nugget, I couldn't take all this babysitting. It's driving me crazy."

"I know. We'll get through it." They exchanged intimacies and hung up.

Atcho woke up with a start. He sat in the dark gathering his thoughts, and then hurried to Horton's room. He found the major sitting on the edge of his bed.

"Are you bein' ate up by the same thoughts bothering me?" Horton asked.

"We didn't see the bombs, did we?"

"Nope. We saw four suitcases. An' Klaus wasn't there. He figured us out and played us." He shook his head. "That little bugger has come a long way." He saw annoyance flash over Atcho's face. He crinkled his brow over a rueful smile. "Sorry."

"So, how many bombs did we burn? Any of them?"

"Well it wasn't like we could open up the bags to find out. I'd guess he had at least one live one there figuring he might get lucky and we'd set one off. He'd know that if we caught up with the guy who placed the suit-cases, we'd have a plan to neutralize the bombs. He ain't no dummy. He tested our security arrangements."

Atcho threw him a quick glance. "Klaus doesn't have to be in a hurry. They're saying the fires could burn on for years."

"Uh-huh, that's right. He could go fishin', get a tan in the Bahamas, take a world tour, and still make it back in time to set off fireworks."

"So, what's he doing now?"

Their eyes met. They uttered a single word simultaneously. "Sofia."

"I'm coming home," Atcho said. His tone implied he had no stomach for argument.

"So, you've caught Klaus and all his firecrackers," Sofia said, with equal force.

"No, but there's a good chance he's coming your way."

"Which says that there's a good chance that he's not. Are you implying that Ivan and I can't take care of things on this end?"

Atcho breathed in sharply. "Of course not. I worry about you. Fault me for that."

Sofia took a moment to respond. Her voice softened. "I don't fault you at all. You're on a job that some people thought no one else could do. Maybe they were right. If the fight comes here, we'll handle things. If you have reason to believe he's coming this way, come home. But while it's conjecture, stay where you can react most quickly."

Atcho smiled to himself. "I guess that makes sense. No wonder I married you. Someone has to keep me thinking straight." His voice took on a somber timbre. "I'm coming home. If something happens, I want to be where you are."

Sofia sniffed. "I know. I wouldn't tell you to stay out there if I didn't believe you'd stop this thing. We'll hold the fort until you get here."

Atcho chuckled. "That's a nice romantic sentiment. Should be good for a novel. The truth is, we don't know where he is or what he's doing."

They were both quiet. Sofia broke the silence. "I'll ride into the FBI office in Austin tomorrow, call Burly on a classified line, and get the full rundown. Maybe he'll have some ideas."

34

Klaus and Yousef met far out in the desert at Bandar's home. They found the pilot inspecting his Mooney. They both came by circuitous routes in nondescript vehicles. Once both were safe behind high walls they met in an inner courtyard.

"My police friends kept watch while we traveled," Yousef told Klaus. "We can never be seen in public together again. US and Saudi intelligence keep an eye on me. The police still ask questions about my car being in Dhahran. I'll be asked about my whereabouts tonight." He saw Klaus react. "Don't worry. As we speak, I am visiting an aunt at a village north of here." He chuckled. "Having large families is a gift from Allah. Tell me what you need."

Klaus leaned in and spoke with urgency. His face contorted with rage as he described his motivation and his plan. "I've already disassembled the components of one bomb and sent them by courier. Except for the plutonium, they are innocuous. They've gone to different addresses, and I'll reassemble when I arrive."

"What about the other bombs?"

"They're in a safe place."

"What do you need from us?"

"Transportation. I need to get into Mexico undetected."

"Why not go straight into the US?"

"Doing that is much more difficult. They'll be looking for me. I need to move the plutonium there. Look." He rolled out a map of the US. "Mexico shares a long border with the US. It's hardly defended. Illegal aliens go through all the time.

"Put me in with the drug cartels, fly me to an isolated runway, or bring me through another country. Do whatever you have to do, but get me in as close to the Texas border as possible. I want to cross some place in Mexico where they have the least migrant traffic, and I want observers on both sides to ensure I get safely across."

Yousef considered the proposal. "Is that all?"

"No." He handed Yousef a list. "I need reliable brothers in the areas of each of these addresses to pick up what I've sent. They must resend to me here." He pointed out the forwarding address. "I'll pick the items up there and assemble them."

Yousef listened intently. He leaned back in his chair, sipping tea while he thought. "The plan sounds workable." He heaved a sigh. "And expensive. That's a lot of trouble and money for revenge against a single man."

"Agreed," Klaus countered, "but the revenge would be against the Great Satan. My personal vengeance is a bonus. Did you read Kadir's report on Atcho and his wife?"

"I did."

"Then you know about their company."

Yousef nodded.

"That technology was used in this war," Klaus said. "It extended the range of vehicles. It made communications more secure. When we blow Atcho's plant, we'll hit a strategic target."

"They'll recover quickly. I'm sure they keep regular batteries in storage."

"But we'll also destroy one of the capital cities in a major state."

"Austin is showing signs of becoming a greater economic center, but it still has a long way to go. The population in the county is only a little over six hundred thousand people now."

Klaus arched his brows. "You've done homework."

"Which should be expected to keep support."

Klaus took note of the comment with a stony expression. He had not expected resistance. He let it slide. "But Austin is becoming a high-tech area."

Yousef saw his expression. He reached over and covered Klaus' hand with his own. "Patience, *habibi*, patience. We haven't said no."

Klaus' head jerked up. "We?"

Yousef smacked his lips. "Usama bin Laden took personal interest in your activities. He wants to help, but first he wants something."

Klaus eyed Yousef with a neutral expression. "What does he want?"

Yousef took his time to answer. "If I've kept track correctly, you still have four bombs. One of those you wish to take to Texas."

Klaus nodded.

"Three of the remainder you have hidden away."

"I think that's best. That way no one can be coerced to reveal their location."

"No argument. But let me ask, have you ever detonated a similar bomb? Do we know from experience that they work?"

Klaus hesitated. "You know I haven't. How could I? But–"

Yousef raised a palm. "We know Dr. Veniamin Krivkov's work in France and Rayner's contributions to Soviet weapons systems. They enjoy sterling technical reputations. The bombs should work." He took a sip of tea. "But do they? They were never tested." Klaus remained speechless.

"Look." Yousef leaned forward. "No one doubts your ability or dedication to *jihad*. You could have taken the money and disappeared to a comfortable life. We want to make sure your efforts turn results. Does that make sense?"

Klaus rubbed his eyes. He nodded reluctantly.

"No one wants to stop you, not even your trip to Texas. But if the bombs don't blow, you've wasted time, money, and effort. If I understood you correctly, all three bombs you set in Berlin failed to detonate. Is that right?"

Klaus nodded. His face had gone slack.

"You still have one of those bombs and it's been rewired. One of your new ones failed to go off in the oilfields…"

"They probably dropped it into one of the oil-well fires and melted the trigger," Klaus muttered.

"Maybe. The point is, it did not detonate." He drew a deep breath. "We'd like to make an offer."

Klaus sat back startled. "What kind of offer?" He barely concealed his skepticism.

"Don't worry," Yousef smiled, "your money is safe. You can have it back at any time and keep your bombs. You'll be happy to know that your investment has grown by two hundred thousand dollars." He watched Klaus' surprised reaction.

"That's nice, but the money is not why I entered *jihad*."

"You proved that. Think of this. The more money you have, the more good you can do. If you accept our offer, we can put unlimited financial support behind you and help you organize. You can pick your targets subject to approval. If your bombs are viable, we'll produce more of them and pressure the black markets for more nuclear material." He studied Klaus.

"I'm listening. What do you want me to do?"

"Detonate a bomb."

35

The conversation with Yousef sent Klaus' mind into a whirl, his nerves on edge. He had never considered that his bombs would not work or that someone might ask for a demonstration. In retrospect, that oversight felt foolish. He had never questioned Veniamin's design since it was first explained to him. The bombs had been affirmed as operational by three East German nuclear engineers, one of whom designed weapons for the Soviet Union.

He had wondered why none of them detonated, but Rayner's explanation seemed plausible—Veniamin sabotaged them with his wiring scheme. Now, Klaus had to demonstrate that they would perform as promised. *What happens if they fail?*

He had little doubt that he could request receipt of his money and disappear with it—as Yousef had said, the word of a *hawaladar* was inviolate. However, taking the money would probably end his access into the levels of influence that opened so many doors so easily. Likely, no other *hawala* would accept his business.

Taking the offer carried other risks. If he tested a bomb and it did not detonate, his standing in the loose organization in which he found himself would be diminished, possibly demolished. He could then be down to two questionable bombs and have to find his own way to Texas.

"I accept conditionally," he told Yousef. "I want to inspect the bombs again, check their wiring, their components and communications systems. If everything checks out, where do you want me to explode one?"

Yousef smiled enigmatically. "Let us know when you're ready. We'll transport you to the site."

Planning and coordination for the trip had been done for Klaus. Several days later, after he had checked the bombs and given the go-ahead, Yousef made a series of phone calls. The next morning, Bandar flew Klaus with one of his bombs to a private airport near Dubai in the United Arab Emirates.

Another pilot picked him up there. They flew in a Beechcraft Baron B58, a twin-engine plane with better than a nine-hundred-mile range. "We're not stopping to clear customs or immigration in Pakistan or Afghanistan," the pilot explained. "Those arrangements have already been made." He did not give his name. "We'll refuel at the destination. I'll wait, and when you're done, I'll fly you back to Dubai. Bandar will pick you up there and return you to Riyadh."

On takeoff, they headed due east over the Gulf of Oman, and then turned north to enter Pakistan. Initially, the outside air was warm. They flew across the Pakistani coast at low level and hugged the western border. As they encountered mountain ranges, they flew higher and higher. Crossing into Afghanistan, they weaved between mountain peaks. The pilot's skill attested to having flown this route before.

Klaus stared down over the Hindu Kush range. Jagged, snow-covered peaks jutted through clouds. Against a misty gray sky, they caused Klaus to shiver in the aircraft's freezing cabin. The pilot said the outside temperature was minus thirty-three degrees Fahrenheit. The heater was on full-blast, but even with heavy boots and jacket, he shivered.

As they descended, the layer of snow on the mountains thinned, revealing bare, rocky slopes. Air became noticeably warmer. They flew over valleys etched by streambeds with winter-resistant vegetation spread out on either side.

Finally, after five hours, they landed in a hidden valley with barely enough room to taxi. Cross-winds buffeted the aircraft as it settled onto the loose-gravel runway. Klaus was more than happy to thank Allah when he finally stepped onto solid ground in weather that was almost warm. He carried his suitcase with him.

The pilot pointed to a group of fifty-gallon drums at the edge of the runway. A tent set fifty meters away. "That's our fuel, and that's where I'll stay until you get back."

Klaus turned in a full circle to observe the mountain peaks and the long, narrow valley surrounding them. "So, this is Tora Bora."

A tall man on a dark horse rode across the field leading another horse. He had a long flowing beard, loose clothing typical of the area, and a *chitrali*, the flat hats favored in Afghanistan by many *mujahedeen*, the fighters for *jihad*. Across his chest he carried an AK-47.

He approached the airplane and reined in. No expression crossed his dark face, but he placed a hand on his chest. "Mahdy," he said.

Klaus studied him and then put his own hand on his own chest. "Sahab."

Mahdy's eyes took in the airplane and the two men. Then, with a sweep of his arm, he indicated the trailing horse.

Klaus secured the suitcase to the saddle, mounted the horse, and rode away with the tall *mujahedeen*.

Long before sunrise the next morning, Mahdy rousted Klaus from his sleep in a bare room inside a compound on the side of a bare, rocky mountain. After breakfast, they set out on foot with an armed escort of five other men. Mahdy led them. They offered Klaus an AK-47, which he gladly accepted. His suitcase went into a bag slung on his back. For the remainder of the day, the group walked along narrow paths, climbing on steep slopes that sometimes gave way to sheer cliffs plunging thousands of feet below them.

They camped that night in a well-used cave and set out again before dawn the next morning. They passed the snow line, and still they climbed, bracing against the freezing wind. Around noon, they stopped at a cave entrance. At first it seemed shallow, but once inside, Klaus saw that

it looped around to his right. Mahdy shined a light and pointed. Klaus'
eyes followed where the light shone.

The roof of the cave arched down. At the point that it should have
reached the floor, it continued down. Mahdy moved closer but held his
arm out to hold Klaus back. The light illuminated the ground at their
feet. Two feet beyond, the floor dropped into a chimney-hole. Mahdy
picked up a loose rock and tossed it into the middle of the chasm. He put
his hand to his ear and gestured for Klaus to do the same.

Seconds passed, then a minute. No sound of a rock bouncing or
hitting the bottom emanated. Klaus looked dumbfounded. He searched
to his rear, found another rock, and tossed it in. No sound. He grinned at
Mahdy and nodded.

They walked out the mouth of the cave, and Klaus looked around in
amazement. The small group had swelled to hundreds, and still more
came from pathways stretching along the mountains.

Mahdy grabbed Klaus by the shoulder and indicated the bag on his
back. Then he pointed at a flat boulder. Klaus nodded. He sat on the rock,
set the bag down, and pulled out the suitcase. Opening it, he removed the
metal plate and entered data into the tiny keypad.

While he worked, the leader issued orders to arriving *mujahedeen*.
Many carried long cords of rope. They knotted the ends together. More
men arrived and added more rope. Other *mujahedeen* brought bags filled
with freshly collected snow which they piled at the back of the cave, and
they kept bringing more.

Klaus finished inputting settings on the bomb. He replaced the metal
plate and closed the suitcase. One of the men brought him a cast-iron
box. He wrapped the suitcase in several blankets and placed the bundle
inside the box.

Two more hours passed. The snow pile in the cave grew until it left
only a narrow passage between it and the chimney-hole. Then the men
piled more snow in front of the cave. Other men began gathering rocks.
Still others rolled in small boulders. Meanwhile, arriving groups brought
more rope and joined the cords together at their ends.

Klaus fought down nervous tension. *If this works... If not, I might not
make it off this mountain alive.* He grabbed the closest end of the rope and

tied it firmly around the cast-iron box, leaving no chance for it to slip out. He entered the cave.

Mahdy had extended two heavy planks over the lip of the hole. Between them at the far end, he had placed a pulley. He and Klaus worked together to feed the rope through the pulley and secure the iron box containing the bomb to it. They pushed the planks to the middle of the chimney-hole and began lowering the iron box with its deadly contents.

An hour went by. Klaus had to check his watch to keep count, and still the rope segments continued down, the snow pile grew, and the rocks stacked up higher.

Then, the rope went slack. They fed more rope. It drooped into the hole's darkness. Klaus and Mahdy exchanged glances. Mahdy instructed his men to pull back on the rope. At first doing so was easy. Then the line grew taut. A long line of *mujahedeen* struggled in unison against the combined weight of all the rope lengths and the bomb at the other end. They pulled back a few feet. Mahdy signaled them to ease it forward. Once again, the rope went slack.

Without waiting to be told, Mahdy commanded the men to start shoveling the snow pile into the chasm. Three hours later, all the snow had been dumped into the hole. Then they dropped in rocks starting with small ones, then larger and larger ones, and finally, the small boulders. When their supply was exhausted, Mahdy shot Klaus a questioning look.

Klaus glanced at his watch. Eight hours had passed since he had set the timer—for eleven hours. Using hand signals, Klaus communicated for everyone to vacate the area—fast.

Klaus and Mahdy's group stopped in the cave where they had slept the night before. Progress to reach it had been much faster since they rushed downhill. They arrived fifteen minutes before the bomb was timed to detonate.

Twilight settled over the long, curved valley. Standing in the cave's mouth, Klaus and Mahdy looked along the massive craggy mountains that marked the way they had just come. Klaus estimated their distance at twelve miles.

They felt the bomb blast before they heard it, starting as a gentle tremor but immediately mounting to a violent lurch. A furious wind whirled through the cave and howled its way toward the bomb site. The group sheltered in the mouth of the hollow, all eyes turned toward the craggy peak at the end of the deep canyon.

As they watched, white-hot light burst into the gathering dusk. For a split second, it pulsed brighter and then did it again, sustaining the hue. The mountain appeared to swell momentarily, then sank in on itself. Red-hot sparks flew into the air.

As quickly as it started, the eruption ceased. No mushroom cloud. Then a deep, throaty roar echoed up the canyon. It shook the ground again, and when it abated, a more muted rumble continued as rocks poured down from the mountains on both sides of the canyon.

Mahdy grabbed Klaus' shoulders and shook him, a huge grin spreading across his face. He raised his voice in a loud cheer, pointed the barrel of his weapon to the skies, and let go a burst of gunfire, its tracers streaming into the night.

"*Allahu-Akbar*," he yelled. His men joined in the celebration. Two hoisted Klaus on their shoulders and danced on the floor of the cave. The others joined in shouting "*Allahu-Akbar*" while firing their weapons into the air.

No one in the group slept that night. Klaus could not understand any of the conversation but guessed that they discussed what this new weapon, delivered into the hands of Allah, would mean to *jihad*. When dawn broke, they peered outside cautiously and then gazed in awe at the sight they beheld.

A deep layer of boulders had filled the floor of the valley for most of its length. Most impressive was the mountain where they had so laboriously inserted the bomb deep into its belly. A gulch had been slashed into its side from top to bottom. The mountain still had its peak, but it had tipped to one side, and it had been lowered by many meters.

Klaus started his trek back to Riyadh.

36

"There's been a tremor in the force," Burly said over the speakerphone.

"What are you talking about?" Atcho replied. Horton arched his eyebrows.

"Sorry. That line fit so perfectly. Have you heard of some seismic event taking place a few countries east of you? We think it was in Afghanistan, but we're not sure. As best we can pinpoint, the disturbance took place somewhere in the area of Tora Bora. That's a mountain range near the Pakistan border southeast of Kabul."

"Why should that interest us?"

"We don't know that it does. Afghanistan is a political vacuum. Since the Soviets left, there's no strong national government. It's become a haven for terrorists and drug traders. The US will have to do something there sooner or later. We're interested from the sense of leaving no stone unturned in pinning down Klaus."

"You think he went to Afghanistan to detonate one of his bombs? Why would he do that?"

"We're keeping all options open. An unexplained tremor of some significance took place. There aren't a lot of seismic sensors in that part of the world. China and India have some. Pakistan too. It was their data that clued us in and gave an idea of the probable area. They have people out checking. We haven't had calls for emergency help and no anecdotal evidence. Maybe it was just a heavy rockslide. I mentioned it to you in case you heard something."

Atcho sighed. "We've heard nothing. Klaus has disappeared from the planet. It's been four days since we dropped his bombs in the furnace. Those fires will burn a long time, and we can't always watch everything. He has lots of time and he can detonate at his convenience."

"Makes sense," Horton cut in. "He knows we're onto him. He could either lay low or hit somewhere else. What do you hear from Sofia?"

"She says it's quiet there. She still has three bad guys watching her. Ivan keeps security tight around her."

Burly sighed. "We're in a lull, and we can't afford to be. We dropped four suitcases in the fire, and as far as we know, none of them were lethal. If that's the case, then Klaus still has five of them. But here's the real hickey. He started with only one. He replicated four. He knows what he's doing now."

"Let's assume that Klaus detonated a bomb in Afghanistan," Atcho interrupted. "Why would he do that somewhere with no strategic advantage?"

"I wouldn't say that Afghanistan has no strategic advantage," Burly replied. "It didn't become the place where empires go to die without good reason. The Mongols fought to a standstill there. Genghis Khan left his progeny. So did Alexander the Great. He was driven back. The Brits lost their mojo there. Most recently the Soviets met their Waterloo and skipped out. No one has ever been able to subjugate the country. It's Muslim, and a great place for Islamic-fundamentalist terrorists to hang out with local support."

"Then why would Klaus explode a bomb there?"

"I don't know. A demonstration? If that's what it was, it's the first of his bombs that detonated. All the others were captured, burnt up, sabotaged. He can't keep claiming he has a lethal weapon if it never performs."

Horton leaned forward. "That's got to be it." His voice gained urgency. "I was an adviser to the *mujahedeen* fighting the Soviets in Afghanistan. The country's got a lot of desert and a lot of mountains. Mostly, it's barren rock. Why it gets fought over so much is beyond me. There's very little vegetation. Only one province can grow enough produce to sustain the country, but it's turning to poppy production. A lot of those mountains have caves, especially down in Tora Bora. If they found a mountain with a shaft going down a thousand meters, they could lower a bomb in there. If they could tamp it somehow, the bomb is small enough that it would do damage, but not enough to throw much radiation into the atmosphere." A fleeting grin crossed his face. "Essentially—now that's a big word—if Klaus could get that done, it would be like running a poor-man's underground test explosion. He'd come out of there a hero."

"What about satellite sensors, or NORAD?" Atcho cut in. "Have they seen anything?"

"The scarce information we have comes from the US Geological Survey," Burly replied, "and that was received from their counterparts in countries neighboring Afghanistan. One of our smart guys picked up the data and relayed it. There were no aftershocks. No warnings, so as an earthquake, it was anomalous."

Horton's brow furrowed. "Burly, you might want to get signal intel to beef up listening in Afghanistan, Saudi Arabia, and Berlin—anywhere that the Islamic-fundamentalist networks operate. If that was a successful test, they'd be shouting *Allahu-Akbar* all over the net. They get careless when they do that."

"Good thinking," Burly said. "I'll get on it."

Atcho had been quietly listening, deep in thought. "If we go forward assuming Klaus ran a successful test, that begs the question, what will be his next target?"

"We have a good idea," Burly intoned somberly. "Atcho, we have the war zone sewed up as tight as we can. Time for you to secure your home front."

"Agreed," Horton broke in. "Go home, Atcho. I'll hold the fort here."

37

Klaus walked into a huge celebration when he returned to Saudi Arabia. Yousef met him at the door of Bandar's palatial house. Many expensive cars were parked in the large courtyard in front. Music played. Laughter pealed from an inner courtyard. "*Habibi!*" Yousef exulted. "You did it. You detonated a nuclear bomb. More like that will bring Allah's vengeance."

He guided Klaus through a side hall. "This party is officially billed as my niece's engagement fest. In reality, it is in your honor. Some important people want to meet you." They moved through the house unseen. "You can clean up in your room. We laid out traditional Saudi clothes for you. Wear them and keep your sunglasses on. We know everyone here. Most guests think this is the engagement party, but treachery is always everywhere. It's best that only a few know your identity and that you are here. We'll talk later."

Late in the evening, Yousef tugged Klaus' arm. "I mentioned a few people want to meet you. They are in another room."

Klaus followed. He was tired from his trip. On leaving the cave the morning after the detonation, he had hiked with Mahdy and his group back to the village. He had spent the night there and then retraced his way along the rocky path on horseback to the Beechcraft at the end of the gravel runway in the narrow valley. The pilot had waited there and had flown him out immediately.

He was glad to be back in Saudi Arabia, but still felt the effects of the arduous trek up and down the mountains and the return flight. Now, he only wanted to sleep.

Five men occupied the sitting room where Yousef led him. They sat on low couches with tea servings on tables in front of them and stood when Klaus entered, lining up in a row to shake his hand and kiss his cheeks. Yousef preceded him, introducing him to each man in turn.

At the end of the line, a tall man stood slightly apart. He had a long, deeply tanned face made seemingly longer by a full black beard that fell to his mid-chest. Instead of traditional Saudi garb, he wore long white robes and a dark vest. On his head was a white turban, and he smiled enigmatically. "You have truly done Islam a service," he told Klaus. "We will talk more. You have the full backing of my *al-qaeda*."

Klaus followed Yousef's example in showing respect. Later, as Yousef showed him back to his room, Klaus said, "I'm sorry, I couldn't hear you well when you introduced me to the last man. Who was he? And what is this *al-qaeda*?"

"That was Usama bin Laden. I mentioned him to you earlier. He fought with the *mujahedeen* against the Soviets in Afghanistan. As I told you, he is furious that King Fahd allowed the infidels to base their military on the Saudi Arabian Peninsula. This is sacred ground. They should not be here.

He grimaced angrily and continued. "'*Al-qaeda*' means 'the database.' He is growing a loose organization that performs tasks by ability. He keeps track of all the fighters and their actions in a database. He is very wealthy himself and draws huge amounts of contributions from faithful Muslims. You are in his database. It now goes by the name of *Al-Qaeda*, and he committed to full financial support for you."

Klaus let the thought settle, uncertain that he understood the full ramifications. "I don't know what that all means. Does he have to approve my missions now?" His tone expressed lack of enthusiasm for the notion.

Yousef chuckled. "You are a wealthy man in your own right. You can take up any mission you can pay for with no one's approval. But think of this: you spent more than a third of your fortune by the time we met, and you had not exploded a single bomb. Getting you inside Texas will be expensive. The cost of plutonium will skyrocket because of your successful detonation, and you'll need someone other than yourself to make regular contact with black-market suppliers. You can do a lot on your own. You can do a lot more with *Al-Qaeda*."

Klaus nodded slowly. "What about my project in Texas. Will he support that?"

Yousef laughed. "You have a one-track mind. That's a good thing for a fighter like you. Never give up." He chuckled. "To answer your question, yes, he supports your mission. I explained to him who Atcho is, the fight between you, the nature of the target, and what you propose. You go to Texas with the blessing and support of *Al-Qaeda*."

Yousef returned to Riyadh that night, and Klaus received a message from him by courier the next morning. "Your travel arrangements are set. You'll fly back to Tripoli under one identity. Your *hawaladar* there, Hassan, will help switch you to another alias. Then you go to Venezuela. Your cover will be that you are in the oil business, and from there, you'll fly into Mexico City. Then, you'll go on a small plane to an unmarked strip south of the Texas border. Travel will be on private carrier for each leg of your journey with arrangements to bypass customs and immigration. Per your request, we've arranged to have observers on both sides of the Texas border. They belong to us. No cartel involved. Brothers are assigned in the US to pick up your shipments and forward them to the address you specified. You are in Allah's hands. I'll welcome you back on your return."

The courier stood waiting while Klaus perused the note. When he had finished, the courier handed him another message from Yousef. "Urgent! I received a call from Kadir in Berlin. The men watching Atcho's wife reported that she made a trip into Austin yesterday, to the field office of the FBI. Proceed with caution. She might suspect that you're going there. If so, no doubt Atcho will be warned."

Klaus read the message through twice, and smirked. *So much the better. I'll get them both at the same time.*

"I'm glad you haven't left yet," Burly said.

"My flight leaves this afternoon," Atcho replied. "What's up?"

"After we spoke yesterday, the chatter on the terror networks went nuts. Looks like our assumptions were correct. Klaus—or someone—detonated a nuclear device in the Tora Bora area of Afghanistan. Whoever it was did it just like Horton suggested. They lowered it into a deep chasm in a cave. We're not sure yet how they damped it. We have a team going in to take a look. But the whole side of that mountain imploded on itself, and the peak came down about thirty to forty meters." He paused for emphasis. "The terrorists now have a nuclear device, they can reproduce it, and they're coming our way."

Silence.

"Atcho, did you hear what I said?"

"I'm thinking. The good news is that now we know what we're dealing with."

Horton chimed in. "Sirs, if you don't mind my sayin' so, this Klaus just became a world-class badass. He'll get as much moolah as he wants and traipse around anywhere he has a hankerin' to. So, what do we do now?"

"Joe," Burly replied. "You're now the designated action guy in the Kuwaiti war zone. I've already spoken with your boss, and the Pentagon weighed in. The commanders will give highest priority and full support. The Saudis believe in the threat. There is a full-on manhunt for Klaus.

"Atcho, some of the chatter indicates a strike in the West, and Texas has been mentioned. Klaus might hit somewhere else, but he just got promoted to top-dog terrorist and can pick his targets. I have to believe getting you and Sofia is chief on his mind."

"I was thinking the same thing," Atcho replied. "What resources will I have?"

"You'll be picked up by helicopter in a few minutes and taken to King Abdul Aziz Air Base. A plane will pick you up there to fly you straight to Bergstrom Air Force Base outside of Austin. I'll meet you there."

Both Atcho and Horton were silent after Burly hung up. Horton spoke first. "Atcho, the next time you want to get together with me, could you arrange it down on Fiji or at Galapagos or somewhere nobody knows us and nobody we know knows we're there?" He grinned.

Atcho smiled wryly. The whir of helicopter rotors sounded through the walls. "That's a date. We'll bring our wives. See you, my friend. My plane's waiting."

38

The small jet screamed onto the runway at Bergstrom, slowed to a halt, and taxied to the terminal. Atcho emerged onto a set of portable stairs. Burly waited for him at the bottom.

"Are you too tired to talk now?" Burly asked after greetings.

"Let's get to it."

They conversed as they walked briskly through cold drizzling rain. "Sofia's waiting at your office. That's a secure location. We can brainstorm alternative plans."

"Any sign of Klaus?"

"None. The chatter died off some. That could be good, or it could be the lull before the storm. For him to come here will take a while—he can't just fly straight in. We've got radiation detectors at all the major airports and at a lot of the smaller regional ones, particularly in Texas. He'll have to come in another way. We have a few days to figure it out, but he has an organization behind him now. He'll have a lot more resources and better intel."

"They suspect something," Yousef told Klaus. "Atcho's wife drove to his company's office. That's the first time she's done that since she returned. Two government sedans entered after she arrived. They seem to be having a large meeting."

"Do we know who was in the sedans?"

"No."

"Do we know where Atcho is?"

"Our people have not seen him in at least two days."

"I'll arrive in Mexico tomorrow. With any luck, I'll be across the border by the next day and at the address where my packages were sent. Be sure I have good security there."

Sofia waited for Atcho in his office at the company plant before the meeting. When the door closed behind him, she rushed to him and threw her arms around his neck. "I missed you so much."

He held her close, and then stood back to look at her. Reaching down, he massaged the swell of her stomach. "Our little nugget is beginning to show." He smiled. Then his face turned serious. "I wish we had more time to visit. People are already assembled in the conference room. We should go."

"I know," she said petulantly, "but when we get home, you're all mine."

Ivan greeted them at the door to the conference room. "I'm insulted that I had to be escorted in," he joked, chuckling. Then he grasped Atcho's shoulder. "It's great to see you home in one piece."

"Thanks for keeping my family safe," Atcho replied, shaking his hand.

Besides Burly, Ivan, and Sofia, the field office director of the FBI and his counter-terrorism special agent, a senior member of the Texas Rangers, and the local chief of the Border Patrol were also present. When all were seated, Burly made introductions. "You've been briefed," he began, "if you have questions, we can start with those, but the emphasis is on what we do about the threat. We believe this is the area where Klaus will strike, but other meetings like this are taking place around other likely targets." He turned to the Border Patrol chief. "Why don't you start out?" he said. "What's being done along the boundary? It's long and porous."

"And difficult to defend," came the reply, "but not impossible. The National Guard is on alert in all the states along the southern border. We have ground sensors and radar that give early warning of movement toward the US."

"Won't those be tripped by animals?" someone asked.

"Animals move more randomly. When we see patterns of deliberate movement northward, we position people to intercept along or near the line of travel." He smiled. "Sometimes we see four-legged animals, and sometimes we catch those of the two-legged variety."

"I'm guessing Klaus will try to cross in areas of infrequent migrant travel. How will you handle that?"

"The border is raggedy. In some places it's flat, in others it straddles the Rio Grande. Mountains sit on top of it in some places, or it plunges into steep gorges. We'll be monitoring the whole stretch in Texas—which is not the same as guaranteeing that we'll catch Klaus if he tries to cross, but we'll be able to move assets quickly when something turns up. Our counterparts in the other states are doing the same thing."

Atcho listened to the discussion with interest, but his mind labored under travel fatigue while processing much of it. After the conversation had continued for an hour, he broke in. "If he hits in the Austin area, what do you think is the most likely target?"

Burly stared as if not comprehending the question. "You know where we think it'll be," he said, "your house."

Atcho nodded. "Maybe," he stemmed back a yawn, "but not necessarily. Klaus wants me dead, that's for certain. My wife too. But he showed us that he's both a tactical and a strategic thinker. He'll want a target he sees as benefitting Islam. So, he'll want to plant the bomb where there's a good chance of taking both of us out, killing large numbers of other people, and doing strategic damage to US defenses.

"Mt. Bonnell sets on a bluff. The company is about a mile away, to the east, on flat ground. I'm no expert on nuclear weapons, but if he gets the house, would he get much else?"

Burly spoke up. "A blast on the side of the cliffs could have the combined advantages of both an airburst and a dirty bomb. It would shape the blast toward Austin. The radioactive debris would cover downtown. All the surrounding areas would suffer from fallout."

"What about the air force base?"

"Bergstrom? That's closing down next year. There's not much left there now. The city of Austin plans to build a new airport on that site, but right now, as a strategic target, it's not much. And it doesn't get *you*."

The room fell into silence as participants contemplated alternatives. Then, Sofia broke in. "Maybe we're giving Klaus too much credit." Questioning eyes swung her direction. "Look, he's wily. He's smart. He's been able to stay a step ahead of us. As Atcho said, he's even proved to be a strategic thinker. But how strategic?"

She paused to collect her thoughts. "He's got a bone to pick with Atcho and he wants that settled. When he tried to detonate the bomb in Berlin, he hadn't tested it. Same thing in Kuwait. We don't know if the suitcases that went into the fire contained bombs, but we do know that his objective was to set off at least one there. We preempted him. Why would he suddenly decide he wants to test one in Afghanistan?

"It's got to be that someone advised or directed him to," Sofia continued, cocking her head to one side as if thinking out loud. "Klaus' objective didn't change. He still wants to kill Atcho—and me. His best bet of doing that is hitting us at our house, but he gets no strategic value."

She paused, pensive "There's another place where he would have a chance to take Atcho and me out and hit what is, at least in his mind, a strategic target." She gazed around the room at the paintings on the wall, and at the sculpture of the cowboy on a bucking bronco on the conference table. "This building. This plant. This is where he has a good shot of meeting both objectives."

Burly looked doubtful. "If he's thinking strategically, this is a light target. He turned to Atcho. "As good as your technology is, it can still be replaced quickly by regular batteries, and he's got no guarantee that he'll get you in the process."

"Think about this," Sofia cut back in. "He's a competent field operator, but his formal education is not extensive. He knows little about the

US. Our stories planted in newspapers about Atcho's trip to Berlin built up in his mind the strategic importance of the power source. We know that in the grand scheme of things, it's not that strategic. But for him, it might be.

"If he can take out this plant and Atcho at one swat, he'd be okay with that, and then come after me since he happens to be in the area. Downtown Austin is only two miles from the house and one mile from the plant. A bomb near this building would not only take out our plant, it would disrupt or destroy part of I-35 and Route 1 and take Camp Mabry with it. He'd get kudos for striking a US Army base. The blast could reach as far as Texas Stadium and a large part of the University of Texas. Austin would be flattened."

"It would hit major neighborhoods on the east and west side of the river," Burly acknowledged. "If the prevailing winds stay constant, the fallout would blow away from downtown, but with a blast that strong, we can't count on that. Besides, upstream is the Mansfield Dam. It supplies drinking and irrigation water far downstream. Commerce, industry, food supplies, and the Colorado River below Lake Travis would remain radioactive for decades."

He heaved a sigh. "While we're being morbid, there's one more element to consider." His tone shifted to one of dread. "I don't think Klaus will drop his bomb from the air. Too much chance of damaging the trigger or some other component. Besides, he'll count on our having the airways sealed. I think he'll plant the bomb.

"Your house, sitting as it does on the bluff, offers some unique aspects. If a nuke detonates high in the atmosphere, you get more heat over a wider area, but a lot of the radiation dissipates in the air. If it's a ground burst, the area will be smaller but the destruction in that area will be greater, and the radiation lasts a lot longer. Detonated on the bluff, he'll get a little of both an airburst and a ground burst."

The room fell quiet again.

Ivan pursed his lips. "We'd better plan to react to both locations," he said. "If he detonates, Klaus would have bragging rights all over the terrorist world. With *Al-Qaeda's* support, he could reverse engineer the bomb design to make improvements. Once he gets Atcho out of the way, he can go about being the master terrorist for Islam he thinks he is. Believe me, his mojo in bad-guy circles would skyrocket."

Burly's brow furrowed. "I hate to do this, but here are two more pieces to the puzzle. We got results back from the team we sent to Afghanistan. They confirmed that the seismic event was a nuclear explosion. The trace material indicates a plutonium bomb with the same origin as the two we captured in Berlin." He exhaled. "That means it was one of Klaus' bombs. Obviously, it was viable. He has at least one more, and he knows how to copy them."

"You said two pieces to the puzzle," Atcho interrupted. "What's the other one?"

Burly sighed. "The president is fully informed. He spoke with the governors in each of the states with likely targets." He grimaced. "There will be no public warnings, no evacuations." He looked around at the concerned faces. "You know why. Mass panic would only create more, easier targets. It's a suitcase bomb. He can blow it anywhere. If Klaus can't get to his objective, he's likely to pick the closest one, get clear of it, and let 'er rip."

No one spoke, most staring straight ahead. Atcho shook his head and then smiled, fatigue lining his face. "I sure do miss Horton."

The others turned to him questioningly. Atcho chuckled. "We're all so somber. Right about now, Horton would tell Burly, 'If you ain't got nothing positive to say, why don't you just quit jackin' your jaw.' Then he'd point his finger at Ivan and say, 'The way you talk, if I didn't know you had been a communist, I'd prob'ly trust you with my girlfriend. So long as you don't tell my wife. Good thing I got you figured out. What do you know about mojo anyways?' Then he'd get tickled at his own joke."

Tension broke as the conference participants laughed. Ivan brought the jocular tone back to earth. He rubbed his chin. "We need to do a better job of coordinating," he muttered. Although he spoke in a low, thoughtful tone, his voice carried. He glanced up and saw that all eyes had swung to him.

"I'm not being critical," he said. "Well, I could criticize myself." He turned to Sofia. "You went to the FBI field office the other day, and we took no measures to hide that, despite knowing you were being watched.

Same thing with this meeting today. A good guess is that Klaus already knows about both events."

Chagrinned, Burly, Sofia, and Atcho nodded their agreement. "What a great bunch of intel pros we are," Burly moaned. "OK, so he knows where your house is, and he knows where this plant is. What do we do about it?"

"He probably already knew those things," Sofia said. "With the information Collins put in his articles, anyone could have figured it out." Her irritation showed, and then she caught herself. "Sorry. Collins was a good man."

Everyone sat in quiet contemplation. Atcho broke the silence again. "What if we give him the target?"

Sofia groaned. "Not again. You can't be the bait again."

"Hear me out," Atcho replied. "He probably doesn't know where I am, but thinks I'm coming here. With the errors made on Sofia's FBI visit and the meeting today, he might think we've either become slack or overconfident. What if we make a few more mistakes? Maybe we could lure him into a target we choose on our schedule."

Burly leaned forward. "Didn't you already try that in Kuwait?"

"We did, but over there, he was the unknown quantity. We didn't know his whereabouts.

"We don't know where he is now either, but I'm betting he doesn't know where I am. Let's keep it that way. We'll dangle me as prey in front of him like holding a treat in front of a dog. When he leaps for it, we'll move it, and keep doing that until we get him."

Sofia stared at Atcho. "Or until he bites your hand off," she said brusquely, "or your head."

Atcho stood and circled the table to stand behind her. He took her shoulders. "I'll be fine."

Sofia tossed her head, unconvinced.

"He won't strike until he knows he can get me," Atcho said. "Let's take him on a wild-goose chase."

39

Klaus' journey from Kuwait had been long and tedious, but uneventful. Hassan had managed his safe passage through security and customs in Tripoli and arranged travel to Caracas. He had rested in Venezuela for a day before continuing on to Mexico. Once again, the network moved him smoothly through authorities to a waiting airplane. Within two hours of arriving in Mexico he landed on a dirt road less than two miles from the US border.

He spoke little to his guides, and they spoke to him only as needed. He leaned against a boulder and scanned the vista of jagged mountains extending out to the horizon. Scrubs were scarce. Only the vast blue sky provided visual relief to the monotony of desert brown. *I might as well be in Afghanistan.*

The leader took a flat parcel from his backpack and tossed it to Klaus. "Here, your new clothes and some equipment. Put those on and listen to me carefully."

Klaus changed while the leader talked to him in English. "This is a good location to cross because the climb is steep. The other side of the mountain is just as rough. At the bottom, the Rio Grande is shallow and on the other side, the ground is flat.

"We expect to be discovered by the US Border Patrol. Don't worry.

We've been caught before. They'll take us to the nearest border crossing and let us go." He pointed to Klaus. "You cannot be caught." He explained in detail what Klaus had to do.

Klaus watched the group prepare. They were well equipped with night-vision devices and small arms.

They waited until well past dusk. Then the group leader approached him. "This is where we leave you. Good luck."

Klaus watched through his night-goggles as the group set out toward the rugged mountain ridge. His guide had chosen well. No moon. Overcast. Ambient light was scarce, but sufficient for the goggles to amplify reflection to see the way ahead.

He checked a pants pocket. His precious package was there—a small, waterproof, lead box containing an infinitesimal amount of plutonium—and now he was only a short distance from the Great Satan. Soon, he would carry death and destruction into its belly.

"I just got a call from the Border Patrol chief," Burly said. They sat in the conference room at the FBI field office. "We've got activity. Unfortunately, it's spread along the border in several places. We have teams heading to each one."

"How many places?" Atcho asked.

"Latest count, seventeen, and that's just in Texas. We also have to contend with illegal aircraft crossings. The pilots will fly in and land on a straight stretch of road marked out with ChemLight or white plastic bags. They'll touch down, let their passengers out and take off within minutes. Or, they'll fly to a private airstrip on a ranch. We can't go in because it's private property. Corporations are buying up ranches for that purpose, so a lot of the time the authorities don't even know who owns them."

Atcho shook his head. "That's a hell of a way to defend a country. You said seventeen ground crossings? Is that normal? And what about the airplanes. How many of those?"

"Hard to tell. The aircraft fly under radar. Seventeen is a high number in Texas for this time of year. Some are hard to get to, but others look like obvious diversions. The Border Patrol still has to check them out though, and that burns up resources.

"A new group just showed up crossing a ridgeline bordering Texas. Six men. They're descending now. Once they cross the Rio Grande, we'll have a welcoming party for them. Hopefully, Klaus will be among them."

Klaus crouched alone in the dark, listening. Soon he heard the sound he sought, faint at first, and then rising in volume as it approached—the roar of an aircraft engine. He could not yet see it, and he felt awed by the daring of the pilot descending low over the face of the mountain. It reached flat ground and settled on a dirt runway marked out with Chem-Light, the group's last act before leaving Klaus alone.

The plane halted on the runway within a yard of him, its engine idling, its propeller spinning. Klaus ran out, mounted the wing, and scrambled to open the door.

Even before he had sat down, the pilot started to taxi, the rugged runway still stretching out to their front. Klaus buckled in and secured the door. He looked across to see the pilot but could only make out a broken profile by the glow of instrument lights.

"Listen and don't talk," the pilot said as he straightened the plane and increased speed. Ahead of them, the ChemLight sticks were adequately visible, marking the path of the runway.

"I'll fly straight up that mountain range and cross in a saddle between two peaks. You won't be able to see. The air will be turbulent. It'll shake us. When we get to the other side, I'll dive down to the flat land to stay below radar. Keep your hands still and don't react. We'll land in thirteen minutes. When I stop, you get out fast, and run to the light. I'll point it out to you, but it'll be the only one. Do you understand?"

Klaus grunted. The plane accelerated to speed and soared into the night sky.

"The Border Patrol caught nothing last night." The Austin FBI field-office chief was clearly disgruntled. "There ended up being nearly a hundred attempted penetrations along the length of the border, from Texas to California, but no Klaus. We kept detainees longer than usual and questioned them but got no leads."

"Aircraft?" Atcho asked.

The bureau chief shook his head. "We had a few blips on radar but caught no one."

"The chatter started up again all over the Islamic world," Burly chimed in. "They keep mentioning the name, Sahab." He frowned. "That's Klaus. They're saying he's in the US and that he's going to visit the wrath of Allah on the Great Satan."

"We are so proud of you," Yousef said over the phone. "You proved your equipment works, and you arrived safely in-country. Did all your shipments arrive?" He was careful to avoid keywords that could trigger listeners.

"They did. A couple were damaged, but they are easily replaced. I've located a machine shop that can do the job. I should be ready in a day or two. What are they saying on the news?"

"No one has explained the seismic event in Afghanistan, at least not publicly. We've heard no speculation about your whereabouts either. My police friends have heard nothing."

Klaus pondered that information. "They would keep that classified anyway. What about Atcho?"

"I saw an interview with him from Berlin last night. He must be there now. An earlier report said he had received an offer to buy his company and he was seriously considering it. The interview was very short. He was entering a hotel, and a reporter stopped him. He said he had finished his study of possible manufacturing locations and was flying to Washington to discuss regulations for exporting the technology or selling the company to a foreign purchaser."

Needles of anxiety poked at Klaus' gut. "I expected him to be home by now. What's his wife doing?"

"Not much. They had that big meeting at Atcho's company headquarters. She went home that night. Since then, she's been doing normal things, going to the store, meeting with her garden club friends, etcetera. She went to see a doctor. Everyone seems to have forgotten about you. That should make it easier for you to move around."

Engrossed in his own thoughts, Klaus barely heard what Yousef had said. "This makes no sense. Atcho baited me in Berlin. He was never there for business."

"The people he spoke with seemed serious. Several stories appeared in business magazines about the worth of his company and its future prospects. They're saying his technology proved itself in Kuwait. Maybe a European company or a major investor took an interest."

"Maybe, but we should have seen major fireworks in Kuwait. He baited me there too. He's doing it again. I can feel it." He paused, gathering his thoughts. "Did you see what the name of the hotel was in Berlin where he was interviewed?"

"No, and the reporter didn't say."

"Then he could be anywhere. I won't play his game." Suddenly, Klaus' mind seized on something Yousef had mentioned. "What kind of doctor did his wife go to?"

"I don't know. Let me see if that's in Kadir's notes." The phone remained silent for a few minutes. Then Yousef came back on. "There's not much information on that. I have the name and address of the doctor, but all it says about him is OB/GYN. Does that mean anything to you?"

"No, but we should be able to find out. Tell Kadir to get me a direct phone number to Atcho."

"What are you going to do?"

"Make him come to me."

40

"It's good to be home," Atcho said, "but I can't stay cooped up like this forever and we can't keep using the riverside entrance for me to come and go. Sooner or later, someone will spot me." He leaned back on the sofa in the downstairs lounge of his home, his arms encircling Sofia. Two days had passed since the meeting in his company's conference room.

He glanced around the room. "So, this is where you intended to tell me about our baby." He smiled. "I should have known—several days of being sick in the morning. A single glass of wine. The romantic setting. How could I have been so blind?"

"You're a man," Sofia said sardonically. She chuckled and squeezed his hand. "You were preoccupied. I knew that." She reached up and kissed his cheek. "I'm glad you're home."

"For now. Klaus is still out there, and I'm still his prime enemy."

"If he or any of his buddies are paying attention, he should think you're on your way to Washington from Berlin."

"That's a big if. He's not stupid. He guessed we smoked him out in Berlin and tried to corner him in Kuwait. Since then he's fired off a nuclear bomb—at least we think it was him. If that's true, his threat on the world stage is real. Right now, he's limiting his own potential with his vendetta against me, but that will wear off. He learns fast and he's shown patience. If he can't get to me soon, he'll either change his tactics or choose another target. Maybe a bigger one."

Atcho's cell phone rang. "Just checking in," Burly said. "We've heard nothing. How about you?"

"Nothing. The bad guys watching Sofia have either pulled back or they've gotten better at it. Ivan's men haven't seen them in more than a day. What about Horton?"

"The same. Chatter has died down again. Illegal border crossings from Mexico have returned to normal. He's disappeared from the CIA's screen, and the FBI has no trace of him."

"But he's in the US." Atcho made his query a flat statement.

"We believe he is."

"All right. Where am I going to show up next?"

"We thought a shot of you meeting with commerce department officials would be good. A couple of their honchos are in Austin now. We rented a room at a hotel. We'll do an interview there and broadcast it on the East Coast as if it happened in DC. The story will be picked up and broadcast through the world's business channels. Anyone watching it should believe you're in Washington. One of the FBI agents will pick you up below your house at the river in a couple of hours."

Atcho sighed. "All right. I'll be ready."

No sooner had Atcho set his phone down than it rang again. Thinking Burly might have called right back, Atcho answered. "Did you forget something?"

A low voice responded. "I don't think so."

Atcho's mind sharpened. He waved to get Sofia's attention, and then spoke into the receiver. "Klaus?"

Sofia's expression morphed into one of horror. She immediately regained control and hurried to the entertainment center at the end of the room and pressed the switch to open the hidden safe-room.

Atcho followed her. While he spoke, she reached up and plugged a wire into the bottom of his cell phone. Then she flipped some switches on a console and put a speaker to her ear. She nodded at Atcho.

"They call me by my real name now, Sahab," Klaus said. "You remember my voice. That's good."

Atcho started to interrupt.

"Shut up and listen," Klaus snarled. "I'm in no mood for small talk. I don't know where you are, and you don't know where I am. That's the beauty of modern technology. I'm on a throwaway cell phone. You won't trace it, and anyway, I'll crush it when we're done talking. Then I'm on the move again. Did you hear about the seismic event in Afghanistan?"

"A few tremors in a remote mountain area. No one was affected. So, what?"

"You know better than that," Klaus grunted. "That was me. My technology works. I proved it and you know it. Stop the crap and let's get to business."

"What do you want?"

"That's better. By the way, I should congratulate you. Your wife is having a baby."

Atcho's heart skipped a beat. His mind spun.

Klaus interrupted the silence. "Do I have your full attention now?"

Atcho struggled to keep his voice steady. "What do you want?"

"You know what I want. You. I want you dead. Revenge is my right. And I want to strike for Allah. Islam will spread over the world, and I will help. Listen carefully.

"The bomb is planted. It's active, tamper-proofed, and set where no one in your house can escape it. If your wife tries to leave the house, the bomb goes off. If anyone that's not supposed to be there comes in, the bomb goes off. I have your house under electronic surveillance. If my cameras are tampered with, I press the button.

"I have the remote, and I'm out of the blast area. You can save your wife and baby. Doing that is simple. All you have to do is go home. You cannot save yourself. You have twenty-four hours.

"By the way, the bomb detonates whether you show up or not. I'll see to that. If I don't get you this time, I will the next. When I see you enter your house, your sweet Sofia will have one hour to get out of the area."

"What's to stop you from detonating before that hour is up?"

"I'm a man of my word. I'll still get her. I'll just do it later. At least she has a chance. You do not. You're already dead."

"I heard," Burly said. "Sofia patched me in. He's put us in a tight spot."

"First things first," Atcho said, his mind focused, his thinking crystal clear. "Send someone to meet Sofia at the bottom of our bluff by the river in twenty minutes."

"I'm not leaving," Sofia broke in.

"Yes, you are," Atcho said steadily. "You have our baby to protect. You can't do that here, and you can't help me. You have to go. Get your things together."

Sofia hesitated.

"Go," Atcho said. He touched her arm. "I'll think better when you're safe." He watched as Sofia left the room, her shoulders drooped. He had never before seen her look forlorn.

"Burly, get Ivan to check out the private investigators that did surveillance on us. We know they weren't good. I want to know where their cameras are and how they're being monitored.

"Next, get Veniamin on the phone. We need to find another vulnerability in the bomb's design. Something we can exploit.

"Get to the news agencies. Flood the airwaves with Klaus' picture. Make up a story. Say he's an escaped prisoner, armed and dangerous. Ask for public help to find him."

"Don't you think that would make him trigger the bomb?"

"Maybe, but he likes to live. He has an escape plan, I promise you. He didn't anticipate having to look over his shoulder every second. You get everyone looking for him, and he'll have to do that. At least it'll be a distraction."

"I'm not crazy about that idea, but I'll run it by others, see what they think. Maybe they'll have other suggestions. What else?"

"I'm almost out of ideas. Do you have radio signal jammers that will work here? Is there a way to interrupt cell phone signal? He can't have known that I'd pick up on his call just now and he doesn't know where I am, so he wouldn't have set the timer. He's going to do it by remote."

"Good thinking. I'll work on those. Do you have one of those NUKEX's with you?"

Atcho's mind raced. "I have the prototype that was sent when I was doing due diligence to buy the company, but I don't know if it's a mockup or a functional device."

"I'll find out. If it's not a working device, maybe we can get one to you."

"OK, but it's not going to do any good until we know where the bomb is. The good news is that if Klaus has already placed it, then it's out of his hands. Is there anything flying that can detect the plutonium from the air?"

"The amount of plutonium is too small, and it's contained in a lead sphere. Hold on a second. I have a call coming in."

A minute later, Burly was back. "That was Ivan. His guys are taking action. Delay Sofia's departure by half an hour. The man who picks her up at the lakeside will bring a working NUKEX. Do you remember how to use it?"

"Someone can call and walk me through it."

"That'll work. Now we just need to figure out where he put the bomb."

"The boat is waitin', it's blowin' its horn," Atcho sang softly. His lips smiled, but his eyes did not.

Sofia slapped his shoulder. "Don't joke. I might not ever see you again." Tears ran down her cheeks.

"I always come out," Atcho said. "We'll beat this." He reached down and felt along her slightly rounded belly. "You make sure our little nugget has a chance at a great life." He took Sofia into his arms. She buried her head in his chest. "Let's go."

Sofia nodded, pulled away, and wiped her eyes. She headed to the small door leading out of the safe-room into the outdoors.

"Stay hidden all the way to the shore. I'll see you soon."

Sofia nodded. When she emerged at the back of the house, she stayed on the barely discernible footpath she and Atcho had laid out when they built the house. It switched back and forth downhill, screened by vegetation, and always within a few feet of rocks that provided solid cover.

A boat waited at the bottom. Sofia scanned the far shore and across the river to her left and right. Then she hurried toward the boat.

A man helped her climb aboard.

A shot rang out. The man slumped, blood trickling from his mouth.

Sofia jumped back in horror. Meanwhile the boat drifted into a turn in the water with its front facing the opposite shore. Keeping low, Sofia ducked behind the engine. Another shot whizzed by her head, and then another, shattering the windshield.

Frantically and keeping low, Sofia searched the boat's interior until she found a small bag that fit easily in her hand. She scooped it up and saw that fragments of a bullet had burned into the bag. She kept it anyway and scampered over the back end.

A hot round hit her leg. She barely registered it as she ran for cover, but oozing blood and the effects of shock settled in as she climbed the twisting path back to the house

Then Atcho was next to her. He grabbed her by the shoulders, pulled her behind some rocks, and checked her leg. The bullet had gone through her thigh. He jerked his belt off, tightened it around her leg into a makeshift tourniquet, and stood her up. Together, with one of her arms over his shoulder and one of his around her back, they finished the climb to the house.

Atcho pulled Sofia through the hidden entrance. Then he pressed a button. Outside, a wall of stones to match the base of the house slid into place.

His cell phone rang. He ignored it. Sofia had already hobbled to the other side of the room and pulled down a first-aid kit. Atcho grabbed it and took out a syringe. He was about to inject her leg with morphine. She stopped him with pain-filled eyes and a shake of her head. "The baby," she gasped. She gritted her teeth, grabbed a pair of scissors and cut her slacks off just below the tourniquet. Straining against the pain, she pulled off the tourniquet and cut the slacks to expose the entry wound.

Atcho opened a small envelope with a coagulant powder and poured it into the bullet hole. By the time he finished, Sofia had opened a pressure bandage. Sucking in her breath against the agony, she held it in place while Atcho tied it off.

Painfully, Sofia dropped to the floor. Atcho turned her over and repeated the process of dressing the exit wound. Then he turned Sofia on her back and placed a box under her feet to keep them elevated. Mercifully, Sofia swooned.

Atcho's cell phone rang again. When he answered, Klaus' voice sounded angry. "Tell your wife that if she tries another escape, I won't wait. I'll detonate the bomb."

Atcho breathed deeply to control his fury. "What did you do to my wife?"

"She didn't tell you? She tried to leave with another man in a boat." His voice turned sarcastic. "Don't worry. Your competition won't bother her again."

"Where is she?"

"Ask her, but I think she made it back inside the house. Who knows? She might still be trying to climb that bluff. Tell her to get in the house and stay there. You'll get no more warning." The phone clicked off.

Atcho returned to Sofia's side. Gently, he picked her up and carried her through the hidden door into the lounge and laid her on the sofa with a pillow under her feet and covered her with a blanket. She groaned. Her eyes fluttered open, revealing her agony.

Atcho caressed her face. "There must be something I can give you."

She shook her head, her face distorted in pain. "No," she whispered. "The baby." Atcho called Burly and relayed the situation.

"How is she now?"

"Unconscious. We stopped the bleeding before she lost much blood, so she's out of immediate danger, but she'll need medical attention. She won't take any pain medicine—she's afraid she'll hurt the baby."

"Did she get the NUKEX?"

"She got it and held on to it like it was gold."

"Right now, it is."

"Listen Burly, Klaus seemed familiar with the backside of our house and the bluff down to the river. The company is less than a mile from here, downstream. There are expensive homes and offices between the two locations on both sides of the river, and most have surveillance cameras. Get a team to collect those and screen them. I'll screen our own. Maybe we'll see him placing the bomb."

"Will do, but didn't Klaus say he had surveillance cameras of his own in place?"

"He's bluffing. When he kidnapped me last year, he controlled Sofia by telling her he had placed a remote-controlled bomb in our hotel room. He never did. He hasn't had time to put in a surveillance system. Between stringing wire, attaching components, and testing, he'd need a few days."

Burly heaved a sigh. "He had time to put a sniper in place."

"That was probably him. Snipers don't grow on trees. The police will be all over the shooting site by now. Tell them to look for surveillance cameras belonging to homeowners and businesses. Maybe we'll catch a glimpse of Klaus. He's moved on."

"All right, we'll assume he has limited eyes on the bomb. I hope you're right." Burly was quiet a moment. "Ya know," he said in a low voice. "He thinks you're flying to Washington from Berlin. Wherever he set that bomb—and he had to have done it within the last day—if he had known that you and Sofia were both at home—"

"I hear you," Atcho interrupted. "Listen, Camp Mabry is less than a mile from here. It's that Texas Army National Guard post I mentioned at our last meeting. They might have mobile jammers that can be wheeled into place."

"Good idea. I'll get the surveillance videos and coordinate with Camp Mabry. Ivan is closing in on the firm that had surveillance on Sofia. One of our guys is working with the cell phone companies to shut down the towers within a five-mile radius of your house on a moment's notice. Between that and jamming, that should cover the field."

"You'd better pinpoint the bomb's location quickly and accurately and let me know where it is. I have no secure radio here and none that could get through the jamming."

"What about a landline?"

"It's been cut. Once you shut down commo in the area, I'll be deaf, dumb, and blind."

41

Klaus cursed Sofia from across the river as he took apart his rifle and jammed it into its case. He had no time to be careful. His objective now was to get out of the immediate area. *Why can't infidel men teach their women to do as they're told?*

He had found a perfect sniper platform near the water's edge. It provided both cover and concealment with plenty of room to lie flat on his stomach far back in the shade so that the barrel of his rifle did not protrude.

He had watched with curiosity through a high-powered scope when a speedboat approached the opposite shore below Atcho's residence. Weather in Austin was turning to spring, but the air was still chilly, and watercraft were few. As Klaus had watched the boat pull in, his attention shifted to a blur of motion over the top of a clump of bushes. Then Sofia had stepped into view, walking swiftly.

Klaus had had little time to think. He had seen Sofia disappear on the other side of the boat, her intention clear. Quickly, he sighted on the vessel's pilot and squeezed off a round. The man had gone down as he pulled Sofia onto the boat. The craft turned in the water. Klaus saw Sofia's head briefly as she clambered over the outboard motor. He had fired off a few more rounds but could not see where they struck.

Sofia had disappeared from view. Then Klaus had seen her again running on the shore. She had ducked behind the same bushes where he had first sighted her. He had fired off another round but did not see her again.

Already, as he scrambled up the shore, he heard sirens closing the distance—fast. He reached his car, hidden in shadows in an overlook, and threw the rifle into the back seat. As he slammed the door closed, two police cars wheeled into the small parking area. An officer from each vehicle threw the doors open and jumped out.

Thinking furiously, Klaus thrust his hands in the air and rushed toward them. "Help, help!" he cried. "There's someone down there shooting. I saw him. He had a long rifle. He shot several times across the river. I think he saw me, so I ran."

The officers reached him. "Calm down," one of them told him. "Tell us again, slowly. What did he look like and which way did he go?"

"He was big, and he had black hair and a full beard. I think he went south." Klaus indicated downriver with his hand.

"I'll go look," one of the officers said to the other. "You stay with him and call it in. Request backup."

The second policeman escorted Klaus to the back of his patrol car. Klaus feigned weakness. He leaned against the car. "I was so scared," he said, wiping sweat from his brow. "I thought he was going to come after me."

"OK. Sit in here and relax while I call in the report." The officer held a back door open.

Klaus stepped in, taking his time. When the first policeman disappeared into the brush, Klaus shoved against the door. His escort sprawled backward, reaching for his gun. Klaus kicked his arm and brought the heel of his boot down into his opponent's face. The officer lay still.

Klaus rushed to his own car. He cranked the engine and spun gravel to get onto the main road, heading north. A quarter mile further on, he turned into a neighborhood on his right, and weaved through it at the legal speed limit. Behind him, he heard more sirens screaming, their wail dissipating as they headed south along the river.

The phone rang in the FBI chief's office. He answered, and then handed the receiver to Burly. "It's for you."

Burly listened a moment. "Put him on."

Another voice came over the phone. "This is Veniamin Krivkov."

"Listen, Doctor. This is very important. Walk me through again the arming sequence for the bombs. We're looking for a vulnerability."

"I understand. I understand," Veniamin said. His aged voice held a note of anxiety. "You see, the trouble is that Klaus rewired it. I don't know what changes he made."

Burly's voice took on greater urgency. "I get that, Doctor, but Klaus is no nuclear engineer. He doesn't understand why the bomb works, he just knows how to put the pieces together. Aside from taking out the dummy wiring, I don't think he would make any changes. So, walk me through the arming sequence."

Veniamin took a deep breath. "Hmm. I'll try. But I'm doing this from memory, and I'm an old man." He chuckled.

"Doctor, please. Think. Concentrate." Burly swallowed his agitation.

"Oh. Yes, of course. Well, let's see. Do you know if he intended to set the timer or use the remote?"

"We're fairly sure he used the remote option."

"Oh. Then he would have to enter a frequency for the remote to communicate with the bomb. He would need to activate the component that regulates the current running between the battery and the trigger mechanism. Let's see. He would also need to set the delay."

"What do you mean by 'set the delay'?"

"What? Oh. Default on that is four minutes, but he could extend or decrease the time if he wanted."

"Doctor, what is it? What does the delay do?"

"Oh, sorry. It's a safety measure. With all the testing done of the battery and the sequence between components, it is possible to arm the bomb accidentally. When it is fully operational, a green diode lights up. If the delay is set, then once the remote activates, the operator has the specified amount of time to shut the bomb down—deactivate it."

Burly's mind raced. "Does Klaus know that?"

"I don't know. I never told him. He was pushing me so hard to show him how to detonate. He wasn't interested in how to shut it down."

Burly breathed a little easier. "OK, Veniamin. This is important. Did I understand you to say that the bomb has no fail-safe? Does that mean that after closing the suitcase, opening it would not trigger it?"

"That's the way I designed it, but that does not mean that Klaus left it that way. He could have booby-trapped it in a way that doesn't disrupt the detonation sequence—just kills whoever tries to open it."

Burly shook his head. "An obvious point. Last question. If the bomb is armed and set to detonate by remote, how would you be able to see the timer? Wouldn't it be closed under the suitcase lid?"

"The first one I built was that way, but I used upgraded components on the newer version. The screen showing remaining time to detonation pops up. I had to cut a slit in the top of the suitcases to accommodate it. If the bomb is armed by remote, that screen will slide up through the slit and show the time remaining."

"So, to be clear," Burly said, "if the screen is up and counting, it shows you how many seconds you have left to disarm the bomb. If you try to open it though, Klaus might have set another booby trap."

"Exactly."

"Got it, Doctor. Thank you."

When Burly hung up, the FBI chief stood in front of him looking grim. "I got a call from the Austin police. They started a manhunt and asked for assistance to find a shooter along the opposite bank of the river from Atcho's house. They've got an officer down, and the shooter killed one of our agents in a boat just below Atcho's house."

Burly rubbed his hand over his forehead to the back of his head, his expression frustrated. "Oh God. I'm so sorry. Is the police officer OK?"

"Touch and go. Klaus did a number on his face. Could be permanent damage, if the officer lives, and that's an open question."

"Are you sure it's Klaus?"

The chief nodded. "The other officer at the scene got a good look at him. Klaus gave them a fictitious description of someone else he claimed was the shooter before he got away."

Burly thought a moment. "If we get too close before we find the bomb, he'll punch the remote." He paused in thought. "Can we do this? Announce a manhunt with the description that Klaus gave. Circulate his real photo to law enforcement. When he hears the news reports, he'll know we're searching, but approaching with caution. He won't have an immediate reason to detonate. He thinks Atcho is still traveling. He'll think he has time to get Atcho where he wants him, and that gives us time to find the bomb. We can close in after the bomb is neutralized."

The chief looked at him curiously. "Sounds like a plan, but are you supposed to be doing this? Aren't you CIA?"

Burly shot him a wry grin. "Retired. It's complicated. You want me to stop?"

"Hell no. Keep doin' what you're doin' and let us know how we can help. I'll get the word out."

Burly nodded somberly. "Good to hear you say that. Some people in our agencies think the real battle is between us about turf."

"We ain't got time for that. If we don't get the job done, Americans are gonna die. Lots of them."

"Atcho, it's Ivan. I heard about Sofia. Is she going to be all right?"

"Yes. The pain is horrendous. She'll need medical attention as soon as we're through this."

"You sound optimistic that we'll beat Klaus."

"Given where you and I have been, why would I think anything else?"

"Makes sense. Look, you might not know yet that Klaus killed that FBI agent in the boat, and he beat a local cop to a bloody pulp. We don't know if he'll live."

Atcho leaned against a wall and rubbed his eyes. "I'm sorry to hear that."

"There's a manhunt going on for Klaus, but the public is being given the description that Klaus made up. I'll tell you the whole story later."

"Now you're optimistic."

"Yeah. I tried to speak with Burly, but he was tied up. I got the sense that things might be heading south in a hurry, so I took an initiative based on a guess that the guys watching Sofia were hired help and not true believers. I had a look at their company's record and client list. They're C-list private eyes at best.

"I went in and threw my weight around. Made them believe I was an FBI investigator coming in on a tip by a state auditor looking at their practices. Long story short, they sang like babies."

Atcho had to smile. "You've adapted well to the scurrilous West. I have a hard time thinking of you as a former KGB officer instead of a good ol' Midwestern boy."

"Hey, I'm a Texan now. I've got my boots an' all. And what about you, my Cuban guerrilla friend? If you could ever shake that slight Latin accent and your unpronounceable real name, some people might mistake you for a real American too."

"OK. Enough banter. What information did you get?"

"Not much, but what I got eases the burden a bit. The wannabe detectives didn't do anything besides watch. They reported their observations to a *hawaladar* in Berlin by the name of Kadir. But they've set up no surveillance cameras or anything of the sort. They've never met Klaus and didn't know really why they were doing the stakeouts."

"Good job, Ivan. Do they know why he pulled surveillance off the house?"

"No, but if I had to guess, he didn't want to have reports called in about a prowler around your house."

"Why didn't your men or our own surveillance cameras pick him up?"

"My men were watching the 'Wannabes,' so when they pulled back, mine did too. An oversight. My fault. The 'Wannabes' provided Kadir with a map showing where your cameras are located and their span of coverage. Kadir must have forwarded the map. All Klaus had to do was stay outside those zones."

"That makes sense. We know who Kadir is. We'll relay that information to Detective Berger in Berlin. He might like to take a look at what else Kadir is doing."

"Is that all?"

"Everything you told me says that Klaus is acting as a lone wolf now.

He had help getting into the country, but either he likes to operate alone, or he's reached the limit of his help on this mission. Given that his primary objective is revenge, that wouldn't be surprising. Anyway, he probably doesn't have eyes on the house now."

"But we don't know that for sure."

"Correct. We'll have to act as if he's watching us, even if he has a limited view. That means no one comes in or out the front door."

"What do you want me to do?

"Listen carefully. We can't get this wrong."

42

Klaus drove through the neighborhoods at a deliberate pace in keeping with the flow of traffic. He wanted to race back to his hotel room, but his greater instinct at this moment was to draw no attention to himself. He was sure that the police officer who had gone to check the riverbank had not seen his car. The other one would not be speaking for a while, if ever.

He arrived at a run-down hotel on the edge of town, hurried to his room, and turned on the television. He flipped though several channels. They all reported breaking news of a shooting victim along the river and a cop-beating at the site of the shooting.

"The policeman is in critical condition at this moment," a reporter announced. "The identity of the victim has not yet been released. The Austin police chief called in the FBI and says a massive manhunt is underway for the perpetrator. Details are scant, but an eyewitness told police that he saw a very large man with black hair and a full beard running from the scene."

Klaus stared at the screen, astonished. That was the description he had given the policemen. He had expected to hear his own description with a photo. He called Atcho. No answer. He paced.

Atcho checked on Sofia. She moaned in semi-consciousness as he leaned over her, then she blacked out again.

He went back into the safe-room and picked up the small cloth bag with the NUKEX that Sofia had brought up from the boat. He slid the device from the bag—and his heart sank. Several tiny perforations showed along the base, the result of shrapnel hits. He took a small screwdriver from his workbench and opened up the casing. Then he called Burly.

"We've got another problem. The NUKEX is damaged. Even if we find the bomb, we can't use this device to neutralize it."

Burly groaned. "Can you see what it looks like inside?"

"I did. Several of the wires and the circuits boards are destroyed beyond repair. Even if we could fix the wires, no operator could hold it long enough for the heat to melt the trigger on the bomb. His hand would be cooked by then. The alloys that transfer the heat and those that protect the operator have been breached. We're talking over a thousand degrees of heat generated in ninety seconds. But if the heat is not contained and focused to the right place, not only can it fail to neutralize the bomb, but it'll fry the operator's hand before the trigger melts."

"What about the prototype? Is it functional?"

"It looks like the casing is real, but the inside is hollow. There's nothing in there."

"What do you suggest?"

"We've still got about fifteen hours, but we don't know where the bomb is, or where Klaus is. We have to find the bomb, or repair or replace the NUKEX—"

"Could your company supply a new one?"

"They're not in high demand, thankfully, so we do limited production. We shipped our inventory to high-value targets three days ago after Klaus crossed the border. Those targets were identified long before today. Austin was not expected to be among them. The one I had was our spare."

A thought flashed through Atcho's mind. "Burly. I have an idea. I'm going to hang up. If you don't hear from me, or if I don't pick up your call, listen for a boom. If you don't hear one, I'm still working."

"Don't joke like that."

"It helps keep my sanity. I learned it from Horton." Atcho hung up. He called the head of his technical division. "Put our best repair tech on the phone." He fended off questions and the call went through. "Mac, this is Atcho. I need your help, but first I need to know, are there any spare NUKEXs lying around?"

"No sir. We had to ship them all out. Real sudden. Something big is going down somewhere."

"You could be right." Atcho grimaced. "Mac, I received one of those NUKEX prototypes when I was looking to buy the company. I opened up the unit a few minutes ago, and it's hollow. Nothing's in it. Is that casing the real thing or is it a mock-up?"

"Let's see. The first casings we sent as souvenirs to investors were real, but they were expensive. We had some mock-ups made out of aluminum."

"How would you know the difference?"

"The real ones were fully functional except that they were missing the electronics. What I mean is, if you look at the three buttons on the outside—there should be a black one, a green one, and a red one. If you see them come through on the inside, you've got the real deal. The mock-ups were solid on the inside, and the buttons on the outside were static."

Atcho's hands perspired. He picked up the prototype and examined its interior. "OK, the good news is that I have the real deal. Now, can I transfer the innards from a damaged unit to the prototype?"

"What's damaged?"

Atcho did his best to describe the tangle of electronics inside the NUKEX. Mac took a deep breath, audible on the phone. "All right, sir," he said, "we'll give this a try, but here's the thing. I'll guide your through some workarounds, but when we're done, you won't be able to test the unit. If you could test it, you'd get a code in the window giving corrective action to make it functional. But with the workarounds, it'll either work, or it won't work. That's the best we can do."

Atcho sat back and stared. From the other room, he heard Sofia moan again. "Let's do it."

Atcho's cell phone rang. He ignored it. Dusk settled in. He had a set of needle-nose pliers in one hand and a solder gun in the other. He peered through a magnifying glass at the insides of the NUKEX and touched a contact with the tip of the solder gun. He held it momentarily and backed off. "I think that's got it," he told Mac. "Anything else?"

"No sir. We're done. But keep in mind that the original prototype has been improved as a result of testing. I don't know which one you have. One thing we did was make the part longer that focuses the heat. We did that to get closer to the trigger. We made the protective shield thicker too. If the unit you have works at all, it should do the trick, but I'd suggest you use a pair of thick work gloves. The heat will be intense."

"And we can't test it."

"No sir, you can't. You've got one shot, and then that's all she wrote."

Klaus felt impatience rising. He had listened to nonstop news reports about the shooting, the victim, the downed cop and all the conjecture about who had done it and why. Obviously, key details had been left out, but he heard nothing to indicate that the authorities had a clue regarding his whereabouts. He was sure that at some point, they would begin to show his photo, *but that's easy enough to fix. When I leave here, I'll look entirely different—and they'll have bigger concerns.*

He tried calling Atcho again. Atcho answered on the third ring. "What are you doing?" Klaus blurted. "Why haven't you answered my calls?"

"What did you expect? I was in Berlin when you started this. I landed in New York three hours ago. I'm in Atlanta now. I should be there in five or six hours."

Klaus leaned back on his bed. "Did you straighten out your wife?"

"I told her what you said. She knows she can't leave."

"She'll be dead if she does, along with a lot of other people."

"She knows that. I have to go." Atcho hung up without waiting for a response. He went to check on Sofia. She was awake, but listless. He dared not touch her for fear of increasing the pain.

A dull knock came from the back entrance. Atcho checked the surveillance monitor and saw Ivan standing outside with two men. He pushed a button to let them in. They all wore black, their faces covered with camouflage.

"These two are combat medics," Ivan said. "They still work EMS jobs. They know what to do."

The two men went immediately to Sofia's side. One carried a folding stretcher. While one medic checked her pulse and eyes, the other prepared a syringe. "This is a local anesthetic," he told an anxious Atcho. "It'll ease her pain but won't go into the rest of her system. It won't hurt the baby." He grinned. "You did a good job, Pops. Once we get her to the hospital, the doctors will take care of that leg, and she'll recover quickly."

Atcho fought off overwhelming emotions. He thanked the medics and hurried to Ivan. "What route did you take coming in?"

"We started three houses down and came in on the cliff side. It was rugged, but on the way in, we scouted a way that should be much easier for transporting Sofia out." He gestured with his jaw toward the two medics. "They're pros. They won't be seen."

"Good," Atcho replied. "Do they know not to come to the road in front of the house too soon? That route might be watched."

"They've got you covered, Atcho, and the ambulance is waiting."

Sofia called weakly from the lounge. He hurried to her. She was already on the stretcher. "Don't let them take me," she cried. "I need to be with you."

Atcho kissed her hand and held it to his chest. His eyes moistened as he spoke, and he bent to kiss her lips. Then he looked at the medics. "We're ready."

He walked with them into darkness behind the house. As he watched Sofia disappear into the night, Ivan drew him aside. "We've got sixty men combing the cliffs below the two houses where we came in, and—"

"Sixty men? Where did you get sixty men?"

A large hand clamped his shoulder from behind. "He called me," a voice said. Atcho looked into the darkness. He could not see the face, but he knew the voice. "Rafael? How, who, what are you doing here?"

Rafael was one of Atcho's oldest friends. The two had fought side-by-side at the Bay of Pigs in Cuba. They had worked several covert operations jointly since then. "Let's go inside where we can talk," he said.

In the safe-room, Atcho greeted Rafael again with a bear hug. He was a tall blond man with an almost perpetual grin and an irascible sense of humor. "Ivan called me," Rafael said. "He told me he couldn't work this by himself." He grinned broadly and clapped a friendly arm around Ivan's shoulder. "Which isn't surprising." He faced Atcho. "I'm a little insulted you didn't call me yourself."

"You live in Florida."

"I know, and only for that reason, I'll let it pass."

"Are these our regulars?" Atcho asked.

"Of course, our men from Brigade 2506, veterans of the Bay of Pigs."

"Rafael is read in," Ivan interrupted. "We've got thirty men on our left flank and another thirty on our right. All are equipped with night-vision goggles. They're combing the ground and working their way toward us."

"Do they know not to touch the suitcase if they find it?"

"They do. They're equipped with radios on frequencies that will be allowed through the jammers, and they'll call in the location when they find anything. Then you'll go do your thing."

Atcho shook his head in disbelief. He cast a glance at Rafael. "Sixty men. How did they all get here?"

"Some live here. Some flew their own planes and picked up buddies along the way. Others drove hard. Not all are with Brigade 2506, but they're all veterans. They know what they're doing, and they were eager to help the famous Atcho."

"I'm not famous," Atcho muttered, "and don't want to be." Otherwise he was speechless. They walked back outside.

Rafael nudged him. "Shhh. Hear that?"

Atcho listened to silence. "I don't hear anything."

"That's the point. You won't see much either, but they're out there, on the job."

Atcho turned to Ivan, concern in his voice. "Do they know the risk?"

"They do."

43

Klaus watched the news reports for the umpteenth time. He paced impatiently. *I gave Atcho too much time.*

Then a news reporter he had not seen before flashed onto the screen. "This is breaking news. Residents in the vicinity of Mt. Bonnell north of Austin are calling into police with reports of strange goings-on there and in the surrounding neighborhoods. Military vehicles from Camp Mabry have moved into various positions, and prowlers are reported moving about below the houses along the cliffs. The police have not acknowledged the calls. At the station, we know about them from concerned residents calling us after having no police response. As for the military vehicles, I've seen them. They are there, but the Army National Guard refuses to comment."

Burly saw the same news report. He whirled to the FBI chief. "Send the order! Jam all radio stations within five miles of those homes on Mt. Bonnell and cut the cell phone towers. Give me five minutes to call Atcho, then do it."

He hurried to make the call. "Camp Mabry's trucks and the movement of your guys on the cliffs were just reported on the news," he said. "That word will spread like wildfire. Klaus will hear it soon. We've ordered the cell towers to be shut down around Mt. Bonnell and the radio signals to be jammed."

"Will I be able to talk to you?"

"Ivan has a radio for you that will be allowed through the jamming. Just so you know," Burly added, "chatter on the bad guy net is screaming. They're expecting something big—tonight."

Klaus flipped through the stations furiously. He saw no similar reports, so he switched back to the first channel. A news anchor appeared on the screen. "We apologize to our viewers," the young lady said, "we've lost contact with our journalist in the field. He was in the Mt. Bonnell area." She pressed a finger against the tiny earphone, listening. "This just in. A large area around Mt. Bonnell seems to have had a communications outage. We hear from people calling on their landlines that their cell phones are dead, and they get no radio signals. Local authorities offered no information or comment. As we understand, cell towers are out, and radio broadcasts are not being received. We'll stay on the story and keep you informed."

Klaus flipped through the channels again. Bits and pieces of detail taken from other reports confirmed the story. Other news stations sent reporters speeding to the locale.

Klaus paced to the window and looked out, thinking. Then he opened a drawer on his bed stand revealing a small remote-control device. He picked it up and stared at it. He had not anticipated being this close to ground-zero when he detonated.

I'll have to retrieve the bomb. Angrily, he tossed the remote onto the bed. He reached into his coat pocket, pulled out his phone and dialed Atcho's cell number. Putting it to his ear, he listened. No sound. He held it in front of his face and watched a digital progress indicator go around and around as the call was attempted but not completed. Realization dawned. *Atcho is here, in Austin, in his house.*

He threw on his jacket, picked up the cell phone and remote, and stormed out the door. Twenty minutes later, he drove off the Camp Mabry exit from Route 1, MOPAC; he drove past its entrance, and wound his way through the adjacent neighborhoods. On the way in, he saw Army communications vehicles. Four police cars with pulsating blue and red strobe lights surrounded each one. *Jammers.*

Klaus pulled his car next to one of the police cars. "What's going on?"

"We don't know for sure. There's been some kind of radio and cell phone disruption. The Army is trying to sort it out, if that makes any sense."

"Can I go on through? I live up the street."

"Show me your driver's license."

Klaus thanked Allah that his Berlin *hawaladar,* Kadir, had been thorough. He pulled a Texas driver's license from his wallet and handed it to the cop.

"You got anything else showing that's your address?"

Klaus pretended to think. "I have an electric bill in my glove compartment. Will that work?"

"Let me see it."

Moments later, the cop handed back the documents and waved Klaus through. He drove to Mt. Bonnell Drive and took a right turn into a parking spot he had found while scouting the area, hidden behind thick brush near the cliff's edge.

He emerged into darkness and listened. Aside from crickets he heard only the movement of air. He stepped onto the road. Far off to his right, he saw another Army truck surrounded by police security. Another vehicle sat close by. It looked like an ambulance.

He put on his night-vision goggles and started down a path on the river side of the road. After a few yards, he stopped to listen. He heard no sound. Not even crickets, and that bothered him. He was about to start off again when he heard footsteps crunching softly on the narrow dusty trail. He ducked off the path and slid down, prone in the dark. Through his night-goggles, he saw the path clearly in eerie yellowish-green light reflecting from shapes.

The footsteps came closer. A man passed by, obviously weighted down. Another passed, also appearing to carry something heavy. He heard someone moan, a female voice. He raised up for a better view as the two men continued up the path. Between them, they carried a stretcher. *Sofia! I must have hit her with a bullet from the river.*

Acting on furious impulse, he stood and stepped into the path behind the group. He pulled his pistol from his belt and raised it, aiming at the trailing medic. Then he squeezed the trigger. For an excruciating few seconds, he held his sites squarely on the closest man's back. Then, his mind overcame his emotion. *If I shoot, the sound will alert everyone. I'll never get close to Atcho, or the bomb.*

He relaxed his finger and started back down the path. As he went, he became aware of other men up and down the slope from him, proceeding in the same direction. They wore dark clothing and night-goggles, and they moved slowly, checking under crevices and bushes. *They're looking for the bomb.*

He moved with them at a slightly faster pace, counting on the notion that anyone seeing him could not tell him from any of the other men. They would not expect him to be among them.

Tom, the leader of Team One, stood uphill from his men at a vantage where he could observe each one of them. Further downhill, he observed another team leader also keeping account of his men as they inched along the steep slope.

As he watched, a new figure appeared in his night-sights. The man crouched, looking downhill to his front. He remained motionless a few minutes and then stood. In his hand, he carried a pistol.

Tom waited until the man was well away from him, but still in sight. Then he pressed his handset and spoke in a low voice. "We have movement that's not ours. An unknown person came from our rear. He has a gun in his hand. He's moving through our sector faster than we are. I have him in sight."

"Copy," Rafael replied. "Is there another team in front of yours?"

"Negative. We're on the left flank, closing into the area below the target house."

"Roger. I'll advise the other teams. Keep him in sight, even if it means leaving your team behind. Tell your men to keep doing what they're doing. Report if he appears to have reached an objective."

Rafael relayed the report to Atcho and Ivan. "He's on one of the high trails crossing below your house."

"Is it Klaus?" Ivan asked.

"Don't know. We don't have a means of recognizing him in the dark, but none of our guys are carrying pistols in their hands. This man has his gun out, and he's moving faster than the team is. Sounds like he knows his objective."

"Let's go outside," Atcho cut in. "Maybe we can grab him before he sees us."

"We'll corral from below," Rafael said. He spoke low into his mouthpiece. "All Teams. Be advised, we have a moving subject. Cease the search. Concentrate on the subject. Teams Five and Six on lower sections. Increase pace. Keep spacing between individuals, but head toward center. Teams Three and Four in mid-sections, maintain contact on your left and right. Teams One and Two, maintain contact with your adjacent team. We're forming a semicircle with the house at the center. We'll slowly contract our perimeter on the house. The subject is detached, away from any team. He's moving alone to the center of the search area. Understood?"

He received quiet confirmations. "Team One, do you still have him in sight?"

"Affirmative. He's on the edge of the property now, about twenty-five yards down on your right. He's stopped, looking around."

"Roger. Don't get too close. We want him to lead us straight to the suitcase."

"Wilco. Out."

Klaus' instincts told him that he might have walked into a trap. His progress had been slowed by rough rocks and brush. From his current position, he saw water glimmering a hundred meters below. Standing very still, he heard scrapes in the rocks and rustling bushes that could not be explained by movement of wild animals or wind. He perceived that many men were spread below him, at least to his rear.

He looked downhill to his front and caught sight of an arm and then a leg moving toward him many meters below. At the same time, he heard bushes rustling above him, also to his front. A clear picture formed in his mind. *They're coming into the center from both directions.*

He turned all the way around, trying to pierce beyond the limits of his goggles. The ghostly shapes that appeared were difficult to make out, and the noise of his movement masked any other sounds. *Better hurry.*

"He's moving again," Tom said into his radio. "He's heading downhill away from me in a southwesterly direction. He's going faster now. If he keeps that direction, he'll run into Team Four, but there is still some distance between them. He might not have heard them yet."

"Keep him in sight," Rafael said. "We're coming your way. We'll stay above and behind you."

Silence descended again, broken only by occasional rolling rocks, broken branches, or the rush of the river. Tom felt his pulse revving, adrenaline coursing through his body. He took a deep breath to calm himself. Behind him, his men moved closer together on a gently curving line extending ahead of him down the slope.

He spoke into his radio again. "He's stopped."

Klaus slid to the downhill side of a scrub-oak where he could not be seen by anyone on his back-trail. He scanned through his goggles down the slope from his left to his right. He thought he saw movement downhill and shifted his view slightly, away from the spot and saw it again, and then another rush of motion from nearby to his left. They appeared to move toward him.

His heart drummed. Perspiration poured from his brow. His breathing came in short, involuntary gasps.

Thrusting his pistol in its holster, he stooped and crawled under the scrub-oak. In a shallow depression below a flat rock overhang lay the suitcase, wrapped in heavy plastic. He pulled it out, tore off the plastic and grasped the handle.

He sat in the dark, weighing his options, cursing himself for not positioning a boat at the river's edge. He took a moment to think. *If I can make it to crowds of people, I'll be safe. No one will recognize me.* Two miles south along the river was a shopping area. It was a tourist attraction with a very popular seafood restaurant.

Getting there would not be easy. He would have to cross a nature preserve where he could be the only human there—until the police arrived. Then he would have to decide whether to cross or go around an inlet from the river. But if he could get that far... He headed out.

"This is Team Six. I think we spotted him. It looked like a guy leaning behind a tree or a bush. Then he crouched and disappeared."

"This is Five. We saw him too. He must be about thirty meters above us."

"OK, Five and Six," Rafael said over the radio, "close in on that location. Tighten your teams. Increase the pace. Weapons hot. The guy is armed. He has killed. Teams One, Two, Three, and Four, maintain your current distance from the house but tighten up between each other. Be advised, Teams Five and Six are weapons hot. Five and Six, keep your shots twenty meters below the house." He listened for confirmations.

"This is Team One. He's moving again, but he's changed directions, and he's carrying something. Looks like it could be the suitcase. He's headed uphill now, on a line that would take him past the southwest corner of the house. He's moving fast."

"Team Two," Rafael radioed, "press him from your side, but keep a distance. Now that we know where he is and where he isn't, we'll get the cops to meet him topside. Be advised again that Teams Five and Six have weapons hot. Stay well away from the southwest corner of the house."

"Wilco. Out."

Rafael turned around to Atcho. "He's headed uphill. It looks like he's carrying the bomb. If he stays on course, he'll come up between your house and your neighbor's." He faced Ivan. "Call the cops and get them moving in. I'll manage things down here." He turned to speak to Atcho again. "Where's Atcho? He was standing right there."

"I can guess," Ivan called over his shoulder. "No use going after him. Keep pressing."

Atcho bolted as soon as Rafael turned to Ivan. Without saying a word, he left the other two men and rushed up the slope to a small path leading along the backside of his house. As he reached the far end, he slowed to a walk, all his senses alert, listening for the smallest sounds, watching for movement. He pulled out his pistol, holding it to his front as he crept past the end of his house into the wide space separating it from the neighbor's.

He reached the middle of the clearing where he expected that Klaus would crest the bluff. Ducking behind some bushes, he peered down the path through his goggles. Nothing. And then, breaking the stillness, he heard the soft pad of running footsteps coming his way.

He keyed his mike. "Atcho here. I've got him. He's coming straight toward me."

Klaus ran uphill, on a path he had scouted. It came out at the top of the slope on the road between Atcho's house and his neighbor's, about eighty feet away. *If I can get there, I can make it to the woods on the other side of the street and loop back to the river.*

His lungs heaved with the exertion of climbing uphill rapidly and running when the ground permitted. Although not heavy, the bomb was cumbersome, and as he climbed higher, it seemed to weigh more and more. He wished he had thought to put it in a bag like the one he had used in Afghanistan. *A next-generation improvement.*

He saw the crest now, twenty meters ahead. *Almost home.*

He slowed to a walk, alert to any movement. A full moon rose, silhouetting every object along the ridge. He thought of skirting below the neighbor's house, but he had not scouted there, *and I could run right into the team over there.* He continued his climb, breathing heavily.

He saw movement ahead to his left. A bush. It swayed with no wind. He stopped and studied it against the bright moon. A dark, indefinable shape at its base seemed too large, too thick to be the trunk of the scrub-oak. He searched the ground for an alternative route behind the neighbor's house.

Atcho held his breath. The footsteps stopped. He peered through the brush. Below him about twenty feet away, he thought he saw two dark boots. They did not move. Then he saw something with straight lines and a rectangular shape, and it dangled, as if being held. *The bomb.*

The boots turned away from him, and he heard the crack of a twig as one boot lifted and set down in another direction. The second boot followed, and then came the sound of branches sweeping against each other as Klaus plunged into all-out flight, crashing through the foliage.

Atcho leaped upright and tore through the slapping vegetation, small branches scraping his face and ripping his clothes. He reached the point where he had seen the boots and suitcase and stopped to listen. To his left, he heard crashing through rocks and shrubs. It stopped, and then started again, heading directly uphill.

Atcho whirled and ran up the path. He reached the top just as Klaus broke into the clearing twenty feet to his right. Atcho aimed his pistol, but Klaus shot first, from a dead run.

A bullet whizzed by. Atcho felt a sting on his earlobe. Blood spattered.

He ignored the pain and the trickle that ran down his neck.

The moon, now higher in the sky, shone radiantly. The light was too bright for the goggles. Atcho tore them off.

Klaus had widened the distance, making straight for the woods across the road. He held the suitcase tightly under his left arm, his right hand gripping his gun.

Atcho darted after him, stopping to fire off a round, but Klaus was beyond effective range. Atcho took off after him again, his breath coming in gasps, but he closed the distance.

Klaus neared the wood line and threw all his reserves into a last sprint.

Atcho thought fleetingly of firing off another shot, but if he missed, Klaus would be in the trees. He burned his last energy in a sprint to catch up and dove at Klaus' feet. His arms wrapped around the ankles, and he held tight.

Klaus went down. He rolled awkwardly and tried to sit up, his arms extended to aim the pistol. He fired, but the angle was too shallow. The bullet hit the ground a foot away from Atcho's torso.

Atcho's arms remained pinned under Klaus' legs, his pistol still in his hand. He could not turn far enough for an effective shot. He pulled the trigger anyway.

Klaus screamed, jerked a leg free, and jammed his foot into Atcho's face. The force slammed Atcho's neck and shoulders backward. He let go of his pistol. It flew yards away.

Klaus kicked again and pulled his other leg free. He struggled to his feet and stood over Atcho panting, the suitcase in one hand, his pistol in the other. He brought the pistol forward to shoot at point-blank range.

Atcho anticipated the move. He swung his right foot around and caught Klaus' ankle from the rear, knocking him off balance.

Klaus' pistol flew into the woods. The suitcase sailed through the air and landed yards away. Klaus recovered his balance. He glanced around quickly, his view landing on Atcho's pistol glinting in the moonlight. Too late. Atcho had already covered half the distance.

From down the street, the wail of sirens rose in volume. Blue and red strobe lights reflected from the ground and trees. Across the street, men shouted as they ran toward the two combatants.

Klaus took in the gathering threat and focused on Atcho who, as if in surreal slow motion, scrambled on his stomach toward the pistol. "Atcho," he called.

Something in Klaus' tone arrested Atcho's progress. He turned.

Klaus stood back a few yards, grinning. He reached into his pocket. When he withdrew it, he held up the remote control. "This close, I don't think those jammers will stop this transmission." He leaned his head back and let loose deep, guttural laughter. "Let's find out." He punched the button.

From a few yards away, a high-pitched electronic tone sounded, emanating from the suitcase. "The bomb is set," Klaus called. "You made me a martyr." He laughed again, evil peals that resonated across the ground. "While you burn in Hell, I'll wave from Paradise." Then he sprinted to the tree line and disappeared into its dark interior.

Atcho stared after him, absorbing the implications. Behind him, he heard running feet and turned to see many men, weapons drawn, heading toward the woods in pursuit.

"Go back," he yelled, leaping to his feet. He waved his arms furiously over his head. "Get out of here. Go!"

Ivan was the first to reach him. He panted heavily.

"Klaus activated the bomb," Atcho roared. "Get everyone as far away as they can go. Tell them to get under something, anything."

He ran to the suitcase, looking for the timer that Veniamin had mentioned protruding through its surface. He saw none. He picked up the bomb and turned it over. There on the right corner nearest the spine, a small electronic display glowed. Atcho stared at it.

Rafael came to his side. "Get out of here," Atcho yelled. "Tell everyone they've got less than four minutes."

Rafael bounded away, running toward the men and the police cars coming his way. He waved his arms and yelled, turning them back to seek shelter over the edge of the bluff.

Atcho set the suitcase down and studied it while watching the seconds click down. He reached into his jacket pocket and removed the small cloth bag containing the NUKEX with its workaround electronics. Too late, he remembered the technician's admonition to wear heavy gloves.

Ivan came to his side. "What else can I do?"

"Get me gloves. There's some on the work bench in the safe-room."

Ivan started at a fast run.

"Ivan," Atcho called after him. Ivan halted. "You've been a true friend. Thanks for everything."

Ivan nodded and took off again.

Atcho looked at the object in his hand. The NUKEX's silvery surface glittered in the moonlight. It fit smoothly in his palm, rounded on the top side to fit the contours of his hand, and flat on the bottom, to be pressed against the bomb. Under his fingers, three buttons protruded. He recalled that the technician said that neither the test-button nor the off-button worked, and he would have only one chance with the button that activated the device. He also remembered that without the extra protection on his hand, the heat from the device improvised from a prototype might be too much to hold before melting the trigger.

He knelt over the suitcase. His ears throbbed from his heartbeat. He drew from memory to recall the orientation of the bomb. "Trigger device at bottom left," he muttered to himself, imagining the metallic tube lying diagonally from corner to corner under the lid. "Nuclear reaction takes place in the lead sphere at top right."

He placed the NUKEX over the bottom left corner of the lid and held it firmly in place. Then he glanced at the timer. It glowed as it continued to count down, passing the three-minute mark.

He pressed the black button. Nothing. He pressed it again. Nothing.

His chest tightened. His heart beat furiously. He took another deep breath. Ten more seconds passed.

Atcho leaned on the NUKEX and pressed the button again. *Did we rewire to the wrong button?* He tried the off-button. Nothing. Desperately, he mashed it again. He felt no reaction. The digital display counted past the two-minute mark.

He tried the remaining button. The lower edge of the device seemed to warm up, but not at a speed to melt anything, and the seconds counted down inexorably.

Atcho leaned back on his haunches and roared his frustration at the night sky. In his mind's eye, he saw a bright flash, then a narrow funnel cloud growing, spreading out into a mushroom while everything about him burned in runaway flames.

He leaned over the suitcase again and mashed all three buttons. Immediately, he heard the NUKEX hum and felt intense heat along the lower edge. He pressed harder while he watched the timer count down past a minute.

The heat spread through the upper surface of the device. At first only noticeable, very quickly it became uncomfortable. Meanwhile, the suitcase began to smolder under the NUKEX, the smell rising, the fumes drying Atcho's nostrils and throat and stinging his eyes. He pressed harder, not daring to ease pressure on the buttons.

He felt a presence at his shoulder, and then another, but he paid them no heed. The counter was nothing more than a blur now, and the burning pain in his hand beyond agony. Still he pressed.

"Atcho, the gloves," Ivan called to him.

"I can't take my hand off," Atcho gasped. "How many more seconds?"

"Thirty," Ivan replied. "If we go, we go together, my friend." He waited beside Atcho, watching, and then started to count down. "Seven, six, five..."

Atcho cried out again and bore down on the NUKEX, tossing his head from side to side in anguish. Mixed with the stench of the burning suitcase and molten metal, he smelled his own burning flesh.

Ivan continued the countdown, "Four, three, two, one."

A pair of hands grasped Atcho's shoulders. "I'm here," Rafael said.

"Zero," Ivan called.

Atcho looked wildly about. Still, he dared not let go of the pressure on the three buttons, pushing with even greater force. He squeezed his eyes shut and roared his torment at the moon.

Ivan jerked Atcho's hand from the NUKEX. "It's okay, Atcho. It's over. You did it. You fried the bomb."

Atcho turned his head, not comprehending what Ivan said. He tried to push back down on the device.

Rafael pulled him back into a sitting position while Ivan slid the bomb and the NUKEX away. Atcho breathed heavily. He looked at his hand, red, swollen, and blistered. "Is this Hell?" He laughed deliriously through the pain as cognizance returned.

"Let's get you to the hospital," Rafael said. "All clear," he announced over the radio. He and Ivan stood Atcho up and held him between them as they headed back toward the house. From down the street, police cars speeded their way, an ambulance behind them, sirens blaring. The men on the bluff ascended back up over its edge.

Atcho watched through bleary eyes. He turned to Ivan. "Sofia?"

"She's fine. She's waiting at the hospital."

Atcho spun drunkenly on Rafael. "What are you still doing here?" he slurred. "You were supposed to get everyone out."

"I did," Rafael replied. He glanced across at Ivan and squeezed Atcho's shoulders. "I should say something like, 'Hey, we're brothers,' but that's too mushy. You know I don't like to be left out."

They guided Atcho past the police cars to the ambulance. "What about Klaus?"

Ivan and Rafael exchanged troubled glances. "The police are searching for him," Ivan replied. He shook his head. "We might have to look for him another day."

EPILOGUE

Klaus crashed through the bushes, searching for anything that would provide shelter from the expected epic blast that would seal his real name, Sahab Kadyrov, among the legion of martyred heroes in the annals of Islam. That was a thrilling thought, although he regretted leaving this life. There was something about breathing, the pulse of blood and his beating heart, and the strain of running through the forest that he found exhilarating. His life had been difficult, but much of the challenge he relished. *And they'll be writing songs about me in Mecca.*

He stumbled in his flight. He had lost his night-goggles during the melee with Atcho, so all he saw were silhouettes when shafts of the bright moon filtered through the canopy of trees. He tripped over a log. On recovering, he sensed that it might be large enough to provide at least a modicum of protection from the flash flame and searing heat of thousands of degrees that would be the least of what he could expect upon detonation.

He had heard Atcho calling to the search party and the police to go back and seek shelter, and as he lay down alongside the log, he grinned. *There will be many dead infidels tonight.* He guessed that Atcho might have tossed the suitcase over the cliffs. If that happened, then Austin would be smothered in radioactive dirt from the mother of all shape charges. In that case, the notion of surviving behind the log was not farfetched, although the aftereffects of burns and exposure to radiation were not pleasant to imagine. *Either way, I'll be a martyr.*

He looked at his watch. *Should be any second.* He buried his face between his arms. A minute went by. Then another. In the distance, he heard the wail of sirens, and realized that there would be no martyrdom for him this night.

More minutes passed, and a new sensation impinged—burning on his left buttock. He remembered screaming when Atcho had fired his pistol and struggling to keep Atcho's wrist from turning for an effective shot. Then Atcho had pulled the trigger.

Klaus sat up in disgust. Obviously, the bomb had not detonated. His brother's death would not yet be avenged. He would have no seventy-two waiting virgins, no celebrations among the worldwide faithful of Islam for the mass of dead and maimed infidels in the greatest strike ever against the Great Satan. All he had to show for his efforts was a seared butt—barely a crease. Worse yet, Atcho and his wife still lived and expected a baby. Klaus climbed to his feet and headed deeper into the forest.

Atcho lay in a hospital bed, his right hand heavily bandaged. Tubes forced oxygen into his nostrils. He lay still. A clear drip-bag fed fluids and pain reliever into his veins.

The nurses had pushed a second bed against Atcho's. Sofia lay with similar tubes protruding from her body, but she had regained consciousness and held Atcho's left hand. Sedatives had reduced the pain of her wound to dull throbbing. Through haggard eyes, she regarded the two men seated at the end of the bed, still dressed in tactical gear, dirty and smelly from the night's events.

"Did you get him?" she asked, her voice faint and hoarse.

Ivan shook his head. "It's a police and FBI matter now. They'll put out an APB and initiate a nationwide search. With any luck he won't get far, but he's smart and experienced."

"No one should underestimate him," Rafael added. "He's learned a lot since Berlin, and now he knows how to penetrate us at home. He came so close."

Burly stepped into the room carrying a bouquet of flowers. "Anyone awake in here?" he whispered. He crossed to Sofia's side and put the flowers on the bed stand.

"Thanks, Burly," she whispered. "They're beautiful."

"How's the baby?"

"Healthy." Sofia smiled and massaged her stomach. "Already impatient..." Her voice trailed off and her eyes closed.

The three men exchanged glances. Ivan and Rafael started to rise, and Burly stepped away from the bed. All three headed softly toward the door.

Sofia's eyes fluttered. "Don't go," she entreated. "It's good to have you here."

"We're all smelly and grimy," Ivan protested.

Sofia smiled. "Like old times."

Ivan and Rafael settled back in their seats. Burly drew another chair close to the bed and sat down. He gestured toward Atcho. "What's the prognosis?"

"Those were deep second-degree burns," Rafael replied. "The doctor said they'll take a while to heal, but he should get back full use of his hand."

"What about Sofia's leg?"

"She'll have scars, but the worst is past. These doctors know their stuff."

"What do you think Klaus will do?" Ivan asked. "Will they catch him?"

Burly shifted in his seat. "I don't know. He's high on the FBI's most-wanted list, but he's proven he can move around undetected. Catching him won't be easy."

"They'd better catch him," Rafael said. "He knows how to get nuclear fuel and put plutonium bombs together. He won't stop, and he still wants Atcho."

"Yeah," Burly sighed. He indicated Atcho with a nod of his head. "He's the guy who knows best how to catch Klaus." He sighed. "Maybe we'll just wait until he wakes up and sic him again."

No one laughed. "Sorry," Burly murmured. "Bad joke."

"Hey Burly," Atcho rasped. Startled, the three men stared. Atcho had not stirred. Sofia turned her head toward him, her eyes half-open.

Atcho's eyes remained closed. "Blow it out your ear."

ACKNOWLEDGMENTS

Writing thrillers full of twists and turns is not difficult—doing so against a backdrop of known historical events is much tougher. The outcome is known. To tell a rapidly paced story that entertains the reader requires detailed research and insertion of elements to raise conflict and add suspense without altering the facts of history. Surprising readers without confusing them or insulting their knowledge of history or procedure is the real art. Then there are the characters....

I'm grateful to the Editors and Beta Readers of Fahrenheit Kuwait for their guidance with the finer points of plot and character, and for their assistance in fighting my natural inclination toward typos: Jennifer McIntyre, Stephanie Parent, John Shephard, Mark Gillespie, Rich Anderson, Paul Smit, Bonita Burroughs, Kevin Clement, Steve Collier, Jerry Warner, Christian Jackson, Anita Paulsen, Margee Harwell, Al Fracker, and friends who cannot be named.

TARGET: NEW YORK

Dedicated to the Victims of Terror

PROLOGUE

Austin, Texas
March 1991

Klaus crashed through the bushes, searching for shelter from the epic blast that would seal his real name, Sahab Kadyrov, among those of the martyred heroes in the annals of Islam. He thrilled at the thought, although he regretted leaving this life. He found exhilarating the feel of breathing, the pulse of blood through his beating heart, and the strain of running through the forest. His life had been difficult, but he had relished much of the challenge. *They'll write songs about me in Mecca.*

He stumbled in his flight. He had lost his night goggles during the melee with Atcho, so he only saw silhouettes where occasional shafts of bright moonlight filtered below the canopy of trees. He tripped over a log. On recovering, he sensed that it might be large enough to provide at least a modicum of protection from the flash flame and searing heat of thousands of degrees that would be the least of what he could expect upon detonation.

He had heard Atcho calling to a search party and police to seek shelter, and as he lay down alongside the log, he grinned. *There will be many dead infidels tonight.*

He guessed that Atcho might have taken the suitcase bomb and tossed it over the cliffs. If that happened, Austin would be smothered in radioactive dirt from the mother of all shaped charges, and the notion of surviving behind the log would not be farfetched, although the after-effects of burns and radiation exposure were not pleasant to imagine. *Either way, I'll be a martyr.*

He looked at his watch. *Should be any second.* He took a deep breath and buried his face in his arms. A minute went by. Then another.

In the distance, he heard the wail of sirens and realized that there would be no martyrdom for him this night. More minutes passed, and a new sensation emerged—burning on his left buttock. He remembered screaming when Atcho had fired his pistol and struggling to keep Atcho's wrist from turning for an effective shot. And then Atcho had pulled the trigger.

Klaus sat up in disgust. Obviously, the bomb had not detonated. His brother's death would not yet be avenged. He would have no seventy-two virgins waiting, no celebrations among the faithful of Islam around the world for the mass of dead and maimed infidels in the greatest strike ever against the Great Satan. All he had to show for his efforts was a seared butt—barely a crease. Worse yet, Atcho and his wife still lived and were expecting a baby. He climbed to his feet and headed deeper into the forest.

Atcho ignored the pain in his badly burned hand, the result of grasping a hot metallic object for too long. He faced the fighters gathered around the conference table at his corporate headquarters. They stank from their search for Klaus and his bomb along the cliffs below Atcho's house last night.

"We can't wait for Klaus to surface again," he said. "He detonated a nuclear bomb. He penetrated the United States. And he hates that I'm still alive. He'll try again."

"What's your plan?" someone asked.

"To hunt him down."

1

Buenos Aires, Argentina
March 17, 1992

A red Ford F-100 pickup truck with a white camper shell rolled east behind a yellow and black Ford Falcon on tree-lined Arroyo in a tranquil neighborhood, heading toward the intersection with Suipacha. The vehicle cut close to the street's edge and parked a few feet from the side entrance of the stately three-story Israeli Embassy. Its tires squealed against the curb, casting off an odor of burnt rubber.

Across the street, those were the last sounds that Father Juan Carlos Brumana heard as he strolled in front of Mater Admirabilis Cathedral toward the adjoining children's school. The blast of two hundred and twenty pounds of high explosives and shrapnel in the back of the pickup hurled a chunk of debris from the church, striking the priest and killing him instantly. It ripped the façade off the embassy and blew through the concrete and marble structure, sending it skyward in a cloud of dust.

The concussive force caught the Ford, heaved it into the air, and shredded it into thousands of unrecognizable pieces that rained to the ground, along with dust and rubble, revealing a gaping emptiness that formerly housed the embassy. The building's rear wall remained upright, still supporting sagging fragments of its corrugated roof. Remnants of the second floor spilled onto the first, bright red splotches identifying where human remains and body parts lay.

The roar of the explosion and its aftermath gave way to moans and cries of agony. Seconds later, wailing sirens joined them as emergency vehicles rushed to the scene. Good Samaritans waded in to rescue those they could, while onlookers formed a wary half-ring at the edge of the debris field.

Among the growing crowd, Klaus watched. He had known the time and place of the attack and had exulted on seeing the truck approach, pull alongside the ceremonial entrance, and disappear in a shock wave of dust and rubble. Now he allowed himself to be jostled aside as police moved in to clear the crowd and make way for rescue teams.

He moved aside to watch for a few minutes and then returned to his hotel to make a call. "It's done," he said. "Where should I go next?"

"Come back here," the deep voice replied. "I'll see you in a couple of days."

Two days later, Klaus climbed the wide stairs into a palatial home on the outskirts of Riyadh, Saudi Arabia. It belonged to Yousef, his *hawaladar,* the man who moved Klaus' money to wherever he needed it on short notice.

"Welcome, *Habibi.*" Yousef greeted him with the traditional exchange of kisses on the cheeks and led him to a seating area in a courtyard amidst swaying palms and tinkling fountains. A boy brought out a brass tray with small, clear glasses and a pot of tea.

"Tell me about the bomb in Buenos Aires," Yousef said, tugging at his traditional white Saudi garb and settling his portly form onto an ornate couch. He tossed his head to move aside the red and white headdress.

"Not much to tell. The operation went like clockwork. The embassy was completely destroyed. Twenty-nine people were killed, including the wives of two Israeli diplomats and two other staff members. Two hundred and forty-two were wounded. I'd call that a success. Thank you for arranging so that I could observe."

Yousef acknowledged his words with a slight head bow. "Let's talk about your next active mission."

Klaus gestured impatiently. "I'm glad to be with Al-Qaeda, but I have my own targets. That was the deal Osama bin Laden promised. I spent most of the last year training his recruits at the camps in Sudan. I'm tired of that. I want to return to action. I have my own money and three nuclear bombs. My name is still Sahab Kadyrov, and I want to strike for Chechnya."

"I know." Yousef nodded despite the slight edge to his voice. "But let's review the deal with Al-Qaeda." He settled his eyes directly on Klaus. "We offered to buy one of your bombs for a particular operation. The agreement included you going to our camps in Sudan to train a team there—and instructing our recruits in advanced military tactics."

Klaus could barely conceal his vehemence. "But that part of the bargain was so I could hand-pick and train my own team for wherever I wanted to use it—and I choose Moscow."

Yousef stirred with a hint of impatience. "I'm your friend. Don't be angry with me. The Soviet Union is history, gone, voted out of existence three months ago. Detonating one of your bombs there would be a waste, and anyway, there is talk that Chechnya will declare its independence from Russia soon."

"Russia." Klaus smirked. "The great northern bear will take only enough time in its cave to lick its wounds. Whoever emerges in the Kremlin as the strong man will not let Chechnya go—it's at the center of too much economic activity that benefits Moscow. We need to strike before anyone there consolidates power."

Yousef took a sip of tea while watching Klaus' face. "I understand, but a bomb in Russia would be wasted. Your goal was to destroy the Soviet Union, but it came down under its own pressure." He reached over and nudged Klaus. "Your higher objective is to spread Islam, is that not so?"

Klaus nodded.

"Let Al-Qaeda help you. Only one superpower remains. After it is brought down, the way will be clear to bring shariah everywhere and mold the Chechnya of your dreams."

Klaus regarded Yousef skeptically. He sat up and leaned forward, and when he spoke, his voice quivered with urgency. "I want to strike for Chechnya now."

Yousef shot him a cryptic smile. "Think of the US nuclear weapons at our disposal. You'll just order Russia to let Chechnya go, and it will have to comply. Can you wait nine months?"

Klaus stared at him in annoyance. "The things I do for Islam," he growled. "What's going on?"

"We're sending you to observe another operation—actually, two of them."

Startled, Klaus nudged Yousef's elbow. "Why? I know how to deliver bombs." He shrugged. "Look, I don't mean to be disrespectful, but I'm a *jihadist*, a son of Islam who proved his worth. I don't have patience for small talk or touring the world. Would you please tell me what you want me to do?"

Yousef cast a somber glance his way and then took a sip of tea. "You are certainly a worthy fighter," he said, "but let's face facts. You have not hit a target successfully. The coup in Moscow failed. The strike in Berlin failed. In Kuwait—"

"I get it." Klaus scowled. "We don't need to go through the history, although, for the record, I was not a principal in the Moscow operation. And you forget that I captured a plutonium bomb complete with fuel, then learned how to make them and get more fuel."

"Granted"—Yousef nodded—"and you're doing an excellent job with our recruits in Sudan. You bring expertise we didn't have." He took another sip of tea. "But that's not your greatest value, and that's not why you joined the *jihad*."

"Exactly." Klaus sipped from his own small glass while gathering his thoughts and then leaned forward again. "Allah put in my hands the means to bring down infidel nations. That's fact, not arrogance. I must live up to the faith bestowed on me."

"I understand and agree." Yousef spoke quietly, firmly. "On the other hand, victory has not yet been yours. We want to determine why. When you strike again, you must succeed."

Klaus leaned back into the couch. "Is Al-Qaeda doubting me?" His eyes burned with frustration.

Yousef waved his hands in a declining motion, then grasped Kraus' elbow. "Not at all. We're trying to help you, and by helping you, we help Islam." He pursed his lips in thought. "What do you think caused your missions to fail?"

Klaus grimaced. "That's easy. Atcho interfered."

Yousef studied Klaus. "He's not a superman. Resourceful, yes. Tenacious, absolutely. But he has no more ability to move about this planet and affect things than you do. He is a private citizen?" He waited for Klaus' nod. "Then how has Atcho managed to be out front each time? If we can determine that, we can limit your exposure so that you reach the target undetected. Does that make sense?"

Reluctantly, Klaus nodded, though his irritation was still evident. "But why did you have me travel all the way to Buenos Aires? That was a Hezbollah operation, and we're Sunni."

Yousef's bulky stomach jiggled under his robes as he chuckled. He shook Klaus' shoulder. "Patience, my brother. We won't win our *jihad* in a day. Hezbollah is not our friend, but it is the enemy of our enemy and will help us destroy the infidel. When that is done, we can settle disputes among Muslims. Meanwhile, Hezbollah will sell us their experience, and they have fought the Jews and their allies for a long time."

Klaus' head jerked up. "You don't call them filthy Jews and godless infidels?"

"Filthy Jews, then, but I don't like to be redundant or get off subject. The point is, we sent you to observe the bombing in Buenos Aires so you could see the operation's successes and failures. We thought maybe you could offer advice or learn something useful from it."

"What's to learn? A guy drives up in a truck and pushes a button."

Yousef frowned. "You're making my point. Planning and executing a mission like that is not so easy. The bombing was revenge for the assassination of Hezbollah Secretary General Sayed Abbas al-Musawi in southern Lebanon by the Israelis back in February. In only a month, Hezbollah conceived, planned, and executed.

"You saw how careful the team was in the South American Tri-Border Region. Hezbollah already has a significant presence there. They have men, equipment, money—they can obtain anything and move it with ease. They knew the embassy's location and the traffic patterns. To this day, the authorities don't know if the driver escaped or was blown up." Yousef paused momentarily, cocking his head to one side. "Let me ask the question again. How did Atcho get ahead of you each time?"

Klaus shook his head. "He's smart, I'll give him that."

"Didn't you tell me that he and his wife were connected to the CIA?"

Klaus nodded.

"Then he had an organization behind him with intelligence capabilities that extended into the army and the FBI. That's why you can't act like a lone wolf. He stopped you in Berlin, Kuwait, and Texas. Walk me through each. We need to figure out how he anticipated your moves."

For the next hour, they pored over the details of the three operations, looking for mistakes Klaus might have made, errant signals he could have broadcast—anything that might have led Atcho and his team to the conclusions that had resulted in Klaus' failures. Finally, Yousef held up a hand.

"Three conclusions stand out to me. In all three places, he knew your objectives and how you intended to achieve them—not down to the fine detail, but enough to guess how you could accomplish them. In Berlin, he knew you wanted to stop the Wall from coming down. In Kuwait, since you were not active during US combat operations, he knew you had moved the bombs to the Middle East and figured out your plan to blow up the oilfields. And in Austin"—he arched his eyebrows—"well, guessing you would come after him at home was not difficult. He knew the nuclear threat you carried in your briefcase, and with that he could get intelligence and logistical support all the way to the president, which he probably did.

"And finally, Atcho knows you—your strengths and weaknesses, your capabilities and habits. Fortunately, you've been out of sight for the last fourteen months, so he must have lost track of you. But if you become visible again…" Yousef leaned forward to emphasize his point. "It is better that you learn new habits and stay invisible."

Klaus, listening quietly while Yousef spoke, now reacted angrily. "He killed my brother. I will have my revenge."

Yousef raised his hands in a placating gesture. "And you will have it. No one will take that away from you. Al-Qaeda promised assistance. But would it not be better to exact your vengeance while killing millions of infidels?"

Stunned, Klaus caught his breath. "Millions? How?"

Yousef leaned in closer. "Listen to me carefully, brother. We have a mission coming up early next year that suits you to perfection. However, it *must* succeed. Since your underground nuclear test in Afghanistan last year, the price of black-market plutonium has skyrocketed. We cannot afford to waste your bombs."

Klaus nodded.

"We want you to observe two more planned bombings." Seeing Klaus react with irritation, Yousef continued, "The emphasis is working in a team, learning new ways to communicate, and keeping operational security. We want you to observe how it's working in other operations." He nudged Klaus. "We are hitting bigger and bigger targets."

Klaus let out a long breath. "If I agree, what then?"

"As I recall, you have three plutonium devices remaining?"

Klaus nodded again.

"We will provide the intelligence, logistics, personnel support, and funds. We have the target. You will place your bombs."

2

"Terrorists have attacked seven times so far this year—and it's only March," Atcho said. "That number doesn't include the attacks Klaus tried to pull off in Kuwait and here in Austin. We know he wasn't involved in the others because he was busy with his own targets. We have to track his location. His bombs make him the most dangerous terrorist on the planet."

"So far he hasn't had a successful attack," Ivan Chekov interjected, "and he's made three attempts."

"That's because Atcho beat him each time," Burly said. "But we can only close him down permanently by getting in front of him—anticipate where he's going next."

The three men sat around a conference room table inside headquarters at Atcho's company, Advance Power-Source Technologies. The company manufactured a battery substitute that was stronger, lighter, and more durable. The product had proven itself in the recent Gulf War in Kuwait to expel Saddam Hussein. As a result, the defense department had doubled its orders and foreign armies were clamoring to purchase it.

A little-known by-product the company produced, the NUKEX, was designed to neutralize briefcase-sized nuclear bombs. The device had low demand but was employed twice.

Atcho's company had developed the NUKEX prior to him purchasing the firm. It worked by generating and projecting intense heat through proprietary alloys to a point several inches below the device itself. The object was to melt the trigger mechanism on small bombs before the radioactive fuel had reached critical mass.

The device's effectiveness was proven, but its operational limitations required it to be applied by hand. Atcho's wife, Sofia, had been the first to use the NUKEX in an operational setting, melting the trigger on a plutonium bomb planted on a cargo plane flying from Novosibirsk, Siberia, to Moscow. Atcho had used a NUKEX to douse a nuclear device planted outside his home, resulting in his badly burned hand.

As he listened to the discussion, Atcho massaged his injured hand. It was healing nicely but still hurt.

He had bought majority ownership of the company two years earlier when its founders had sought second-round financing, selling many of his real estate holdings in Washington, DC, to secure funding. By then, his background was legendary: West Point graduate, native of Cuba, airborne ranger, resistance fighter against Fidel Castro, freed political prisoner, successful entrepreneur, honored by Ronald Reagan... The passage of years had creased the corners of his eyes and mouth and added lines to the strong features of his face. Silver strands streaked his hair. He leaned his muscular frame across the table.

"How do we track Klaus?"

The door opened, and Atcho's wife, Sofia, entered. She moved lithely across the room, her hair falling in dark, lustrous locks that framed sparkling green eyes over a delicate nose and full lips parted in a smile.

"How's the baby?" Atcho asked. *I still catch my breath every time I see her.*

"He's fine." She grinned. "Isabel is watching him, along with your granddaughter." She laughed as she spoke, and her eyes sparkled.

Isabel was Atcho's daughter from his late wife who had died in child-birth. Kidnapped at the age of four and returned while Fidel Castro had held Atcho in prison, she had not known her father again until ten years ago—by then a fully grown woman. She was now visiting Austin with her small daughter while her husband, a US Army officer, traveled to Europe and the Far East on military business.

Atcho laughed. "My six-month-old son and three-year-old grand-daughter playing together. That should be interesting."

"It's fun to watch." Sofia chuckled, then turned to greet the others in the room. "What have I missed?"

"We started discussing how to track Klaus," Burly said, arching his eyebrows as he addressed the group. "Let me point out that because both Sofia and I are officially retired and neither of us is currently contracted with either the CIA or the State Department, our access to classified information is limited to nonexistent. That won't change unless we get one or more of the intelligence agencies on board, and that won't happen unless we come up with something solid."

"I still have my clearances through the company," Atcho said.

"You don't have the designation for sensitive compartmented infor-mation that would keep you current on this case," Burly replied.

"Got it." Atcho had known Burly since they had fought together at the Bay of Pigs in Cuba thirty years ago. In the last two years, they had worked jointly on four black ops in concert with covert agencies. Burly was a big, balding man, proud of his Irish ancestry and his years at the CIA. He had been Atcho's case officer.

Atcho turned to Sofia. "What do you think?"

She had been a covert CIA field officer, her cover being a senior intel-ligence supervisor at the State Department, and she had participated in all four of Atcho's operations with Burly. During a recent cutback in CIA personnel, she had taken an early retirement package in order to raise her baby boy.

She rubbed her forehead. "This one is going to be tough. We might get cooperation from the agencies on an informal basis, but without clearances or a need-to-know, any of their employees giving us classified information would be breaking the law. That could mean prison time for them. Let me think about how to do this."

"While you're thinking, let me add something," Ivan broke in. As a former KGB officer who had defected to the US two years ago, he had risked his life to save his family during a coup attempt in Moscow before the fall of the Soviet Union. Because Ivan was instrumental in averting the conspiracy, the Chairman of the Soviet Communist Party, Mikhail Gorbachev, had allowed him to emigrate with his wife and son to the US. He had worked with Atcho, Burly, and Sofia in their joint operations and won their friendship, loyalty, and respect. When Atcho had bought the company, he had helped Ivan form a security firm and contracted with him for those services.

Watching him, Atcho smiled. Ivan reminded him of a tough, physically fit version of the comedian Bob Newhart. "Go ahead."

Ivan glanced up. He had always been intrigued with and loved American Western lore. To him, Atcho brought to mind Gary Cooper's character in *High Noon*, a man with the cares of the world on his shoulders who could wreak untold destruction at any second. He pursed his lips.

"When the Berlin Wall fell and East Germany opened up, thousands of Stasi officers headed west." He spoke with a perfect Midwestern American accent, courtesy of extensive training. "The Soviet Union is winding down, and the same thing could happen with KGB officers." He shook his head. "Much as I hate to admit it, many of my former colleagues are known for low ethical standards. Between ex-Stasi and ex-KGB, that could mean selling off state secrets and assets to criminals—including nuclear technology and fuel."

"He's right," Sofia added. "With the Soviet breakup, we have high concern about safeguarding nuclear stockpiles. If black-market guys want to buy some, now's the time to put out feelers and bids."

Atcho grimaced. "And Klaus already knows how to get it."

They sat in silence for a few minutes. "Let's start with what we know," Sofia broke in. "Klaus' real name is Sahab Kadyrov. He became known as Klaus after he deserted the KGB and went to East Berlin before the Wall fell. He's a Chechen Muslim who hates the Russians and the Americans as much as he hates Israel." Her gaze bored into Atcho. "He hates you most of all."

Atcho nodded grimly. "That's what I get for killing his brother."

"He managed to get to the Middle East and hook up with Al-Qaeda," Sofia went on. "He brought along five nuclear suitcase bombs and several million dollars he stole from the East German government just before the Wall fell. We think he ran an underground test with one bomb, and we believe he can replicate them. Our best guess is that he still has three of them."

"He escaped both the local police and the FBI here in Austin," Burly chimed in. "We assume either he slipped out of the US or is lying low."

"I think he left the country," Ivan said. "He only brought one bomb into the US. He wants to secure the others and re-set for another target."

The other three nodded.

"How do we find him?" Atcho asked.

"We know he got his bombs into Saudi Arabia," Sofia replied. "That's probably where he hid them. That's a starting point."

"Agreed, but I had another thought," Atcho said. "I'm sure you all heard the report about a car-bomb attack on the Israeli Embassy in Buenos Aires last week. The driver wasn't found, and authorities don't know if he escaped or blew up in the vehicle. The street was empty except for one priest who was killed by flying debris, so there were no eyewitnesses. Israel is the main target of *jihadists*. Maybe we should take a look there."

Burly listened attentively. "I have a few contacts in the Mossad. I'll call. If they don't know about Klaus yet, we should clue them in."

"That's a long shot," Sofia cut in. "Hezbollah claimed credit for the Buenos Aires attack. It's a Shia organization. We think Klaus is Sunni; Al-Qaeda is too. They would compete with Hezbollah."

Burly arched his eyebrows. "Hold on. We can hope things stay that way, but Al-Qaeda is a new organization, while Hezbollah has been around awhile. That guy, Osama bin Laden, brings a lot of cash, and Hezbollah has built up experience and technical skill in their strikes against Israel in Lebanon. If those two groups can agree on who the enemy is, they might help each other. Klaus proved that he can penetrate the US and bring a nuclear bomb with him."

The others eyed Burly grimly.

"Make the call," Atcho said.

3

Tel Aviv, Israel
April 1992

Eitan Chasin hurried down the hall into his boss' office at Mossad headquarters. Tall, slender, and in his early thirties, he was younger than his fresh face and dark hair suggested. He carried a dust-covered open cardboard box with electronic devices and dangling wires protruding from the top, and he scrunched a thin file between the side of his chest and arm.

"Sir, you should look at these."

The head of operations, Jaron Bryk, glanced up from documents he had already been reading, clearly annoyed. "You're new here. I get that. And you came over from the Kidon department. We're impressed. That doesn't mean you can barge into my office at will. I spent time there too."

Eitan fought down an urge to retort. Kidon was the most secret of Mossad's numerous departments. Often characterized in the media as a band of assassins, its operators were posted worldwide to combat terrorism and anyone posing a threat to Israel. Only the best operatives from Israeli special forces were recruited into Kidon.

"You're right. I apologize," he retorted. "You can see these later." He started toward the door. "Don't wait too long."

Bryk caught Eitan's irritation. "Wait." He leaned forward in his seat and waved Eitan to a chair in front of his desk. "I haven't been out of the field long myself. Sorry. This must be urgent."

Eitan crossed the room but remained standing. "It's about last week's bombing in Buenos Aires. I've gone through some of the rubble brought here for analysis. I might have found something." He set the box down on the desk.

Bryk peered at the jumble of electronics and then looked up at Eitan. "That's a little below your pay grade, isn't it? We've already had people take a look at this material."

Eitan sat down. "Have you heard of a terrorist the Americans refer to as Klaus?"

Bryk leaned back, searching his memory. He was approaching middle age as if the concept did not apply to him—full of energy and always ready for the next turn of the screw. His trim build and toned muscles were at odds with the headquarters' collegial air. Despite his current billet, he dressed for the field, ready to hit the streets at any moment. He understood the concept of having experienced operators in leadership positions and the existential need to gather intelligence accurately and analyze effectively. Knowing that, however, did not make coming into the sedate atmosphere any easier.

"Show me what you've got."

Eitan set the box on the desk and took the file from under his arm. "These are the remnants of the embassy's video surveillance machines." He gestured at the wreckage of electronics. "As you can see, they were pretty much destroyed, including the storage cards and backup units. I sent them to our technical geniuses for analysis anyway, and they managed to extract these." He opened the file and spread three blurry photos across the desk. "You can't make out any detail on these, but you can see down the intersecting streets, and we captured the timestamps. Look at this dark blotch. It's located catty-corner from the embassy and down a little way. From there, a person could easily observe the side entrance without being threatened by the bomb, and that blotch looks like it could be a man."

Bryk peered at it. "So?"

"I sent a message to the embassy security personnel—obviously, they're working from a different location. I asked them to check with authorities to see if any other surveillance picked up an image at that time and place. They sent back this."

He moved the spread-out photos aside and showed Bryk an image of a man in profile.

"That's a close-up of the blotch. Look at how he stands backed against the wall and the direction of his view. He's watching the embassy."

Bryk picked up the photo and brought it closer to his eyes. "Light complexion. Curly hair. Heavy mustache. It's not very clear, though. What time was it captured?"

"Two minutes before the blast. He stays there the entire time, and that is not a sightseeing area."

"Maybe he was waiting to be picked up."

Eitan nodded. "Maybe, but look at this." He slid another photo forward. "Here he is among onlookers. He's an able-bodied man, on site at the moment of impact, and he does nothing to help. On the contrary" —he showed Bryk another image—"he walks away."

Bryk studied the photographs a while longer. "Who is Klaus, and what makes you think that's him in the pictures?"

Eitan exposed one more image, this time showing a man whose facial features undeniably resembled those of the subject in the other photos. "This is Klaus. He is a terrorist known to German intelligence and the CIA—a deserter from the old Soviet KGB who trained with the Spetsnaz. He escaped from the East when the Berlin Wall fell. He is confirmed to have participated in three failed bomb attacks."

Bryk shrugged and tossed the photos he was holding back on the desk. "Do you think he triggered the bomb in Buenos Aires?"

Eitan shook his head. "He doesn't come up in any of our monitoring before that event. I think he was there to observe the attack and its effects."

"Trying to improve his craft," Bryk mused. "Pray that he doesn't. If he keeps failing, he can't present much of a threat to us. What's our interest?"

Eitan took a deep breath and let it out slowly. "He's a Chechen and an avowed Muslim. He hates the US and Russia equally, and of course he hates Israel too. His bombs failed because the Americans stopped him before he could detonate—but they were never able to catch him. They put concerted effort on him because"—he took another deep breath—"his bombs are nuclear."

Bryk sat upright in his chair, his attention now fully engaged. He picked up the pictures and studied them again, one by one. "Where is he now?"

"We don't know for sure. We have sightings of someone who looks like him in the Sudan training camps, but no confirmation that he's there."

"How did you come across him?"

"A retired CIA friend was brought in twice to stop this guy. He contacted me about Klaus, who disappeared after each attempt and stayed hidden until the next attack. Klaus almost detonated one in the oil well fires in Kuwait last year, and then in Texas a few weeks later."

Bryk's eyes narrowed. "I heard about that one in Kuwait. Is he part of Hezbollah? They claimed bragging rights for the embassy job."

Eitan sucked in his breath and blew it out. "Well, no. He's Sunni." He watched Bryk's reaction. "We think Klaus is closer to Al-Qaeda, but in fact, he's somewhat of a lone operator. He could be a catalyst for more cooperative action between Hezbollah and Al-Qaeda."

"Hmm." Bryk examined the clearest photo. "The CIA thinks he's the guy in those pictures in Buenos Aires?"

"That's jumping a little ahead. Since the Texas event, the Americans kept up an active search for him, but until this came in, they didn't know where to look, and we didn't know about him." Eitan indicated a few pages stapled together in the file folder. "I've summarized the situation for you in this report."

Bryk scanned the first page. "What do you want us to do?"

"Assign me to the case. Let me meet with my CIA contact. I'll suggest to him that we go together to Buenos Aires to see what we can figure out."

"What specifically are you looking for?"

"We need to understand the tie-ins. The Buenos Aires operation belonged to Hezbollah. If that was Klaus, then he links Al-Qaeda to Hezbollah. Hezbollah's focus is Lebanon, but now they're hitting us in Argentina. That means two things: Hezbollah is going for a global strike capability, and they are moving toward cooperation with Al-Qaeda. That should be worrisome. The two organizations are fierce enemies on opposite sides of the Sunni-Shia split. If they start collaborating..."

Bryk sat forward, disturbed. "What do they bring to each other?"

"As the old saying goes," Eitan said, "'the enemy of my enemy is my friend.' They both seek the destruction of Israel and the US. Al-Qaeda brings lots of money. Hezbollah contributes training and technical experience. They might revert to fighting each other at some point, but between now and then, they can wreak havoc on us and our allies."

"Any chance that Klaus was in Buenos Aires on his own? He seems to offer know-how."

Eitan pursed his lips and shook his head. "I don't see it. For him to be there at the precise moment of the bombing, he had to be informed by Hezbollah. Despite his technical skill, he's a newcomer on the terror scene. He wouldn't have the contacts to know about that hit on his own. A Chechen wouldn't gravitate to Hezbollah because of his Sunni background. Regardless, he has suitcase nukes, and that should worry us."

"Because you think Klaus will eventually make his way to Israel with his bombs?"

"That's a given. My CIA friend thinks he's Al-Qaeda, and he has the ability to devastate us in our homeland."

"If he can get through our defenses."

"Many have."

Bryk eyed Eitan. "I thought your CIA friend was retired. What's he doing in the middle of this?"

"He *is* retired. He was a senior officer and goes active on a contract basis for specific missions. He was on the case for each of Klaus' previous attempts and helped thwart him. This tie-in to Buenos Aires was generated by his own initiative. He knew about the bombing and got curious—

a 'leaving no stone unturned' inquiry. He pointed me in the direction of what to look for."

"Why not let the Mossad teams down there handle it?"

"Because they're concentrating on Argentina and the Muslim population in the Brazil/Argentina/Paraguay border region. This looks like a global thrust, and we're still gathering information. There's no operation on the table yet, and I know the background and parties. Faster ramp-up."

"What about the Sudan connection? Who found Klaus in the training camps?"

"We did, but we haven't confirmed the ID yet. My CIA friend doesn't know about that detail. Since the US is moving toward electronic snooping, with less reliance on boots on the ground, we have more access into Sudan. I sent several of these images to operatives in Kabul, and they located the man we think is Klaus in one of the camps."

Bryk scanned the remaining two pages of the report. "You've been busy. When did you want to leave?"

Eitan grinned. "I have a reservation on El Al for this evening."

Bryk smacked his lips skeptically as his eyes bored into Eitan's. "Keep in mind who you work for. Give up as little information as possible and get all you can." He signaled his approval with a nod and a wave.

Eitan rolled his eyes even as he shot Bryk a thumbs-up on the way out the door.

Burly called Atcho's office on a secure line from an FBI field office outside Washington, DC. "We might have a nibble in Buenos Aires."

"When do we leave?"

"You tell me. You could be gone a while. Do you have someone who can run the company in your absence?"

"He's already on the job. Let's leave tonight."

4

Atcho gazed across the magnificent Iguazú Falls spanning the border between Argentina and Brazil. Tons of water rushing furiously over rugged cliffs on both sides of the river created clouds of spray as far as he could see, their pounding on the surface below filling his ears. The resulting droplets worked their way into his hood and down his back, soaking his shirt despite a heavy rain slicker. He shivered.

Only ten miles to the left of where he stood with Burly and Eitan was the border of Paraguay. "This is gorgeous," he yelled at Eitan over the roar of the falls, "but what are we doing here?"

"Enjoy," Eitan called back. "We're tourists, and we need to look like tourists. Smile, take pictures, look amazed. Point at things. We'll talk later."

Atcho's shoulders slumped. As he turned to view the falls again, he caught Burly's eye and telegraphed his skepticism.

The three men sat in a small hotel in Puerto Iguazú, Argentina, on a veranda away from prying ears. Two hours had passed since their trip to the falls.

"Why are we here?" Atcho asked politely, though his impatience showed. He refrained from glaring at Eitan, who appeared twenty years his junior.

Startled, Eitan shifted his eyes toward Burly. "I thought you wanted to track the man you showed me in the picture."

Burly leaned back and smiled. "Sorry. Atcho flew down from Texas, and I came in from DC. We flew separately from Buenos Aires to the Tri-Border Region. We haven't had a lot of time to talk."

Eitan looked back and forth between Atcho and Burly, his expression inscrutable. "I know some of your background," he said to Atcho. "Burly sent a summary and I went through what's in the public record. He told me some of your training and operational experience. I'm taking his word that you can handle yourself. I should tell you that we are already in the middle of intelligence gathering, and mistakes here could be fatal."

Atcho sat back, feeling chastised but not quite understanding why. "I'm sure you know what you're doing," he said with a tinge of sarcasm, "but we're after a man with powerful weapons intending to lay waste to both of our countries. He specifically threatened me and my family. I don't have time for sightseeing."

Eitan fought down exasperation, but his expression did not change. He turned to Burly. "Are you sure he's up to this?"

Burly froze, and so did Atcho. Burly alternated his view between his two companions. The air suddenly felt thick despite the seasonal chill of approaching winter and the high altitude. "This is my fault," he said. "Atcho is new to working with the Mossad. I should have taken time to explain."

"Then let me enlighten at the outset," Eitan cut in, his voice icy. "We wouldn't be having this conversation here, in this place, if members of the local team hadn't already cleared it. I don't know who they are, and we'll probably never meet, but if we do, we'll use aliases. They are out now, as we speak, gathering the intelligence we need, and they're doing it at personal risk. I'll get a report tomorrow via a dead drop.

"Meanwhile, our job is to get a ground sense of the area. We're tourists, and we'll drink and laugh and act silly, but not so much that we draw attention. While we do that, we'll take in every detail we can. Do you know anything about this place you're in?"

Dumbfounded, Atcho returned Eitan's steady gaze with an unfamiliar feeling of uncertainty. "I-I can't say that I do. I—"

With barely concealed disgust, Eitan cut him off. "Then let me educate you. It's important for you to know what you've wandered into."

Atcho leaned forward. "Go ahead," he said evenly.

Eitan glanced quickly at Burly before addressing Atcho. "This area is called the Tri-Border Region because—"

"That much I know," Atcho said. "It's bounded by Puerto Iguazú in Argentina, Foz do Iguaçu in Brazil, and Ciudad del Este in Paraguay."

"Exactly," Eitan said, his agitation ebbing a bit, "and if not for the borders, the three towns would almost form one good-sized city. This is an area where all three countries are sovereign, but no one rules. Laws are not enforced except as required to protect the tourist trade, and the bad guys will even help out on that when needed, like the mob did in the early days of Las Vegas. The intent is to keep tourists in the dark about nefarious activity.

"This is where Nazi war criminals escaped to after World War II to evade trial, so it has a history. The borders create opportunities and attract illicit activity. Hell, you can walk between the three countries here without carrying papers."

Eitan paused, gathering his thoughts. "Most people can't show you on a map where Paraguay is, but this Tri-Border Region is a big deal. The population is over half a million and growing at boomtown rates. It's a free-trade zone with established banks, but the area is largely lawless, a great environment for terrorist and criminal activity, and when their interests meet, well..." He shrugged. "The Brazilians and Argentines like it because it's a cheap place to buy electronics. The region is a melting pot of cultures, including Portuguese and Spanish, of course, but also Chinese and Korean.

"One of the largest Muslim populations in South America is here too; most are from Lebanon, but a lot are Palestinian. They have their own schools and clubs, and they live in gated communities, so penetrating them is difficult. We have specialists who take care of that. On the Brazilian side are Syrians, Egyptians, and some from other Arabic countries. They are prosperous and influential here.

"We're getting reports of duty-free transactions conducted by both Hezbollah and Hamas. They supply Colombian consumers with cheap products, and the profits fund their terror enterprises." He leaned back and wiped his eyes as if to shut out the scale of what he had described.

"Tourism is big," he continued, "especially with the Iguazú Falls only ten miles away, so the population is always transient. That's the legit side, and the authorities, such as they are, cooperate with the darker elements to ensure an atmosphere that won't turn tourists away.

"On the illegal side, drug smuggling, money laundering, gunrunning, prostitution, human trafficking, and document forgery are everywhere, but most of the money coming into the area is from Lebanese donations —Hezbollah. Paraguay has a weak, corrupt government, and all three countries have poor banking transparency laws. That makes this a perfect place for terrorist and organized crime financial networks to operate undetected, exchange tactical tradecraft, raise and launder money, and cover their trails, with huge sums sent out every day. In fact, we've identified local agents of Al-Qaeda, Hezbollah, Al-Jihad, and al-Muqawama. Iran's active here too."

"I get the picture," Atcho broke in. "What does that have to do with us?"

Eitan inhaled, curbing a retort. "We think this is where the planning and coordination for the attack in Buenos Aires took place. If Klaus had any involvement with it, he would have been inserted into the operation here." He stopped talking, eyeing Atcho in silence.

Atcho leaned back and stretched, looking out at the cold night sky. "I understand. Now, will you tell us what's going on while we're being tourists?"

Eitan smiled wanly. "Burly told me some of your story. I know you came from Cuba, and about your actions at the Bay of Pigs, your years in prison, and the assassination plot you aborted. I know what you did in

Siberia, in Berlin when the Wall came down, and what took place in Kuwait."

"That's great. I know nothing about you."

"I'm not important. What is important is that you understand how Mossad works. We admire your confidence and successes, but if we were to describe them in a word, it would be 'cowboy.'"

Atcho chuckled. "A Cuban cowboy. You wouldn't be the first. My wife accuses me of rushing in where only fools go. In my defense, I didn't get involved with intelligence willingly, and I never sought out a mission. They always seem to find me." He tilted his head in contemplation. "Come to think of it, I did set out on this one deliberately. We have to find and stop Klaus. Get those bombs away from him."

"I'm going to brag on you a bit, Eitan," Burly interrupted. "I think Atcho would feel a lot better knowing your pedigree." He chuckled. "You *do* look a little wet behind the ears." Without waiting for a response, he turned to Atcho. "Are you familiar with the Kidon?"

Atcho shook his head.

"'Kidon' means 'the tip of the spear.' It's the name of the most secretive department of the Mossad. There's a lot of myth mixed in with some truth about foreign operations, assassinations, and the like, but when those activities are ascribed to Mossad, most people don't know that they mean Kidon. To apply for Kidon, a prospective recruit will have been active in the Israeli Defense Forces for many years, culminating in training and serving with the Israeli special forces. Out of the best of those, Kidon takes its few. Eitan is one of those."

Atcho turned to study Eitan while Burly continued.

"Once selected, the new Kidon recruit goes through two years of extensive training on surveillance, counter-surveillance, and hand-to-hand combat more intense than your basic commando. They learn and practice spy craft from every angle, and when finished, they're assigned to teams, mostly operating far from home, and usually for a three-year stretch.

"The Mossad believes that the people at the top must come from field operatives, because only then can they make smart decisions based on first-hand experiences. They know what their people in the field go through.

"Eitan has already done all that. He's assigned to headquarters because it's his turn. My point: he knows what he's doing."

For a few moments, the veranda was quiet. Atcho regarded Eitan with new respect.

"Wow," Eitan quipped, breaking the silence. "I'm impressed." He laughed. "Burly, how much do I owe you for that story? I don't know where you're getting your information and I won't confirm any of it." He turned back to Atcho. "Seriously, our service is charged with gathering intelligence and executing operations to keep our tiny country safe, and we're surrounded by people who openly swear to wipe us off the map. We can't take unnecessary chances. Sometimes, we seem slow and overcautious, but we get the job done, and usually, our people come home."

Atcho held his gaze. "Tip of the spear, huh?" he muttered, then broke into a wry grin. "So, now will you tell me why we're just twiddling our thumbs?"

Eitan laughed. "Fair enough. I'm a guest here during our Mossad team's intel gathering mission. The members know the streets, the personalities, and the locations. For me to insert myself would be the height of arrogance and could prove counterproductive, if not catastrophic, to our undercover guys. We provided them with all the information they needed to find out what we want to know. Tomorrow, they'll give back a data dump of everything they've learned. Specifically, they'll find out if Klaus was here, and why.

"Meanwhile, we acclimate. This region is unlike any other. Not everyone thrives here. More crime of every sort is probably committed here per square mile than any place in the world, including terrorist activity, but because of the tourist trade, the local powerbrokers keep a lid on it. It's a good place for introductions into the underworld."

The next evening, the trio met again on the same secluded veranda. "This is what we know, but it isn't much," Eitan said, opening the conversation.

He pulled out a clear photo of Klaus. "He was here. That's been confirmed. He was seen by two of our operatives and a few of their informants. He was here only a day or two, but he sat in on a couple of the coordinating meetings before the Buenos Aires bombing."

"Do they know where he went from here?" Burly asked.

Eitan shook his head. "Obviously he went to watch the mission, and that's why he was here—strictly to observe. We don't know where he went after that. His presence is significant, though. It's the first known instance of Al-Qaeda and Hezbollah collaborating. And we suspect we know his current location." He put another photo on the table between them. "This was taken at one of the Al-Qaeda training camps in Sudan."

Burly peered at the photograph. It showed a close-up of hooded trainees, their arms stretched between the overhead bars of a combat obstacle course. At the base was a man's uncovered face, observing the trainees. Burly looked closer. "Makes sense," he muttered, "and that looks like him." He lowered the photo. "If Osama bin Laden is looking to Hezbollah for technical know-how, he'd want to approach someone who's already in his own camp. How recent is this photo?"

"Within the past few days. I sent out inquiries right after you contacted me."

Atcho examined the grainy photo. "You're sure it's him?"

"We'll do a final confirmation, but I'm quite certain."

"Get me that verification," Burly said. "With that, I can get a contract with the CIA and bring in more assets. It's been less than two years since I left the last contract, so renewing my clearance should not be an issue."

5

A light blue 1964 Chevrolet Impala navigated through the tight streets and heavy traffic. When it reached the three-lane, one-way Jirón Luis Sánchez Cerro in the Jesús María District, it turned right and headed toward the upscale thoroughfare, San Felipe Avenue.

The driver wiped sweat from his brow. It ran in rivulets, stinging his eyes, but not from summer heat—the windows were closed, and the air-conditioner blasted cold air in his face. His breathing came faster, even spasmodically, as the intersection came into view. He hoped no one noticed that the car hung low over its tires, weighted down as it was with one thousand pounds of dynamite.

He had scouted this area thoroughly but had been unable to find a suitable parking space near his target to accomplish the job, meaning he had to take extreme action. His heart pounded as he turned right onto the high-end thoroughfare. As soon as he rounded the corner, he saw the brand-new headquarters of Frecuencia 2.

The television broadcast company, founded in 1957, was one of the oldest in Lima and had gone through several changes in management, name, and program format. Most recently, it had moved from its original headquarters; and, most dangerously, it had begun transmitting a ninety-second news report that was repeated and updated throughout the day with a longer, more in-depth version in the evening.

Unfortunately, the ownership and management were independently minded people who called the news as they saw it and proffered opinions counter to the cause that the driver served. Further, they had ambitions of becoming the first station to broadcast all across Peru. With their philosophies and supporting actions, that could not be allowed to happen.

The Impala drew nearer to the station. To his right, the driver saw full-color images of the television personalities side-by-side on huge placards lining the front of the building for at least half a block. He passed the side cargo entrance, a place he had discarded as a detonation point because it was far from the organization's heartbeat.

He maneuvered into the right lane. A fountain on his left marked the T-intersection with Olavegoya Avenue. He continued on San Felipe, past the fountain, intersection, and the Frecuencia 2 stars' smiling faces.

When he reached the end of the placards, the curb gave way to a driveway leading into the headquarters' inner confines. This was as close as he would get to the offices where the station management mingled with its talent.

The driver pressed a button to turn on his hazard blinkers and pulled across the driveway. He exited the car, raised the hood, and pretended to make adjustments to wires and hoses on the engine. Moments later, he left the car, crossed San Felipe, backtracked toward the fountain at Olavegoya, turned right, and walked briskly along a row of multi-colored high-rise apartment buildings. Thirty seconds later, he ducked into one of them. Just before the door closed behind him, he reached into his jeans pocket and pushed the button on a small remote control.

The explosion tore off Frecuencia 2's face, shredding the placards, ripping into the depths of the edifice, and sending shockwaves and dust clouds along the streets, stripping leaves off the tall trees in the medians along the avenues. When the noise receded, the dust cleared, and people dared to emerge from their shelters, Frecuencia 2's new headquarters lay in ruin, its news editor and two security guards lying in bloody heaps.

6

Riyadh, Saudi Arabia
One week later

"What did you think about the operation?" Yousef scrutinized Klaus' face, observing a subdued expression of disgust. They were once more sipping tea on the couches in Yousef's courtyard.

"I don't understand why we're working with these people," Klaus retorted. "The *Senderos*." He snorted his disgust. "They are not dedicated. They're infidels. And they leave too much to chance. What was I supposed to learn there? Three people dead—that's all—and the station was back on the air within twelve hours."

Yousef smiled, amused. "My brother, you can be so impatient. I'm glad you had a safe trip back."

"Please, explain. Why are we working with them? They're communists. I escaped Soviet communism. They have no god. They are worse than most infidels."

Yousef chuckled. "We aren't working with them. We are learning from them. We share common enemies and the objective of bringing down the last remaining superpower. Pressures in Washington are growing. What did you learn?"

Klaus sighed. "As I said, the *Senderos* are not dedicated. I watched from the top of a building down the street. I saw the driver park the car across the driveway, open the hood, and fiddle with the engine. Anyone could see the car was weighted down beyond its capacity—it's a wonder the axles or the suspension system didn't break.

"He parked too far for maximum damage, and then he walked away. He's lucky a station guard didn't come out to see why he blocked their driveway. As it was, someone might have seen him and given investigators a description. Has he been caught?"

Yousef leaned back. "I don't know." He sipped his tea. "What would you have done differently?"

Klaus sat up, resting his elbows on his knees, his hands clasped loosely between them. He sighed. "I've thought a lot about that. It's important to control all aspects of the attack right up to the moment of execution. In this case, the driver should have detonated as soon as he parked across that driveway."

"A suicide bombing? You don't want to be a martyr. Why should he?"

"I'll gladly be a martyr for the right target," Klaus retorted. "With my weapons, I won't waste my life on a small-time hit—he only killed three people and didn't even put the station out of business." He shrugged. "There wasn't closed-in parking that could assure the driver's getaway without his being stopped or seen. And he should have used a truck, not a car. If he had broken down on the way to the target, he would have failed the mission."

"You failed. Three times."

Klaus grimaced. "You keep reminding me."

"What would you have done differently on your missions?"

Klaus took a deep breath. "Day and night, I think about that." He tilted his head to look at Yousef. "In Texas, I should have detonated as soon as I knew Sofia was in the house. If I had done that, Austin would be a wasteland, the entire Colorado River below Lake Austin would be contaminated, and Atcho would be a widower grieving not only his wife but also his unborn child. By waiting, I left him time to figure out what I was doing and take counter-action."

He looked down at his hands and shook his head. "In Kuwait, I should have sent in suicide bombers—I could have been one myself. I missed that opportunity." He looked up again and made eye contact. "I let my desire for revenge get the best of me."

Yousef pursed his lips and nodded somberly. "And in Berlin?"

Klaus smirked. "I was an underling then, but that's where I learned the lesson of staying in control. I set the bomb, but the Russian general held the remote two miles away. We should have detonated as soon as I was a safe distance from the blast area. If we had, the Wall would still be there, East Berlin would still rule East Germany—"

"And that Russian general might have made the Soviet Union stronger and able to survive," Yousef said. He gripped Klaus' shoulder. "Don't trouble yourself, *habibi*. Allah's will was done. You learned from those experiences—and more importantly, you brought us the bombs."

The phone rang in the basement lounge of Atcho and Sofia's house on the bluffs overlooking Lake Austin. Atcho looked up from playing on the floor with his ten-month-old son, Jameson, and his nearly four-year-old granddaughter, Kattrina.

Sofia, sitting on a sofa with Atcho's daughter, Isabel, answered. "It's Burly," she said after a moment, and handed him the receiver.

Atcho arched his brow. "What's up, Burly?"

"Can you get to a secure line? We had a sighting. We need a teleconference."

"Give me two hours. Can I bring Sofia along?"

"We'll need her insights."

Two hours later, Atcho and Sofia sat in a secure conference room inside the FBI's Austin field office. He called Burly on a speakerphone over a classified line to an office in the Old Executive Building within the White House compound.

"I've got Eitan on the line at Mossad headquarters," Burly said as soon as contact was made. "This is a difficult connection, so we'll skip niceties. Eitan, I have Atcho and Sofia on the speakerphone." He gave a quick summary of Sofia's background. "Based on what we learned on our trip to

Argentina, I've accessed CIA resources. I'm under contract again. Both Atcho and Sofia are cleared. Since we're chasing a nuclear threat, interest here goes all the way to the top. Tell us what you've got."

"Greetings from Israel," Eitan enthused. "And Sofia, congratulations on the baby. Atcho told me about him in Argentina." They heard rustling papers, and then Eitan continued in a serious tone. "I called about last week's bombing in Lima. The Shining Path terrorist group claimed responsibility. The Spanish term for the group is *Sendero Luminoso.* They call it *Senderos* for short.

"They hit a television station that was growing rapidly in influence, killing a news editor and two security guards. That's tragic, but beyond the deaths, their success was marginal. The station was back up within twelve hours."

"Excuse me," Sofia broke in. "The *Senderos* are a communist group. What do they have to do with Islamic terrorism?"

"We asked the same question," Eitan said. "It's an interesting turn of events. We saw evidence of Al-Qaeda cooperating with Hezbollah in Buenos Aires, and now with the *Senderos* in Peru? It's an open question, but when you see what I have to show you, you'll know it's a question we have to pursue. Did you look at the pictures I sent?"

"I saw them. They looked like they could be Klaus," Atcho said. "I'm not certain."

"No problem," Eitan said. "I only sent two for ease of transmission, but all of them were time- and date-stamped just before the bombing took place. Klaus took a walk south along the sidewalk in front of the television station. He crossed the street just past the driveway where the car had parked, then headed east on Olavegoya and entered the closest apartment building. It was out of the blast area. Fortunately, the station's surveillance cameras' storage devices survived, and we were able to extract these and others. Klaus seems not to be much aware of the electronic surveillance capability. One of the pics captured a long shot down Olavegoya and caught him on the roof. We had to magnify it considerably and it came out grainy, but it's him, and he's watching the TV station."

"Do you have any other confirmation?" Burly asked.

"From our undercover guys," Eitan replied. "Based on these photos, we had them pinning down whether he was in the area and why."

"What did you get?"

"Not much. He flew in, stayed a few days, and flew out shortly after the bombing. The Shining Path guys didn't like him much. They described him as aloof—like he thought he was better than them."

Eitan smirked. "That's the Muslim-among-infidels coming out in him. Where did he go?"

"We don't know. He didn't fly on a commercial carrier. At least not from Lima. He didn't arrive that way either. We're checking private flights, but so far nothing. Keep in mind that crossing borders in Latin America is easy. He could have driven anywhere and then taken a commercial or private flight."

"What's your take on his cooperation with Hezbollah and the *Senderos*?"

"If I may," Sofia cut in, "this is from a purely analytical point of view. We know he's a hero within Al-Qaeda, meaning he's firmly ensconced with them. He might like to be a lone wolf, but they provide financial and logistical support he can only dream of on his own. They're moving him around. That's why he enters and leaves countries at will.

"He's a fighter and wants to be in the thick of things. He wouldn't choose to be an observer of his own accord. That's against his instincts. Since that's what he did, Al-Qaeda must be handling him, and he's acquiescing. The question is: what are they up to? Is he the guy forging relations with these other entities? Is he advising these groups? Or, is he scouting out or learning techniques for a mission of his own, sponsored by Al-Qaeda in cooperation with another group? We need to figure that out."

"You zeroed in on those fast," Eitan said in an admiring tone. "Those are the same questions our analysts came up with."

Sofia shrugged off the compliment. "Any guesses about where he is or where he'll show up next?"

"I wish. The best we can say right now is that the plot thickens."

Atcho had sat listening quietly to the discussion. The conversation receded to silence, and after a beat, he broke it.

"Eitan, how much presence does your organization have in Lima?"

"Not much. I can't give you exact figures, but there's no organization in Peru that threatens Israel, so we monitor through the embassy. We sent a couple of guys up from the Tri-Border Region to ferret out the confirmation on Klaus. They have dual capability to interact as Arabs or Latin Americans."

Atcho thought about that a moment. "So, you already have inroads to *Senderos* in Lima?"

From his right, Atcho felt Sofia fix her stare on him.

"We do," Eitan replied, "but I wouldn't call them extensive."

"What about CIA, Burly? What are its assets in Lima?"

"We've kept active surveillance on *Senderos'* activities. President Fujimori is fighting them hard. He suspended Peru's constitution and its congress last month—he's promised elections to restore constitutional government next year. Meanwhile, he's going after them in force, but they're fighting back."

"Do we have undercover assets there?" Atcho asked. He looked up and met Sofia's eyes; they flashed horror and anger.

"No!" she pronounced before Burly could answer. "You're not going down there. Get that out of your head."

"But—"

"I don't want to hear 'buts.' You have a baby son and a toddler granddaughter who need you, not to mention a wife and daughter who have already had you ripped out of their lives for too long. You can handle this from a distance."

"Honestly, Atcho, I don't know what we have in Lima," Burly interjected cautiously. "I'm sure we have sufficient people there to do anything we need done."

"You didn't have enough to stop the bombing the other day or the one in Buenos Aires," Atcho retorted. He held up a hand to stop Sofia from speaking. "Listen to me. We stopped Klaus three times because we know him—how he thinks, what he can do, and how he does it."

He stopped and returned Sofia's dismayed expression. "We're talking about a nuclear threat. Truck bombs are a poor man's air strike, and they're effective, but so far nothing compared to what they would be if they included a plutonium bomb. I promise that Klaus hasn't given up on hitting the US or getting revenge on me. He was in Lima for a reason, and we need someone on the ground to figure out what he's up to. Who else is better qualified than me?" He chuckled. "I even speak the language."

The conversation descended once again to silence. This time, Burly spoke first.

"Are you thinking of going undercover?"

"That's the plan."

"I'm not sure I can get support for that. You're a private citizen."

"CIA didn't mind using me for bait in Berlin," Atcho countered. "What about Mossad, Eitan?"

While he spoke, Sofia left her seat and circled behind him. She cradled his head with her arms and pressed against his back. "Please don't," she whispered.

Atcho reached up and squeezed her arm.

"We don't even know where Klaus is," Burly interjected.

"That's easy," Atcho replied testily. "He's either in Lima or back in Saudi Arabia, close to his bombs. I suggest you increase surveillance in Lima and get our own guys or Mossad's to act independently of the Saudi government to put eyes on that *hawaladar*, Yousef. We need to know what contact he's had with Klaus."

"Atcho, this is Eitan. I don't know if Mossad would support your mission. It's irregular, and we succeed by being deliberate, leaving nothing to chance. I'll run it up and see what happens."

"You do that. Tell your guys that my neck's in the noose, not theirs." Atcho stood and turned to embrace Sofia. She buried her face in his chest.

"Hear me well, CIA and Mossad," he said into the speaker. "My mind's made up. The only question is, will either of you support me—or not? I leave in two days. Get back to me with a cover story by then, or I'll figure I'm on my own." He reached for the phone and terminated the call.

———————

"Eitan, are you still on the line?" Burly asked.

"I'm here. Atcho's a willful guy."

"He learned that from hiding his identity in Cuba's prisons for nearly two decades, and then being forced to be a sleeper agent in the US for the Soviet KGB for seven years. He had no one to rely on but himself. He's been incredibly effective—"

"I know. I read the CIA dossier on him. Sad what happened to his family. Castro took everything from them. What are you going to do now?"

"I'll raise it upstairs and see what happens. Our president knows him and what he can do, so we have a good shot. What about you?"

"Operating Atcho's way is outside the Mossad's modus operandi, but we're better positioned to support him—our undercover guys are already placed in the Tri-Border Region. They could insert him, but if he trips up, they could be exposed. That could ruin years of asset development in that area. I'll push my boss, but I can't promise anything. Even if I could get it done, it could take a few days, and he leaves in two. We're on the other side of the world. That means he could go within thirty-six hours from now. That doesn't give us much leeway."

"Keep me posted. I'll do the same."

Atcho and Sofia rode home in silence. When they arrived, Isabel had already put the children to bed and sat alone in the ground-floor living room, watching TV. She sensed the tension when they entered.

"I have to speak with Sofia," Atcho told her brusquely. "We'll go downstairs."

In the lounge, Atcho crossed to the entertainment center at the far end of the room and felt along the wall behind it until he found a button. When he pushed it, the console swung away, revealing a room stocked with weapons, ammunition, water, food supplies, and other items required for an emergency.

They stepped in and closed the door, and Sofia whirled on him. "How could you do this again?" Her cheeks flushed with anger and her eyes flashed. "We're in no immediate danger."

"That we know of," Atcho responded, holding his own irritation in check. "We don't know Klaus' location or plans."

"Good point. So, what do we do if he comes here while you're gone?"

Startled, Atcho stared at her, then broke into an involuntary laugh. "Who are you, and what did you do with Sofia?" He reached up and caressed her cheek. "I'd pity Klaus in hand-to-hand combat with you, but I'll read Ivan into the situation and get him to increase security around the house. I'll tell him to put a tail on you when you're out and about. When are Isabel and Kattrina going back home?"

Sofia's expression had morphed to sheepishness. "They leave in a few days. I'll hate to see them go." She reached up with both arms and hugged his neck. "I'll worry about you, and there's not much I can do to help you from here."

Atcho embraced her. "Are you kidding? You've got the biggest job of all—keeping those kids upstairs safe and making sure I have a home to come back to."

He brightened. "My gut tells me I'm yesterday's news to Klaus. He still wants revenge, but he wants his major strike against the US just as much. Otherwise, he wouldn't be tooling around in South America. He's not going to waste another bomb on me—he'll try to get me another way, another time."

7

Eitan hurried into Jaron Bryk's office. Mossad's head of operations looked up with feigned annoyance.

"Do you ever set an appointment, knock, or wait to see if I'm busy?"

"Sorry, sir," Eitan responded while striding across the room with an attitude that belied his apology. "We need fast action." He related his conversation with Burly, Atcho, and Sofia.

Bryk leaned back in his chair, hands clasped behind his head. "If we support Atcho, we could blow some assets. If we don't, this Klaus character could do incredible harm to us. Is there another way?"

Eitan sighed. "Probably, if we had time to ferret out all the risks and planning factors. We don't. Klaus could strike anywhere at any time. We have to find him and get those bombs away from him. Atcho knows his mind and is the best chance we have of getting him soon." He glanced out the window, continuing to think out loud. "The undercover assets in the Tri-Border Region must be protected. What do you propose?"

"That we detach two of our covert guys to insert Atcho. Spanish is his first language, and we can build a cover story that puts him working for Castro—the *Senderos* will like that. I'll go down to run the op…"

Bryk listened intently as Eitan explained his plan. When he had finished, Bryk contemplated a few moments before speaking.

"We'll need a longer-term plan in case Atcho fails. I'll handle that. Before exposing the undercover assets, I'll need minister-level approval and probably the prime minister's too. My boss will have to inform them anyway, since we're talking about a nuclear threat. I'm sure the PM will want to confer with the US, so I'll get a briefing prepared." He shook his head. "We're talking bureaucracy. This could take a few days."

"That might be all the time we have."

"I know." Bryk leaned over his desk, pressing his fingers into his forehead. "Let's do it this way." He lifted his eyes to meet Eitan's. "Fire off a warning order to the case officer in the Tri-Border Region and tell him to extend it to the undercover guys. You go down there ASAP, but don't do anything until you hear from me. I'll get our director to speak with the head of the CIA and tell him our plans and status. Let your counterpart at the CIA know, so he can prepare. What's his name?"

"We call him Burly. Can I pre-position our undercover guys in Lima?"

Bryk took a deep breath. "That's even more risky. They'll have to explain their absence from the Tri-Border Region and their presence in Lima. Can you live with just the warning order until we know when and how they'll link up with Atcho?"

Eitan nodded, his reluctance evident.

"Then go. I'll move things along here as fast as I can." He lifted the phone and punched a button. "Get me an appointment with the boss," he said, then turned back to Eitan. "I'm on it."

8

Two days later, Klaus and Yousef once again settled on the couches in the inner courtyard of Yousef's palatial mansion. A light breeze floated through the palm trees, and the fountains babbled. Yousef's servant hurried away for tea servings.

"We need you to return to Lima." Yousef's face tightened in anticipation of Klaus' reaction. "That's where the next strike will be. We want you to observe again."

Klaus took in the implications, expressionless. "Do you think I'm a trainee?" he said at last. "I know what I'm doing."

"No, no, no." Yousef extended a fleshy hand, palm out, to assuage Klaus' irritation. "You know that part of every successful operation is exploitation—extending the effect. The *Senderos* did that in Lima. They've been in running gun battles with the government all over the city since the attack on the television station. A major crisis is brewing there." He nudged Klaus. "The next attack will be huge. We want to see the effect first-hand." He smiled enigmatically. "Think of it as a rehearsal for a future strike."

Before Klaus could respond, Yousef reverted to a businesslike demeanor. "We have another reason for sending you."

The boy with the tea tray appeared, poured the hot liquid into little glasses, and handed them to Klaus and Yousef. The aroma of mint floated on the vapor.

"You know we've made inroads with Hezbollah in Argentina," Yousef resumed after the boy had retreated.

Klaus acknowledged his words with a nod.

"We want to establish a presence in Peru as well. Islam has been there since 1560, but the Catholic Church persecuted it almost out of existence. The faithful claimed to convert, but they secretly kept Islam alive. It resurrected in 1948 thanks to Palestinians and Lebanese fleeing the Arab-Israeli war. Both Sunni and Shia are there, and we think we can use *Senderos* to recruit Muslims into their cause, and then convert the effort to *jihad*. The organization's leaders have already met you. This will be a second contact. You can stick around awhile afterward."

Klaus, leaning back in his seat, now studied Yousef with steady eyes. "Do I have to stay there?"

"Go in early, watch the big event, and stay a few weeks afterward. Make contact in the Sunni community beforehand and meet with them after the explosion to show solidarity with *Senderos*. We will make good Muslims out of the communists after we kill the Great Satan. You are going to play a big part in that."

Klaus rested his chin on his chest and gazed at Yousef. "Do I have time for a stopover in Texas?"

Yousef frowned. "We would rather not risk the mission. As soon as you return, we will start preparation for your operation. Believe me, it will be worth the wait."

Klaus groused, "You can't tell me anything about it now?"

Yousef shook his head. "I don't know anything about it, but Osama bin Laden sent a personal message to beseech your patience."

Klaus folded his arms across his chest and scowled. "Give me something," he exclaimed. "I've been babysitting at the camps in Sudan for more than a year—most of those recruits are only good for cannon fodder. I didn't join the *jihad* to go on a world tour or watch others carry out operations." His eyes flashed. "You want me to wait until next year for my next mission? Allah give me patience." He looked up at the ceiling and then glared at Yousef. "I have a right to revenge. I'll leave Atcho alone for now, but I want to take care of him personally. Meanwhile, let me send someone to take out his wife and son."

Yousef peered at Klaus, then poured himself another glass of tea and stirred sugar into it. He shifted into a more comfortable position on the couch and fixed his eyes on Klaus again.

"We are not ready for highly visible killings in the US," he said. Then his face broke into a benevolent smile. "The operation has to be clean. No beheadings, no yelling 'Allahu Akbar,' or anything of the sort. If you can make it look like an accident untraceable to us, that would be perfect."

"There was a man in the camps. The Soviets had trained him to spy in Texas. Supposedly he looks, acts, and sounds like a Texan, and he won't hesitate to kill. I want him, and he'll need a team who can watch Sofia at her house."

"Consider it done."

"You'll handle it for me?"

Yousef met Klaus' anxious eyes with a look of benevolence. "If you can hold your impatience in check, that's the least we can do. I will coordinate through Kadir, our friend in Berlin. He is familiar with the parties in Austin and will know how to direct the team. That way we keep the plan as far away from here and Osama as possible."

Klaus stood and looked around the courtyard, taking in the palm fronds swaying in the breeze and listening to the fountains' musical notes. Then he turned back to Yousef. "When do I leave?"

9

Lima, Peru
Late June 1992

Atcho spun on the ball of his right foot in the waning light of dusk, then crouched low, extended his left leg, and swept the feet from under his first assailant. The other attacker grasped at the empty air formerly occupied by Atcho's upper body, lost balance, and fell into his partner. The first one pushed off, leaped to his feet, and stood back in a fighting stance while studying Atcho, who had backed off a safe distance to prepare for the next onslaught. The man remaining on the ground sprang up, and Atcho noted that both were agile and physically fit trained fighters. He looked for an escape route but, seeing none, waited to see which man threatened first.

The attack had occurred within minutes of leaving Jorge Chavez International Airport. Atcho had arrived dressed down and immediately altered his clothing to blend in with the general population. He thought he had done well, but something must have stood out.

Intending to find a cheap room in a downscale place to stay, he had headed toward the town's poorer areas, but was attacked immediately upon entering the edge of a slum. The assailants had chosen a place where foot traffic was light, and their initial assault had driven him into a vacant building, dark and out of sight.

One of the men moved in. The other stood his ground but blocked the exit. Atcho prepared to fight.

As the first man edged in, Atcho half-crouched, ready to deliver a blow.

"Eitan sent us," the man hissed in Spanish. "We're here to help."

Startled, Atcho stared at him while holding his stance. "What?"

"Eitan and Burly sent us. Don't fight. Follow us."

The man straightened and stood watching Atcho. He was tall and lithe with deeply tanned skin, a narrow face, and dark eyes.

"You can call me Jaime," he said, then gestured toward his companion. "You can call him whatever you want to. I call him Danilo." He chuckled. "It means 'God is my judge,' and that keeps him in a sober mindset."

In the half-light, Atcho could see only that Danilo wore loose clothes over a medium build. He said nothing, keeping a wary eye on Atcho.

"We can't talk here," Jaime said. "We'll lead you to a safe house." He grinned. "Look hurt. Stagger a little. Keep a distance, but don't lose us."

Atcho remained silent, still crouched, ready to fight, and keeping a close eye on both men.

"I hear you prefer Glocks," Jaime said. "I'm going to reach to my belt, pull one out with two fingers, and hand it to you. It's fully loaded, and if we don't measure up, you're free to use it." He moved one hand to his side.

"Put it on the ground and back away," Atcho growled.

Jaime complied. Atcho picked up the pistol, checking the magazine and chamber before sliding it in his belt.

"Lead away."

Atcho sat on a wooden chair at an empty table with Jaime and Danilo in the kitchen of a sparsely furnished safe house. A lone clock ticked above a refrigerator humming in the corner. A lightbulb hanging from a bare wire provided the only light. "Why didn't you just come up and talk to me in the street?" Atcho asked. "I wouldn't have attacked."

"We couldn't know that," Jaime said. "You were in a strange city, alone, and as far as you knew, you were on an unsanctioned mission. You had to figure that someone might be watching you, and we had to see it that way too. Fortunately, you walked straight into a part of town where we could make it look like a mugging, and no one was going to interfere."

"From what I've seen of Lima so far, that's easier to do than walk into a safe area."

Jaime nodded. "Sad but true."

Atcho considered Jaime's words. "Are you telling me that I now have support? From whom?"

"Mossad at your service, for what it's worth." Jaime grinned, and Atcho noticed the wild look in his eye. "Out here in the field, we can be crazy. Especially him." He gestured at Danilo.

Atcho scrutinized Danilo. "Does he talk?"

Danilo scowled.

"Sometimes too much," Jaime said with a laugh.

He stood, moved behind Danilo, and clapped him on the shoulder. "You can come out now."

Danilo jumped up, whirled behind Jaime, threw a chokehold around his neck, and jerked his head down.

In a flash, Atcho sprang to his feet, pulled the Glock from his belt, drew back the slider with a metallic click, and trained it on the two men. They looked at him and burst into laughter. Danilo released Jaime's neck and the two shoved off from each other jovially.

For the first time, Danilo spoke. "You can fight *and* use a gun. That's good to know." He extended a hand to Atcho. "In our world, we like to know all we can about anyone we meet, especially if we're supposed to work with them."

Atcho accepted the handshake with uncertainty. "Should I be amused or angry?"

Danilo crossed to the refrigerator. "Sorry. We don't have a lot of time to size people up. You left the US without touching base with either Eitan or your guy Burly. You want a beer?"

Atcho nodded. "One of those two guys was supposed to get back to me with a cover story," he groused. "Neither of them did. I figured I was on my own." He sat back down at the table, and the other two men followed suit.

Danilo slid the cold beers across the table. "They both tried to reach you on your cell phone in Austin, but their calls went straight to voicemail."

"Damn cell phones," Atcho growled. "Austin is in hilly country and reception is spotty. I should have guessed."

"They spoke with your wife on your landline," Jaime cut in. "She couldn't reach you either."

"Regardless, we've never met Burly or Eitan, and don't want to," Danilo said. "I'm sure neither of them uses his real name. Our commo with them comes through our handler in the Tri-Border Region. My cover story is that I'm a *Senderos* fighter willing to cooperate with the Islamists to bring down Fujimori's government.

"Jaime's is that he's Lebanese and a member of Hezbollah. He's here to offer support to *Senderos* and help connect it to the Muslim community. For this mission, he speaks no Spanish and I speak no Arabic, so in public we'll communicate in broken English. By the way, we both speak Spanish and Arabic fluently, and either of us can pass for an Arab or a Spaniard. For this mission, I'm a Peruvian from the far north. We were here a few weeks ago in our aliases and made our way up the *Senderos* chain, so we can get back in without difficulty.

"Our story is that we were both in Cuba for training and brought you back with us. Your cover is that you're a mid-level instructor in guerrilla tactics for the Cuban Army. The tale goes that Castro had come to our site to observe training. He had been impressed with the June 5 bombing in Lima and the running gunfights since then. When Castro heard that I was from Peru and Jaime was from Hezbollah with an interest in Peru, he asked to meet us. You introduced us, and he immediately assigned you to come as his emissary to offer training and tactical assistance."

Atcho sucked in his breath. "That might work. Won't *Senderos* check?"

"Maybe," Jaime chimed in. "We'll use a slow-fast approach. Danilo and I will go in together for a couple of days to re-establish contact. We'll talk about our training in Cuba and meeting Castro and his interest. We'll say you're on your way and talk you up. By the time you arrive, they'll think they know you."

"Why aren't I on scene already? Won't they ask why I didn't come back with you?"

"You're a great son." Jaime chuckled. "You stopped in to see your ailing mother before you came down."

"Are we talking about *Senderos*? They're vicious. They boast about having no regard for human rights and killing anyone who opposes them. They push for social rights, which means Maoist theory. Remember Mao? He choked the Yalu River in China with tens of thousands of dead bodies."

His face grim, Jaime shrugged. "They'll hold you in high esteem because you come from Castro. Either they'll accept your story about caring for your mother, or they'll give up the technical expertise Castro offered by sending you. If they do the latter, they risk offending him. At least, that's what they'll think."

"I'm sure they'll check me out more thoroughly."

Danilo laughed. "They'll do their best, but their capabilities are limited. We'll run interference. On the other hand, if they find you out, the time until your extraction will be unpleasant."

Atcho crossed his arms, blowing air out of puffed-up cheeks while nodding. "Who extracts me?"

"The CIA. This is a cooperative mission. They don't have undercover officers here, but they do have an active presence that can mount a rescue. We don't. We'll walk you through the signaling methods and give you time to study the details of your cover story. That's why your mother's sick, God bless her."

"One thing I'm not clear on yet," Jaime interjected. "What exactly is your objective? Don't tell us anything more than what we need to meet our mission—the less we know, the less we can give up if we're compromised—but make sure you're thorough." He grinned. "And by the way, when you go back to the US, we will never have known or heard of you, and don't want to see you again until after we retire."

Atcho grimaced, then took a moment to consider how best to

respond. "If you hear of a Chechen anywhere around *Senderos*, let me know ASAP. That's critical."

Danilo scraped his chair back, rose to his feet, and disappeared into an adjoining room. He reappeared moments later holding a photo and tossed it on the table in front of Atcho. "Is that him? We got this just before we came after you. We're supposed to be on the lookout for him."

Atcho stared down at Klaus' black-and-white face. "That's him. He's why I'm here. If you see him or find out what he's up to, get to me quick."

The other two men studied the photo. Only the tick-tock of the clock and the hum of the refrigerator broke the silence. Then Jaime slammed a hand down on the table. "Let's talk about how we do this."

10

Austin, Texas
Early July 1992

"Rawley" spoke in rapid Arabic to Kadir in Berlin. "I've contacted the surveillance team. They tell me that Miss Sofia has guests staying with her—another woman and a child."

"Do you know who they are?"

"We're working on it. I'm going over to observe for myself."

"Don't include them. Hitting Atcho's wife will be a sensational news story. We don't want it traced."

Rawley hung up and walked into the convenience store in a strip mall where he had made the phone call. He was a gangly blond with light blue eyes and wore enough Texan attire to look authentic without pressing the point—denims with work boots, an untucked Western shirt with sleeves rolled to the elbows, and a Houston Astros baseball cap.

"Where's the beer?" he called to the clerk in a flawless Texas accent. As he paid for a six-pack of Lone Star, he asked, "Can you give me directions to Mt. Bonnell Road? I need to make a delivery."

Rawley's journey through life to arrive at this point had been long and circuitous. He was born and raised in Afghanistan to a tribe with features that sprang from Alexander the Great's ancient foray there. The iconic general's soldiers had dallied with local women before being among the first great armies brought to heel in that barren land. They left behind a large progeny.

During the Soviet's ill-fated adventure there, Rawley had caught the attention of military intelligence officers, who took note of his looks and cleverness and recruited him as an interpreter. While he was still young and malleable, they sent him to Moscow to train for assignment in Texas. Upon completion, he infiltrated the menial labor ranks of contractors serving NASA's Johnson Space Center south of Houston.

Rawley also trained as an assassin and had been diverted for short-duration operations in other parts of the world. His skill of blending in with Texans and sending treasure troves of space-related secrets back to Moscow had earned him respect within Soviet clandestine services.

With the dissolution of the Soviet Union foreseen by its retreat from global engagement and its withdrawal from Afghanistan, Rawley sought other sponsors. Having strayed from Islam, he made overtures through several mosques in Houston to rejoin the faith and make inroads into Middle Eastern terror groups, pointing out his value as a field operator with a successful background in representing himself as a Texan.

Before long, he caught the attention of both Sunni and Shia organizations and found he could operate as a freelancer, doing jobs for the highest bidder. He did not care to aim his weapons at women and children, but after speaking with Klaus in the Sudan camps and learning of Atcho and Sofia's incursions against Muslims in Berlin and Kuwait, he was happy to oblige.

The convenience store clerk directed him to Mt. Bonnell Road, and Rawley made his way back to his delivery van. He drove to the address he had memorized, Atcho and Sofia's home overlooking Lake Austin. He drove past it, noting the horseshoe driveway lined with mature oaks, the shrubs in front of the house, and the wide expanse of lawn. *If I can find the right place, this should be an easy shot.*

He waited an hour, and then drove past again. This time, he observed two women arrive in a sedan. They parked the car under a *porte-cochère*, exited, and removed two children from the back of the vehicle—a toddler boy and a little girl a year or two older.

Rawley left the neighborhood again, deciding that he had taken enough risk of exposure for one day. Then he thought better of his decision. *I've got to hit the right woman. She's there now.*

He first went to check that his getaway car was undisturbed and had plenty of fuel. Then he drove nineteen miles to Lakeway Airpark. He walked out to the single-engine, red-trimmed Cessna Cardinal he had parked there, opened it, and ran through the pre-flight checklist—twice —to save time later. That done, he retraced his route.

Rawley had considered bringing in a team but decided against it. Doing so would take time. Not only would that increase the odds of discovery, but Kadir had also impressed on him that the hit was urgent. He knew of Sofia's background but felt that, with surprise on his side, he should be able to handle the job on his own.

The sun had begun its slide on the western horizon, meaning he would have to take off illegally from Lakeway—the runway shut down at sunset. But he did not expect to fly far on the first leg—just enough to be out of the immediate search area.

He drove back through the neighborhood, his heart beating faster, his hands sweating. Between houses, he saw the waters of Lake Austin, a widening of the Colorado River forced by a dam farther downstream. He approached the driveway and turned in.

A green-lettered sign on Rawley's van read, "Mt. Bonnell Flowers." He parked so that it was easily seen from the front door. Circling to the back of the van, he removed a bouquet and carried it to the house.

Rawley rang the doorbell and stood back, his hand checking the Beretta 70 in his belt at the small of his back. He heard a female voice call, "I'll get it," and then the door swung open.

As soon as Rawley's van left the neighborhood for the second time, Sofia's phone rang. "This is Ivan. We've seen some unusual activity in your neighborhood. Stay alert."

When Sofia hung up, Isabel asked, "Who was that?"

"Ivan. He's keeping watch while your father's gone."

"Anything to be concerned about?"

"Maybe. His security guys noticed a van that didn't belong circling the neighborhood."

Isabel's expression became fearful. "Is it that serious? The children."

"Exactly. Right now, it's only a heads-up, but there are people who would like to do your father in, and they're not fond of me either. We're taking no chances. Ivan will move his guys in closer, we'll turn on our outside surveillance, and you need to move into the safe room."

Isabel nodded, her eyes wide.

"Good. Get the kids and bring them down. I'll open the room and switch on the security cameras. If the doorbell rings, don't open it. I'll handle that. You make sure the kids are inside the safe room and then close it. Ivan will send someone to the hidden exit at the back corner to take you down the path to a boat on the lake. Got all that?"

When Isabel nodded again, Sofia saw that she was trembling. She cupped Isabel's face in both hands. "It'll be all right," she said, looking into her eyes. "It might be nothing, but if it's something, we have a great team to help us. Ivan is one of the best in security, and all the people who work for him are combat veterans. They love your father. I pity anyone who threatens his daughter, granddaughter, or son."

"What about you?"

Sofia chuckled. "Me too, but they know I can take care of myself. Now go."

Isabel hurried away, and Sofia went to the safe room. There, she turned on all the cameras, checked the monitors, and called Ivan.

"We're set. Have you checked the waterfront?"

"We have, and there's no sign on either side of the lake. Our guys are watching for other team members in the neighborhood, but so far there's nothing suspicious."

"Good. Get that boat over here. We have to get Isabel and the babies out."

"And you?"

"No one's going to push me out of my home. If this is a real threat, we're going to deal with this guy. Did you find out anything more about that van?"

"It has a sign on the side—Mt. Bonnell Flowers. Looks nice, except there is no such flower shop. I checked."

"Keep me posted. I've got to keep Isabel calm. She's not used to this."

"I'll have her taken to my house. Lara would love to see her and the kids."

"Sounds like a plan. If this flower guy comes here, let him get to the door. I'll have my weapon out and my headset on. You'll hear whatever is going on and be able to speak to me."

"That'll work. I'll reposition several men to within yards of your front door. The rest will be on the lookout for accomplices. Our guys will be invisible."

"I think we have all the angles covered. Now it's a waiting game."

As the sun sank in the western sky, Ivan called Sofia again. "We've spotted him. He's headed your way. My guys are in position. We'll notify authorities as soon as he makes his move. There's still no sign of others working with him."

"That's fine, but Ivan, don't mention this to people at the company or to Burly. Do you understand? I don't want Atcho hearing about this."

Ivan sucked in his breath. "You're putting me in an awkward position."

"Humor me. He doesn't need to worry about what's going on here. He's got his hands full, and we can handle this. Where's the boat?"

"It's almost there."

"Tell your man to cut the engines and come in silently. Does he have an electric motor?"

"He's using it now. Take a look at your driveway monitor. Your visitor just turned in."

"I see him." Sofia grabbed a Glock from the gunrack and headed out of the safe room. "Get in there and close it," she told Isabel. Together, they hurried the children into the room. Sofia watched to make sure the entertainment center swung back into place before heading upstairs.

"You're my eyes now," she said to Ivan through her headset.

"We've got him. He parked the van in front of your entrance."

Sofia reached the foyer and unlocked the door. "Tell me when he's on the other side."

"He's taking flowers out of the van now."

Sofia's heartbeat thundered in her ears.

"He's almost at your door. He's reaching for the doorbell."

Sofia took a deep breath and pressed herself against the wall beside the entrance. She jerked involuntarily when the doorbell rang.

"I'll get it," she called out.

"He's taken a step back," Ivan intoned in her ear. "His hand is going to his back. Gun!"

Sofia threw the door open and leveled her pistol in Rawley's face. Simultaneously, two men moved out of the shadows with guns aimed at his chest.

Astonished, Rawley froze, taking in the weapons, his pistol still gripped behind him. He dropped the bouquet and opened his other hand, moving his finger away from the trigger. Then, he lowered his weapon carefully to the ground.

Sofia glared at him, her cheeks crimson with rage. Without a word, she stepped forward and delivered a solid kick to Rawley's groin. He screamed in pain and reached for his crotch, but before he could drop to the ground, Sofia high-kicked and brought her foot crashing down on the side of his face. He dropped, barely conscious.

Sofia grabbed him by the hair and jerked his head up. "Do you know what happens to *jihadis* who die at the hands of a woman?" she hissed in his ear. "No Paradise." She shook his head. "If you come near me or my family again, you're going to find out what that means. Make sure your buddies know it." She thrust his head down onto the concrete and stood over him.

Ivan appeared, walking up the driveway. "The FBI is on the way to pick him up. They'll decide what to do with him."

"Tell them I'll be at the interrogation, and you can cancel the boat."

11

Isabel emerged from the safe room, her eyes wide with uncertainty. The two children clung to her legs.

On seeing his mother, Jameson rushed to her, arms extended upward, begging to be picked up. She scooped him up and buried her face in his neck.

"Is it over?" Isabel asked.

Sofia took a breath to regain her composure. "We got him," she said. "He won't bother us again. I'm sending you home, though. Someone else could show up, and you don't need to be around if that happens."

"Bob's not home yet," Isabel objected.

"Then go stay with a friend." Sofia faced Isabel, placing both hands on her shoulders and meeting her eyes. "You have a child to think about. This place just became dangerous. You need to leave."

"You have a little boy to worry about too," Isabel retorted. She reached up and caressed the toddler's back. "At least let him come with me."

A look of horror crossed Sofia's face at the thought of being separated from her baby. She started to object, but then the germ of an idea formed in her head.

"Let me think about it. Make your travel arrangements. I have to go to the FBI office."

Ivan was still briefing the FBI agents when Sofia arrived at the field office. Above them, a TV monitor showed Rawley sprawled in a chair in an interrogation room.

"He's still recovering from that pounding you gave him." Ivan grinned.

"What do we know about him?" Sofia asked. "Who is he?"

"A bit of a mystery," one of the agents replied. "We already know that he's worked on a maintenance contract at Johnson Space Center for a number of years. We have documentation of a minimal background check that had to be run for that job, but because he was not expected to be in contact with classified material, it was a cursory check looking for criminal activity. He came up clean. He has a record of other jobs before NASA, but when we dug in, we found closed companies, unavailable references... Based on Ivan's briefing of who his target was—you, with your background—we sent a team to his apartment in Houston. They should be there by now."

Sofia looked up at the screen again. Rawley had not moved.

"Let me question him," she said. "There's one piece of information I want."

Startled, the agent raised his palms in protest. "Ma'am, I can't—"

Sofia stepped toward him. "That man just threatened my family," she said tersely. "I want to know—"

Before she could finish her sentence, the phone rang. The agent answered, and when he hung up, he turned to Ivan and Sofia.

"That was the lead investigator in Houston." He gestured toward the monitor. "This guy's careless. As soon as they entered his apartment, they spotted stolen and forged IDs giving access to classified areas of the space center."

Without another word, Sofia strode to the interrogation room door and entered. Surprised, the agent watched her go but did not attempt to stop her.

On hearing the door close, Rawley looked up. Seeing Sofia, he leaned back and grinned. His hands were cuffed to the table in front of him.

"Wow, lady. You sure know how to greet a guy. All I was doing was delivering flowers." He lowered his jaw to his hands and rubbed the spot where Sofia's foot had struck him. "I'm going to love the lawsuit I'm bringing against you and..." He looked around. "Were those FBI guys who brought me in? Deep pockets. That's going to be a great lawsuit." He laughed.

Sofia walked over and yanked his head back. "You attacked my family. You're on video pulling a gun from your belt before I opened the door. Attempted murder. You're going away for a long time.

"Let's talk about your background. You came out of nowhere, got a job at Johnson Space Center, and somehow got all those IDs to access classified areas, then left them on the nightstand in your apartment.

"You're a foreign agent, bud. Your attack on me was a terrorist act." She extended her right hand, palm up, and shoved it near his face. "You just disappeared." She blew air over her hand and splayed her fingers wide. "Like a puff of wind."

Rawley scoffed. "I know my rights."

"I'm sure, but I just gave you your safest option. Another thing we could do is spread the word that you exposed a plot to assassinate me. Who knows what else you might have told us? We could drop you in Moscow, Iraq, or Saudi Arabia. How about Palestine? You don't exist in the United States, so who's going to miss you?"

As she spoke, Rawley visibly stiffened. His expression turned sullen, but he remained silent. Sofia headed toward the exit.

"The first option is only good until that door closes behind me. Then I'll get the word out and prepare your transportation. Do you have a preferred destination?"

She walked deliberately to the door and made a show of opening it.

"Wait." Rawley's voice sounded hollow, desperate. "I'm low on the totem pole. I don't know much."

Sofia stopped. "Don't waste my time. Give me a name."

Five minutes later, Sofia told Rawley, "You're about to be dead to your Islamic masters. Unless you want to be dead for real, I would never let them know you're alive. You're not the type for the martyr thing."

She left the interrogation room and found Ivan. "Kadir sent him— Klaus' *hawaladar* in Berlin." Then she turned to the FBI special agent. "He's all yours."

"I don't understand why you don't just stay with us," Isabel protested. "You're going to fly with us to New York, leave Jameson, and go home?"

"This isn't easy." Sofia sighed. She picked up Jameson and held him close. "I want more than anything to stay home and be a mother. But I want him in a safe place, and you don't need to be handling two small children in airplanes and airports by yourself. But I need to be home. The bad guys could come again."

"Exactly," Isabel retorted, her eyes flashing in exasperation. "You should stay with us, where it's safe."

"No place is safe while Klaus is out there," Sofia replied distantly. "I'm trained for this, and I can't stand by and wait for the threat to reach our doorstep again." She finished packing the car for the trip to the airport.

12

Berlin, Germany
Two days later

Sofia walked off an early morning Lufthansa at Berlin's Tegel "Otto Lilienthal" Airport in the capital of a reunited Germany. She'd last visited the formerly divided city a little over a year ago, shortly after reunification, and wondered now what changes she would see. Certainly, the sense of traveling freely into the former East Berlin would feel strange, and she guessed that international investment and West German largesse had already begun transforming those streets closest to the old Wall site.

Almost as soon as she stepped into the terminal, she saw a grinning Joe Horton, a US Army major and the man she had called to await her arrival. Dressed in his uniform, he commanded respect, and he nudged through the crowd to greet her.

"Little lady," he chortled, his Texas accent cutting through the air. "What brings you back to this side of the lake? Cain't be good, since you came without Atcho or the baby. If it was to see my smilin' face, you're gonna have to take that up with my better half."

Sofia could not help laughing. "Ah, Joe. I've missed you." She hugged him, leaning her face into his chest. "I *wish* I were here only to see your smiling face."

Horton stood back and held her at arm's length. "So, it ain't about a trip to Tahiti? I told Atcho last time we was together that I didn't want anything to do with either of you unless we was all going for rest and relaxation on Tahiti. My wife is lookin' forward to that." He studied Sofia's somber face. "Oh no. Are you here for another one of them clandestine things?" He glanced up at the ceiling in mock vexation. "Figures. I should've guessed when you wouldn't tell me anythin' on the phone. Let's go somewhere where we can talk."

Horton sped a Peugeot through Berlin's streets. "Sorry about this little clunker. Since you're not here on official business, I couldn't get an army sedan to pick you up." He pointed down the street. "You'll get a kick out of seein' somethin' I want to show you."

Ahead, the thoroughfare widened in front of the magnificent Brandenburg Gate. He pulled to the side of the street and parked.

"Ya see, little lady, it's gone. The Wall." He jabbed a finger at her and then himself. "We did it. You and me. We brought it down." He grinned and pointed toward the gate. "Right over there's where you had the temerity to make me an' Atcho wait while you greeted your long-lost family from East Berlin—and me bein' all shot up an' all." He laughed, and then the corners of his eyes creased as they tightened into mock seriousness. "Did you notice how I just threw in that big word, 'temerity?'"

Despite her somber mood, Sofia laughed. "No wonder Atcho loves you so much," she said. "You lift spirits at the worst times." Her eyes misted as her face tightened.

"Don't you start doin' that on me, ma'am," Horton said. "Let's get out and walk around and you can tell me what's eatin' you."

As they walked along the sidewalk toward the gate, Sofia told Horton about Atcho's intent to hunt down Klaus, the sightings in Buenos Aires and Lima, Atcho's trip to Lima, and the attack in Austin. "They sent an assassin to our house," she concluded, her fury palpable.

"Let me guess," Horton said. "Atcho doesn't know you're here, and neither does anyone else."

Sofia wiped her eyes and nodded.

Horton looked up at the gate's tall pillars towering over them and put his hands together as if in prayer. "Hell, little lady. Ain't you ever gonna learn that goin' off on your own ain't never a good idea? You get folks all worked up and worried."

"Don't go there, Joe," Sofia said evenly. "I've done it before, and things worked out." Her face broke into a smile. "Remember, you and I brought down that Wall because I went off on my own."

"Sorry to correct you, Miss Sofia, but that was one time you didn't go off on your own, and you got all shot up too."

"You're making my point."

Horton's eyes widened, and he nodded sharply. "Oh. You're right. Well, what have you got planned this time? I thought you was retired."

"I am, but I need to find that *hawaladar,* Kadir. He's the one who hired Rawley, the hitman who came to my house. As I recall, you and that German police detective, Berger, pressured him to tell you that Klaus had moved his money to Libya."

Horton looked dismayed. "That's true, we did. But you need to understand that things have changed in Berlin. I don't have the same authority. We're not even doing the Flag Tours anymore. There's no East German and West German governments. There's just Germany, and the federal government here is firmly in control." He cocked his head. "You know I'm retirin' in four months. I'm so short now I cain't barely see over the tops of my boots. Are you gonna go and mess that up for me?" He chuckled. "Not that it would matter, but Ziggy might object."

"Ziggy?"

"My wife."

"I never knew her name. Of course I'm not going to mess up your retirement. I'll tell you what I have in mind, and you tell me the boundaries."

"Hell, you already know the boundaries—whatever we can get away with." His face broke into his unique grin.

Sofia laughed. When she had finished describing her idea, Horton scratched the back of his head and scrunched his face.

"If I help you with this, Atcho will skin me alive."

"If you don't, he might do that anyway."

Horton bobbed his head with a blank expression. "That's reasonable. Just so ya know, I'll have to bring in Berger. If all's we need is muscle"—he flexed his right bicep and chuckled—"I can do that, but if we need legal clout, it's his show." His expression morphed into a pout. "I sure miss the old days when we ran this place." He shook his head in fake regret, and then his face brightened. "Berger might want to bring that German intel guy in too."

"Whatever it takes to get the job done. Will either of them object?"

"Doubtful. Remember"—his eyes crinkled in another grin—"you and me, we brung the Wall down. We're heroes. You turn that charm of yours on them, and they'll melt like soft butter on a hot griddle at high noon on a summer day in South Texas. I'll call and get 'em to meet us here."

While they waited below the Brandenburg Gate for Detective Berger and Gerhardt, the German intelligence officer, Sofia contemplated Horton. She was frequently surprised at yet another element of his past or a skill he possessed that neither she nor Atcho had known about. As he was somewhat old to be a major, she had correctly surmised that he had enlisted in the army and later earned a commission as an officer.

His promotion into the officer ranks, however, had come after a nearly full career as an enlisted man, where he'd risen rapidly to sergeant first class. While still a young enlisted soldier, he served several tours with Special Forces in Vietnam, was on loan to the CIA for covert missions, and trained the Montagnards in the Vietnamese highlands. In addition to Vietnam and Germany, he served in Saudi Arabia, Afghanistan, and who knew what other parts of the world. He spoke German and Arabic fluently, with a smattering of Pashto.

Most endearing to Sofia was that he had rescued Atcho out of East Berlin just weeks before the Wall fell. He had then been the team leader for the US Flag Tours, a special intelligence unit of the US Army housed in the former West Berlin. His job was running patrols inside East Berlin to maintain US rights to freedom of movement authorized under the Four-Power Treaty, which had governed Germany post-World War II until reunification a little over a year ago.

Horton then accompanied Atcho on a raid into the dreaded Stasi headquarters on the night the Wall fell. The mission was dangerous and impossible, but they had succeeded and survived, although Horton took a bullet in his leg.

Subsequently, they had gone on a perilous mission to Kuwait. Once again, Horton carried a sense of humor that sometimes seemed ill-suited to the current situation. His humor was generally self-effacing, and he sometimes befuddled his superiors with an air that was simultaneously irreverent and completely respectful. Regardless, they often described him as the man they would most want with them in a foxhole.

"That's his secret," Atcho had once told Sofia. "Horton lulls people into underestimating him, but he's always alert, aware, knows what to do —and is deadly effective. He pulls it off because he's got a big heart, but he spares nothing in meeting his mission. He's a legend within army ranks on both scores."

Sofia noticed that Horton's humor had rubbed off on Atcho, and for that she loved him. Atcho's years in Cuban prisons and living in shadows as a Soviet sleeper agent had left him impenetrably serious, self-reliant, and almost humorless.

Under her nurturing, Atcho's personality had softened, but not his physical capability or skill. Around Horton, he had learned to poke fun and receive it, to joke, and to converse just for the sake of conversation.

She had loved Atcho from their first meeting for his nobility despite the incredible pain he had endured. But pulling him out of his shell so that he could enjoy life had been beyond her. Horton had accomplished that, and she could never thank him enough.

"What are you thinking so hard about?" Horton asked, interrupting her thoughts.

Sofia smiled. "That I'm glad to see you and that you're still here in Berlin."

Horton glared at her. "Don't you go gettin' mushy on me." He grabbed his chest. "My heart cain't take it. Besides, those guys just arrived."

The two men who approached both spoke flawless English with the peculiar German accent that was almost British. Sofia had noticed on a prior mission with Gerhardt that he invariably preferred to use proper grammar, almost never condescending to contractions or colloquialisms. Berger shared no such qualms.

They exchanged pleasantries before Sofia launched into her explanation of the current situation. They expressed concern for Atcho and the family.

"Thanks. We don't know Klaus' plans, but we do know what he's capable of. And he still has those nukes—we think three of them."

"What do you want from us?" Berger asked.

As Sofia told them, the two men exchanged looks of Germanic solemnity. When she had finished, neither spoke for a few moments. Then Gerhardt broke the silence.

"You have no official position here, is that correct?" he asked Sofia.

She nodded. "That's true, but I think we can construe one, and do it in such a way that Major Horton can participate in his official capacity."

Horton's head swung around to her in surprise.

Berger asked, "What do you have in mind?"

"The way I see it, this man Kadir ordered a contract on me from here in Berlin. That makes it a criminal matter in which the Berlin police should have an interest. I was the intended victim, so of course Detective Berger will want to interview me and learn all he can. We know from last year's operation that Kadir is somehow tied in with terrorist groups in the Middle East, but we don't yet know the ins and outs.

"Same with Rawley. He does a good Texas act, but he was born in Afghanistan, has Soviet and Middle Eastern backgrounds, and was contacted for the job by Kadir. That should bring in German intel, and since Rawley is stateside, that brings in US intelligence and Horton. He knows the situation and the players."

The three men listened intently. No one stirred when she finished, each thinking through her analysis.

"Remind me never to be on the opposite side of a situation with her in it," Horton said at last. "On second thought, no need." He tapped his head and smirked. "I'll remember." He glanced back at Sofia. "I'm in. I'll square it with my boss."

"The BND will cooperate," Gerhardt said. "Of that I can assure you."

"We've kept a close eye on Kadir for over a year," Berger said. "We haven't seen him do anything criminal. This might be what we need to reel him in."

"This might be an opportunity to turn him," Sofia added.

Horton regarded her with a smirk. "Like I said, I never want to be on the side opposing you—for any reason."

"I'll set things in motion," Berger said.

13

Lima, Peru
Same day

While Sofia discussed plans with Horton, Berger, and Gerhardt in Berlin, Atcho drummed his fingers on the kitchen table at the safe house in Lima. Danilo eyed him from across the room while Jaime rummaged in the refrigerator.

"Was that run-through good enough?" Atcho asked with a slight edge to his voice. "I didn't come here to sit around for days."

"Don't let impatience get in the way of success," Danilo said.

Atcho held back a retort. "I've been in secret operations in Cuba, Berlin, Siberia, and even Washington, DC. None failed, and none had time for preparations like you're imposing."

"Imposing?" Jaime slammed the refrigerator door and ambled to the table. "I hope we're not imposing." He sat down and scooched his chair forward. "We're trying to keep all of us alive in a sensitive operation. Tell me if I'm wrong: this guy Klaus knows you. He would recognize you and maybe your voice."

Chagrined, Atcho nodded. "Any sign of him?"

Danilo shook his head. "No, but we can't inquire about him. We're not supposed to know he exists." He locked eyes with Atcho. "Let me ask you a question. Did you ever operate undercover in any of these other operations? Were you ever among enemies, passing yourself off as one of them?"

Atcho lowered his eyes to his outstretched feet and shook his head.

"These are not nice people," Danilo said. "They'll cut your heart out and feed it to you in a second. If you hesitate about a single detail of your backup story, or if you say something in a language you're not supposed to know, that could be enough for someone to cut you down. This group is not well-disciplined. The leaders might take a second longer to allow for human frailty, but some of their hot-headed followers will look for any excuse to blow you away—and they would rather apologize for a mistake than ask permission."

"We trained for our roles for two years, and we've been in them for three," Jaime interjected. "If you're found out, we're exposed. That would be bad for Israel. We won't let that happen." He reached across and grasped Atcho's hand. "Listen to me carefully. If we think you're about to do something stupid that will reveal our cover, we'll take you out ourselves."

Atcho looked into two sets of unblinking eyes, then leaned his elbows on the tabletop and rubbed his eyes.

"I hear you loud and clear."

"Good." Jaime grasped Atcho by the shoulder and shook him. "Nothing personal. We like you, but mission comes first."

"I wouldn't have it any other way."

Danilo locked eyes with Atcho. "You're as ready as you can be for a short-notice mission. We just gave you our 'go forward and do great things' graduation speech. We'll take you in tonight."

"Let's go over this one more time before we head in," Jaime said. "Who is Abimael Guzmán?"

"He's the founder and leader of the *Sendero Luminoso*. His fighters refer to him by his *nom de guerre*, *Presidente* Gonzalo. He was a college professor who split off from a sub-group of the Peruvian Communist Party. Lots of young Peruvians joined his classes, drawn by his radical Maoist views. In 1980, he formed the Revolutionary Directorate with both political and military objectives. He sent guerillas into strategic areas of Peru with orders to start an armed conflict, and he set up a military school to teach strategy, tactics, and weaponry."

Atcho continued to recite the history of Gonzalo and the Shining Path, finally ending with, "He's a ruthless man running an equally cruel organization whose followers will kill anyone without blinking."

"In your undercover role, he's a hero you admire," Danilo cut in. "Got that straight?"

Atcho nodded unhappily.

"You could meet Gonzalo tonight," Jaime said. "He asked for an introduction. Be ready. Why are you here?"

"Fidel Castro sent me to offer technical assistance as an expression of solidarity with *Senderos*."

"Have you ever met Castro?"

"Twice. Once in Havana when I helped capture and kill a traitor of the revolution, and once at the training facility where my two companions, Jaime and Danilo, trained. He observed my class and asked to meet them. When I introduced them—"

"What is Jaime's Islamic name?"

"Abdul Kareem, but he prefers to use 'Jaime' in Latin American operations in order not to draw unwanted attention to himself."

"What name do you answer to?"

"Domingo Suarez."

"Who is Atcho?"

"I've never heard of him."

Danilo questioned him on Domingo's place and date of birth, parents' names, number of siblings...

"Why is Jaime here?" Danilo asked. "He's Hezbollah, not a communist."

"But Hezbollah wants to bring down the US. Besides, in economic philosophy, Islamic tribal practices are not far removed from communism, and we share similar strategies and tactics."

"That's good," Jaime broke in. "You said 'we.' That means you've internalized your role. Be sure to lean into your Cuban accent. It adds authenticity." He stood back and looked Atcho over. "Your hair and beard grew out. You look like a Cuban revolutionary." He handed Atcho a well-worn Cuban Army cap and a pair of shaded wire-rimmed glasses. "Wear these. Keep the glasses on. They hide your eyes. If you run into Klaus, they could be the difference between life and death."

At dusk, Danilo parked a battered Volkswagen along a street on Lima's eastern edge, then the three men walked two blocks to a house. Atcho noted dark places along the way where gunmen could hide.

Danilo knocked on the door. They heard movement inside, and then someone uncovered a peephole and peered through.

"Get your weapon out and be ready to hand it over when we go in," Danilo instructed. "Better you give it to them than they find it."

Atcho complied. The door opened, and the three men entered. Inside, three armed guards stood, feet spread apart, rifles held loosely pointed at them, fingers on the triggers.

Atcho watched Jaime and Danilo surrender their weapons to one of the guards, and he followed suit.

Wordlessly, the guard turned, indicated for them to follow, and led them down a dark hall. The remaining two guards trailed them. The lead man opened a door into a medium-sized, poorly lit room and gestured them inside. Furnishings were sparse, but a few chairs were set around the periphery.

"Wait here," he told them in Spanish, then left, closing the door behind him.

Atcho, Jaime, and Danilo sat down. No one spoke. Five minutes passed, and then ten.

Winter air had permeated the room and now seeped through Atcho's clothing. He shivered. The room reminded him of the dank prison cell he had occupied in El Moro in Havana.

The door opened, and three men entered—two of the guards and a third man who bore an air of authority. He stopped inside the entrance to study Atcho, the guards flanking him on either side.

"*Capitan* Domingo?"

When Atcho nodded, the man approached, hand extended.

"I am Carlos Marka, chief of operations for *Senderos*. *Presidente* Gonzalo sends his regrets that he could not stop in tonight. He's busy with the gunfights in the city."

Atcho grasped Marka's hand and shook it. "I'm not here to get in the way."

Marka grunted and glanced at Jaime and Danilo without comment. "We have a technical issue we hope you can help us with. We have an operation coming up, but we have not run one like this before. Are you an explosives expert?"

Atcho steeled himself against a reaction. "I've worked with them, but that's not my area of expertise. I train soldiers in hand-to-hand combat and small arms targeting. Fidel thought that might be most helpful with your city-fighting."

"We're trying to build bigger bombs," Marka growled. "Transporting them safely on these rough roads and ensuring they detonate at the target is a challenge. Would you take a look? I'll have these guards take you to the building site."

"I'll do what I can."

Marka turned to Jaime. "One of your fellow Muslims is on his way to observe the operation. He's overdue, but should arrive within the next few days. If *Capitan* Domingo can't resolve the issue, maybe he can. You might know him. His name is Sahab Kadyrov. He was here to watch the bomb attack last month. He says American intelligence calls him 'Klaus.'"

"Your progress seems slow," Yousef told Klaus over the phone.

"You picked this route and mode of travel," Klaus groused. "I had a weather delay in Algiers, I'm sitting on a long layover in Caracas, and I still have to go through the Tri-Border Region and then overland to Lima. That could take days."

"I know. I apologize. We would have sent you on a private jet, but that is expensive for an observation assignment. The issue we have now is that our friends in Lima have a problem with their latest project. The objective is much larger than the last, and they are hoping you might have expertise to finish it out."

Klaus grimaced, hoping he had correctly deciphered Yousef's words. They conversed with caution in case intelligence monitors were listening to telephone conversations. "I might be able to help, if you can get me there sooner."

"We have a large community in Caracas. Let me see what I can put together. Maybe you can go straight into Lima and avoid the Tri-Border segment. Have you heard from Kadir?"

Klaus' ears perked up. "What's up?"

"Call him, but whatever he says, keep the communication directly between you two and don't mention me. I can't say more."

Annoyed, Klaus hung up and called Kadir. He related Yousef's comments. "Tell me what's going on."

Kadir breathed heavily into the phone. "Our man in Austin disappeared."

"What do you mean he disappeared? How could he disappear?"

"He had the highest recommendation, as you know. On the day he went to complete the job, he called to inform that he was on the way. That is the last we heard from him."

"Did he do what he was supposed to do?"

"We don't know. We sent a local contractor to observe the place. No one was home. It has been empty for days. If he completed his task, he was in and out and did not report back."

Klaus, burning with anger, called Yousef again. "When this project is over," he snapped, "I'll take care of that matter personally."

"I understand," Yousef said in a soothing voice. "You are owed that. Do us a favor, though, and come back here before you take action. We're prepared to brief you on the next project, and it might give you a different perspective—one you'll like."

"Fine," Klaus snapped. "Get me to Lima, and get word to that chief of operations, Carlos Marka, about when I'm supposed to arrive."

14

Kadir controlled his annoyance as he sat alone in an interrogation room at BND headquarters. He was a large man, swarthy, with fleshy facial features and big hands, and he was dressed in a crumpled business suit without a tie. He wiped a hand over his thinning curly dark hair.

Sofia watched him over the closed-circuit television monitor, one arm across her waist, her opposite hand at her mouth. She turned to Horton, standing next to her. "He's upset."

"Let him stay that way a while longer," Gerhardt interjected. "He has no idea why we brought him in. His business associates will wonder where he is. That will be a good thing."

An hour later, Detective Berger arrived. Together with Sofia and Horton, he watched the monitor as Gerhardt entered the room carrying a Styrofoam cup.

"I thought you might like some tea," Gerhardt said.

Kadir scoffed but took the drink and sipped it. "It's barely warm," he said in disgust, setting it back down. "Why am I here?" They both spoke in German.

Gerhardt smiled. "You were a big help last year in tracking down Sahab Kadyrov, otherwise known as Klaus. We want your help again."

Kadir half rose from his seat, obviously angry but also nervous. He glanced around. "You threatened my business," he snapped. "I only told you about a pilot who had recently flown to Greece. You did the rest. I'm done."

"Shut up and sit down," Gerhardt growled. He walked around the table and shoved Kadir into his seat. "You participated in a terrorist act. Don't tell me what you will or won't do."

Watching from the next room, Sofia raised an eyebrow in surprise. Gerhardt always spoke so politely and properly. She had not considered his ability to get rough with detainees. Berger entered the interrogation room and stood over Kadir.

"What is this?" Kadir demanded, his eyes baleful. "I'm a businessman. I don't have time for terrorism." He smirked. "But I wish I did."

"You solicited murder," Berger said.

Kadir's head jerked up. "Are you crazy? My business runs on trust. I can't afford to kill people." He smirked again. "Lucky for you."

Berger leaned down and put his face close to Kadir's. "You're going to help us," he said, "and you'll do it happily. That's my prediction." He straightened up and looked at his watch. "It's lunchtime," he said to Gerhard. "Let's go. I'm hungry."

Anger rising, Kadir stood up. "I'm a German citizen," he stormed. "Charge me or let me go."

Gerhardt pushed him back into his seat. "I'll tell you when you can get up."

"Spend the time thinking about your recent activities," Berger added. "The criminal case will come later. Right now, the BND is concerned with an intelligence matter. Sit there and enjoy your tea. We'll get back to you."

Four hours later, Sofia, Berger, and Gerhardt watched Kadir on the monitor once again. He paced back and forth, periodically glancing at his watch.

Gerhardt re-entered the interrogation room while the others observed.

"You're costing me money," Kadir bellowed. "My customers will wonder where I am and why I'm not responding to them. Tell me what you want."

Bemused, Gerhardt gazed at him. "That's simple. We want you to work for us."

Kadir stared at him. Then his face broke into a grin, and he guffawed. "You want me to spy? Should I get a business card marked 007?" His expression turned sullen. "Let me out of here, now, or the lawsuit against the German government will be epic."

Gerhardt shook his head, exhaled, and gestured toward the overhead surveillance camera. "I think you'll change your mind."

The door opened, and Berger walked in with a set of handcuffs. "Kadir Dogan, you are under arrest for soliciting the murder of Sofia Stahl-Xiquez." He circled around and grabbed Kadir's wrist from behind.

"Forget that," Kadir said, jerking his hand away.

"If you want to add resisting arrest to the charges," Berger said, "go ahead. You might want to consider more carefully, though." He waved at the camera. Moments later, Sofia entered. Astonished, Kadir stared at her.

She stood across the table from him, arms crossed. "We've never met," she said in fluent German, "but I know a lot about you. Rawley gave you up."

The blood drained from Kadir's face. He leaned over the table, eyes fixed on Sofia's face, and offered no further resistance when Berger pulled his wrists behind him and cuffed him. Then he slid into his seat.

"We know you arranged the hit on me," Sofia said. "We know about your connection to Yousef in Saudi Arabia, and his links to Osama bin Laden." Her stern voice gained ferocity. She moved around the table and brought her face close to Kadir's. "Rawley came to kill me at my house. My baby was there." Her eyes burned with rage. "Was Rawley going to kill him too?" She grabbed Kadir's lapels and jerked him forward. "Did you order my baby to be murdered?"

Gerhardt moved behind Sofia and held her by the shoulders. "We have it now," he said gently in English. "Let us do our jobs."

Sofia shoved Kadir away. Berger sat down opposite him.

"If we take you to trial," Berger told Kadir, "we'll win, and you'll be in prison for years. Even if we lose, your associates will wonder how we learned about Rawley and where you've been all day today. Either way, your business is finished, and you could die a slow, painful death.

"Have you ever seen a pig gutted? They start just under the sternum, stick a knife in and pull it down through the stomach. All that stuff comes rolling out, making a squishy mess—and it's worse when you're alive. All the blood." He paused for effect. "Then again, your friends could just slit your throat or behead you."

He watched as sweat beaded across Kadir's brow and ran freely down his face. The man's eyes looked dull, almost trancelike.

Gerhardt sat on the table and grasped Kadir's shoulder. "We're here to help," he said softly. "We don't want to destroy your life or disrupt your business."

Kadir raised his eyes, despair mingling with hope. "What do you want me to do?" he croaked.

"We've arranged for you to be released from the emergency room close to your house. You were brought there after collapsing on the street this morning. You fainted from dehydration after an attack of acute gastroenteritis. You'll go home or to your office and carry on normally. You will willingly inform us of anything and everything that involves terrorist activity that comes your way—and we have a lot of catching up to do on what you already know. You'll volunteer for bugs on your phone, in your house, in your car, and you'll wear a wire whenever we tell you to. You will also wear a tracking device, so we know where you are. If you disappear, we will find you and start the criminal case. Is all of that understood?"

Kadir nodded. "What happened to Rawley?"

"We got him," a new voice responded.

Kadir's head jerked up. He had not noticed the bull of a man enter the room.

"I'm just another intelligence guy at your service," Horton said in fluent Arabic, smiling, "and we own Rawley, just like my German friends own you. He's in a safe place, but the official record will show that he was hit broadside by a drunk driver and didn't survive the accident. It was in all the newspapers. You didn't hear about it?"

"He folded fast," Sofia said.

"He's soft," Horton replied. "He's peripheral to terrorist activity, valuable for moving money and services but not ever getting his hands dirty. He never thought Rawley would get caught and point at him."

He nudged Sofia's shoulder. "What now, little lady? We got this situation tucked in. If Kadir sends someone after you again, we'll sock the guy away somewheres." He squinted, and then laughed. "This could be good for business. If Kadir kept sendin' bad guys, we'd keep catchin' them and puttin' them away."

Sofia smiled through her fatigue. "I haven't thought far enough ahead about what to do next. My main concern was turning this guy into an early warning system. Now we need to get the information that Rawley had about the camps in Sudan. He trained with Klaus in one of them."

Horton's eyes widened and he whistled. "Well ain't you full of surprises. Why didn't you tell Burly?"

"I didn't want him to know what I was up to over here. He'd try to stop me. Maybe you can get the information to him."

"I can do that—and also into the intelligence channels far and wide." Horton turned with a genuinely serious expression. "My advice to you is to go home. Your baby needs you."

Sofia nodded but said nothing.

Horton studied her face. "You listen to me and you listen good. It's like my mama used to say." He chuckled. "Hell, I don't remember anything my mama used to say, but it was good advice, and you should take it."

Sofia laughed in spite of herself. "You used that joke on me a year ago."

"Huh? Oh well, it was still good advice." Horton chuckled again, then grew serious. "Listen to me. Go home. We got things in hand in Berlin, and Atcho knows what he's doing."

He watched her face, which remained expressionless. "I don't know what you got cookin' in that noggin'," he said, 'but whatever it is, let it go." He leaned back, hands on hips, as another thought struck. He peered at her more closely. "Don't you even think about doin' nothin' without me. Tell me what you got goin' on."

Sofia stared into his eyes. "Remember last year when the reporter, Tony Collins, was murdered in Saudi Arabia?"

Horton nodded. "Yep. I was in Collins' room when Atcho found the note leading to the identity of Klaus' contact in Riyadh, Yousef the *hawaladar*."

"We *think* Yousef is Klaus' main contact," Sofia corrected him.

"So now you're gonna get all snippety and accurate with me." Horton grinned. "You win. We haven't proved a connection between Yousef and Klaus." He widened his eyes. "But it's damn close."

"I know. I think it's him too." Sofia took a moment to compose her thoughts. "What I'm seeing is that Klaus is connected to Al-Qaeda through Yousef. Kadir is just a messenger. He moves things under orders or as part of his regular business, but he's not connected as an active participant of Al-Qaeda.

"The reporter saw Klaus and Yousef together in the hotel. That's probably why Klaus killed him. After Klaus met up with Yousef, his 'career' accelerated. He suddenly had Al-Qaeda backing his moves. But I don't think he's been around long enough to be fully trusted at the highest levels. He's still a maverick."

"I'm intrigued." Horton grinned. "Did ya see how I used that word—'intrigued?' So, where are you headed with this?"

"If we're going to stop Klaus for good—get his bombs and stop him from coming after Atcho and my family—we've got to isolate him. Cut him off from his support. We need to find out where he's keeping his personal money and close down his access to it, and we have to separate him from Al-Qaeda."

Horton pulled back and whistled, looking at the sky in disbelief. "Lady, you sure don't dream small. Just how are you fixin' to pull all that off?"

"I'll need your help and Burly's, and we have to go to Saudi Arabia."

"Ain't you forgettin' one thing?"

"No," Sofia replied. "We still have to recover three nuclear bombs."

15

"Were you able to help those guys with the explosives?" Danilo asked.

"No. I had to maneuver fast to keep my credibility," Atcho replied. "I taught them some street tactics. Nothing fancy, just things they weren't doing, like using rendezvous points and maneuvering at night without losing anyone." He shook his head. "I worry about the good guys who will die because of what I showed the bad guys."

"You can't think about that. Did you get a good look at the bomb?"

"Two. Big trucks. Big bombs."

"We'll get word back through our contact in the Tri-Border Region," Jaime interjected. "Did you get an idea when or where they'll detonate?"

Atcho shook his head. "They've got the technical issue with the bombs and they're waiting for Klaus to get here, hoping he'll resolve it. Meanwhile, they're happy to keep up the gunfights in the streets. I tried to get close enough to do some damage, but once I convinced them of my limited knowledge on explosives, they wouldn't let me near them again."

"And they don't know when Klaus will arrive?"

Atcho shook his head. "He was held up by weather and missed his flight connections."

"So, we don't know when to watch out for him."

"We do," Atcho countered. "All the time."

Jaime raised an eyebrow and pursed his lips, then nodded. "We're going to have to destroy those bombs."

"I'll go in again this afternoon," Atcho said. "I promised to teach some techniques in hand-to-hand combat."

"We'll come along for the camaraderie." Jaime laughed at the irony. "Maybe we can damage it." They put their heads together over the kitchen table to brainstorm.

———

Two hours later, the three returned to the house at the edge of Lima. On entering, they noticed an air of expectancy, an energy not previously present. The guards exuded enthusiasm.

"Why the excitement?" Danilo asked one of them.

"The Al-Qaeda man," he replied. "He arrived last night and fixed the bombs."

Instinctively, Atcho reached up, touched his darkened wire-rimmed glasses, and pulled his service cap as low as possible on his forehead. His hair had grown below his ears and his beard hid most of his face. He slumped and walked with a lumbering gait.

"Marka wants to watch your hand-to-hand combat class," the guard said, leading the way. "He said he might stop in to observe. Right now, he's working with the bombs."

———

When Atcho started the class, Jaime and Danilo hung around until the guards returned to the front and then ducked out. They moved quickly through the house and grounds, not concerned about being seen—they had been around enough to be recognized as friends of the *Senderos'* cause. They noticed that the headquarters, usually teeming with people, was almost empty.

Atcho had given them directions to the garage where he had seen trucks loaded with bombs, but when they entered, it was empty. They quickly retraced their steps and headed off in a different direction.

The house, though narrow, was three stories high. *Senderos* had taken over several adjacent buildings, including the garages. Jaime and Danilo pressed through the buildings, searching unobtrusively, but found nothing. The backyards were tiny but opened into a wide field that stretched far into the distance and was used for training. It too was empty.

After an hour of searching, as Danilo and Jaime returned to the training room, they saw Marka walking with another man. Before he noticed them, they turned into an adjoining hall and pressed into the shadows. After Marka and his companion had passed, they entered the training room.

"Come at me," Atcho urged a volunteer from among the *Sendero*s fighters. "What's your name?"

"Basilio."

"Use your knife and come at me, Basilio. Don't pretend. Attack to kill me."

Basilio looked dumbfounded, but then he grinned and turned for his comrades' approval.

"I never liked Cubans," he said. "They think they know everything." He turned back to face Atcho, knife in hand, eyes gleaming, and half-crouched, ready to pounce. Slowly, he circled, maintaining eye contact with Atcho, watching for an opening.

He lunged.

Atcho blocked with crossed wrists against Basilio's forearm. He slid one palm behind the knife-wielding hand and pressed a nerve. Basilio yelped and opened his fingers. Atcho seized the knife handle while simultaneously jamming a foot behind Basilio's ankle and throwing his shoulder into the man's chest.

Basilio fell to the floor on his back. Atcho straddled his chest, pinning his arms, and held the knife at Basilio's throat.

The other fighters were silent in astonishment, and then roared their approval. Atcho patted the downed man on the shoulder, released him, and stood up.

Basilio took his defeat good-humoredly and climbed to his feet, grinning. "Next time," he said.

Atcho turned to address the group. Just then, Marka appeared in the door with a companion whose muscles bulged under loose clothing.

Atcho sucked in his breath. *Klaus.*

Atcho cleared his throat and proceeded to fake a coughing fit. He stooped slightly, dropped his hands onto his knees, lowered his head, and continued to cough. Then, raising his head, he called in a hoarse voice, "Dust in the throat. Pair off while I drink some water."

He walked into the shadows on the opposite side of the room, lifted a clay jug over his head, and poured water into his mouth.

"I liked your demonstration," a voice behind him called. "I saw the end of it."

Atcho turned to find Marka and Klaus facing him. He fought down his shock, silently thanked Jaime for the dark glasses, and acknowledged the comment with a nod. "Please excuse the dust in my throat," he replied, keeping his voice hoarse.

"Teach my soldiers well," Marka said with only a touch of irony, "and you'll be forgiven. I want you to meet Sahab Kadyrov. He's here to observe our next bombing operation. He fixed our technical problem. His English is as bad as yours, but at least you two can say hello."

Marka turned to Klaus and made introductions in broken English. "This is *Capitan* Domingo Suarez. Fidel Castro sent him to train our fighters."

Klaus shook Atcho's hand perfunctorily. "Castro is a good man."

Atcho hoped the rapid beat of his heart did not show through his shirt and that his forced breathing was not too apparent. He thanked Klaus, generated another coughing fit, and drank again from the water jug.

Marka and Klaus moved away. Atcho watched them until they disappeared through the door, noting an urgency about them. Then he reassembled the class. A few minutes later, Jaime and Danilo appeared. They made eye contact with Atcho and shook their heads.

The three men discussed what they had seen and heard as Jaime maneuvered the little Volkswagen through Lima's crowded streets to the safe house. The sun slid to the western horizon.

"They moved the trucks carrying the bombs," Danilo said. "We looked all over for them. Nothing."

"Marka said that Klaus had fixed the problem with the bombs," Atcho said. "They're probably staging the trucks now."

A strange expression crossed Jaime's face. "Atcho, what were they trying to fix?"

Atcho reflected momentarily. "I know the fundamentals of demolitions, but not much beyond that. In addition to their concern about its stability—getting it from here to there without blowing it in the wrong place—they were concerned about shaping it." He suddenly looked stricken. "Oh my God, that's it. I should have seen it before."

His strident tone caused Jaime and Danilo to turn toward him abruptly. "What?" Jaime asked tersely while keeping his eye on the road.

Atcho spoke slowly, pulling his thoughts forward. "If the two trucks contain an equal distribution of explosives and all they've done is load them into the vehicles with no other preparation, the detonation will be immense, but the shock wave will spread evenly in all directions. The damage will be massive, but they must have been looking to cause even greater damage."

He put his hand to his chin while he reflected. "They want damping on the same side of both trucks, and they want the main shock of the explosion to hit high, well above the trucks' height. The force has to hit along a vertical band."

"A skyscraper," Jaime muttered. He jammed the little car into a lower gear and shoved the gas pedal to the floor. "That's what they're going for. With so much destructive power shaped that way, they could bring down almost any of Lima's tall buildings." He glanced at Atcho. "The US and Israel are organizing a joint op with Fujimori's troops to raid *Senderos* and seize the trucks. They'll get here too late."

"Did you notice that hardly anyone was at the headquarters?" Danilo cut in, his voice anxious. "We didn't expect to be confronted, but there was no one to challenge us."

"Even the group I had to work with was small," Atcho observed.

On arrival at the safe house, Jaime hurried into the operations room to radio his contact in the Tri-Border Region.

"Those are garbage-size trucks," Atcho called after him. "We're talking two tons of explosives. President Fujimori needs to mobilize everything he's got to stop them."

Danilo turned on a television in the living room and stood watching news reports. The screen repeatedly flicked from scene to scene of running gunfights all over the city.

"You need to see this," he called. The warning tone in his voice brought Atcho and Jaime to his side. "They've had constant shootouts since the June 5 bombing," he said. "But this is different. Today they executed nonstop simultaneous attacks all over Lima. The police are spread out, trying to keep up."

"They're keeping the police busy," Danilo said. "The cops can't respond effectively to any specific attack."

Atcho took a deep breath. "*Senderos* is going to blow those bombs tonight."

16

Esteban, the driver of the lead truck, looked about nervously. Traffic was relatively light at this time of night, but still moved slowly. He looked in his side mirror for the umpteenth time. The second truck was following a few cars back.

Esteban had already made his final turn onto Avenida Larco in Lima's Miraflores district. His target was a few blocks ahead. He reflected on the fact that he was not far from the location of the June 5 bombing and grinned. *No one's seen anything like this.*

He honked at a car blocking his path and cursed at the driver. While he waited for traffic to clear, he listened absently to radio news reports of the gun battles that had plagued the city all day, but he was not worried. He knew no shootings would take place within many blocks of him.

The driver of the car in front of him gestured obscenely and drove away. Esteban took his foot off the brake and pressed the accelerator. As the truck struggled forward under its heavy load, he checked his mirror again for the second truck. Satisfied that it was still following, he proceeded along Avenida Larco.

Three blocks later, Esteban pulled to a stop next to the Central Bank of Peru at the intersection with Calle Schell. He punched on his emergency blinkers and climbed down from the cab.

Behind him, cars honked and drivers yelled. Esteban stood in traffic to hold open the next lane until the second truck lumbered in behind his.

A security guard hurried out from the bank. "You can't park here," he yelled, face red with aggravation.

"It's only for a few minutes," Esteban called back. "We have to make a delivery."

"Deliveries are on the other side of the building," the guard insisted. "Calle Schell is a one-way street, so you can't turn there. You'll have to cross over, turn right at the next intersection, and take another right on Calle Alcanfores, which will bring you to Calle Tarata. You can park there."

Esteban sighed. "Come on," he implored. "That's a lot of maneuvering for trucks this big, and it's a small delivery. This will take only a minute."

Although he could still hear horns and shouts behind him, Esteban ignored them.

"I can't let you park here," the guard said. "Look, a policeman is coming this way. He'll tell you the same thing."

Esteban looked up sharply and spotted a nearby police car flashing its lights. Esteban signaled to the other driver to follow, then hurried back to the cab. He looked at his watch. Five minutes after nine o'clock.

Ten minutes later, both trucks lumbered onto Tarata. Esteban and the other driver left their trucks in gear, allowing them to drift into the intersection with Avenida Larco. Then they jumped from their cabs and fled.

Three hundred meters down the avenue, a young couple was kissing goodnight when the blast shockwave hit them, hurling them against an apartment building. They slid to the pavement, arms interlocked in an eternal embrace, never hearing the thunderous explosion that rocked the city. The concussion tossed cars into the air, ripped the faces off nearby high-rises, and sliced a vertical gash many stories high in the Central Bank before its entire glass front crashed to the ground, sending dagger-like shards flying in all directions. The floors at its base lay demolished, reduced to heaps of dust and rubble.

Miles away at the safe house, Atcho, Jaime, and Danilo heard the explosion.

"We got here too late," Jaime murmured.

"We should have known," Danilo whispered. "When they told us that Klaus was on his way, we should have known that the bombing was imminent."

Atcho sat on a kitchen chair and buried his face in his hands. "I could have stopped it. Klaus was right there in front of me. I shook his hand."

"Don't do that," Jaime warned. "We were there too. We saw them both in the hall. Think about the timing. The trucks weren't there. They must have been on the way."

"Besides," Danilo said, "stopping that bomb wasn't our mission. We were here to locate Klaus and learn what we could about cooperation between Al-Qaeda, Hezbollah, *Senderos*, and the local Muslim community."

"And get Klaus' nukes and track him back to wherever he hangs out these days," Atcho interjected. "Got it—but understanding that doesn't make me feel better. We should have been able to stop it."

Danilo regarded him thoughtfully. "Time to move on. Let's walk back through each step we've taken. If we find something we could have done differently, we'll learn from it and then let it go. If we find we would have done things just the same, then we'll have to accept that nothing else could have changed what happened. Does that make sense?"

Atcho looked at him through haunted eyes and nodded.

"That includes not being heroic inside the *Senderos* HQ today," Jaime added. "With that many fighters, including Klaus, you'd have been overwhelmed. You'd be dead, the bombing would still have happened, and Klaus would still have his nukes."

Horrified, Sofia watched the news of the explosion with Horton in his Berlin office. "My God," she said, "a hundred and eighty-three homes demolished, sixty-three cars destroyed, four hundred businesses ruined, twenty-five people killed, and a hundred and fifty-five wounded." She stared at the screen. "It looks like Berlin at the end of World War II."

"Those guys are serious," Horton said without a hint of humor, "and they don't care who they hurt."

The phone on Horton's secure line rang. He answered it and then held the receiver out to Sofia. "It's Burly, returning your call."

Sofia grabbed the phone. "Have you heard from Atcho? Is he all right?"

"We heard from the case officer in Lima. Atcho is safe. He was miles from the explosion. The CIA was on alert to extract him. They weren't needed."

Sofia closed her eyes and breathed a sigh of relief. "What's his plan now?"

Burly hesitated. "Uncertain. He saw Klaus. He intends to go after him."

Sofia squeezed her eyes shut and shook her head. She felt her gut tighten and steeled herself to remain calm and clear-headed.

"Did you understand the proposal Horton relayed from me? I'm putting you on speakerphone so he can join the conversation." She flipped a switch on the base instrument.

"I heard it. I won't claim to understand it yet."

"I'm taking Horton with me to Saudi Arabia. His boss has already approved his travel. We turned Kadir, the *hawaladar* here in Berlin. He identified Klaus' contacts in Libya and Riyadh and confirmed that Yousef is Klaus' conduit to Osama bin Laden. I want heavy surveillance on Yousef without Saudi knowledge. If we're going to put Klaus out of business permanently, we have to isolate him from his own money and his Al-Qaeda support. We need something on Yousef to make him work for us."

Burly whistled. "You don't ask for much, do you? I'm still ticked off about your trip to Berlin without telling me."

"I got good intel for you," Sofia retorted. "Can we stick with the business at hand?"

"Fine," Burly replied angrily. "But you're suggesting that we spy on a private citizen of an ally. If we're caught—"

"We do it all the time," Sofia said. "If there's a threat, we need to know about it. The threat is confirmed." She felt anxiety rising and fought it off. "Listen to me, Burly. This is the third bombing in Latin America we know about where Klaus was present to observe. He has no interest in that part of the planet. He wants to strike Russia and/or the United States.

"I think he's been less aggressive coming after Atcho because Al-Qaeda has been holding him off. They're the ones who keep sending him on these observation missions. Why would they do that?"

Burly grunted. "I'm sure you're going to tell me."

Sofia ignored the jab. "Multiple reasons. Buenos Aires was a Hezbollah-backed attack, but they arranged for Klaus to observe. He's Al-Qaeda. The mission was arranged through the Tri-Border Region where Hezbollah and *Senderos* share relations. The first bombing in Lima last month was *Senderos,* and so was this one. Klaus' presence there had to be arranged through Hezbollah, meaning that it is cooperating more and more with Al-Qaeda. A logical conclusion is that both organizations seek areas of cooperation and want to extend relations into the Muslim communities in South America. Are you with me so far?"

"That's a little hard to follow, but it makes sense at this point," Burly said. "Go on."

Across the room, Horton sat down in a chair, leaned back, and extended his legs, then stared at the ceiling, expressionless.

"In Buenos Aires, the target was the Israeli Embassy," Sofia continued. "The cathedral and school were collateral damage. Last month, the target in Lima was a television station. This time it was the high-rise headquarters of the Peruvian Central Bank. They're learning to strike strategic commercial and communications assets—targets that do more than kill people in the immediate vicinity: they disrupt economies. The bombs are getting bigger, and so are the targets. This latest one was a quantum leap."

"Agreed," Burly interjected. "Where are they going with it?"

"Burly," Sofia said, her voice hollow, "Klaus was studying the effectiveness of delivery systems. The vehicular bombs keep getting bigger and bigger. Think of the devastation if one or more of Klaus' nukes had been in those trucks." She took a deep breath. "Al-Qaeda is planning something bigger than we've ever imagined. It intends to use Klaus' bombs, and I doubt the target is in South America."

Burly remained quiet a moment. "You know that getting into Riyadh isn't easy. You'll need visas and they don't take tourists. Maybe someday they will, but not now. Arranging your travel will take some time—we're talking days, possibly weeks."

"Work your magic," Sofia cooed. "This should be high priority. You got your contract with the CIA, right?"

"I did." Burly let out a resigned sigh. "I'll have to do some arm-twisting to arrange that travel."

"Then do it. Take it to the president. He already knows who Klaus is and what he can do. Remind him that sources inside the Saudi police have assisted in keeping Yousef beyond our reach already."

"Right. Out." Burly clicked off the line.

17

Horton looked grim when he swung by Sofia's hotel for the drive to the airport. They met in the lobby.

"You're in an unusual mood," she said. "What's up?"

"Our trip got nixed," he responded.

Sofia's eyes widened in anger, and her nostrils flared. "What happened?"

"You ain't gonna like this," Horton said, opening his palms in a defensive gesture. "Don't shoot the messenger. The CIA pulled its support. The Germans did too. My boss reversed his approval. I'm supposed to give you a message. This comes from whoever Burly worked with in DC. He said you won't be allowed into Saudi Arabia. If you go there, you'll be deported back to the US. Atcho is on his way back home. Burly said you should meet him there."

Sofia stared blankly at Horton, the flush of anger draining into dread as she struggled with the inevitable.

"We could get this guy," she rasped, her voice shaking. "I feel it. Yousef is the key. When we get the goods on him, he'll work for us, and he knows where Klaus is."

"I know, little lady," Horton said in mock solemnity, a twinkle returning to his eye. "I agree with you. I'm on your side." He rolled his eyes to one side and scrunched his lips together in an expression of jovial skepticism. "I have to say I thought the CIA lettin' you traipse into the Kingdom and spy on a Saudi citizen was a long shot, but I didn't want to say nothin'." He rubbed his balding head. "I value my scalp. My guess is the president didn't jump up and down with enthusiasm either."

Sofia stared at him, expressionless.

Horton held her stony gaze, his own face frozen in comical indignation.

The corners of Sofia's mouth crinkled slightly in a suppressed smile. Then she burst into quiet, involuntary laughter.

"Does anyone get to stay mad around you?" she said, then cuffed his shoulder. "I'm not ready to be pleasant."

"Well, ma'am, I got an idea." He looked around as if checking for anyone who might overhear them. "Let's you an' me go into one of them lounges across the lobby and down a bottle of Conee-yak. You know that's my favorite liquor. I'll call Ziggy and tell her to come pick us up off the floor when it gets late. Then she can truck you up to your room and drive me home. By tomorrow afternoon, after the hangover, we'll both feel better, and I'll drive you to the airport."

Sofia stared at him. "Major Horton, are you making a pass at me?"

Horton chuckled. "You ain't never met Ziggy, or you wouldn't ask. Besides, I know Atcho, and I'm partial to my hide. You could use a friend right now. I thought I was one. We won't talk high principles 'cuz I ain't got none."

Sofia grabbed Horton's shoulder and tugged him. "I could use a strong drink right now." She started across the hotel lobby. "Let's go. You're paying."

18

"That was more like it," Klaus told Yousef enthusiastically on greeting him at the front door of Yousef's house. He embraced his portly friend and kissed him on the cheeks. "We killed some infidels."

"And did damage to Peru's economy and weakened its president." Yousef smiled warmly and led him into the courtyard. "That was the main objective, and the *Senderos* were happy with the technical solution you provided." He signaled to his servants to bring tea.

"I didn't do much," Klaus replied, taking a seat on the couch. "They were competent with the explosives configuration. I showed them how to stabilize the platform better and how to shape the charge to accomplish their objective. They had most of it figured out and wanted confirmation."

"Well, they are lifelong friends now. We have a staunch ally in South America, thanks to you."

The tea arrived, and both men sat quietly while a young boy poured it. After the servant had retreated from the courtyard, Klaus leaned forward. His eyes burned with enmity.

"Now, tell me. What's the big target?"

Yousef smiled benevolently. "I said I would tell you on your return, and I will." He held up a hand, palm facing Klaus, face solemn. "First, you must promise not to breathe a word to anyone. I am allowed to tell you only for the purpose of managing your impatience, but then you will leave Saudi Arabia and not return until after the mission, and perhaps not until months or years after that."

Astonished and almost angry, Klaus leaned back. "You said the attack wouldn't take place until February. That's seven months away. Where will I go? What about my bombs?"

Yousef leaned forward in a placating gesture. "You have them in a safe place?"

Klaus nodded.

"Leave them where they are. You can make one trip back to Riyadh to retrieve them when the time is right. We'll make the security arrangements to get you to your destination."

"Meanwhile, what? The camps?"

Yousef assented. "Our recruits need to know what you can teach them."

Klaus sat quietly, his eyes flickering as he studied Yousef while controlling his own annoyance. "Let me hear what the target is."

Yousef shook his head. "You must agree first and swear an oath never to speak of it. You will be held to it." He gazed steadily into Klaus' eyes. "You know what that means."

Klaus leaned forward and dropped his arms between his knees. He held Yousef's gaze. "And if I don't agree?"

Yousef breathed heavily. "No one will blame you, my friend. You have done much for Islam. I will place your personal funds in a bank of your choice where you can access them. Your balance is over four-and-a-half million dollars now. And you are free to retrieve your bombs.

"However, *habibi*, think carefully before acting. If you choose that path, our association ends. We cannot provide you safe passage out of the Kingdom or into any country. Al-Qaeda will no longer support you, and I will not be allowed to be your *hawaladar*."

Klaus regarded Yousef with an expression indicating he had anticipated that response. "Those are tough conditions."

Yousef sighed. "You're an unusual fighter for Islam," he said. "Your training in the Soviet Spetsnaz makes you more of a lone actor than we usually see. That's not a criticism. It's a fact, and your talents are extremely valuable. But we're not looking for individual hits, despite how large they might be. We look at a longer strategy. Once your bombs are proven in action and we can reproduce them reliably, they will fit in."

Klaus looked around at the swaying palms and babbling fountains, the spray falling like diamonds in the sunlight. He exhaled.

"Can't I at least kill Atcho?"

Yousef frowned and shook his head. "Too much risk right now."

Klaus leaned back against the couch, his hands cupping the back of his neck and his legs splayed out in front of him. He stared up at the blue sky.

"All right," he said at last. "I swear on all that's sacred to Islam that I will never mention the target until you direct me otherwise. I will go to the camps in Sudan and train Al-Qaeda recruits until I am called for this great mission." He glanced at Yousef. "Does that satisfy?"

Yousef nodded.

19

Sofia watched through Atcho's conference room window as a metallic-green compact rental car stopped at the security gate below. A guard approached the window and spoke with the driver briefly, then checked a clipboard and waved the car through. It traveled a short distance to a parking lot and slid into a space. Then Burly's bulky, balding figure squeezed out of the small vehicle and headed toward the building carrying a valise.

Atcho stood next to Sofia, also watching Burly's arrival. "Are you still mad at him? It's been two months, and he's a good friend."

"I know," Sofia sniffed. "But I can't let him off the hook so easily. We could have had Yousef and maybe Klaus by now. What's he doing with that tiny car?"

Atcho chuckled. "He's on his own dime. And I don't agree that we would have caught those guys by now. With or without Burly, your mission in Saudi Arabia would have been scrubbed. The director was never going to sanction that, and if he had, the president would have had his neck. Anyway, Burly wouldn't tell me on the phone why he's here."

LEE JACKSON

"Don't worry." Sofia kissed Atcho on the cheek. "I'll be good."

They watched Burly enter the building before turning from the window and taking seats at the conference table. Sofia poured coffee from a pitcher and added cream and sugar.

A few moments later, a secretary showed Burly into the room and closed the door, leaving him alone with Atcho and Sofia. They rose to receive him.

Burly greeted Atcho amiably, and then turned to Sofia. "You still mad?" He exaggerated a look of anxiety.

"Depends on what you have to tell us," she said with a pert smile. Then her expression warmed, and she extended the cup to him. "Your coffee, sir, just the way you like it."

Startled, Burly took the coffee and grinned. "A peace offering?"

"A truce, until I hear what you have to say."

Burly groaned. "Fair enough." He glanced around the room at the Western art on the walls and a bronze cowboy-on-a-bucking-bronco statuette on the table. "I'm always amazed at how a lifelong Cuban adapted so well to life in Texas," he told Atcho, then addressed Sofia. "We've located Klaus. Will that do?"

"What? Where?" Sofia replied, startled.

Atcho's eyes narrowed, but otherwise he showed no expression.

Burly moved toward the conference table. "I'll show you." He sat down and took a key from his pocket, then unlocked his satchel and pulled out another bag, which he proceeded to unlock as well. He looked up and caught Atcho's questioning glance. "The travails of carrying classified material," he muttered. Then he took a quick look around the room. "This is still a secure facility, right?"

Atcho nodded as he took a seat next to Burly. "We have our defense department contracts."

Sofia sat down on Burly's other side.

"We believe this is Klaus," Burly said, extracting a photo from the file folder. "This was taken a few days ago by Mossad at one of the camps in Sudan. It's a bit grainy, but the agent on the ground assured his headquarters that this is our guy."

He turned to Sofia. "That was good information you got from Rawley.

I passed it on to the Israelis, and they located him." He paused. "I didn't shoot down your mission to Riyadh, but I didn't give it much probability of being cleared either. You must have anticipated that."

Sofia stared at him, then sighed and nodded in acquiescence. "Every time I try to do things by the book, I get shot down. That's why I go off on my own."

"Please don't do that this time," Burly replied. "Eitan Chasin's man in the field got this for us. He put his neck on the line—for real. Need I say more?"

Sofia shook her head. "Just so we get Klaus. What's the plan?"

Burly chuckled. "You'll be happy to know that I'm a bit off the reservation myself this time. I knew that the CIA higher-ups would nix your request for intel support in Saudi Arabia, but I keep my backchannels to members of the Mossad. They kept an eye on Yousef in Riyadh, watching him and monitoring his communications. One call came through that helped in finding Klaus. So, your conclusion that Yousef is Klaus' conduit to Al-Qaeda is confirmed, and now we know Klaus' location."

"Okay," Sofia cut in. "I'm properly chastened and you have my thanks. Again, what's the plan?"

"Israel's going to mount an operation to grab him. Obviously, since he has nukes, Israel feels threatened."

"The world is threatened," Atcho said. "Why doesn't the US go after him?"

Burly shrugged. "For the same reasons Sofia goes rogue. Bureaucracy. Al-Qaeda isn't perceived as much of a threat. Osama bin Laden is seen as a rich kid with a fortune to spend who likes toys that go boom."

"What makes anyone think Mossad can mount a mission before Klaus disappears again?"

"The Mossad is a bureaucracy too," Burly countered, "but because they're so much smaller, they have to conserve resources, including manpower. They have their own challenges with intransigence, inertia, and careerism, but not as severe as in the CIA. They eliminate as much risk as possible and have backup plans on top of backup plans to ensure success." He furrowed his brow and pursed his lips. "Frankly, they have an enviable record."

"I want to be there," Atcho said.

Sofia's eyes flashed.

Burly nodded. "And they want you there to confirm they've got the right guy."

"This is insane," Sofia said as she paced in their bedroom.

"No more insane than your intent to go to Saudi Arabia. My presence is sanctioned." As he spoke, Atcho stuffed articles of clothing into a light bag.

"By Mossad, not the US."

"By the people who are running the mission." Atcho's impatience flared. "They've done all the prep work, and my only task is to confront Klaus after they've nabbed him."

"You're going into Sudan," Sofia stormed. "That's a hotbed for terrorists. If you get caught, the things they'll do to you would be beyond imagination—except they've already done them: beheadings, hangings, crucifixions..." Her voice trailed off.

Atcho tried awkwardly to comfort her. "I've seen as bad," he replied gruffly. A scene replayed in his mind of a fellow prisoner being bayonetted next to him and left to bleed out while Cuban guards stood around and watched. "I know what to expect from evil people."

Sofia's expression softened and then became stoic. She crossed the room, embraced Atcho from behind, and buried her head against the back of his neck.

"I know you do," she whispered. "I want you home, safe and sound."

Atcho turned to wrap her in his arms. "I'll be back. Make sure I have you and Jameson to come home to."

Sofia held him closely and then pulled away, the fire back in her eyes. "What do you even know about Sudan?"

"Not much," Atcho admitted, "but I'll be with people who know it intimately."

"It's a hell-hole." Sofia's voice rose. "It had a great civilization centuries ago. That's long gone. It's where Egyptian and Turkish traders snatched people to sell into slavery. The Brits took over Sudan more than a hundred years ago and set up a democracy, but they mucked it up with more lines on a map, like they did when they created Iraq out of whole cloth."

Atcho noted the anger in her voice, unsure if it was aimed at him or history. She continued unabated.

"The Brits criminalized migration from the south to the north and vice versa, and then opened the south for Christian missionaries. In no time, Christians and Muslims started fighting each other. The civil war killed people by the millions, and the last coup happened only three years ago. Omar al-Bashir is a dictator, and he just aligned with Osama bin Laden and let him set up terrorist training camps outside the capital. Do you even know what the capital city is?"

Atcho started to shake his head, but before he could say anything, Sofia put her head close to his, her eyes boring into his own, her inflection becoming more pronounced. "It's Khartoum. I was on the desk for that part of the world for several years. I studied Sudan. Khartoum makes the Tri-Border Region look as organized and civil as Switzerland. Sudan isn't Cuba, and it isn't Latin America. They kill people on the streets over any excuse. That's what you're wandering into."

Atcho held Sofia by her shoulders. "This isn't like you. Aren't you being a little extreme?" As he gazed at her, he saw that, under her ferocity, she was fighting back tears.

"Extreme?" Sofia jerked away. "I'll tell you what's extreme. It's the culture you're going into. They hate us because we're infidels. It's the culture that murdered my first husband." She whirled on him. "I won't lose another husband, and we have a baby son and a granddaughter to think of. I'm begging you. Don't go."

Atcho, feeling helpless, reached to comfort Sofia, but she tensed and stepped away.

"Why can't they bring Klaus here, or to Israel?" she blurted. "Somewhere safe."

"Burly explained that. They'll snatch him out of Sudan when they are sure they have the right person. If they have the wrong one, Klaus could get wind of it and disappear again, and they might expose informants and operators."

"You always have a reason why you have to be the one going in." Bitterness had crept into her voice. "Why can't you just stay home for a change and let someone else get their hands dirty? I'm starting to think you like the adventure."

Stunned, Atcho searched for words. "Adventure? Like it?" He held his creeping anger in check. "Have you forgotten that an assassin came to our front door? That the man we're going after has a sworn vendetta against me? He's aligned with Al-Qaeda, Hamas, and Hezbollah. They're hitting bigger and bigger targets, and he has a nuclear bomb. If I don't go after him, I'm consigning my family to death." He glanced at his watch. "I'll miss my flight. I have to go."

Sofia stood, unmoving.

Atcho kissed her on the cheek, then picked up his case and headed for the door, stopping at the threshold to face her. "Promise me you'll stay out of this." He paused, his face a mask of conflict. "Take Jameson and go stay with Isabel. She'd love to see you, and the two kids will have fun together. It'll be good for all of you."

Sofia walked over, embraced Atcho, and kissed him. "I love you," she said softly, and then turned away.

20

"I trust your flight was pleasant? Burly, that tip you gave us about Klaus' whereabouts was terrific." Eitan turned to Atcho. "We'll take today to let you get over jet lag." He sat across from the two men in a bungalow along a broad stretch of beach by the Mediterranean. In the distance, skyscrapers reached into the heavens, and on the road between them, multiple-lane traffic bunched up as cars traversed both ways. Near the water's edge, vacationers soaked up the sun.

"Our men are rehearsing, and you"—Eitan indicated Atcho—"will need to be inserted into the team and brought up to speed quickly on your role during the operation. The next moonless night is in a week. That's when we go in."

Atcho stood, stretched his arms over his head, and stifled a yawn. "I'll be fine. Let's get on with it." He crossed the room, cup in hand, to refill it with coffee from a steaming pot on the kitchen island.

"We'll take it slow," Eitan responded, an edge to his voice. "We need you at your most alert. Things are rough in Khartoum, especially now. This is a difficult operation without much room for error. As we speak, a crew is preparing a dirt airstrip in the desert, capable of handling a large cargo jet. They have to work undetected—not an easy feat."

He turned to Burly. "We've set up an operations center on a nearby military base where we'll monitor preparations and the op as it progresses. Your living quarters are there. You won't have access to the rest of the base, and you'll have to enter and leave under escort. I hope that's acceptable."

Burly chuckled. "Nothing I didn't expect. Can you bring us up to speed on what's going on in Khartoum?"

"You'll get more in-depth briefings later. Atcho will rehearse how to interact with the team and members of the Sudanese public and security forces he might encounter, but I'll give you the quick and dirty now." He sipped his coffee. "Sudan has been in a deadly civil war for seven years, essentially between the Muslim north and the Christian south. When the Brits were here, they poured huge amounts of money into developing the north but very little into the south. That raised resentment on top of the religious divide.

"Since al-Bashir's coup, he's been merciless, killing off rebels and political opponents, and he made the strategic mistake of supporting Saddam Hussein's invasion into Kuwait. That's left him very little foreign support. The US is furious with him. He had a huge military parade three months ago to celebrate independence from British rule, but about the only dignitary who came to celebrate was Yasser Arafat from the Palestine Liberation Organization.

"That said, oil was discovered a few years ago across the line that separates north from south. That should have benefited the south, but the pipelines are being built north through Khartoum. China is investing heavily there, and with projected oil revenues, al-Bashir expects plenty of money to finance his military operations."

Eitan sighed and crossed his arms. "So, al-Bashir's going nowhere soon, and in fact, he not only knows about the training camps outside Khartoum, he welcomed Osama bin Laden to set them up. They share similar views about infidels and establishing a caliphate."

"I heard," Atcho broke in. "My wife informed me."

Eitan nodded. "I recall that she's great at intelligence analysis." He shifted in his seat. "For your purposes, the result of that history is that Sudanese society is in chaos, riots and killings occur regularly, and al-Bashir's henchmen are everywhere. To give you an idea of the danger, if Beirut is threatening to Westerners and Israelis, Khartoum is about ten times so. That's the environment our covert operators live in." Eitan fixed his eyes on Atcho. "That's the environment you're going into."

Atcho held Eitan's gaze. "Fine. I get that. But I'm curious: why Khartoum? I understand the interest in oil, but that's recent. I read up a little on the area during the flight over here. From what I can see, it's in the middle of the desert without much else going for it."

Eitan stretched and took another sip of coffee. "It's got the Nile going for it, and don't let the bleakness or current situation fool you. The history is ancient and rich. Egypt ruled here for centuries, and then Sudan ruled Egypt for a while. There's even a kings' graveyard here, with pyramids that no one ever hears about. Suffice it to say that before the Brits gave it up, Khartoum was the Paris of eastern Africa—before Sudan descended into chaos."

Atcho sighed. "A common theme the world over. So, let's get down to specifics. How are we going to pull off nabbing Klaus?"

Eitan smiled. "Two words. Think Entebbe."

"What's Entebbe?"

Startled, Eitan stared at Atcho. "You haven't heard of Entebbe?"

"He was in prison then," Burly cut in, "courtesy of Fidel Castro."

"Sorry, I forgot." Eitan looked sheepish, then studied Atcho. "Operation Thunderbolt was a rescue mission by the Israeli Defense Forces based on intelligence from Mossad. A group of terrorists had captured an airliner with 248 passengers, including 114 Israelis. The hijackers flew it to Entebbe in Uganda and threatened to kill every passenger if Israel did not release forty Palestinian prisoners. They wanted to free thirteen men in other countries too."

"The operation was sensational," Burly added. "The Israelis flew several C-130s at night, barely a hundred feet off the ground, for about 3,600 miles. They landed undetected but were eventually seen. To make a long story short, in a ninety-minute engagement, they freed most of the hostages with minimal casualties and brought them back to Israel. When you consider that they had to bring along armored personnel carriers and other heavy equipment and refuel along the way there and back, it was one hell of an operation."

Atcho listened, entranced. "And that's what we're going to do in Khartoum?"

"A variation," Eitan replied. "The planes will fly at night below radar. We have longer-range aircraft and less than half the distance to go than we did for Entebbe, but the aircraft is larger, and detection technology has advanced considerably. It's a high-risk mission."

He took another swallow of his coffee. "Most of our operators are already inside the country, and they've acquired vehicles for ground travel, but the operation is high cost. When it's over, we'll have blown the cover of several undercover agents and will have to take them home.

"We know where Klaus is. Two of our men are in the camp. You'll be inserted into Khartoum a day ahead of the mission and make your way there with an in-country operator. On the night of the mission, the assault element will take care of subduing Klaus and any resistance and get him to the full extraction team. You'll wait with the team leader. Whether or not Klaus leaves the country is on your say-so. If it's Klaus, the entire team will bring him back to Tel Aviv."

Atcho mulled over the plan. "What if it's not him?"

"You and the rest of the team will leave the way you came, and the aircraft will return with just the combat-support elements."

"What should I do between now and then?"

"Rehearse, rehearse, rehearse. Our guys will tutor you. Unless you can learn Sudanese Arabic in a few days, you've got to look and act like a Sudanese who is both illiterate and mute." He studied Atcho's jawline. "You'll need to grow some facial hair, get dirty, and start smelling like a street person. I suggest that if you take a shower tonight, it becomes your last one until mission complete."

Atcho shot him a wan glance. "Sofia would love that."

"One other thing," Eitan said. "Go on a starvation diet. You need to look hungry."

21

Sofia tossed in her bed at Isabel's house at West Point in upstate New York. She was worried about Atcho, but even more, she felt frustration at being unable to help him. A week had gone by since he had flown out to meet Burly and Eitan in Tel Aviv. He had called the night he arrived, and since then he had gone dark. She did not know where he was, where he was going, or any details of the operational plan. With Burly also gone, she had no way of gaining information and determining if there was a role she could play. She had exhausted her sources in the CIA and State Department, and she sensed that she was wearing out her welcome in both organizations.

She got out of bed and went to the kitchen to make coffee. There, she found Isabel sitting alone in the dark, already sipping a freshly brewed cup. The warm aroma took the edge off the tension. Sofia flipped on a soft light over the table.

She greeted Isabel with a hug. "You can't sleep either."

"No. Grab a mug and help yourself. There's plenty."

The two sat in silence for a time, each with her own thoughts. Then Sofia eyed Isabel with curiosity.

"Do you do this often? Get up to have coffee by yourself in the dark?"

Isabel gave her a distant smile. "More often than I'd like to think about." She sighed. "Bob's teaching assignment at West Point was supposed to be a break for us, but he's constantly gone. All I know right now is that he's in South Korea doing some kind of special study he can't talk about. He'll be gone a few weeks." She laughed without mirth. "I'm surrounded by people who can't talk to me about what they do. You can't, Dad can't, Bob can't, his associates can't. And there's the not knowing what's going on with family members. Bob might be in danger. I don't know. Dad seems always in danger, I don't know where he is, and you're here because your home is threatened." She suddenly seemed on the verge of tears. "I admire you, Sofia, I really do, but I don't know how you do the things you do, and that's just the things I know about."

Sofia reached across the table and clasped Isabel's hand. "You have a daughter, our granddaughter—if I'm allowed to think of Kattrina as mine."

"Of course," Isabel murmured through teary eyes. "She loves you. I do too."

"Being a great mother is every bit as important as the things Atcho and I do. I'm falling down in that department. I know it." She sniffed as her eyes moistened. "If you weren't available to fill the breach, I'm not sure how I'd take care of Jameson in this situation." She squeezed Isabel's hand. "Never forget that our families are why we do the things we do."

"You're a wonderful mother," Isabel broke in.

Sofia sighed. "A lot of people think I'm a know-it-all bitch."

Isabel leaned forward and grasped her hand. "You're not. You're a very capable woman who loves her country and has put her life on the line over and over in its defense. And you're a wife and mother who will fight for your family with everything you've got. I wish I could be more like you."

Sofia wiped away a tear. "Being a mother is the best job I've ever had," she said, dropping her eyes, "but under these circumstances..." She brought her hand to her face and rubbed her forehead. "I took an early retirement package to be with Jameson, and I love taking care of him. But now this..." She sat quietly, her expression conflicted. "I'm a threat to him just by being around. I can't let that go on forever."

She sat quietly a moment. "I want to be a real mother to him," she continued, her voice catching. "I'm torn between staying put while Atcho and the others handle things..." Her voice trailed off as she struggled with her thoughts. "But I'm trained and good at what I did in my past life. I couldn't live with myself if something terrible happened because I didn't do everything I could."

The two women sipped their coffee in the quiet morning. Isabel broke the silence with a chuckle. "It's hard to think of Jameson as my half-brother—we're nearly thirty years apart. But you're so capable of defending him. If someone broke through my door—"

"You'd do whatever it took to protect your daughter. Do you have a gun?"

Isabel nodded.

"Do you know how to use it?"

"Yes."

"Keep it handy. My role, your father's role, and Bob's role is to widen the safety perimeter, to go after the bad guys before they get to your door. Between us and you are our military and police forces. Someone has to make sure the kids are warm and fed. And if the bad guy gets inside your door and we're not there, it's up to you. Otherwise, what we do is for nothing."

A look of horror crossed Isabel's face. "Sweet Jesus! You're scaring me." She crossed herself.

"I'm sorry. That's the reality of what we live in. It's better that you're prepared."

Isabel acquiesced with a nod, then looked thoughtful. "One thing I don't understand is why you go off on your own so much. I don't know a lot of details, but I overhear things sometimes, and you have a reputation for going rogue. You go off without telling the rest of your team."

Sofia laughed. "Guilty," she exclaimed. "I guess I've done that a few times."

"Why?"

Sofia was slow to respond. "It started when I met your father, although the instinct developed several years earlier." She paused, and the hurt in her eyes expressed her reluctance to continue.

"You don't have to say anything," Isabel said.

Sofia shook her head. "It's better that you know. I never want you or Kattrina or Jameson to think that I put anything above my family." She wiped tears from her eyes. "My first husband came home from a covert operation in a body bag. The funeral was closed casket because he was so mauled, but the CIA would never give me a straight story about what happened.

"When I started dating your father years later, I could tell something was wrong. He was so strong and noble, and people loved him, but he pushed everyone away, even me."

"I remember," Isabel interjected. "I thought he was crazy."

Sofia smiled. "My intel instincts kicked in. I went to Burly for help, and as things turned out, Atcho was being coerced to be a sleeper agent for the Russians, and he was resisting by doing the only thing he could—becoming a recluse."

"But he got out of that."

"True, but he almost got killed in the process, and a year later, the president wanted to send him into Siberia with no support. I was furious when I heard about it. We were engaged to be married, and I refused to accept that I might lose another man I loved to a spy mission. I was trained and capable and had some ideas about what to do. As things turned out, what I did helped.

"We had two more missions where I saw things that others didn't and felt like I had to act. Some people thought I was careless. I saw it as using the skills I had trained for and the experience I had gained to protect those I love most, your father and our family." She sniffed. "That might seem like an emotional approach, but"—she shrugged and laughed—"I'm a woman."

Isabel closed her eyes as if to shut out a fearsome world. "Are you going to stay with us this time?" she said, an edge to her voice. She opened her eyes and looked directly at Sofia. "Or do you plan on taking off again to places unknown? I know you didn't go home last time around. You went to Berlin."

As soon as she spoke, Isabel looked as though she wished she could take the words back. Sofia regarded her without expression.

"How do you know that?"

"I'd rather not say," Isabel replied, her tone slightly defiant. Then she softened. "I don't want to get anyone in trouble."

Sofia's mind furiously worked through a mental list of all her acquaintances who might have known about her trip to Berlin. She settled on one name.

"Ivan must have told you. There's no one else who could have."

"Don't be mad at him," Isabel cried. "I tried to reach you after you left here. Dad was wherever he was, and Bob was on travel. You were supposed to be at home, and when you weren't, I pushed Ivan to tell me where you were."

"It's all right." Sofia rose and moved to the other side of the table to reassure her, wrapping her arms around Isabel's shoulders. "Ivan is the one guy who can usually figure out where we are," she mused aloud. "How would he have found out?" She thought a moment. "He must have called Horton. He and Ivan worked with us on a mission in Berlin two years ago. They know each other and are close to Atcho and me."

"Who's Horton?"

"Never mind." Sofia's mind whirled as she considered who else might have information leading to Atcho's current location and activity. She released Isabel and downed her last bit of coffee. "I have to shower and get dressed. I'll be gone most of the morning."

Startled, Isabel called after her, "Ivan's not in trouble, is he?"

"No, but you gave me an idea."

By nine o'clock, Sofia was waiting outside the office of the West Point history department director. When she was finally shown in, she got straight to the point.

"Colonel Morgan, I believe my son-in-law, Bob Bernier, teaches in your department?"

The colonel nodded. "How may I help you?" He was an amiable man, tall with dark hair tinged gray, and he was in remarkable physical shape. Despite his warmth, he carried an air that brooked no nonsense.

"I need a secure line to call Berlin."

Morgan stared at her. "I'm sorry. I accepted this unscheduled meeting out of courtesy to Bob, but I—" His voice was firm, his speech refined.

"I'll tell you exactly why I need it," Sofia interrupted. "Does the name Atcho mean anything to you?"

Their conversation lasted fifteen minutes, after which Sofia sat alone in an office waiting for the secure phone to ring at the opposite end.

"Horton here."

The major's big, friendly voice brought welcome relief.

"Joe, it's Sofia. I'm glad you're still in Berlin. I know you're supposed to rotate out soon."

Horton grunted and Sofia smiled. She could almost see him leaning forward in his chair, his face mischievous as he calculated how best to respond.

"Yes, ma'am, I'm still here, holdin' the line against the Mongol hordes. Great to hear you." A moment passed. "You ain't never called me from stateside before — just to chat. This cain't be good. Are you aware that I'm gettin' ready to retire? You ain't gonna mess that up for me—"

"No." Sofia laughed. "I just need your help."

Horton huffed into the receiver. "Somethin' tells me that your no-account husband got hisself in trouble again. Cain't you put a leash on that guy?"

Sofia brought Horton up to date. "I just need you to get someone, anyone, to keep an eye on Yousef in Riyadh. Twist that *hawaladar* Kadir's arm there in Berlin. He can tell you how people come and go at Yousef's house. If this Mossad mission in Sudan gets close to Klaus and fails, he's going to be hopping mad, and he'll go to Yousef pushing for vengeance. Unfortunately, his revenge is aimed at our family."

"I see what you mean, little lady, but I wouldn't be bankin' on the Mossad failin'. They got a pretty good record."

"I'm not banking on it," Sofia said, stifling her impatience. "I'm playing 'what if?' If they do fail, they'll go home, make a report, and look for the next chance. But my family is likely to pay the consequences. I can't wait around to find out."

"All right, ma'am, I'll see what I can do." He sounded deliberately world-weary.

"Get the Germans to help," Sofia urged. "They're bound to have assets in Riyadh."

"I got it."

"Get them to interrogate Kadir again."

"I said I got this," Horton said brusquely. Then he laughed. "You know, if you mess up my retirement, there's gonna be hell to pay with Ziggy." He paused a moment. "Where are you?"

Sofia told him.

"Well, I suggest you stay right there and get to know your son a little bit. Your stepdaughter and her daughter too. Cain't hurt. And don't worry. I got your backside from here."

After hanging up, Horton stared at the phone. "What are you gettin' yourself into this time, Major?" he grumbled to himself. He rose, walked across his office to a cabinet, and extracted some blank forms. Returning to his desk, he grabbed a pen and filled them out.

Twenty minutes later, he was sitting in front of his boss, engaging in a heated exchange. Ten minutes after entering the office, Horton emerged with a satisfied grin, his request for a special intelligence mission to Riyadh approved.

"I'll push it upstairs," his boss said, "but it'll take a few days."

Horton's conversation with Ziggy that evening went as he expected. At first dismayed, then angry, then mollified as he cajoled her, she finally acquiesced with tears and hugs to an outcome she had known at the start was inevitable. Three days later, Horton boarded a plane for Riyadh.

Two hours after landing, he entered the headquarters of the General Intelligence Presidency just off Said As Salmi, a major Riyadh thoroughfare. He presented his US Army credentials and asked to see a particular officer. Then he sat and waited in a reception area.

An hour passed, then two. By that time, Horton had tired of studying the intricate design on the ceiling, discerning repeated patterns and counting their number while twiddling his thumbs. Another hour passed, and Horton took note of various people crossing the reception area and throwing glances his direction.

At last, he heard his name called in a heavy Arabic accent and looked up. A short, barrel-chested man walked toward him, hand extended. His smile wrapped from ear to ear over a jutting, clean-shaven jaw, and he had a straight nose with flaring nostrils and eyes a peculiar shade halfway between green and brown. His hair was cropped short.

"My brother," the man said, and laughed. "You should have told me you were coming. I would have told my wife to prepare a room for you at my house."

"Which wife, Iqbal?" Horton chuckled and shook Iqbal's hand. "The last time we met, you only had two."

Iqbal's face turned deadpan. "Yes, that's a serious issue, and now I have three." He looked skyward. "They all give me trouble. I should have stuck with just one—or maybe none." He broke into laughter again. "What are you doing here?"

"You already checked me out, so you know I'm here in official capacity."

"But you came straight to the Kingdom's intelligence headquarters without checking in at your own. How can I help my best brother?"

"Don't flatter me," Horton joshed. "You tell everyone they're your favorite brother. I'm tired. You could offer me some refreshment in a quiet place where we can relax."

Iqbal's eyes narrowed and he looked about. "Of course. You had a long flight. I'll take you to my favorite tea room."

They left the building and Iqbal drove Horton to a nearby plaza with a smattering of shops and eating establishments. Entering one, he greeted the owner like a long-lost relative and introduced Horton as his very best brother. Then he asked for a room where they could relax quietly without being bothered.

When they were seated in front of a pitcher of steaming tea on a low table, Iqbal glanced around the room. "These walls have no ears," he said. "My good friend, the owner, would not dare to compromise me." He fixed his gaze on Horton. "What brings my best cousin to Riyadh?"

"I thought I was your best brother." Horton grinned.

Iqbal poured the tea. "Brother, cousin, friend—it's all the same. I would give my right arm for you. I would take a bullet in the chest and—"

"Got it," Horton interrupted. "I've never had so much fun workin' with anyone than when I was assigned here—what was that, ten years ago?" He sipped his tea. "I need to call in a favor."

Iqbal's expression dropped. "You don't need to call in any favors," he said with an edge to his voice. "You are my brother, my friend. You have only to ask. If I can do it, consider it done."

Horton took a moment to order his thoughts. "There is a *hawaladar* here in Riyadh. His name is Yousef."

Iqbal nodded. "I know who he is. We track all the *hawalas* in Saudi Arabia. He is very well connected."

"Do you also know of a terrorist by the name of Sahab Kadyrov? Western intelligence calls him Klaus from a previous alias."

"We're cognizant of him. Tell me what you know."

Horton related his first awareness of Klaus as a Soviet Spetsnaz deserter and rogue operator in Berlin. He went on to describe Klaus' activities in Kuwait in the days after Saddam Hussein's invasion during the time when the wells burned, including his suspected murder of Tony Collins, an investigative reporter covering the war. He finished with details of how Klaus had attacked Atcho's home in Austin and later sent an assassin to kill his family.

Iqbal listened attentively. When Horton finished, he asked simply, "What do you need from me?"

"We believe the *hawaladar* Yousef is Klaus' conduit to Osama bin Laden."

"Saudi intelligence believes the same thing. Osama is a thorn in the royal family's side, but he has so far done nothing to cause us to take action against him."

"Do you know about his activities in South America?"

Iqbal shook his head. "Only peripherally. Maybe someone else in our agency knows more."

"He's been involved at a high level on each of three bombings." Horton related the details of the Israeli Embassy bombing in Buenos Aires, along with the television station and huge bomb in Lima. "That one killed over eighty people and took out a whole neighborhood and dozens of businesses. Klaus was present each time. We have positive identification."

Iqbal sat in silence for a while, then said, "What do you want from me?"

"Klaus is in Sudan now. We think he might have reason to come through here soon. If that happens, I need to know. He'll go straight to Yousef."

"Why hasn't US intelligence made a formal request for cooperation?"

"We tried that when the newspaper reporter was murdered, but your police force protects Yousef."

"Ah, yes," Iqbal agreed. "We do have that problem."

"I ain't askin' for nothin' fancy," Horton pressed. "I just want to know if Klaus comes through here in the next week or two. If that happens, I'll know why and where he's likely to go."

"And you won't tell me how you'll know his purpose?"

"Are you goin' to tell me everythin' you know?"

Iqbal chuckled. "That would take years. Why don't we just arrest him here?"

"If you can, please do. He's become wily, enterin' and leavin' countries at will, undetected. I'm expectin' that by the time you find out he's been here, he'll already be gone." *Besides, we're hopin' he leaves with the bombs. We don't want those fallin' into your hands.*

"All right. I will tell you only this: we have an informant in Yousef's house. We turned one of his house servants after a US intel request a few months ago."

Horton's eyes narrowed. *Thank you, Sofia.*

Iqbal continued. "I'll bring this matter under my personal attention. If we hear that Klaus has come to Riyadh, I'll call you. But"—he raised a finger—"we will also attempt to arrest him."

"Fair enough." Horton grinned. "You must have been promoted a few times since I last saw you."

"Once or twice," Iqbal said noncommittally. "How's your family?"

22

Khartoum, Sudan

Atcho struggled to keep Jaime in sight, following from a distance as they wound through the crowded city streets. He had placed a small pebble in his shoe to induce a limp, and he wore a long, dirty, pastel robe—a *jalabiya*. Unkempt hair protruded from below his soiled turban. He stooped heavily over a worn walking stick, and he kept his head bobbing oddly to one side while his eyes burned with apparent madness. His week of fasting had left him looking gaunt—he did not have to pretend. That morning, he had eaten enough to take the edge off his hunger and keep himself mentally alert, but he still felt lightheaded.

As Atcho passed the teeming crowds, he noticed buildings that evoked the grandeur of a time long past, their walls cracking and crumbling and surrounded by lean-tos and shanties. Water pooled in low spots in the middle of the dusty streets, and the stench overcame that of his own unwashed body.

The condition of Khartoum reminded him of Havana the last time he had seen it, just after his release from prison: a formerly proud city, brought to ruin by Castro. Atcho wondered which part of Khartoum's history had brought it to this disorder.

Dismissing his thoughts, he looked ahead to keep Jaime in sight. So far, no one had approached Atcho, but he had practiced how to indicate that he could neither speak nor hear, emphasizing his feigned plight by throwing in a few unintelligible grunts.

A car had brought him to the edge of town at dawn. Atcho knew nothing of the driver, and they did not speak. He had already been in character, and on reaching their destination in an alley off of Omduram Souk, the largest marketplace in Khartoum, he had waited in the shadows for the car to disappear before emerging into the teeming masses poring over open displays of vegetables and other produce and haggling in a constant cacophony.

As he struggled through the throngs, he held his hand in front of him like a beggar and took up a position near a mosque on the edge of the *souk*. He stood there for nearly half an hour, begging, and a few kind souls had dropped coins into his hand.

At last, Jaime had come along. Atcho knew that his former teammate from Peru had been selected for the task because Atcho would recognize his face.

Jaime was dressed to pass as a Sudanese farmer. He had stopped in front of Atcho, muttered a recognition phrase, dropped a few coins in his hand, and moved off. Atcho followed.

As they trudged through the streets, Atcho relaxed into his role, recalling how he had similarly disguised himself to meet with a Soviet intelligence officer in Cuba a lifetime ago. *We're in a never-ending battle.*

He looked ahead. Jaime had just rounded a corner. Atcho hurried to catch up, reminding himself to do so in character.

He turned the corner. Jaime was nowhere in sight.

Atcho wheeled about slowly, searching. Then he heard a hiss.

Jaime's head protruded from a short stairway leading under a row of buildings. He made eye contact with Atcho and then disappeared down the stairs.

Atcho waited a short while and then followed. He entered a dark, dank, smelly passage that led into deeper darkness and made his way carefully, shedding his pretense of physical disability as he went. At the end, he found a door leading to another tunnel-like passageway that crossed at a right angle. He took the branch to the right as he had been instructed and followed it until it curved again to the right. Then he saw light ahead. Moments later, he stumbled into a wider space, where Jaime was waiting.

"Great to see you," Jaime exclaimed. "We're safe here. If anyone comes in, we'll get warning, but it's doubtful anyone will." He led Atcho through a door to the side. "These are access tunnels to the city's sewer system, but it's antiquated, so the tunnels are not used much. We've cleaned out a maintenance room for our use."

The chamber was sparse, nothing more than a table with light communications equipment and a few cots set against the walls. "We'll rest here for the day and move to the staging site after dusk. You'll meet the rest of the team there and run through a few brief-back rehearsals. Do you have any questions?"

"I'm glad to see you. Is Danilo on this mission too?"

Jaime shook his head. "We both volunteered, but as you Americans say, I got the short straw." He grinned. "Besides, I do a better Sudanese than he does. Any other questions?"

Atcho shook his head tiredly. "I've been thoroughly rehearsed." He hesitated. "Well, just one question. What was the point of my disguise and walking all that way through the city?"

"Simple. If we get separated tonight, and you don't make it to the extraction point, you've got to take care of yourself until we can get you out, and you don't speak the language. You needed to get the feel from the ground. Do you have that transmitter you were issued in Tel Aviv?"

Atcho nodded.

"Good. Tonight, we'll cross the Nile west of here and meet up with the assault team a few miles east of the camp. Anything else?"

Atcho shook his head.

"Good. Then get some rest. I'll wake you up when it's time to go."

23

A Training Camp Outside Khartoum, Sudan

Klaus raised his head and listened. Something in the pre-dawn hours had awakened him, but he could not discern what. His gut stirred. He sniffed the air, but nothing unusual drifted in the light breeze. Across the room, other men snored and puffed in their sleep, but no other sound caused alarm. From afar, he heard the call of a rooster, soon to be followed by the call to prayer.

Thinking of the latter, he rolled to his other side, annoyed. Although he considered himself devout, he sometimes admitted to himself that his religion's demands could be onerous. *Prayer five times a day!*

He dispelled the thought, but soon the sense of unease returned. *Am I becoming paranoid, or are my instincts warning me?* He reached under his pillow and grasped his pistol, then sat up and tried to look through the darkness. Only the sound of sleeping men accompanied their unwashed malodor.

Rising to his feet, Klaus thrust the gun into his belt and reached for his AK-47 leaning against the head of his bed. He headed for the door, opened it, and looked out. Behind him, two men rose from their cots and joined him.

Klaus looked across the compound. The sun, still below the horizon, cast its pre-dawn light against a sky just turning blue with wisps of elongated red clouds above the distant ground level. Seeing and hearing nothing amiss, Klaus was about to turn back when strong arms seized him from behind. One hand went immediately to his face and clamped a wet cloth with a sweet-smelling substance across his nose and mouth.

Klaus only had time to sense that his assailants were hardened, trained combatants before he slipped into unconsciousness. The two men behind him grabbed him under his shoulders and dragged him forward into the compound's open ground.

A small white pickup truck was parked beyond the door. The two Israelis pushed Klaus into the middle and took seats on either side of him. The man on the driver's side cranked the engine and drove at an unhurried pace toward the main entrance. Although vigilant, he was not worried about meeting resistance. Other members of the team had subdued security across the camp, including the main gate.

Once outside the compound, the driver mashed the accelerator and headed west into the desert at high speed, leaving a trail of dust billowing behind them. Aided by a flashlight and map, his partner navigated through the dunes and craggy, sparsely vegetated hills. After ten minutes of driving, they crested a ridge and descended into a long, flat piece of hard ground. At the near end, a Black Hawk helicopter idled, its blades whipping the air and throwing up dust around it.

The pickup came to a halt a safe distance from the aircraft. Behind it, other vehicles pulled in with the rest of the assault team and formed a perimeter around the small truck.

Klaus stirred. His eyes opened. He looked around, taking in the full scene, as comprehension dawned. He heard the steel-on-steel sound of weapons being armed. On either side of him, his captors held pistols to his head.

As full consciousness returned, he heard another sound, the low roar of an idling jet engine. Then he saw a C-17 cargo jet a short distance behind the helicopter, idling on a rough, makeshift runway. Its rear cargo hatch had been dropped to the ground, exposing a cavernous interior. Crewmen hurried about making preparations for taking on freight.

Meanwhile, a man emerged from the Black Hawk. He wore the tattered clothing of a Sudanese beggar, and although he looked gaunt, he walked with authority. He was joined by another man in Western garb.

The two men guarding Klaus exited the truck while keeping their weapons trained on him. He sat motionless, watching the Sudanese beggar and his companion approach. The two guards stood aside while the newcomers thrust their heads in to take a closer look.

"Is that him?" the team leader asked.

The sun had risen to the point that no additional light was necessary. The Sudanese beggar stepped closer and gazed into Klaus' eyes.

For seconds, Klaus and the beggar stared at each other. Startled recognition crossed Klaus' face, but his mind could not yet believe what he saw.

The beggar turned to his companion. "It's him," he said simply. "He goes with us."

On hearing the voice, Klaus reacted. "Atcho!" he screamed, and lunged, wrapping his hands around Atcho's throat.

On the other side of the truck, the driver leaned in swiftly. He crooked one arm around Klaus' neck, and his free hand brought the pistol to Klaus' head.

"Let go," he growled.

Meanwhile, Atcho landed a punch in the middle of Klaus' face that stunned him, causing him to release his hold. With the gun at his head and surrounded by overwhelming firepower, Klaus stared at Atcho, hatred glistening in his eyes. "I will kill you," he said. "You and your family."

Without expression, Atcho turned his back on Klaus and walked away. Next to him, Jaime thrust an arm into the air with a circular motion. Immediately, the vehicles ringed around the white pickup started moving toward the C-17. The Black Hawk's idling engine began winding down. Two crewmen prepared to fold its blades and winch it into the hold of the cargo plane.

The pickup driver grabbed Klaus by the shoulder and pulled him from the truck, while the guard on the passenger side rounded the truck and held his weapon steady, aimed at Klaus' chest. The driver pointed to the C-17 and shoved him toward it.

Suddenly, gunfire erupted from the left ridgeline above the aircraft. Klaus' two guards went down and did not move.

Next to Atcho, Jaime fell, a clean bullet hole through his chest. Atcho heard the spit of rounds whizzing past him, ran to a sand berm, and dove behind it.

The helicopter's engine spun up again, and armed men returned fire and ran from their vehicles to clamber aboard it. Others scurried to the back of the nearest C-17 and ran up the cargo hatch. Within seconds, the helicopter soared into the air, spun in the opposite direction, dipped its nose, and gained speed as it climbed into the sky and out of range of small-arms fire. Meanwhile, the large aircraft leaped into forward motion and began taxiing even while the cargo hatches were raised.

Klaus wasted no time. As soon as his two guards collapsed, he ducked, ran back to the pickup, and sped off. As Atcho watched from his hidden position, the little truck vanished in a cloud of sand.

Within minutes, the aircraft had disappeared. Except for the sound of wind springing up over the desert sand with the rising sun and morning heat, all was silent. Deathly silent. Atcho reached into a pocket and activated the tiny transmitter that would send out a location beacon.

24

Nessim had slept fitfully that night in the chamber next to the one Klaus occupied. His room was small, no more than a closet, and it doubled for his place of work during the day. His job was to keep records of each trainee's progress.

He longed to be a fighter as well, but his slight figure made that improbable. He was well regarded in the camp, even considered to possess superior intelligence, but no one thought of him as being effective on a battlefield. Perhaps he could be a martyr if the appropriate mission came along, but doing so did not require training in the other military skills, and he was not sure he wanted to take such extreme action before contributing to *jihad* in some other meaningful way.

Nessim's ambition had always been to be a *jihadist*, and he had arrived at the camp with that intention. However, he soon learned that the training cadre looked for trainees of at least average physical build, and his frame was slight. They humored him by allowing him to stay and take part in training if he did not get in the way, but they gave him noncombatant jobs that prevented him from being a full participant.

His favorite trainer was Sahab Kadyrov, the Chechen who had been a KGB officer trained by the Soviet Spetsnaz. Rumor circulated that he was wanted in the West, where he was known by an alias he no longer used, Klaus.

Sahab maintained a distance from trainees and other instructors, but Nessim found the man's breadth and depth of knowledge fascinating. Whether the subject was hand-to-hand combat, small-arms targeting, demolitions, land navigation, or any other of a myriad of subjects, the Chechen seemed to know all of it to a superior degree. Students also muttered that Sahab had a personal connection to Osama bin Laden, a distinction that gave him an almost mythical aura.

Nessim had contented himself with attending lectures whenever time allowed, and he took part in skills exercises every chance he could. His perspicacity had been recognized despite his size, so he maintained the respect of trainees and cadre.

He heard the rooster crow and anticipated the call to prayer that would follow. He sat up in bed, yawned, stretched, and got up to prepare for the day. He heard the door creak open in the next room and went to see who might be up. Entry to his room was on the opposite side of the building, but his window was angled such that he had a clear view of the door to Sahab's room. Nessim was pleased to see that Sahab was the first to rise and had stepped outside just beyond the door. *Not surprising.*

As he observed, two other men appeared behind Sahab. One Nessim recognized. He was a trainee who had been in camp for many months and did well at all his lessons. He was quiet and kept to himself for the most part, but he was friendly when addressed, and he helped other students who did not grasp training tasks as easily as he did.

The other man was one Nessim did not recognize. That surprised him because the man had not registered with him, yet he slept in quarters reserved for trainees and cadre. For a guest at the camp to stay in that room was unusual.

As Nessim watched, one of the men stepped closer and threw a hand over Sahab's face. The other immediately grabbed Sahab's arms and held them until they went limp. Then both men dragged Sahab to a white pickup truck.

Before the truck's engine had turned over, Nessim ran out his door, heading around the building. As he reached the front, the pickup drove off.

Nessim darted into the room where Sahab had slept. He tried to wake the other men there. They had been drugged.

He sprinted to the office near the front of the camp where someone was always on duty. He arrived there with heaving lungs in time to see the pickup clear the gate without being challenged.

Inside the small room that served as the duty office, a young man, really a boy, was slumped in his chair, also drugged. In desperation, Nessim ran to the headquarters building, yelling all the way. He pounded on the door until a tall bearded man opened it. From other buildings, men poured into the compound to see what had caused the commotion.

Speaking in precise terms despite being out of breath, Nessim told the camp commander what he had seen. With a wave of his hand, the commander ordered the camp to be rousted. Within five minutes, a quick reaction patrol of twenty trucks with heavily armed men rolled out of the gate in pursuit.

Nessim rode in the lead truck with the commander. The trail of dust lingering in the air made following the pickup easy. Looking ahead, they saw by the abrupt end of the dust cloud where the intruders had halted.

The commander ordered his patrol to the left of a ridge that would hide their actions. Then all the fighters dismounted and climbed up the hill, Nessim with them.

At the crest, they looked over. Several military vehicles had circled the white pickup. Two men, one in traditional Sudanese clothes, leaned into it, and two other armed men stood on either side of it. A Black Hawk helicopter idled below the ridge, its blades spinning. Beyond it, a huge cargo jet faced away from them, its cargo bays open.

Nessim pointed toward the white pickup and spoke into the commander's ear.

"Who is the Sudanese?" the commander asked.

"I don't know," Nessim responded. "He was not in the pickup when they took Sahab."

The commander designated targets to three snipers, set his other men in a line along the crest of the ridge, and gave the order to open fire.

25

When the mayhem had subsided, Atcho remained still for nearly ten minutes, listening. Then, from the far ridge, he heard voices. When he dared peek over the top of his meager cover, he saw armed men descending the steep, craggy slope on foot.

He eased back down, his mind racing. The only plan that came to mind was impersonating a deaf and mute Sudanese beggar again—he was already in costume and knew the part.

The weakness in his plan was that snipers had already seen him. That had been evident when they'd picked off Jaime and the two men in the pickup but had left Klaus and Atcho unscathed. *Did they shoot at me and miss, or did they assume I was a captive? Either way, they'll spot me. I can't beat them all, so I'd better join them until a better plan comes along.*

The ground behind him was flat, aside from a few low sandhills. He pushed himself backward on his stomach down a shallow sandy slope a few yards and stood up. Then, assuming the posture and gait he had used while traversing Khartoum on foot, he started up the bank toward the site of the firefight.

He first headed toward Jaime's limp body to check for breathing and to pretend to scavenge. On his way, he waved wildly at the men still struggling down the embankment. As he neared Jaime, he saw clearly that there was no life.

Casting aside remorse for the moment, he spotted Jaime's sidearm still in its holster. He reached for it, and then heard the rhythmic chopping of helicopter blades slicing the air, followed by long bursts of machinegun fire. From the back side of the ridge, the Black Hawk wheeled around and veered to the front, firing withering bursts that cut through the men, who now ran headlong down the slope seeking cover. Atcho estimated that they numbered between seventy and a hundred.

Its machineguns still doing their deadly work, the Black Hawk settled back to the ground. Immediately, armed men jumped out of each side. The ones nearest the enemy advanced toward them, sending a hail of bullets. The ones on the opposite side sprinted toward Atcho and the three dead Israelis.

Moments later, Atcho found himself running toward the helicopter among a group of rescuers who carried their dead between them. On reaching the aircraft, they clambered aboard, while the other element retreated to the opposite side and climbed on. All the while, the door gunner kept up his prodigious rain of steel.

The helicopter lifted into the air. Atcho took in the simultaneous roar of gunfire, thunder of engines, and odors of fuel, gun smoke, and bloody corpses. He glanced down at Jaime's still face, remembering their time together in Lima, in the rancid streets of Khartoum, and now on the bleak sands of the Sudanese desert. Against the chopper's throbbing vibration, he felt overwhelming sorrow.

He looked into the faces of the men who had mounted the original assault and risked their lives to rescue him and bring back their fallen comrades. Some watched the bodies. Others stared far away into the empty desert. All carried the same expression of unspeakable grief and failure buttressed by stoicism. No one spoke.

At the far end of the desert runway, the ground spilled into rough terrain, all but impassable for ground vehicles. Then it spread into flat, hardscrabble ground.

The helicopter flew on for a few minutes, then settled on the surface and cut its engines. Ahead of them, the C-17 waited with cargo hatch down. Even as Atcho and the soldiers jumped from the Black Hawk and transferred to the larger plane, a crew ran to the helicopter to fold its rotor blades and winch it into the cargo hold.

Fifteen minutes later, the C-17 taxied over the rough desert floor and lumbered into the sky. Atcho settled in with the rest of the team for the long flight back to Tel Aviv, each man alone with haunting images.

26

A panel truck with three coffins awaited the C-17 when it taxied to a stop on a remote airstrip outside Tel Aviv. Atcho stood with the rest of the team to pay respect as the bodies were transferred. Burly, Eitan, and the head of Mossad operations, Jaron Bryk, joined them.

When the panel truck had departed, Burly and Eitan escorted Atcho to a waiting car while a bus drove the rest of the team away. Bryk and the mission leader walked separately to another waiting car, already in deep discussion.

Eitan shook his head sadly as he watched them. "Heads will roll over this cluster. What happened?"

Atcho described as best he could.

"What happened to the overwatch?" Eitan pressed. "And why was the Black Hawk on the ground? It was supposed to be providing air cover."

"I don't know what happened to the overwatch. I can say that the dust kicked up by the returning assault team hung in the air and created a smoke screen. A good guess is that the overwatch couldn't see the force in pursuit."

"Which the Black Hawk *should* have seen. So again, why was it on the ground?"

"It had a mechanical problem. The crew considered that it wasn't

mission-threatening, but it took longer to fix than expected. It had something to do with locking the blades in place once they were unfolded. So,
the assault got a late start. The leader decided to go for the capture rather
than wait for air cover. Another few minutes and he would have had to
scrub the mission because daylight was already dawning."

"He should have scrubbed it," Eitan observed. "We wouldn't have
captured Klaus, but we could have had another chance. That's why the
Mossad is deliberate." He closed his eyes momentarily and leaned his
head back. "As it is, we lost three good operators, one on loan from Lima
and two from Sudan. That's a huge intel hole in both countries, and we
still don't have Klaus. Worse yet, he knows we're closing in on him."

He opened the car door. "There'll be an investigation. I'm sad to say
that the mission leader is likely to see the end of his career. He'll live with
this for the rest of his life." He sat in the driver's seat and started the
engine.

"What now?" Atcho asked, settling into the back seat.

"Klaus has already scooted, I'm sure of that." Burly turned in the front
passenger seat to look at him. "Who knows where?" He grimaced.

"He recognized me," Atcho said. "Now more than ever, he'll want
revenge. He'll come after me and my family." He leaned forward and
grasped Burly's arm. "Please get word to Sofia to stay put at West Point."

Burly nodded. "What are you going to do?"

"I don't know. I'll need time to think." He sat quietly a moment, and
then leaned forward to speak to Eitan. "Out of curiosity, where did the
Israeli Air Force get a C-17?"

"What C-17?" Eitan replied without turning his head.

27

Eitan pushed into Bryk's office uninvited and sat in a chair in front of his desk. Bryk barely acknowledged his presence, continuing to scribble notes on a pad. Eitan waited him out. At last Bryk looked up.

"Is there something I can do for you?"

"I've been debriefing our recovered undercover asset from the raid in Sudan. He's the guy who got our picture of Klaus in the camp."

"Any surprises?"

Eitan shook his head. "He said Klaus was a good instructor for technical competence, but he stayed aloof. Our guy tried to get close to him, but Klaus held him at a distance. It was as if Klaus was there against his will and biding his time."

"For what?"

"We don't know. Another bombing, maybe. But where?" Eitan shook his head again. "He's a bit of a legend inside the camp, with supposed contact with that new terrorist rich kid, Osama bin Laden, but so far we haven't been able to pin him against any known plans. Rumors there credit him with exploding a nuclear device in Afghanistan last year that caused those tremors we heard about, but that's not confirmed."

Bryk eyed Eitan irritably. "Then what are you doing in my office?"

"I'm trying to piece together Klaus' next move. Here's an interesting aspect. Before the raid, chatter was building with references to a Chechen, a bomb, New York, and the financial district. That all stopped after the raid."

"What do you mean 'that all stopped?'"

Eitan sat quietly a moment. "You know how it goes. The chatter is just that. Snippets of conversation along the lines of 'he saw,' 'she said,' 'I heard,' and the like. Quite a bit of it seemed to point to Klaus, and much of it was associated with New York and the financial district."

Bryk leaned back, his expression skeptical. "All the bad guys want to hit New York City, including King Kong and Godzilla. Do we have any confirmation or corroborating evidence of something imminent?"

"No, but there is a difference between what we have and chatter."

"And that would be...?"

"What our asset overhears inside the camp is a step up from chatter. He's hearing the same things, but not from anonymous sources on a phone line many miles away. He's hearing from flesh-and-blood people he trained with. And what he heard is that something big is going down in the New York City financial district."

"Then I ask again, what are you doing in my office?"

Eitan smirked. "Seeking the wisdom of greater experience?" He leaned forward. "Seriously, we haven't encountered a threat from terrorists as great as the one Klaus represents. Shouldn't we at least be making preparations?"

"That's been done. Anything else?"

"How about warning the US?"

"That's been done too. They've been tracking him as much as we have. How seriously they take the threat is on them."

Eitan nodded. "Do you mind if I back-channel Burly and Atcho? Klaus has a personal vendetta against Atcho. They're likely to pay more attention."

Bryk let out a long breath. "I don't see how that would harm anything. We're really just talking about your gut instinct, right?"

Eitan acceded, and Bryk went back to scribbling notes on his pad. He looked up a moment later. Eitan still sat in front of him.

"Is there something else?"

Eitan sighed. "Sir, what is going to happen to the mission leader on that raid?"

Bryk dropped his pen on the desk impatiently, though his eyes held compassion. "It's out of our hands." He picked up the pen and toyed with it a moment. "I hate losing good people, but he showed remarkably poor judgment against all his training. He can never be allowed to lead an operation again. Beyond that, I don't know." He glanced at Eitan's face. "Is he a friend?"

Eitan looked down in resignation. "No," he said slowly. "I just feel bad for him. He risked his life; he was the guy on the ground. I just wish we allowed for second chances."

Bryk rose from his seat, a gesture to end the discussion. "I understand, but when life and death are at stake, as they were on this mission—we lost three good men, and who's to say that if allowed another chance he wouldn't exercise similar judgment, or overcorrect by being too cautious? He's damaged, and we can't risk other lives for his sake."

Over eyes half-closed with regret, Eitan nodded and rose to his feet. "I suppose you're right. I also wish we could find a way to even the score with Klaus."

"Get that out of your head." Bryk spoke sternly. "We gather intelligence. We share it when and where appropriate. We mount operations. We even retaliate, but when we do, it's after careful thought about possible outcomes by taking or not taking action. And we never allow a desire for revenge to cloud our thinking. That's the way to ruin. Do you understand?"

Chagrinned, Eitan nodded. "Yes, sir."

Bryk gestured that he would walk Eitan to the door. "I've given you your leeway. If you want to see justice for the failed mission, put the information where it can best be used. That includes your gut instinct. And then back away."

Eitan thanked Bryk and returned to his office. There, he put in a call to Burly, but connected with an answering machine. He left a message.

28

Yousef awoke with a start. A light shined in his eyes, and he felt a hand clamped against his lips. Around him in his bedroom, all was dark.

"Shh, it's me, Sahab. Don't set off alarms." Klaus lifted his hand from Yousef's mouth.

Bewildered, Yousef looked about wildly. "Wh-who? H-how did you get in here?" He struggled to pull his wits together.

"Never mind that. I'm here. Or rather, I'm not here." Klaus snickered. "You taught me well how to move in and out of countries without being seen."

"What are you doing here?" Yousef hissed, suddenly angry. "You put us both in danger."

"Don't worry. I'll be gone before the authorities know I'm here. I've already transferred my money to my own control, and my bombs are safely outside the country."

Fully awake now, Yousef stared at him. "Why are you doing that? Did we do something to gain your mistrust?"

"Haven't you heard?" Klaus growled, matching Yousef's anger. "They came for me in Sudan, right in the training camp. They were taking me away on a jet. I came face to face with Atcho." His face contorted with rage. "If one smart trainee had not been alert, who knows where I would be right now." In vivid terms, he described the raid on the camp. "Our snipers killed three of them."

Yousef listened, almost disbelieving, except that Klaus' fury was genuine, and here he was, in the dead of night, having entered Saudi Arabia undetected on his own, not once but apparently twice—and he had taken possession of his money.

"I see why you're upset," he entreated when Klaus finished telling his story, "but don't blame us, and don't throw away our *jihad*."

"I'm throwing nothing away," Klaus stormed, "but someone is to blame. How did they know where to find me?"

Yousef thought for a few moments. "It had to be either the Americans or the Israelis. I think the Israelis. They have covert operators all through the Middle East and parts of Africa."

"But Atcho was with them."

"Maybe he was on loan."

"I'm going after him. I'm tired of his interference. He blew the operation for us in Berlin and then in Kuwait, he stopped me in Texas—and he killed my brother. He needs to go."

Yousef pulled his bulky frame out of bed, crossed the room to switch on a lamp, and then sat in an overstuffed chair. Klaus remained sitting on the edge of the bed.

"I understand your anger," Yousef said, "but why are you blaming us? Why did you pull your money and take your bombs away? We're on your side."

"I'm tired of waiting," Klaus snapped. "I spent months in the Sudan training camps. I made three trips to Latin America and then spent more months in Sudan. I want Atcho dead, and I want to blow a hole in America that will never be forgotten. I have the ability to do both, and I don't need Al-Qaeda's permission."

Yousef saw that Klaus would not be easily placated. "Then why did you return to see me? You have your money and your bombs. Why not just plant your bombs?"

Klaus took his time to respond, choosing his words carefully. "Because I have enough enemies. I don't need more." His tone seemed almost wistful. "When my brother was alive, we relied on each other. If I go alone now, I am truly alone. I don't wish to alienate you or Osama bin Laden. I just want my revenge and to hit my own targets, and I don't want to wait for anyone's permission. I think we can still cooperate."

Yousef studied Klaus from across the room. He observed a rare ferocity in him, but also a dampening of spirit, as if Klaus felt his isolation for the first time, or at least the depth of it. He climbed from his chair, walked over to Klaus, and leaned over, placing his hands on Klaus' shoulders.

"*Habibi,*" he said, "you are one of us. You have no need to ever be alone. We fight for the same things."

Klaus looked up at him defiantly. "You gave me ultimatums."

Surprised, Yousef pulled back. "I did," he said. "Maybe that was the wrong approach. You seemed about to take hurried action. We've succeeded by careful planning and execution.

"You know the operation we have coming up. We've prepared for years, but moving the pieces into place took a lot of time. It's almost ready. We didn't want you to do something impulsive to jeopardize it."

Klaus dropped his head into his hands. Yousef returned to his chair and sank into it. "So, what do we do?"

Klaus raised his head and regarded Yousef for a moment. "Just let me take care of Atcho. Now. More than two years have passed since he killed my brother, and he's taken a wife, and they've had a son. He's living life while my brother lies cold and desecrated by infidels in an unknown grave."

He cast a beseeching glance at Yousef. "I can make Atcho's death look like an accident. I'll even let his wife and son live, if you prefer. And whether I succeed or fail, I'll turn over my bombs to the people you already have in the US, and they can add them to the ones they're building. I'll show the leader how to detonate them. In return, I only ask for help locating Atcho. I doubt he went home to Texas. This way, I get my revenge, your plan goes forward, and we both get to strike a huge blow for Islam—the biggest ever."

Yousef's eyes widened in surprise. "You would do that?"

Klaus nodded. "You've already scouted the target. You know where to place the bombs for maximum destruction. I'll be happy to help."

Yousef sat in disbelief. "What happens afterward?"

Klaus shrugged. "I'll give you back my money to manage and go wherever Osama directs. I'll be his most loyal soldier. If the bombs work, I'll make as many as we can get plutonium for, and I won't ask for another thing." He stood and faced Yousef with fierce determination. "Atcho must die."

29

Sofia hurried into Isabel's house to answer the incessantly ringing phone while Isabel helped the children from the car.

"You were right, little lady. If I ever doubt you again, please remind me to check my sanity."

Sofia recognized Horton's voice and smiled despite the warning implied by his words. "What's going on?"

"Get to a secure line. I'll fill you in."

An hour later, Sofia sat in the same West Point office where she had previously called Horton. He picked up on the first ring.

"The mission failed," Horton said. "Klaus got away."

Sofia's heart dropped into the pit of her stomach. "Atcho—"

"He's fine. But the Israelis lost three men. Klaus went back to Riyadh."

"How do you know?"

"I have a friend in Saudi intelligence. Thanks to your shakin' the bushes when you came to Berlin, they recruited an informant inside Yousef's home in Riyadh. A man arrived there in the middle of the night, unannounced. He didn't use the doorbell. He broke in. It was Klaus. The informant eavesdropped." Horton chuckled. "Ya really shouldn't take the domestic help for granted."

He coughed and continued. "We have a second source. The *hawal-*

adars had a conversation. Yousef in Riyadh called Kadir in Berlin, who called us. You and the Germans turned him good. A guy by the name of Sahab wants help to locate Atcho."

"That's Klaus."

"Right. As I was piecin' this together waitin' on your call, I remembered that last year, here in Berlin, Kadir checked out you and Atcho for Klaus. He hired a detective agency in Austin and got pictures of you from an announcement in the Austin newspaper about your joinin' a garden club." He chuckled again. "Somehow, I have a hard time seein' you putterin' around in the roses and weeds with muddy gloves and rubber boots."

"Not now, Joe. What are you getting at?"

Horton's tone turned serious. "Klaus already has loads of information on you and Atcho. It's only a mental hop, skip, and jump for him to find out that Atcho has a daughter and granddaughter and where they live. He'll figure that Atcho will come to wherever his family is to protect them. It's good that you're at West Point. You should be safe there."

"I'm not so sure about that. Security is pretty loose here."

"Well, when you hear from Atcho, there are a couple of other things to talk about. There's some big operation planned inside the US. No mention was made of where, but it's been in plannin' for years, and they're goin' to execute soon." Horton sighed heavily into the phone. "I don't like tellin' you this, but you got to know."

"Just spit it out."

"Klaus offered to contribute his bombs to the operation in exchange for being cut loose to come after Atcho. At last count, he has three left. He'll deliver them to the stateside honcho for this operation, show him how to arm and detonate them, and then head Atcho's way. You nailed it, Sofia."

Sofia felt pressure against her temples and a roar in her ears as a sense of dread descended. Her hands became clammy. She took deep breaths to regain emotional control.

"Has our intelligence been advised?" she asked.

"The CIA, military intelligence, and even the FBI are hittin' their sources hard for whatever this operation is. So far, there's not much to go on, but they've heard chatter about it for months. I don't know where Atcho is now. Presumably, he's headed home. My guess is you'll hear from him today or tomorrow."

Silence ensued. "Ma'am, are you there?"

"I'm here. I was trying to think through all of this. Thanks for the help, Joe. You're a good friend to our whole family."

"That's mighty nice of you to say, little lady. Ziggy is just glad I get to stay home nights now, and soon we're headed into that promised land of retirement." He laughed. "Anythin' else I can do for you? Keep in mind that's just a nice way of endin' a phone conversation." He laughed again.

"Nothing for now, Joe. Thanks again."

"Seriously, if you need somethin', alls you got to do is ask. Us Texans got to stick together."

When Sofia arrived back at the house, Isabel looked anxious.

"Burly called," she told Sofia. "He wants you to phone him back first chance." She handed Sofia a piece of paper with numbers neatly written on it. "He wouldn't tell me anything."

"Don't worry. I'll fill you in." Sofia took the number and called Burly. "What's up?"

"Atcho's on his way home. We landed in the US a little while ago. He's fine. He asked me to get a message to you to stay where you are."

"I'm not so sure that's a good idea. I'm read into the situation. Security here is not great."

"Got it," Burly said, then chuckled. "There's no reining you in, is there? Just do me a favor and keep me in the loop."

"I will, Burly, but you've got to do me a favor. Call our friend Joe Horton and get him to brief you on what he told me. Then call Bob, Isabel's husband, on a secure line and fill him in. He needs to be home with Isabel while this is going on."

"Shouldn't that come from you, or Atcho, or Isabel?"

"Maybe, but you can locate him and get on a secure phone easier than I can, and we don't know how much time we've got."

"Roger. I'll shake some trees."

"Thanks." Sofia hung up and turned to face Isabel.

When Atcho arrived at Isabel's house that afternoon, he was surrounded by the overjoyed embrace of his wife, daughter, young granddaughter, and toddler son. He could not help thinking of the stark contrast in atmosphere and living conditions between being among loved ones at this stately home above the Hudson River and roaming the streets of Khartoum.

Isabel chided him. "Dad, those gray hairs on your head are multiplying. When are you going to stop this dangerous hobby of yours?"

Atcho did not reply. He caressed the side of Isabel's face and hugged her tightly. Then he stooped to pick up Kattrina and Jameson. With one under each arm, he bounded out onto the lawn, dropped to his knees in the grass, and rolled over onto his back amid the children's happy squeals.

Watching them, Sofia's chest swelled and her eyes moistened. She turned to Isabel. "Atcho has never had a malicious bone in his body. That's the life he yearns for and deserves."

Later, when they were alone, Atcho and Sofia exchanged details of their activities since Atcho's departure. Sofia related her conversation with Horton that morning.

"Your analysis was dead-on," Atcho told her. He took her in his arms. "No wonder they paid you the big bucks."

"Right," Sofia replied, snuggling against him, "and now we have to figure out what we're going to do. Klaus has something big planned inside the US, and he will never stop coming after us. We're going to have to end it."

30

Klaus called Yousef from Tripoli, Libya. "I'm in a safe place now."

They spoke in cryptic terms.

"Have you moved your cargo?" Yousef asked.

"It's on the way. I broke the individual objects into their component parts and sent them the way I did before. I'll find machine shops to do the parts of the frame I couldn't send."

"How will you travel?"

"I'll take exactly the same route." *Well, not exactly, but I won't tell you that.*

"When you get there, I'll put you in touch with our contact."

Klaus hung up and crossed to a window, deep in thought. He watched the blue waves of the Mediterranean crash against boulders far below. This was a moment of introspection, as if observing himself from outside his body.

Deciding not to reveal his real travel plans to Yousef had been an impulsive decision, based, he suddenly realized, on mistrust. Not that he believed Yousef would do anything to harm him or any other member of Al-Qaeda—the *hawaladar's* entire existence was based on trust. If he violated that, his fortune would collapse, and that would be the least of his problems. *But somehow, Atcho found me in Sudan.*

Klaus realized an emerging sense of independence greater than any he had known before. He had money, he had weapons, he knew tactics, and, just as importantly, he knew how to move around in the Western world unseen.

For a moment, his mind's eye glimpsed the man he had been, crawling through the smelly tunnels under Berlin—a fearsome warrior, no doubt, but one taking direction from a higher authority and relying on brute force to take down enemies in his immediate vicinity. Now, he knew how to disappear into the fabric of societies as far-flung as Afghanistan, Peru, and even the United States, whether the occasion called for a *jalabiya,* tourist clothes, or a business suit. He smirked. *I've grown.*

Later that day, he met with Hassan, a local *hawaladar* who had introduced him to Yousef on Klaus' first trip to Saudi Arabia. So much had happened since then. Klaus had flown over the burning oil fields of Kuwait, he had smuggled himself with a lethal packet of plutonium into the United States, and he had traveled into several countries in South America to watch three separate bombing attacks.

"I need to move money and have it ready in three cities," he told Hassan, getting down to business after courtesies. "Make it one hundred thousand dollars in Caracas, the same in Montreal, and half a million in New York City."

Hassan made a note. "Anything else?"

"Get me a Libyan passport, an Argentinian passport, and a US passport. I need highest quality, and they should be well used with proper stamps. The Libyan one needs a visa to enter Argentina, and that one needs to get me into Canada too. The American one needs to show that I've passed through a legal port of entry—I don't care where."

"These could take several days."

"That's fine. One other thing." Klaus pulled a sheaf of papers from his jacket. "This is information that Kadir pulled together for me when I was in Berlin. There's a photograph of a man known as Atcho. You'll see his real name in these documents. They include newspaper articles about him and his wife, Sofia. I want to know everything about him, what family he has, where they live—"

"Should I go through Kadir?"

Klaus shook his head. "You'll see the name of a detective agency in Austin that Kadir used. Get a different one. I'll make my own travel arrangements. No one can know my movements."

Still taking notes, Hassan nodded as if doing routine business. "Anything else?"

"Just one. I need a contact in Montreal with a mosque that is sympathetic to *jihad*. Is that something you can arrange?"

Hassan nodded without looking up.

Klaus headed for the door. As he opened it, he turned back to Hassan. "I'll pick them up in three days." He glanced at Hassan's notepad. "Burn those notes."

31

Klaus looked about the small coffee shop on the Jersey City waterfront. The early morning crowds were finishing their last mugs before heading off to work. The buzz of chatter quieted amid the aroma of fresh brews mixing with cinnamon and nutmeg. *This is not an unpleasant place.*

Klaus had never heard of the man Yousef had directed him to meet, nor would Yousef tell him anything about the contact except to say that Klaus would be approached at this time on this date in this place. Despite the coffee shop's pleasant atmosphere, Klaus felt persistent unease, surrounded as he was by tall skyscrapers and roaring traffic on a scale beyond his experience, even in Berlin. Nevertheless, he was impressed with the opportunity that presented itself: *My bomb in this place would kill huge numbers of infidels.*

He reveled in the thought, but his mind turned to Atcho. *How do I get Atcho into the area where I'll place the bomb?* He dismissed the notion with a shrug. He could take out Atcho at any time. The hit did not have to occur in conjunction with the bombing, and Atcho might suffer even more knowing who had planted it and that he had been powerless to stop it. Klaus smiled.

He felt someone nudging his shoulder. A stoop-shouldered man stood there, young despite his posture. He had reddish hair that curled around his ears and an unkempt beard.

"Excuse me, sir. Do you mind if I read your paper—the part you've finished?"

Klaus studied him. The man had just given the recognition signal, but he was nervous in a way that bothered Klaus, as if that was his habitual demeanor rather than one generated by this clandestine meeting taking place in public view.

"I'm finished with the sports page. Is that the part you wanted?" Klaus replied, completing the sequence.

The man nodded and looked around, again in a manner that was too furtive for Klaus' liking. *He'll attract attention just because of his silly manner. Who sent him?*

"I'm sitting with a friend over there. Would you like to join us?"

Klaus stared at the man angrily. "No, I would not," he retorted, registering the man's startled expression. "I have a meeting to go to."

He shoved the newspaper into the man's hands, stood, and made a quick exit. He made his way to his hotel a short distance away and called Yousef in Saudi Arabia. It would be mid-afternoon there.

"They sent me a fool," he blurted when Yousef came on the line. "If I'm going to work with these people, I need to see someone with competence. Anyone would have noticed and remembered that idiot. If that's who's carrying out your mission over here, it's already a failure."

"I'll take care of it," was all Yousef said. He entreated Klaus to return to the same coffee shop at the same time the next day.

Klaus spent the rest of the morning walking the city streets. Around noon, he crossed to the other side of the Hudson River through the Holland Tunnel in a taxi. There, he asked the driver to point him to the ferry that would take him out to the Statue of Liberty.

He meandered along the waterfront opposite the coffee shop, taking in the sights and sounds of the bustling city. As he skirted by the World

Trade Center, he stared up at the towers, taking in their full height and might. Then he scoffed. *Your days are numbered.*

His reaction was similar as the ferry broke the wavelets while approaching Liberty Island with its grand statue, the most famous in the world. Without emotion, he watched the people gazing up in awe at the crown, torch, and visage. He viewed them in the same light as a home-owner observing an anthill spoiling a back yard—a nuisance to be removed. *And I have the pesticide.*

The next morning, Klaus returned to the coffee shop. He arrived a little earlier this time so that he might have a better chance of getting a seat in a corner with his back to the wall, where he could better observe the morning crowd. Several minutes later, he noticed a man enter alone.

The newcomer was nondescript, wore tinted glasses, and dressed neatly in clothes typical of the area. He moved easily among the other customers, excusing himself politely when bumping into someone or having to reach across for items like sugar or cream. He did not look around, yet he seemed aware of where everything was in the room, circling tables, chairs, and other people with unobtrusive ease.

When he had paid for his coffee and a pastry, he made his way to a table not far from Klaus and sat with his back toward him. He lingered there as the crowd grew, satisfied its morning caffeine craving, and then thinned out—the rhythm of the city.

After a while, the man stood and walked into the restroom. When he came out, he stopped by Klaus' table.

"Excuse me, sir, if you are finished with parts of your newspaper, would you mind if I read them?"

Klaus looked up into a set of calm eyes. The man had removed his glasses, and he smiled mildly. "I don't mean to bother you," he continued. "I'll return them if you like."

Klaus studied him quickly. "Please sit. You can read them here."

"Thank you. My name is Ramzi Yousef."

The two men stayed in the coffee shop only long enough to ensure they had not been observed. Then they departed and walked along the street edging the waterfront, speaking in Arabic.

"I apologize for Salameh yesterday. He's my useful idiot."

"He needs a leash. He has no subtlety and he's all emotion. People will notice him, his strange behavior, and the people with him. I could not stay."

Ramzi nodded. "You are right. He's exploded things in my workshop and he even put me in the hospital."

"He what?"

"It's true. He drives like a maniac. One night a couple of weeks ago, he drove through an intersection on a yellow light. He was going too fast and was rammed by another vehicle. I was a passenger and had to be taken away in an ambulance." He grasped Klaus' arms. "These Americans are so stupid. I had all the bomb-making materials in the trunk of the car. Would you believe it? The police never checked. A few days later, two of our men went to the impound lot and told the attendant they needed to get some personal items from the car. The guard let them. They got everything out. No problem.

"I was in the hospital for a few days, but I had a telephone right by my bed and just kept working. I ordered some powdered metals I need to make the bomb more powerful. They will multiply the explosive effect by many magnitudes."

Klaus stopped Ramzi with a hand on his shoulder. "You're the bomb-maker?"

"I thought you knew that."

Klaus shook his head. "They wouldn't tell me much. Only how to make contact and that I would be briefed when I arrived."

They walked to the water's edge. "And there," Ramzi said, "is the target."

Across the river, the twin towers of the World Trade Center rose into the sky, gleaming in the sunlight.

"Can you believe it?" Klaus exulted. "Allah be praised."

"That's it," Ramzi affirmed. "In a little more than a week, we'll topple both of them."

"How?" Klaus asked, barely able to contain his excitement.

"Simple. We'll park the van next to one of the outer walls on an upper floor in the parking garage. We've already scouted and have the location selected. When the bomb blows, it will be of such power that it will damage the foundational structure of the first tower, causing it to fall into the second tower." He rubbed his hands together in exultation. "We'll get them both."

Klaus' eyes glowed with excitement. He leaned back so he could see the full height of the towers and imagined them collapsing into the Hudson River.

"Do you know why I'm here?" he asked.

Ramzi pursed his lips. "Not really. I was told only to expect you, how to find you, and that you should be treated as a peer. You come with the blessing of Osama bin Laden."

Klaus nodded. "True." As he explained his purpose, Ramzi's eyes grew wide with amazement. Klaus explained to him about his bombs, how he had come into possession of them, and how he had transported one into the US on a previous occasion. "I'm building a new one here," he said. "I'll have some parts machined in local shops; the other parts were delivered to an address here in New York. I think that address is yours."

Ramzi's cheeks contorted as he held back a smile. "I didn't know what they were for." He stood back and took a new measure of Klaus, then pointed across the river at the towers. "That," he exclaimed, "is the financial heart of the US economy. When we bring those buildings down, this abominable country might never recover. And with your weapon added to mine, thousands of infidels will die, perhaps millions. The black hole a mile wide in New York City will be a warning to all mankind of the power of Islam." He closed his eyes and breathed out slowly. "Surely, Allah brought you and me together for his *jihad*."

Then a questioning look crossed his face. "What about the nuclear fuel? Do you have it already?"

Klaus chortled. "Are you ready for some irony? I have it, and I stored it in a bank safety deposit box in that tower." He pointed at the one with the television antenna protruding from its top. "I think they call that the North Tower."

Neither man spoke for a few minutes, both taking in the sight of the soaring edifices across the river. Then they turned and retraced their steps past the coffee shop toward Ramzi's workplace.

"How did you enter the country?" Ramzi asked.

Klaus smirked. "It was so easy. I flew into Montreal on an Argentinean passport and took a boat from Kingston across Lake Ontario. I have a US passport that shows I traveled outside the country a while ago and re-entered a few weeks back." He laughed. "I'm legal. What about you?"

"I've been here since September. I came in on a fake Iraqi passport and was arrested coming through immigration at the airport. I claimed that my life was in danger in Iraq and requested political asylum." He shrugged and laughed. "I went in front of some minor official who scheduled a court date for me and let me go on my own recognizance." He guffawed. "I think I missed my court date."

They reached a long alley and turned to walk through its shadows. "You know what's even funnier?" Ramzi continued. "I came here with one of our men. He's more like Salameh, not the most intelligent person. The passport he presented at immigration had his own picture pasted over someone else's, and he had three other passports. He was arrested and sentenced to six months in jail and fined fifty dollars."

"Fifty dollars? That's all? In Saudi Arabia, they would have tortured him."

"Here's the funniest part," Ramzi continued. "He was carrying bomb-making manuals with him, complete with his own drawings. At his trial, he claimed that he had them because he was researching how to spot them among terrorists. The judge not only ordered that the manuals be returned to him, but also that if any of them were damaged or missing, the arresting officer would have to pay to replace them."

He shook his head. "Only in America. Anything goes here. He has a week or two remaining on his sentence, but we can't wait for him. If he's not out in time, we'll blow the buildings anyway. I don't worry about him, though. He's comfortable. He says the inmates just sit around watching

TV or porno videos." He chuckled. "He claims to turn his head so he doesn't see and be corrupted, but I don't believe him."

They continued on through the alley. Then Klaus stopped. "I need help with another project."

Ramzi gave him his full attention.

"This project is sanctioned by Osama on condition that I don't let it interfere with our joint mission here." He recounted his running battle with Atcho, the death of his brother, and Atcho's interference in his other attempts at raining death on infidels.

"Yes," Ramzi agreed when Klaus had finished. "This Atcho must die, and all those close to him. What do you want to do?"

"If I can't get him into the bomb blast area, I'll deal with him afterwards. Meanwhile, I want him to feel my reach, to fear the power of what I can do, to tremble at the knowledge that I am coming for him."

"How can I help?"

"I want to send him a message. He's at West Point. Have you heard of the place?"

Ramzi nodded. "Of course. It's about fifty miles upstream from the Twin Towers."

Klaus' eyes burned with malevolence. "That close? I hadn't realized that."

"What do you want to do?"

Klaus hesitated only a moment while he gathered his thoughts. "Let me have your best man. Atcho has a son and a daughter. They are at West Point now. I want them kidnapped and brought to me."

Ramzi shrugged. "We can do that, but do you think it's wise so close to executing our mission?"

"It will be a distraction for Atcho. He expects me to come, but he won't expect that. He'll be so busy trying to find them that he won't have time to get in our way."

"How old are the children?"

"His daughter is fully grown, and she has a daughter as well. Your man can bring her too, if he can manage all three."

"What about the son? Will he be a problem?"

"Only if you run out of diapers. He's a toddler."

"What will you do with them?"

"Sell them into the sex trade," Klaus said without hesitation, "or you can take Atcho's daughter back to Pakistan with you, if you like. Consider her a bonus. The son we can sell to a trader in Afghanistan. He can be a dancing boy there."

32

Atcho cleared security without difficulty at FBI headquarters in the Jacob Javits Federal Building on Lafayette Street in Manhattan. The largest federal building in the US, it was an imposing edifice with many small windows that made it look like an enormous, vacated beehive.

Burly met Atcho in the lobby and escorted him to an upper floor. "We're not getting a lot of takers on our story," he said as they rode the elevator. "Most people in the intelligence community or the FBI have never heard of Al-Qaeda or Osama bin Laden, and the notion of Hamas and Hezbollah cooperating with each other seems outlandish to them. That goes back to the Shia–Sunni chasm. If they killed every last infidel on the planet, that still wouldn't stop their *jihad* because they'd kill each other until one or the other of their belief systems reigns supreme."

"So, what are we doing here today?"

"Klaus threatened you and your family. We have to make sure we get all the federal protection we can. The special agent in charge at the FBI office in Chicago, Tom O'Brian, is an evangelist for counterterror and spends a lot of time researching it. I spoke with him by phone when we got back from Israel. He's proposing to his superiors to form a counter-error task force. He's a bit of a dandy and he rubs his bosses the wrong way. Rumor has it that he was granted the Chicago assignment to sideline him—get him out of his boss' hair."

Atcho's agitation sparked. "I'm not understanding. Don't they know that a ring of terror is closing around us, and if we don't stop it, we're going to be hit here at home, big time?" He took a deep breath and swung around to face Burly. "Three explosions. Three of them in the last year when Klaus was there, near the site, and they keep getting bigger. That doesn't even count the failed attempt by my house last year. The terrorists are testing methods and probing weaknesses, and they're getting better by the day. Do these smart intel guys think we're invulnerable?"

The elevator reached its destination, the doors slid open, and they stepped into a corridor. Burly led the way into a conference room. The view beyond the glass was dramatic, showing the vast cityscape that was New York City with its crown jewels, the twin towers of the World Trade Center, gleaming in the sunlight against a deep blue sky.

"The man we're meeting with is skeptical about the size of the threat," Burly said, ignoring the vista. "He'll be here in a few minutes to put us on speakerphone with O'Brian in Chicago."

"It's not just Klaus," Atcho said in exasperation, continuing their prior conversation. He glanced around the conference room and took note of the magnificent view, but he stayed on point. "Klaus is the tip of the spear, and an incredibly lethal one. Bad people are coming our way, and they intend to convert or kill us. In their view, we're all combatants: women, children, mothers, fathers—it doesn't matter. If we're infidels, we should die. That's the way these *jihadists* see things."

Burly gave him a sideways glance. "Do you think you might be getting a little paranoid?"

"Paranoid?" Atcho whirled on him. "You were the case officer when that suitcase nuke got loose in Siberia. You were in Berlin when the guy we're chasing right now, Klaus, escaped with one just like it. You came back out of retirement last year when he had ideas about using it in the Kuwaiti oilfields, and he had learned to make copies. And in each of my last three missions, including the attempt to capture Klaus in Sudan, *you* came to *me*."

Burly listened to him patiently. "Correct on all counts." He sighed.

"I'm your friend, Atcho. We're on the same side. We have to stay objective, though."

"Meaning what?" Atcho fought to control his anger. Images crossed his mind of a dank cell in Siberia where he had been held captive in the dead of winter, of being aboard the near-crash of a huge cargo jet in Moscow, of crawling through dark tunnels under Berlin, and of flying through the black smoke clouds in a Black Hawk helicopter amid the flames of burning oil wells in Kuwait.

He squinted. "I've put my life on the line at your request several times, and you call me paranoid. Even if I were, that doesn't mean the danger isn't real."

Chastened, Burly backtracked. "Poor choice of words," he said. "But take another look. Siberia and Moscow were purely East-versus-West situations. Berlin was too, and only involved *jihad* because Klaus was part of that conspiracy.

"We're after one man with a bomb, not a whole movement. I'm not saying that there isn't a group of bad people wanting to do bad things to us, but their resources are limited. They can't pose a major threat to us."

Atcho's eyes bulged. He slid both hands over his ears to massage the back of his head. "I can't believe I'm hearing this. You thought the threat credible enough when Klaus put that suitcase nuke by my house last year —and activated the countdown."

Burly blew out a breath, his own patience waning. "Yes, I did, and the threat was real—from one man, with a weapon that still has never been proven."

Atcho contained his exasperation. "Are you serious? Do you recall that I nearly burned my hand off taking care of that bomb?"

"Agreed," Burly said, restraining himself, "and the device had plutonium, but we can't say definitively that it or any of Klaus' bombs were viable. They were never tested."

"What about the tremor in Afghanistan at Tora Bora? I recall you thought that might have been caused by a 'poor man's underground test.' I think that's what you called it."

Burly nodded. "We still think that might be the case, but we don't have proof. Some radiation leaked into the atmosphere, but that could have been naturally generated, and our teams couldn't go deep enough to find trace materials that would tell us the origin of any nuclear device, *if* that's what caused the tremor in the first place."

Atcho shook his head, defiant. "Then what am I doing here?"

"Klaus poses a real threat, particularly to your family. His device might actually work, in which case the danger extends far beyond you. As you said, you came to warn the authorities. I'm here for the same reason."

Burly paused. "There's one other thing I wanted to tell you when we got into a secure facility, like this one." He looked around the room as if double-checking. "Eitan called last night. He passed along that their asset inside the camp overheard that Klaus plans to hit the New York financial district. Mind you, that information is not confirmed and it's just above the level of chatter in terms of reliability."

Before Atcho could respond, the door opened, and a well-groomed man in a dark business suit walked in. "Gentlemen," he greeted them. "Sorry to run late. We're going to have to get right to the call. My name is Jim Dude." He extended his hand.

Atcho and Burly stared at him.

Dude returned their gazes with a shrug. "I get that a lot. That's my real last name. Will you please take your seats? My secretary has already placed the call and will put it through." A green light on a speakerphone in the middle of the table blinked. "That should be our man." He reached over and flipped a switch.

"O'Brian here," a disembodied voice intoned.

Dude introduced Atcho and Burly.

"It's an honor to meet you, Atcho," O'Brian said. "I watched the night President Reagan introduced you at the State of the Union Address."

"Thank you, but that was long ago. Can we get to business?" Atcho felt the heat of his anger still simmering and forced himself to be civil. "A few weeks ago, I was in Israel, where I participated with the Mossad in a mission to snatch a Chechen terrorist from Sudan. The man has a suitcase nuclear bomb, maybe as many as five, and his stated aim is to harm the US and, more specifically, me and my family. And I just learned he's planning an attack right here in New York City."

As Atcho spoke with passion, even fury, Burly leaned back in his chair and arched his eyebrows. Dude leaned forward in his seat, thunderstruck.

"If he succeeds in harming my family," Atcho went on, "he will simultaneously kill many other Americans. Depending on where that happens, we could be talking millions of casualties. Sorry to be so blunt, but I learned on the way here that the FBI doubts the severity of the threat."

A stifling cloud seemed to have descended over the room.

Dude cleared his throat. "Mr. Atcho," he began, his reluctance to speak evident. "This mission you say you went on with Mossad"—he glanced at Burly—"are we supposed to know about that?"

Burly shook his head slightly, looking dismayed. "Not necessarily," he said, just loudly enough for O'Brian to hear over the speakerphone. "I filed a full report with the CIA. If it's relevant to your efforts, you'll get the details through channels."

Startled, Atcho looked back and forth between Dude and Burly. "I don't understand. What do you mean you're not 'necessarily' supposed to know? How are you supposed to protect—"

"This is exactly what I've been talking about," O'Brian cut in over the phone. "That silly practice of not sharing information between the CIA and the FBI is going to get people killed. Lots of *American* people."

Atcho rose to his feet and leaned on his fists over the table. "Will someone please explain to me what the hell we're talking about?" He glared at Dude. "I came in to tell you about a man who has a nuclear device he intends to use inside the United States. The threat is taken seriously by the Mossad, and you talk to me about practices and whether you're supposed to know about something that could be critical to protecting our people? What kind of crap is that?"

"It's complicated," Dude responded in a low voice.

"Try me," Atcho snapped. "I'm just a dumb yokel from the general public, but I've been known to understand a thing or two."

"I'll handle this," O'Brian called, "and Atcho, I'm on your side. That's why I'm consigned to the hinterland in Chicago instead of meeting with you in person there in New York."

"Now, Tom—"

"I said I'd handle his question." O'Brian's voice assumed an icy quality. "I still outrank you, Jim, and I'm a participant in this meeting."

Dude started to protest.

"I want to hear him," Atcho said. He straightened to full height, crossed his arms, and cast a challenging glare at Dude. Burly said not a word.

"You know the CIA and the FBI have different missions," O'Brian said.

"Yes."

"The CIA is restricted to intelligence gathering outside the US, and the FBI is responsible for investigating crimes inside our borders."

"Got it. Tell me something I don't know."

"Because of the rise in terror worldwide," O'Brian went on, "I started this counterterror unit, but it doesn't have wide acceptance within the bureau."

"Now, Tom—" Dude interrupted.

"I'm just giving him the lay of the land," O'Brian said tersely. "I won't air our dirty laundry.

"Atcho, the hickey comes in when defining the dividing line between what is a threat to the US outside our borders and when it becomes a domestic concern. Your guy Klaus illustrates the problem clearly. He's on foreign soil, but he threatens us here, and more specifically you and your family. As you pointed out, if he succeeds, many people will die. I understand he attacked your house with a device a few months ago—"

"There's no physical evidence that was Klaus," Dude protested.

Atcho's head swung around, his anger palpable. "I fought with him. He killed one of your agents and beat a cop nearly to death."

"You say so," Dude retorted, "but where's the proof that Klaus did those things? You fought him at night, and no one else saw him." He looked at Burly. "So far there is no physical evidence confirming that Klaus was involved at all. Is that correct?"

Looking sheepish, Burly nodded and turned his attention to Atcho. "We found your fingerprints on the bomb last year. That was expected, because you fought with the assailant—"

"The assailant," Atcho glowered. "That's all he is? You and I joined in a full manhunt for him in Germany and Kuwait."

"That was overseas," Dude cut in. "Different ballpark, different game. Here, inside the country, we need evidence of a crime to investigate. As I understand, the assailant"—he emphasized the term—"got away, and there's no physical evidence to say who the man was." He turned to Burly. "There was no match for the other fingerprints on that case. Is that right?"

Burly nodded. "Besides Atcho's, there was only one other set of prints. They were smudged, and there was no match in the database for the partials that were lifted."

Atcho stared in disbelief. "Burly, you were there. You know it was Klaus. You just got a call from the Mossad about an intent to attack here in the city."

Burly caught Dude's glance. "The call I got was unofficial," he said, his reluctance clear. "I was there when Atcho fought whoever it was, and I think it was Klaus, but I didn't see him, and we can't prove it."

Atcho had never seen Burly look so uncomfortable, even awkward.

"We think he's overseas now," Burly continued, "and involved with a terrorist organization that we know very little about. That makes it an intelligence matter, which is CIA."

Atcho's exasperation was unbridled. "So, the FBI is going to sit on its hands and do nothing in the face of a known threat? The same set of people blew up the Israeli Embassy in Buenos Aires. They did the same thing to a TV station and then a major bank in Lima. Their bombs are getting bigger, and they're hitting targets that are higher and have greater economic impact. To think they won't come here is silly."

"That's the battle I'm fighting," O'Brian growled.

Dude rolled his eyes. "It's not that we'll do nothing," he said. "We're a country of laws and we have a protocol. To protect our own people's rights, the CIA is not allowed to operate inside the US—we don't want the agency spying on citizens." He warmed to his argument. "When they've developed intelligence of a threat they judge to be credible, severe, and imminent, they'll let us know through proper channels."

"With all due respect," Atcho replied in a tone that indicated his respect had dissipated to a breaking point, "terrorists are not operating on your timeline or observing your protocol. They train, they rehearse, they improve every day, and they are gaining funds, technology, and advanced methods. You'd better stop regarding them as third-world wannabes and start seeing them for what they are: an increasingly sophisticated fighting force that wants to kill us. And you'd better find a way to get information back and forth between you and the CIA or..." He paused as though considering the gravity of what he was about to say. Then he straightened, looked directly into Dude's eyes, and pointed a finger at him. "Or you'll have lots of American blood on your hands."

He turned to Burly. "I'm done here. If I want to waste my time, I can find better ways to do it." He faced the speakerphone. "Mr. O'Brian, I wish you luck."

He looked Dude rapidly up and down. "Don't worry about protecting me or my family. I can do a better job without you."

With that, Atcho walked out.

33

Burly barely made it to the elevator before the doors closed. Atcho was already inside, staring straight ahead. They rode in silence down to the first floor. There, Atcho exited without a word and strode toward the street. On clearing the door, he kept going without slowing down.

Burly struggled to keep up. "Atcho, would you please stop? Let's talk," he called.

"I've heard enough talk for one day," Atcho retorted. "I have things to do. A thug is coming after me and my family, or hadn't you heard?"

"Atcho, don't do this." Burly stepped up his pace and turned in front of Atcho, stopping him. He lowered his head so his eyes were level with Atcho's and placed a hand on Atcho's shoulder, his lungs heaving. "I'm your friend," he panted. "After all that we've been through together, I shouldn't have to prove that."

Atcho looked away, his irritation still keen. "What do you want? I really have to go move my family. That's not idle talk."

"I know." Burly leaned back. "Let me catch my breath." Pedestrians moved around them on the sidewalk while morning traffic whooshed by only feet away, filling the air with the heavy smell of exhaust.

"I'm sorry about what happened up there," he said when he had regained his composure. "I saw it coming. It was worse than I thought."

"You mean the pigheadedness? What's wrong with those people? If they think that war we fought in Kuwait makes the world safe for democracy, they are incredibly naïve. Klaus and whoever sponsors him are breeding and training more goons like him every day."

Burly nodded. "Not exactly like him. There aren't any more we know of with their own money, expertise, and fighting experience."

"Maybe. Burly, I watched the training in Lima. Hell, I gave classes in close-in combat, and the guys who attacked us in Sudan were good. Not as good as the Israelis, but they'll get better. Their snipers took out three men with three shots. You can't ask for better than that. I didn't see inside the camp in Sudan, but they put together a quick reaction force in a matter of minutes." He shook his head and looked around at the tall skyscrapers looming overhead before returning his gaze to Burly. "If we don't recognize and identify the threat, we're in trouble. And if we won't share information with everyone who needs it, we're lost."

They headed up the street toward the parking garage.

"You surprised me up there," Atcho said. "I hadn't expected pushback from you."

"I didn't say I agreed with the practices," Burly replied. "I was trying to alert you to the facts of the world we live in."

"You called me paranoid."

Burly chuckled. "Lord help me for choosing the wrong words. I already apologized for that. Do you still want your pound of flesh?"

Atcho relaxed a bit. "No, but that policy had better change, or it's going to create the world we all die in together."

"What are you going to do now?"

"Get my family to a safe place, and then figure out how to get Klaus. We poked a sleeping tiger in Sudan, and he's mad as hell. He's coming. I can feel it."

"You don't think West Point is safe enough? By now, the superintendent has been alerted and will augment security. With the general terror threat elevated, that would happen anyway. There's a quiet alert going out. I'll speak with Dude and O'Brian again, and I'm sure they'll line up behind providing greater security for you."

Atcho scoffed. "For how long and to what degree? I'm not leaving my family's fate in their hands. My son-in-law will arrive home the day after tomorrow. We'll figure out what to do with Sofia, Isabel, and the kids. I'll get Rafael to put protection around the extended family, and Ivan can increase security around the home and our manufacturing plant. In Texas, we can still protect our property with guns, and those will be combat veterans pulling watch. If the country makes it through, so will we.

"Tell Dude not to get in my way. I won't do anything illegal unless I have to, but I'll do whatever it takes to protect my family, and I won't apologize for it. The government might not do its job, but I'll do mine."

They reached the parking garage and the point where they would part ways. Atcho paused. "I appreciate you, Burly, I really do. You've always been there for Sofia and me. Sorry I got hot under the collar."

Burly grabbed Atcho in a bear hug. "No need to apologize. We've been through lots of crap together. We'll get to the end of this. Anything I can do?"

Atcho thought for a moment. "Put me in touch with O'Brian. I want to know what he knows. Tell him I'll fly to Chicago if that's what it takes."

"I can do that. Mind if I tag along?"

Atcho smiled. "If you can get us there tomorrow, I'll buy the ticket."

34

Chicago
January 25, 1993
The next day

"I'm happy to meet you in person, Atcho," Tom O'Brian said, and then turned to the other man standing before him. "Should I call you Burly?"

"Might as well." Burly chuckled. "That's the name Atcho hung on me in the swamps of Cuba."

"I want to hear the story," O'Brian said. He was a tall man with a dark complexion, heavy facial features, and a receding hairline. His manner contrasted with his clothes: he was brusque, albeit courteous, though dressed immaculately in an expensive Italian suit with a pocket kerchief and matching tie, and perfectly coordinated soft leather shoes. "Come in. Sit down."

They were at the door of the special agent's office at the FBI Chicago field headquarters on Roosevelt Road. They crossed to a seating area with a couch and two leather chairs and sat down.

"Dude filled me in on the details of your personal situation," O'Brian told Atcho. His brow furrowed. "You rode him hard yesterday." He chuckled. "Not that he didn't deserve it. Now, what can I do for you?"

"I want to know what you know," Atcho replied. "Why are you met with such stiff opposition inside the FBI?"

O'Brian bobbed his head while considering how best to answer. "My bosses don't want to hear from me on the subject of terrorism mainly because our hands are already full, there's a wide ocean between us and where most of the bad guys hang out, and the CIA and department of defense are responsible for what's beyond our shores and borders. Our job is solving crimes already committed inside our borders. Once the terrorists act within our country, it becomes a crime and we investigate.

"I've been making the case that terrorists aren't just spies. They're fighters: they infiltrate, they don't wear uniforms, and they don't discriminate between civilians and military or police forces. To them, every man, woman, and child is a combatant." Passion rose in his voice as he spoke.

"I've been agitating to get ready for terrorism in the US because I think it's coming," he said. "The powers that be put me in Chicago to shut me up. They'd probably get rid of me if they could, but I'm the guy who broke that Tylenol case—you know, the one where this jerk wanted to off his wife, so he put Tylenol laced with cyanide in bottles and planted them on pharmacy shelves. He killed several people just so his wife would be among the dead, and since the victims got the pills from a pharmacy, he figured the investigators wouldn't trace the case back to him. Well, we did, and forever after, people are stuck wrestling with almost impenetrable plastic wrappers to get at their pills."

He smirked. "That's heinous. Anyway, that case protects me. Can you imagine the headlines if I'm fired?" He drew an imaginary banner in the air. "'FBI Sacks Agent Who Cracked Tylenol Case.' I'd get more attention and then maybe my ideas on terrorism would get out. That might be great in the short run. More people would hear about them, but the FBI would be embarrassed, and then I'd fade, and no one would listen to me." He furrowed his brow, winked, and wagged a finger in the air. "But mark my words, the terrorists are coming. They'll make an entrance in a big way, and I can do more good by staying in the FBI than I can if I leave it." He heaved a sigh. "Besides, I like my job too much."

He sat back in his chair. "Does that answer your question?"

Atcho leaned forward. "Something got you started thinking that

LEE JACKSON

terrorists are coming this way. What was it? I need to know everything you know on the subject."

O'Brian laughed. "That's precious little. I didn't say I knew a lot. I said I've been stewing that we don't know enough, and we'd better get up to speed before the threat becomes a tragedy.

"Look, those guys in the Middle East hate us. They hate us because we support Israel and because we don't embrace Islam. We're infidels—nonbelievers. To them, that's a sin punishable by death. This guy Klaus hates you because you killed his brother, but he'd hate you anyway."

He looked at Burly. "Is the New York office helping out with security?"

Burly nodded. "They've assigned a special agent to coordinate with local law enforcement and the MPs up at West Point."

O'Brian nodded. "And law enforcement is on a raised alert nation-wide," he said. "So, it's not like nothing is being done." He regarded Atcho with an appraising look. "I think I've been a disappointment."

Atcho shook his head. "I hoped that you knew something that could lead to Klaus and what he's up to." He looked around the office, formulating his thoughts. "What made you think that terrorists are coming to the US—to the extent that you've alienated your bosses?"

O'Brian laughed. "Hey, I'm a charming guy," he quipped. "People like me—if I'm not working for them." His smile disappeared, and he became serious. "It doesn't take a rocket scientist."

He extended his arm and pointed in the air. "Over there, they've been chanting 'Death to America' for years. They call us the 'Great Satan.' They hit US facilities in other places because they can get to them. But their targeting and delivery systems are becoming more sophisticated, and their bombs are getting bigger and more destructive." He jabbed a finger in the air to make his point. "Those two oceans won't protect us much longer. Our borders are wide open, and the bad guys are getting better educated and more technologically savvy." He shook his head. "It's only a matter of time, as your personal experience demonstrates."

He gave Atcho a curious look. "Do you really believe that was a nuclear bomb Klaus planted at your house last year?"

"No doubt about it," Atcho stated flatly.

Burly nodded in agreement. "We have the designer under protection," he said. "Atcho saw Klaus escape with one of the bombs, he was confirmed to have shown one to a credible source in Berlin, and the one he brought to Atcho's house was the same design. We took the plutonium out of that one and two others we captured."

He inhaled and exhaled audibly. "Klaus knows how to replicate them. His only limiting factor is getting the plutonium. The price has gone sky-high, but he's backed by huge petrodollars. As long as there's a source, he can get the money."

"What I don't understand," Atcho broke in, "is why the FBI isn't taking more concerted action. The president knew what was going on in Berlin and Afghanistan. His national security adviser coordinated support for the missions to stop Klaus in both places. Why doesn't he cut through the red tape and order closer cooperation?"

"It's comp—" O'Brian began.

"Don't tell me it's complicated," Atcho cut in. "We're talking about the safety and security of our country, and more specifically about my family."

O'Brian relaxed and chuckled. "You're right. The national security adviser is a friend. He's one of the few allies I have in the government, but he's overridden by the director of the CIA and the secretary of defense. Neither believes a threat to be imminent."

"So, we leave ourselves open to attack until one happens," Atcho said disgustedly. "Would someone please remind them of their oaths and their jobs?"

The room fell silent.

A knock on the door interrupted the brooding atmosphere. A secretary entered, brought a note to O'Brian, and left without saying a word.

O'Brian blanched. He stood and went to his desk, then picked up a remote and aimed it at a television on the opposite wall.

"More bad news," he muttered, "and it might be pertinent."

The television screen lit up to a scene of a multi-story building with large windows. Burly sucked in his breath. Scrolling text at the bottom of the screen read, "Shooting at the front gate to the CIA's Langley head-quarters leaves two dead and three wounded. No suspects."

A young woman spoke into the camera. "We are told that a man steered his car into one of the two left lanes off the main highway that leads into the headquarters complex. Witnesses say he exited his car with an automatic weapon and walked down a line of cars, shooting into them. He shot only men, and when he was finished, he returned to his car. On the way back, he executed a man who was already wounded. Investigators currently have no suspects."

"It's begun," Atcho murmured.

"We can't say that for sure," Burly cautioned.

"Figure it out," Atcho said. "That was no spontaneous act. The man knew where he was and what he intended to do. Mark my words. The perpetrator will turn out to be an Islamic fundamentalist, and our august defenders will be afraid to call him that."

"I'm with you," O'Brian said, "but we do operate within constraints. Jumping to conclusions helps no one." He studied Atcho's face. "This attack might have nothing to do with your situation, but if they *are* related, we'll want to know about it. Meanwhile, you have a direct threat to deal with."

He stood next to his desk, hands in his pockets. All three men continued watching the television report.

"I'll tell you what," O'Brian said after a few moments. "A young special agent named Sam is assigned there in New York. I mentored him while I was there, and he stays in touch. He's kinda my back channel to know what's going on there, and he believes in my instincts. He's been chasing down the facts around the guy who shot and killed a Jewish rabbi a couple of years ago, keeping tabs on the shooter's acquaintances. I'll put Sam in touch. You might be able to help each other."

He turned to Burly. "What do you think? Does that make sense?"

"Can't hurt."

They continued to stare at the carnage at the entrance to the most vaunted intelligence agency in the world.

35

When Atcho returned to Isabel's house at West Point the next morning, his son-in-law, Bob Bernier, had arrived home from Korea and greeted him with open arms. Bob was tall and blond with blue eyes. He wore a perpetually friendly but skeptical grin, and his manner projected a warm heart constantly attuned to danger. Atcho knew him to always be ready to defend his family and his country: he had once broken the jaw of a man he had thought posed a threat to Isabel.

"Great to see you, Atcho," he boomed. "Sofia's been filling me in. That was some bad stuff that went down at the CIA headquarters yesterday. Do you think that's tied in with Klaus?"

Atcho shrugged ruefully. "I don't know. It could be a lone wolf acting spontaneously. Let me say hi to Sofia and Isabel. Then we can take a walk and I'll brief you on the details."

A few minutes later, they stood on the front porch of the stately house on a hillock near Michie Stadium, home of the West Point football team. From their vantage, they saw the rays of the waning sun glance off the waters of Lusk Reservoir, and far below, the wide expanse of the Hudson River carried its burden of broken ice chunks toward New York City.

Bracing against the cold, they started off at a good pace, walking through a thin layer of snow, past the reservoir and stately cadet chapel, and then descending a steep set of concrete stairs built into the side of the bluff overlooking the cadet garrison. Below them on a road skirting the rear of the barracks, young men and women in athletic gear ran together in small groups.

Atcho stopped and watched them with a melancholy expression. "It seems so long ago that I jogged that same road to the gym." His face brightened. "Would you believe I used to run these stairs to condition my legs for soccer?"

He turned and looked back up at the magnificent Gothic revival stone chapel, now outlined by the sky. His face receded to somberness. "The last time I climbed them was with my father on graduation day. We attended the wedding of a classmate." He sighed. "So much has happened since then."

"You were a better cadet than I was," Bob said. "I never attempted to run these stairs." He clapped an affectionate hand on Atcho's shoulder. "Let's keep going. I want to hear about this conundrum you've gotten us into."

They reached the bottom of the stairs and turned right toward Thayer Road. Now on flat ground, they could talk more easily, and Atcho recounted the entire series of events that had led to his visit to the New York City FBI building.

———

Sofia and Isabel watched as Bob and Atcho headed off together.

"They get along so well," Sofia said. "We're lucky for that."

"They admire each other," Isabel replied. "When Bob was still a cadet, he studied Atcho's actions in Cuba. That was before we knew each other."

"He mentioned that years ago. Time passes so fast." Sofia started toward the back door. "I need to run some errands. If you don't mind, I'll go while they're out."

Isabel shot her a skeptical glance.

"No, really," Sofia said, and laughed. "I need to get some things at the store. I won't be long."

Isabel consented with a smile, and then stood at the window

watching as Sofia pulled the car out of the driveway. Below, the two children played on the front lawn. Isabel watched them for a few moments after Sofia had disappeared, and then took in the view of the sun filtering through the trees on its descent, reflecting off the surface of Lusk Reservoir.

She was about to turn away from the window when motion at the edge of the trees across the road caught her attention. Thinking she might see a deer or some other wild animal, she focused her attention in that direction and then froze.

A man emerged from the woods. He wore a deliveryman uniform, but Isabel could not make out the company, and no vehicle was parked nearby. As she watched, the man looked up and down the street, but his actions were furtive, as though he was checking to see if he had been seen rather than deliberately seeking an address.

A pit formed in Isabel's stomach. The man stared at her house and began walking toward it.

Spurred into action, Isabel rushed outside and called to Kattrina and Jameson. Her tone startled them. She ran to them, grabbed their hands, and hurried them back to the house. As they climbed the steps, she glanced over her shoulder.

The man was walking rapidly now. "Mrs. Bernier," he called. His accent was thick but indeterminate.

"Mrs. Bernier," the man called again. "I must speak with you."

Isabel pushed the children in front of her, then slammed the door and turned the deadbolt.

"Go to my bedroom," she ordered. Sensing her urgency, the children ran.

Isabel crossed the room to the mantel over the fireplace. Reaching behind a plate on a display stand, she pulled out a pistol and chambered a round. Then she hurried to the kitchen to lock the back entrance. Even before she returned to the living room, the man knocked on one of the front door window panes.

"Mrs. Bernier," he called, "I have a letter for you. I need your signature."

Isabel ducked behind the couch, grabbed the phone, and dialed.

"Go away," she yelled. "I'm calling the police."

She heard the door knob rattle as the operator answered her call.

"There's a man at my door trying to break in," she screamed into the phone. "I have children here and I'm armed. I'm Major Bernier's wife and we're in the residential area by Lusk Reservoir."

She heard glass shattering. A man's hand protruded through the broken window and reached for the deadbolt.

Isabel aimed the pistol and pulled the trigger. Her ears rang from the explosion. "He's coming in," she yelled to the operator. "He broke the window and he's trying to unlock the door."

"Help is on the way," the operator yelled back. "Can you get to a safe room?"

Meanwhile, Isabel dropped the receiver and stood up from behind the couch. She took aim with both hands, then steadied her stance and fired off three more shots at the man's hand. Then she raised the barrel and fired several more times through the door. She heard a groan—and a click as her pistol's magazine ran out of bullets.

Through a shower of glass, the man burst through the door, his left hand dripping blood and his eyes burning with fury. He strode across the room, grabbed Isabel by the neck, and shoved her toward the door. Her pistol clattered to the floor.

Isabel screamed, and then she heard Kattrina and Jameson whimper in terror from the other room.

"Shut up," the man snarled in Isabel's ear. He grabbed her hair and jerked it around, forcing her to look at him. "Or the children will die." Then he pushed her outside and down the steps to the woods.

By the time Atcho had finished relating the details of the threat Klaus posed, he and Bob had walked a full mile along Thayer Road overlooking the river, almost to Thayer Hotel. They turned right on Mills Road to head uphill and back to Lusk Reservoir from the opposite end.

"I think I've got a handle on the whole shebang," Bob said. "I'm not sure I agree that we need to leave West Point. What about Sofia? What's her role in all of this?"

Atcho grimaced, hesitating before speaking. "I need your help on that. I need you to keep her out of it. She has to stay with Jameson."

Bob pivoted in mid-stride and held his hands up by his shoulders, palms open, facing Atcho. "Whoa, buddy. I'll do almost anything you ask, but I'm not tangling with that lady. You want me to handcuff her to a radiator in our living room? Hog-tie and hand-feed her?" He belted out a laugh. "If she thinks you or Jameson is in danger, she'll be a hellcat, and short of putting my own life at risk, you tell me how I'm supposed to keep her out of anything."

Atcho heaved a sigh and smirked. "You're right," he said, a note of pride deepening his tone. "She's a handful and she's absolutely the reason our past missions succeeded. But..." Atcho's voice became serious, almost pleading. "If something happens to me, Jameson can't lose us both. She has to be here for him."

Bob placed both hands on Atcho's shoulders and lowered his head so that he looked directly into Atcho's eyes. "Count on me for this," he said. "I'll protect Jameson along with Isabel and Kattrina. Leave that to me and don't worry about it anymore. Your mind needs to be free so you can concentrate on Klaus. If anything happens to either you or Sofia, Isabel and I will take care of Jameson. He'll always have a home, and we'll treat him like our own child.

"I'll give Sofia my best advice, and I'll pass on to her what I just told you about Jameson, but if she's determined to do her thing, I won't stand in her way." He chuckled. "Not that I could anyway."

"Fair enough," Atcho said, his reluctance obvious. They resumed walking up Mills Road. "I talked with Rafael after I left Burly. He'll get security out to your extended family—"

"Your old Brigade 2506 buddies?"

Atcho smiled. "We're getting a little long in the tooth, but our guys can still fight. I wouldn't want to be on the opposite side of them."

Rafael Arteaga was one of Atcho's oldest friends. They had met more than thirty years ago in a firefight at the disastrous Bay of Pigs invasion in Cuba, when the US had deserted Brigade 2506. The unit had been a fighting force of more than one thousand men the CIA had trained to re-take the island country from its dictator, Fidel Castro.

Years later, after they had both been released from captivity in Castro's dungeons, Atcho and Rafael had reacquainted and worked together in several black operations. In the first, Rafael had organized and provided security to Atcho's extended family when they were threatened by a rogue Russian spy seeking to coerce Atcho's cooperation. He had recruited from among the veterans of Brigade 2506.

"I sure wouldn't object to any of them being in a foxhole next to me," Bob agreed.

"Ivan will secure our home and the manufacturing plant in Austin," Atcho went on.

"It sounds like you've got your bases covered."

"Not quite," Atcho responded. "I still think you should leave West Point."

Bob shook his head. "The superintendent knows the situation. He's beefed up security on the post, and he's specifically increased patrols around our house. If Klaus shows up here, we'll get him."

Atcho whirled around. "Listen to me, Bob. When there was still a wall in Berlin, Klaus found a way under it to go back and forth at will; he kidnapped me out of a hotel with US State Department security at my door; he moved around the battlefield in Kuwait freely; he smuggled a nuclear device into the US; and he escaped the country despite a nation-wide manhunt. He's gained knowledge and experience, and since I killed his brother, he has a vendetta against me. He'll kill everyone close to me if he gets a chance, and that includes you, Isabel, Kattrina, and especially Sofia and Jameson." Atcho's voice became urgent. "If we screw up, those we love will die."

Bob studied Atcho in the gathering dusk.

"Criminy, Bob," Atcho rolled on, "he tested a nuclear device in Afghanistan. It lowered the top of a mountain by thirty meters." He caught himself. "That's classified, and neither the FBI nor the CIA will confirm that's what happened, or that Klaus was behind it, but they know it and we know it."

They were about halfway up the hill, still on Mills Road, at a point where it curved left and continued uphill. Suddenly, they heard a single popping sound, followed by several more in quick succession. They could not be certain of its direction, but they both knew the sound from close-up experience: gunshots.

They glanced at each other, eyes wide, then turned and raced up the hill. Before they reached the crest, a military police sedan sped by, its blue strobe lights blinking. Moments later, another swept past them, its siren blaring.

Their lungs heaving, Atcho and Bob pushed uphill until they reached flat ground. Then they raced across a footbridge over the reservoir and loped the remaining distance. Four MP cars were already ringed in front of the house, their roof lights flashing.

As they sprinted toward the house, two MPs stepped in front of them. Bob pulled his ID from his pocket and thrust it at them. "I'm Major Bernier. I live here. This is my father-in-law."

Satisfied, the officers let them through. As they mounted the stairs, an MP captain walked out the front door.

"Major Bernier?" he said to Bob and introduced himself. "There are two children inside, very scared. You should talk to them. They're afraid of us."

"Where's my wife?" Bob demanded, still breathing hard.

The captain shook his head. "There were no adults in the house, and there's blood on the door." He spoke in rapid, clipped tones. "Shots were fired. The blood trail leads into the woods." He glanced at Atcho. "Who are you?"

Atcho jutted his jaw toward Bob. "His father-in-law. The little boy is my son."

Just then another car screeched to a halt down the street. Sofia jumped out and ran toward the house. An MP stepped in front of her.

"That's my wife," Atcho said. "Tell them to let her through."

Another MP emerged from the house. "I got the little girl to talk some," she said. "She says a mean man came to the door and took her mother away."

Sofia ran up the stairs in time to hear the MP, then rushed inside without stopping.

Bob and Atcho followed her. Inside, Sofia stooped to comfort the children while Bob strode into his bedroom. When he emerged, he was carrying a holstered Smith & Wesson Model 3 Schofield top-break revolver. He slapped the belt around his hips and, without breaking stride, headed for the door.

"This is the best I can do on short notice," he muttered, "but this just got personal for me too. I've got plenty of bullets."

Meanwhile, Atcho picked up Sofia's pistol from the floor. "Where's the ammo for this?"

Bob showed him. "Let's go."

The MP captain blocked their way at the door. "My people are on this. The post is already on lockdown. No one moves from wherever they are right now except for my MPs. We'll get this guy."

"That's my wife," Bob growled, shouldering past him. "Try to stop me."

"That's my daughter," Atcho echoed, and followed.

Isabel's heart beat wildly as she crashed through the underbrush down the steep slope of the bluff below her house. Her breaths came in short gasps and her feet stumbled over loose rocks and downed branches.

Her captor followed closely, prodding her in the back and cheek with a pistol he carried in his good hand. A good distance below was another row of houses, but rugged terrain and thick vegetation impeded their way. Whenever Isabel would pause to catch her breath or see where to take her next step in the waning light, he shoved her, causing her to stumble to the ground. Then he jerked her upright and pushed her forward again, down the mountain.

Above them the wail of sirens had risen to a crescendo and then ceased. Others sounded from every direction. Below them, the rush of the river mixed with leaves beating against each other in a swift wind, and the smell of half-decayed winter vegetation assaulted the nostrils.

Isabel barely noticed, her mind focused on a single thought—survival. Then, after several minutes that felt like hours, she heard the crashing of bushes and rolling of rocks above them. Her rescuers were on the way.

Another thought struck. *Will he shoot me before they can get to me?*

Her senses now fully engaged, Isabel pictured the ground ahead—steep, overgrown, rocky—and then a sheer drop-off behind the row of houses below, if she could steer their flight to the left of their current direction.

In the twilight, judging direction was difficult, but Isabel recognized the main area of the cadet barracks glowing to the left. She deliberately stumbled again, and when the man jerked her up, she turned slightly so they would veer closer to them. Two more similar falls and recoveries allowed her to move in her intended direction, and her captor seemed not to have noticed—his panic now evident as he reacted to the sounds of a narrowing pursuit from behind.

Two voices called, "Isabel!" She recognized them both. Atcho and Bob.

The man shoved his gun against her jaw, driving it into her teeth, and pushed his face close to hers while bringing one bloodied hand to his mouth as a sign to remain silent. They crouched and waited. The sounds of stumbling and the voices receded to the right and continued below them.

The man pulled Isabel up and pushed her to the left, away from the pursuers.

The pause on the slope had given Isabel a brief chance to study him. In the dim light, she couldn't make out any of his features but saw that he was not much bigger than her. The pain in his hand must have been growing—he had shifted his face to lean over and nurse it.

They continued downhill at a more deliberate pace, and Isabel noticed that his panic had waned, and he was now paying more atten-tion to their direction of travel. She only hoped she had managed to steer them far enough to the left to provide her the advantage she sought.

Down, down they went, and she no longer stumbled or fell. Doing so could spell the end. She tolerated the jabs in her back as she stepped downhill, placing her feet carefully until she saw a break in the vegetation outlined by the glow from the distant barracks—and the edge of a sheer, high drop-off.

She deliberately stumbled again, and when the man reached for her, she rolled away, sprang up, and rushed him, her head low, aiming for his wounded hand.

She careened against him, jamming his injured palm against his leg. As he cried out in pain, she dug her heels into the rocky ground and shoved harder, driving him to the edge of the bluff.

Too late, the man realized her intention and teetered on the edge. He swung his arms wildly, then brought his pistol around to train on Isabel and pulled the trigger.

As his gun swung toward her, Isabel threw her arm up, deflecting his. The shot went wild, the sound muffled in the stiff breeze.

Isabel dropped to the ground, threw her arms around the man's ankles, and pulled with all her strength. Her breath came in gut-wrenching gasps.

With a scream, the man fell over the edge. Scarcely a moment later, Isabel heard a thud, and then all was quiet aside from the sounds of the wind, the leaves, and her own labored breath.

Isabel stayed in her prone position, breathing hard, until the icy fingers of winter began to wrap around her body. Then images of the children entered her mind and carefully, gingerly, she rose to her feet and began the climb back up to her home.

The entire family left that evening, including Atcho and Sofia, flying by military helicopter to nearby Stewart Air National Guard Base. They spent the night in guest quarters secured by Marines.

Many hours later, unable to sleep and still seething with anger, Atcho asked Sofia, "How do you think Isabel is handling this emotionally?"

"She's shaken up," Sofia replied. "She's never killed a man before."

Atcho nodded. "And when she climbed back up the hill, she didn't know he'd broken his neck. As far as she knew, he could still be after her. She's traumatized."

Sofia caressed his cheek, hiding her own rage. *Klaus attacked my family where we live—twice.* "She's strong. After all, she's your daughter. She'll be okay. Her confidence should take a jump. She knows she can protect her child. She's done it, and she kept her wits and saved her own life."

Atcho nodded. "Klaus won't stop."

Sofia shot him a glance. "We have to get him."

Atcho pulled back and studied her face. Her tone had carried uncharacteristic menace.

"What are you going to do?" she asked.

"I'm going back to the New York FBI office in the morning. We've got to figure out a way to draw Klaus into the open."

"You mean to make him come after you," Sofia said flatly, then sighed. "I suppose I can't stop you."

Atcho locked eyes with her. "I have to do this. He's not after just us. He wants to deliver a crippling blow to the US, and he can do it. If he needs to, he'll put me on a back burner, but he's still going to come after us personally. If I don't finish this fight, we'll always be checking our back-trail—after he's massacred millions. The more important question right now is what are *you* going to do? Isabel and Bob will have the same worries about Kattrina."

Sofia pulled back and gave him a preoccupied look. "Don't worry. Our kids come first. I'll help Bob stave off any onslaughts. Where he's taking us, Klaus won't know how to follow. Our family is off the table as a pressure point for Klaus to threaten you."

Atcho nodded. "That ranch of Ivan's up in Montana came in handy."

36

"I should have gone myself," Klaus groused. He had just listened to a news report about the death of a would-be kidnapper at West Point.

"You know that wouldn't have been a good thing to do," Ramzi replied. "If you had been captured or killed, your part of our plans would be dead."

"Why can't these infidel men teach their wives how to behave?" Klaus said in exasperation. "Their women dress to provoke when they go out in public; they go to jobs and drive to get there. And this daughter of Atcho's killed Aban. I should have known she could do that. Atcho's wife is a she-devil who beat up six men at once in Berlin last year."

"She did what?"

"Six men tried to detain her in Little Istanbul last year. She left all of them lying on the street."

"You're joking."

Klaus shook his head.

Ramzi grinned lasciviously. "Give her to me for an hour. I'll teach her proper respect. The daughter too."

Klaus heard him distantly. He pulled himself back to awareness and shook his head dismissively. "We'll never get close to Atcho's family now. He's warned and he'll move them. I'll deal with him later. For now, we'd better concentrate on the plan. We need to coordinate to make sure we get the most effect."

"And to make sure that if one bomb doesn't go off, the other does," Ramzi interjected.

Klaus looked at him sharply. "What do you mean?"

A cautious look spread over Ramzi's face. "No offense. I mean that if one system doesn't work, we've configured them so neither one interferes with the other."

Klaus' expression hardened. "Which system would you expect not to work?"

Ramzi's gaze turned stern. "We're brothers working for the same *jihad*," he said. "I meant no insult. I know what you did in Afghanistan, blowing up that mountain. If your bomb works like that one..." He shook his head. "You already have the respect of Al-Qaeda, Sheikh Omar, and Osama bin Laden, but the bomb is not proven operationally yet. We can't risk this mission. My bomb must have every opportunity to succeed, with or without yours."

Constrained anger clouded Klaus' expression.

"The same is also true about your bomb," Ramzi added. "Think, brother. We'll bring down those twin monsters across the river."

"You've been talking to Kadir," Klaus muttered.

"I don't know Kadir," Ramzi replied neutrally, "but I can tell you that while your weapon's potential is recognized in the Kingdom, it hasn't worked in a real situation yet, despite three attempts."

Klaus' eyes narrowed. "Because of Atcho," he hissed. "He's interfered every time."

"Which is why we can't let him get in the way this time."

The two men eyed each other for extended moments. Then Klaus nodded.

"What do you suggest?"

Ramzi exhaled. "The two bombs should be set to explode nearly simultaneously. Mine will go in the parking garage of the South Tower and detonate first. You should put yours a couple of floors above ground level. If it fails, mine will still topple one tower into the other one. If yours does succeed..." His eyes widened as a grin spread across his face. "It will have the effect of an airburst. Instantly, everything within a mile of the World Trade Center will be covered with radioactive fallout raining down on the city. Millions of infidels will be dead, and the US financial system will be crippled. Our bombs together will leave a black hole in the floor of Manhattan a mile wide, with nothing but rubble and dead infidels. That will be the beginning of the end for this wretched country."

Klaus listened, mesmerized. His eyes shone with the fervor of his mission.

"*Habibi*," he said, "it's so good to finally work with someone as dedicated to our *jihad* as I am. In Saudi Arabia, many men speak of *jihad* and they put their money in, but they leave the fighting to untrained fighters with no experience. You are here with me, and you have the wisdom, expertise, and experience to *do* something besides talk or throw money your family got out of the oil wells."

Ramzi smiled, a faraway look in his eyes. "Thank you, my brother. This is sacred work we do." He pulled himself from his thoughts. "How long until your bomb is ready?"

"About two weeks. I've located the machine shops that can manufacture the structural parts, but the tolerance levels are tiny, so I don't want to rush them, and I want plenty of time to test the bomb. I'm waiting for some electronic parts too, but they should be here by then."

Ramzi nodded in contentment. "That's good. My shipment of powdered metals should arrive around the same time, and then my bomb will be complete."

"What do we do until then?"

"Lie low and wait."

37

Sofia fidgeted.

Bob noticed. "Set a spell. Take your shoes off,'" he quipped, quoting the character Jed Clampett from the closing theme song of *The Beverly Hillbillies*. "We're going to be here awhile. Might as well relax."

Sofia studied him. Behind his jocular greeting resided an undertone of anger. Dressed in warm woolen winter clothing, he sat in a rocking chair on the wooden porch of a ranch-style house built on a rise looking across a vast expanse of snow-covered rolling prairie to distant peaks. Behind the house to the north, the ground swept up into a towering mountain. Set as it was with the sun rising to Bob's left and setting to his right, when the weather was clear, the house basked in sunlight the whole day. Halfway to the mountains outlined against the far southern horizon, the town of Livingston nestled in rolling hills, and a frozen lake glimmered off to the west. A long, cleared driveway with a few ice patches led from a secondary hardtop road up the gentle slope to the house.

"Nobody's getting in here that we don't know about," Bob went on. "We'll see 'em coming for miles, and if we miss 'em, we have sensors and monitors behind every bush, and local authorities are on the lookout." He took a sip of coffee from a mug in his hand while patting a Winchester rifle lying across his lap. "If Klaus sneaks in somehow, we'll deal with him." He brandished the firearm. "We've got plenty of ammo and lots more weapons."

Sofia pushed off from the rail she had been leaning against while she drank her coffee. She turned to look out over the vista.

"Ah, Bob," she said. "You know me too well. I can't help worrying about Atcho."

"Concentrate on feeling sorry for that Klaus guy," Bob said. "He's not going to get away again. Mark my words. Atcho is setting up an endgame."

"I have full faith in Atcho, but anything can happen."

Bob eyed her closely. "You're conjuring up something. I can see it in your eyes." He turned and leaned the rifle against the cabin wall, then picked up his coffee and stood, ambling over to Sofia. "Atcho figured you'd try to do something. He asked me to stop you."

Sofia chuckled. "And what did you tell him?"

Bob laughed. "That I might as well try to hog-tie a mountain lion. I said I wouldn't attempt to stop you because it would be useless."

Behind him, the front door opened, and Isabel emerged with the two children. They ran across the porch, squealing with excitement, and bounded down the stairs to play in the snow.

Isabel wrapped her arms around Bob and leaned her head against his shoulder. "What's up?"

Bob put an arm around her back, then gestured toward Sofia. "She's thinking she has to do something, and a plan is already forming in that head." He turned to Sofia. "Am I right?"

Sofia set her coffee cup down on the flat rail of the porch and rubbed her eyes. "Your family is here," she said. "You're safe. My husband—"

"Can take care of himself," Bob finished for her, striking a kind note. "And Jameson is here. He needs his mom."

"I know." Sofia's fatigue showed in her drawn face and sunken eyes. "He needs his dad too." She exhaled. "Atcho believes the government isn't taking the threat seriously. The FBI acknowledges the personal danger to us, but the larger threat seems beyond their comprehension. If someone doesn't do something, Klaus will blow that bomb."

"Why did Atcho go back to New York?" Isabel asked. "Why not DC?"

"Two reasons: Klaus wants Atcho, and he traced us to West Point; and Burly got word through backchannels at the Mossad that the New York financial district is Klaus' target. By now, he must know the plan to hit us failed. He doesn't know where we are now, but he'll still go after his larger target."

"So again, sit back and relax. You can help me handle things here."

Sofia shook her head. "I can't, Bob. I'm a veteran analyst and operations officer. Klaus is after big targets. I can feel it. That's what he does. He tried to hit the embassy in Berlin and the oil wells in Kuwait. He's not after penny-ante stuff."

"I'll let you two hash this out," Isabel said. "Just know, Sofia, that Jameson is safe with us."

"You proved that," Sofia said warmly. "We're proud of you."

Isabel smiled appreciatively. Then she disentangled herself from Bob and headed toward the stairs while Sofia took a deep breath to regain control over moistening eyes and lips that had begun to quiver.

"I have to go," Sofia rasped to Bob.

"I know. But let me help you think through things. Do you have any idea what the target might be?"

Sofia gathered her composure. "I do, but it seems too outlandish to say out loud." She took in a deep breath. "Tell you what. I'll go over what I've been thinking, and you tell me your conclusions."

"All right. Try me."

Sofia dropped her head in deep thought. "Klaus was first spotted this time around in a video of the explosion at the Israeli Embassy in Buenos Aires." She paced the porch as she spoke. "Then he witnessed the one that took out the television station in Lima, and then the headquarters of the largest bank in Peru. Each explosion was larger than the previous one, and they're no longer striking just to make a political statement. That bomb in the Marine barracks in Beirut ten years ago was a huge strike, but it didn't do lasting injury to US capability. Now, they're hitting to inflict far-reaching economic damage beyond the carnage."

"I'm with you so far, but how does that lead us to now?"

Sofia spoke slowly, thinking out loud and choosing her words carefully. "The US has always been the target. Strikes in other places have been to train, try out new methods, and develop tactics. Now we're seeing evidence of collaboration between local terrorist groups with both Al-Qaeda and Hezbollah—and they're working together.

"The local groups unwittingly"—she arched an eyebrow—"or maybe wittingly, help spread fundamentalist Islam while they forward their own aims. That's what they think they're doing. And Burly says there's been a build-up of chatter about New York."

"That chatter has been going on for years."

"And the terrorists have been getting better for years. When do we start believing that they'll at least try to do those things they've chanted about for decades?"

"When do we start believing that we can't stop them? That's when the game is over." Bob caught the sharp glance that Sofia shot his way. He waved his hands above his head. "Hey, I'm just playing devil's advocate. I'm the last guy to pooh-pooh the idea that bad guys are coming our way. One came to my house two days ago, threatening my wife. But since we've got limited resources, we have to think through every possibility."

Sofia had stopped pacing. She glanced at her watch and then stood still, her eyes fixed on Bob.

"That's right," she said. "Rummage around with those thoughts for a while and see where they lead. I have to go. I have a plane to catch."

Startled, Bob jumped up from his chair. "You what?"

Sofia had already started down the stairs. "I packed early this morning," she called over her shoulder. "My luggage is in the car." With Bob trailing after her, she plodded rapidly through the snow to where the children played.

"Listen, sweetheart," she said, picking up Jameson and hugging him to her chest. "Mommy has to go away for a while."

"No-o-o," the little boy protested, tears welling in his eyes. "I want you to stay here. When is Daddy coming?"

"I'm sorry," Sofia replied, burying her head against his shoulder. "Your sister Isabel and Uncle Bob will take care of you, and you can play with Kattrina."

"No-o-o," Jameson wailed. "Don't go."

Isabel edged up to help comfort the child. Sofia handed him over, her face a mask of anguish. The little boy kicked and cried. Sofia's eyes reddened, and tears ran freely down her face.

"I'll be back soon," she whispered, kissing Jameson's cheek one last time.

Kattrina, who had continued building a snowman, now pulled at her mother's leg. "Mommy, where is Gigi Sofia going?"

Fighting back her tears, Sofia walked to her car. Bob followed at her shoulder.

"Don't do this, Sofia," he pleaded. "Everyone knows your instincts are good. Work through the analysis with me. We can feed whatever you come up with to the guys in New York and let them handle it."

Sofia swung the car door open and slid behind the wheel. "We don't have time to convince people and wade through red tape." Her tone was labored. "No more time to discuss. Think through what we talked about. If you come up with any conclusions, get them to Atcho."

"What do I tell him about you?"

"Tell him I love him, and I'll see him when this is all over. Tell him the target is obvious, but unthinkable. If I can confirm what I think, I'll get that to him." With that, she rolled up the window and, sliding over the ice patches, sped down the long driveway.

As she drove to the airport, Sofia reviewed her analysis. *Klaus is in New York, or at least in its vicinity. He's going after big targets that affect the economy. His weapons can take down any building. The last hit where he showed up was a skyscraper. There is no building more emblematic of US economic power than the Twin Towers. If he can lure Atcho there, he'll see it as a plus. That's where he's going.*

38

The next morning, Sofia dressed to draw attention. Strikingly beautiful with her fine features, green eyes, long dark hair, and elegant figure, she took care to look her best—to stand out in a crowd in such a way that anyone who knew her would surely recognize her.

As she sat in front of the hotel mirror primping her hair, she thought of the last time she had seen Klaus. That had happened only once, just over three years ago in Berlin, but she knew she would never forget his face, those burning eyes, and that voice that simultaneously commanded and mocked.

She recalled seeing Atcho disappear at Klaus' gunpoint into the hallway outside their hotel room, where a State Department security officer had lain unconscious. Across the hall, the rest of the security detail had been locked in their room and hit with pulverized tear gas, incapacitating them.

She hoped Klaus had equally vivid memories of her.

He had certainly succeeded in identifying and tracking her down fourteen months later, when he tried to have her detained in Little Istanbul, the Turkish enclave in Berlin. Months after that, he shot her in the leg across Lake Austin with a sniper rifle, though she doubted that he had actually made out her features. *He knows me, but he won't be expecting me to expose myself.*

As she rode a taxi into Lower Manhattan, she thought of Atcho. She had left a note in her room in Montana for Bob or Isabel to find, and she was sure that one of them had read it to Atcho by now.

"Stay focused and don't think about me," it read. "I'll call when I have something to tell. Klaus must be stopped. I love you."

Atcho would be angry, but despite the fact that all of his covert operations training had been gained on the job, and much of that by working alone, he was professional. He would weigh the risk she posed to herself against the danger to the nation if they did not succeed. He would proceed, stone-faced to be sure, but he would pursue the objective that must be met, and his thoughts would be on saving his family. They would work out their differences afterward.

She smiled. *Something to look forward to.* Then her expression became somber again. *If there is an afterward.*

The taxi arrived at her destination. She paid the driver, exited, and then looked up at the tall twin towers of the World Trade Center. Even on this overcast winter day, they gleamed in the cold light, their wide concrete expanse softened by trees, displays of art, and lower buildings. They stood proud, stately, evoking power and prosperity. *The very elements that the terrorists hate—when they belong to someone else.*

The cold February wind swirled around Sofia as she began her trek along the periphery of both buildings. She wore a white, heavy overcoat, styled for fashion as well as warmth, and she held her hair in place with a maroon scarf. On her feet, she wore knee-high leather boots with two-inch heels. *If they're still scoping out the place, they'll see me.* An image of Klaus' face formed in her mind. *I'll smoke you out, you bastard.*

After the third loop around the buildings, the cold whipped through her coat, especially on the Hudson River side. She ducked inside the North Tower and rode an escalator to one of the underground levels, where she found a coffee shop and warmed up.

When she felt sufficiently resuscitated, she took another loop around the Center and then rode the elevators in both buildings, stopping off for a drink in The Greatest Bar on Earth, one of the establishments that made up the Windows on the World complex at the top of the North Tower.

As she gazed across the cityscape and then over at the mighty structure of the South Tower, she wondered about the plausibility of bringing them down. *Maybe I'm crazy. It's unthinkable.* She shook off the thought and gazed again at the South Tower, magnificent in a now-waning sun, standing firm against the freezing winter wind that moaned against the glass. *Then again, building these towers was unthinkable in the first place. But someone conceived the idea.*

She returned to her hotel for the night feeling glum and alone. Calling Atcho would serve no purpose, so she went to bed early and slept fitfully.

The next day, she repeated her pattern, wearing the same overgarments. She moved quietly among busy New Yorkers on their various errands and visitors gawking at the sights. In some places, clumps of Asians grinned as their countrymen snapped away on cameras. She smiled. *Seems like everywhere you turn these days, people have cameras.*

On the third day, she did the same thing, alighting from her taxi and beginning her trek around the Twin Towers.

39

"She did what?" Atcho felt his normal self-control slipping away to dread.

Bob explained again what had transpired with Sofia. "She wouldn't tell me where she was going but made it plain that a good guess is New York City. That's where you are because you think Klaus is in the vicinity. That's as much as I know. She could be anywhere within the five boroughs."

"Why wouldn't she tell you where she was going?"

"You know why. You'd try to stop whatever she's doing. She aims to help and is dead set that you stay on mission until Klaus is neutralized. That's my word, not hers."

"But appropriate anyway." Atcho fought off despondency. "It might come to that."

"Hey, I'm not suggesting anything. I'm just saying that, regardless how it's done, Klaus has to be—"

"I get it," Atcho interrupted. "What else did Sofia say? Walk me through her analysis. Can you think of anything she said that would give a hint of what she's up to?"

The line was quiet as Bob put his thoughts together. "She was sure that you would stay focused and on the job."

"Great. What else?"

"She said that the target was obvious, but unthinkable."

Atcho felt his irritation grow. "Is she kidding? In New York City? It's all unthinkable. We've got the New York Stock Exchange, the Federal Reserve Bank, all of Wall Street. Klaus' bomb could take out a whole mile in diameter. If it's planted in the middle of Manhattan, he'll kill a lot of people and cut the US financial system off at the knees."

"That stacks up with what Sofia said about going for targets that cause long-term damage." Bob repeated her observation that the targets and the bombs had become larger and directed at destroying economic hubs.

"That's been my conclusion too." Atcho blew out a breath. "Finding and stopping him will take drastic action."

Atcho remained silent a moment, listening to the soft whirring of the telephone receiver. Then Bob asked, "What will you do?"

"I don't know, but if we don't stop him, let's hope the bomb is a dud."

40

"There's a woman circling the towers," Ramzi told Klaus. "She was spotted yesterday, and she's back today."

"You have people watching the towers?" Klaus asked. He had just come in from a workout at a local gym and was streaming sweat.

"Of course," Ramzi replied. "We keep several brothers posted around the center to notice changes in security."

"So, what's special about this woman?"

"Maybe nothing, but she walks around the buildings and inside them for no apparent reason. One of our men noticed her yesterday when she kept appearing. After the third sighting, he followed her. She's alone and doesn't seem to be waiting for anyone or have anything to do. She just walks around, sits for a while in various places, and continues on."

"Maybe she's a tourist."

"Could be, but she doesn't pay attention to the art pieces scattered around or take pictures. She just roams around the buildings. We didn't see how she arrived yesterday or today, but she left by taxi last evening."

"What's your concern?"

Ramzi sighed and raised an eyebrow. "Everything is my concern as we get closer. I mentioned the woman to you by way of thinking out loud.

You have more experience." He closed his eyes and tossed his head back, surrendering a bit to stress. "Maybe I'm becoming paranoid."

Klaus studied Ramzi's face. "Allah the merciful, peace be upon him, put us together. He must mean for us to collaborate. If you think this woman could be an issue, we should consider her carefully. How are your other preparations coming along?"

Ramzi smiled, relieved that Klaus had not considered his angst to be ridiculous. "Everything is going according to plan." He sighed again. "However, our brothers are becoming too eager. I only hope no one talks too much. You know our security is not the best when it comes to that." His face took on a comical expression. "Then again, the Americans are so stupid. They underestimate us. They'll listen to our brothers talking on the phones to *jihadis* at home and think they're hearing the rantings of madmen, and they won't believe anything is happening until it does."

Klaus chuckled and put an arm across Ramzi's shoulder. "I pray that you are right, but anyway, disinformation is a tactic. Lots of repeated stories will camouflage our real plans." He glanced at his watch. "It's late. I'm going to clean up and go to bed."

He turned away, then added, as an afterthought, "What about the woman?"

Ramzi waved a dismissive hand. "That's probably nothing—just me being more anxious the closer we get to execution."

"Caution is a good thing," Klaus said. "If she shows up again tomorrow, have your man take a picture. We'll circulate it and have the other men watch out for her. If she's doing something that'll get in our way, we'll deal with her."

A distressed expression crossed Ramzi's face. "Ah, I almost forgot. One of the men took some pictures. Polaroid. They're grainy, but you can make out the woman's features."

He reached into his pocket, pulled out several photographs, and handed them to Klaus. "You can see that she is dressed for show. Scandalous. Walking around like that alone? We can only hope that she and all like her are taken down with the towers."

Klaus began flipping through them. The first two showed a tall woman at a distance away from the photographer. Klaus peered at them closely but saw nothing concerning. Then he turned to the third picture and gasped. There, in close relief, was Sofia Stahl-Xiquez.

"It's her," he exclaimed. "That woman."

Startled, Ramzi took the photo and held it for close examination. "You know her?"

"That's Sofia." Klaus' face shone with malicious excitement. "That's Atcho's wife."

Ramzi looked up from the photo. "What do you want to do?"

"If she shows up again tomorrow, take her," he replied in a raspy voice, his eyes gleaming. "Put a team together. Be ready. Make it a public spectacle."

Ramzi eyed him with concern. "Do you think that's a good idea? The police will search all over for her. With this mayor—"

"David Dinkins?" Klaus snorted. "We'll give him big crimes to worry about, and while he oversees a search for Sofia, we'll blast a gigantic pothole for him to fill in." He laughed again. "We'll even give him a new worry to think about—radioactive air."

He whirled on Ramzi. "Bring this infidel witch to me, and while the authorities search for her, we'll put our plans in motion." He clasped his hands together and rubbed them in exultation. "Before the bombing, we'll leave her mutilated body in a public place for the television cameras. Atcho will know I did this."

41

Atcho fretted. He hadn't known helplessness in many years. Isabel, Kattrina, and Jameson were safe in Montana, but the woman who had restored joy and meaning to his life had gone to places unknown. Meanwhile, Klaus threatened the huge population of New York City with a nuclear bomb.

"Can't crumble now," he muttered under his breath, while admitting to himself that crumbling was all he felt like doing. His other instinct was to wring Sofia's neck the next time he saw her.

He sat across the conference table from Jim Dude in the New York City FBI offices at the Javits Center. Burly sat next to him. A window on the opposite wall opened to a cityscape, the Twin Towers glistening in the late afternoon sun.

"Exactly what do you want me to do?" Dude asked. His voice remained businesslike, professional. "Your wife is a grown woman, free to come and go as she pleases. When did she leave?"

"A little less than forty-eight hours ago." He took a deep breath while collecting his thoughts. "My wife is a retired CIA operations officer," he told Dude pointedly. "She left a note to tell me that Klaus must be stopped. I think that clearly indicates her intent."

"And you think she came here, to New York City." Dude's tone was flat.

"That's what my son-in-law thinks based on the last conversation he had with her as she was leaving."

"Did you check the airlines?" As Dude spoke, he leaned back in his chair and picked at the end of a pencil in his hand, his expression indicating that he anticipated the answer.

Atcho nodded. "She must have used one of the many aliases she has stashed away. There's no record of her having flown."

"Now that, we could investigate."

Atcho bristled. Burly placed a calming hand on his forearm.

Dude reached across the conference table and picked up a telephone receiver. "Let me show you something," he said while tapping in a number. He spoke into the phone in a low voice and then hung up.

"You think we're not sensitive to threats against us," he said, "but that's not fair. Our charter is to investigate crimes already committed, not—"

"I got it," Atcho interrupted, his voice laden with disgust. "We know who the attacker is, the general area where he intends to strike, and the weapon. But you can't do anything about it." He leaned forward so that his eyes locked with Dude's. "Or won't."

Dude held his glare.

A secretary knocked on the door, carried a thick file to Dude, and left without saying a word.

"This," Dude said, holding the folder up for Atcho to see its thickness, "this is a fraction of the threats that we have on file." He opened the folder. "Here, I'll read you some snippets of conversation:

"'...we're going to bomb the George Washington Bridge. Watch for it, brothers.'

"'...we're going to bomb the White House.'

"'...two of our glorious *jihadis* will fly a plane into an office building. They will be martyrs...'"

He flipped through several pages. "Here's a doozy. '...we're going to bomb the Statue of Liberty.'" He looked up at Atcho. "This file is from two years ago. Shall I go on?"

Atcho sank back in his seat and shook his head. "I get the picture."

Dude's expression softened. "I'm sympathetic to your effort, Atcho, I really am. But how many agents do you think I have to chase all this down? If I assigned all of them to do that, we still wouldn't have sufficient coverage, and no crimes would be investigated. That includes rapes, murders, bank robberies, kidnappings..."

Atcho heaved a sigh and nodded.

Dude shifted his attention to Burly. "What is the CIA saying?"

"Pretty much the same things as you are. I'm retired from the CIA and on contract. I don't speak for it, but I can tell you that it is not perceiving an imminent threat."

"Even in light of the attack at Langley the other day?"

Burly nodded. "They see that as a lone wolf attack."

The three men sat in silence a few moments, and then Dude redirected his gaze to Atcho and raised an eyebrow. "Atcho, I have to ask another question. I wouldn't be doing my job if I didn't." His reluctance hung in the room.

Atcho regarded him with a stony look.

"How are you and Mrs. Xiquez getting along? Has it occurred to you that the pressure might be getting to her?"

Atcho's chair fell to the floor as he shoved it back and sprang to his feet. "You think my wife abandoned our son and granddaughter? You think she left me?" He whirled on Burly. "Let's go. This was another waste of time."

As Atcho and Burly walked into the freezing February air, a man followed them closely. When they reached the sidewalk, he called to them.

"Mr. Atcho, may I speak with you?" He called two more times before they heard him and turned to face him.

"Mr. Xiquez—uh, Atcho. My name is Sam Shook. Tom O'Brian in Chicago suggested I meet up with you. I saw you leave Jim Dude's office a minute ago."

Atcho studied the young man. He was lanky, in his late twenties, and had dark hair, sharp features, and an expression that dripped sincerity.

"Mr. O'Brian filled me in pretty thoroughly, including"—he glanced momentarily at Burly and then back at Atcho—"what's going on with your wife. Mr. Dude had briefed him."

"What are you supposed to do?"

Sam picked up on Atcho's impatient tenor. "I don't know that I'm supposed to do anything, or that I can, other than listen. I think O'Brian told you that he mentored me. That included keeping me at his side while he developed his sense of terror and counterterror. Meager as I am by myself, I'm the main counterterror effort here in New York. Sometimes I go undercover. I get into the mosques, and I listen."

He looked around at the passing crowd and blew into his cupped hands to warm them while shivering against the cold. "Can we go somewhere to talk? Maybe we can share ideas and spark some more."

Atcho looked him over and nodded. "I don't have much time. I need to find my wife."

"No one here would take O'Brian seriously," Sam said. The three men sat in a coffee shop on West Broadway. "He let me work closely with him because I speak Arabic fluently and can pass as a Middle Easterner."

"How did that happen?" Burly asked.

"I grew up in Lebanon, back when Beirut was still the Paris of the Mediterranean. My father was a construction superintendent. I ran the streets with the Arab kids."

"When did you return stateside?" Atcho asked.

"I came for good in my early teens. I'd been going back and forth for most of my life, but my parents decided I needed to finish my education here."

"How did you wind up in the FBI?"

"O'Brian recruited me. He'd known my father from a couple of cases he worked in Lebanon. He knew my academic record and that I was fluent in Arabic. I won a couple of athletic awards too, so he knew I could handle the physical requirements."

Atcho glanced at his watch. "This is all very nice, but how can you help us? I know the threat, but I really want to get Sofia away from here."

Sam gave him a tentative glance. "O'Brian routed her file to me. From where I stand, she can probably handle things on her end."

His face a mask, Atcho stared at Sam. "You checked out my wife's background?"

With rounded eyes and a taut jaw, Sam nodded. "I'm trying to help," he said. "Look, I'm the only FBI special agent in New York City who will give you more than lip-service support. We all know you're a national hero, so any of us will talk with you. But I'm the only one who knows fundamentalist Muslims. O'Brian tried to elevate attention on the questionable activities of some of them, and our superiors trotted him off to another city. If you want help, I'm it."

Atcho's eyes bored into Sam. He said nothing.

"Look," Sam went on, still sincere but flashing impatience, "something is going down here in New York City soon. I can feel it. When I go to the mosque, men clump together and talk in whispers. I've tried to break into inner circles and I'm making progress, but I'm still not trusted. I glean only what I hear when people talk in close proximity, but I can't appear to be trying to listen. The polite thing for me to do when they stare at me is to move away, and I do."

Burly leaned his heavy frame into the table. "What are you hearing?"

Sam exhaled, looked around the small coffee shop, and shifted toward Burly.

"Let me take a few steps back." He dropped his face into his hands and his shoulders drooped as if they carried a great weight. When he looked up again, his eyes revealed a haunted expression.

"A lot of Muslims hate us," he said, and glanced around again as if wary of unwanted listeners. "They hate our culture, our lifestyles, and mainly they hate us because we are infidels. They don't intend to assimilate into our culture. The aim of these extremists is either to change our culture or kill it—meaning, kill us."

Atcho looked at him skeptically. "Aren't you being a little extreme?"

Sam pulled back, startled. "You, of all people, say that?" He tossed his head back and forth in frustration. "You languished in a prison for seventeen years because a madman in Cuba wanted to play God. You took on a mission in Siberia because a lunatic wanted the Soviet nuclear arsenal.

You were instrumental in liberating millions of people from behind the Iron Curtain and the Berlin Wall, and you stopped the disaster in Kuwait from becoming a global calamity, and you ask me if I'm being extreme?"

He blew out a breath. "You've seen what extreme people do, and they don't move quietly like I do. They don't live within the confines of a constitution and the laws promulgated under it, and they don't respect the rights of others. They kill and they burn, and they enslave by the millions, and that's what they want for our country. You've seen it, and I've seen it."

Atcho crossed his arms and studied Sam. The young man reminded him of himself at a younger age, roughly thirty years ago, in the jungles of Cuba when he had so passionately confronted Burly, the same man who now sat by his side and had participated with him in so many life-and-death situations.

"You've done your homework on me too," he said gently. "Sorry. I didn't mean to minimize what you have to say." He glanced at his watch. "But please get to the point about how you can help."

Sam pushed his chair back, leaned over, and rested his elbows on his knees. He looked up at Atcho, his air almost one of despair. "They're here," he said. "New York is going to get hit, hard. I feel it in my bones, and your wife might find herself in the middle of it."

"Explain."

Sam dropped his head and closed his eyes. "There's a man here in New York, a blind man his followers call Sheikh Omar. He preaches all the time at a local mosque. What comes out of his mouth is venomous. He hates the United States and rails against us. Frankly, I'm finding the line between the practice of free speech and advocating for the violent overthrow of our government to be incredibly thin. I think this guy crosses the line routinely. I've reported him. O'Brian tried to have our superiors investigate his activities, but we both got shunted aside like we're being ridiculous."

"The point," Atcho goaded Sam. "Get to the point."

Sam sighed. "Sorry. The sheikh is acting different now. He's more circumspect in what he says. The groups of men whispering to each other have grown tighter, and the chatter has fallen off. It's as if they're cautioning each other to silence. At the same time, you can see a zeal in their eyes, like they know something is about to happen but don't dare mention it outside of their own groups."

"And that's what you think Sofia might be wandering into?"

Sam drew himself back, closed his eyes, and inhaled deeply. "I don't know," he said. "I'm going on what I know of her disappearance. I think you told Jim Dude that she left a note suggesting she was going to head things off at the pass, so to speak."

Atcho nodded.

"Do you mind sharing what she said in her note?"

"She told me to stay focused and not to worry about her. She said the target was unthinkable."

"Aren't they all," Sam observed, a touch of irony in his voice. "Do you think she's identified the target, or thinks she has?"

Atcho put both hands against his forehead, clasped his fingers together, and dragged his hands through his hair, his concern manifest.

"That's what I think. And she doesn't want to raise alarms until she's sure. She won't want to divert resources and then find out she's wrong. But knowing her"—Atcho heaved out a breath—"she's probably nailed it."

The three men sat in silence for a spell. Atcho broke it.

"Do you know about Klaus and his bomb?"

"Only water-cooler talk. I know some believe he detonated a suitcase nuclear device in Afghanistan—a poor man's underground test. But that's never been confirmed. He supposedly tried to bomb three different facilities with similar devices, but you stopped him each time." He grinned tiredly. "You're a legend, Atcho."

Atcho shook his head. "Sure. One that no one listens to. One of those facilities he tried to bomb was my house. What do they say about his attempts?"

"That maybe his bombs are the problem. Maybe they just don't work."

Atcho folded his arms again and pursed his lips. Visions flashed through his mind of a huge cargo plane almost fatally landing in Moscow, of himself at the flight controls while Sofia applied a heat-generating device to the trigger mechanism of a suitcase bomb, hoping to melt it before it detonated.

He recalled ducking behind a heavy concrete wall inside the headquarters of the secret police in East Berlin when a rogue Russian general mashed the remote for one of the bombs. And only last year, Klaus had placed a similar bomb outside Atcho and Sofia's home in Austin.

"Maybe the critics are right," Atcho said. "Lucky for the terrorists, they only have to be right once. We have to be right every time. So, what do we do?"

"Tell me about your wife. Tell me how she thinks. She said the target was unthinkable, but you both thought it will probably be somewhere in New York City. Which target, in her mind, would be more unthinkable than any other one?"

Atcho regarded Sam with new respect. "I can see why O'Brian likes you." He glanced up to the ceiling while he thought. "There are so many possibilities. We thought we had seen a pattern." He paused. "Burly got information from the Israelis that narrows the field a bit. They think he intends to hit the financial district to cripple our economy. But we know that they also like to hit targets that are symbolic. They'll hit one that does the best of meeting both of those objectives."

He related his forays into Argentina and Lima. "The three times Klaus went there to observe, the bombs kept getting bigger and their economic effect more pronounced. These terrorists are not satisfied with thousands of small strikes that cause a little damage and then people forget. They want to make a statement that everyone will have to hear. They want to eviscerate the physical landscape and the economy. They want to strike a blow that will make the country reel and one they can then exploit for PR and further attacks on a similar scale. In short, they want to see our utter destruction."

"And which target in New York City gives them that opportunity more than any other?"

Atcho stared out the coffee shop window. The sun had begun its rapid descent, and gloom had already settled onto the long street. At its end, the Twin Towers rose above the dark outlines of the smaller buildings.

As Atcho ruminated, the sun glanced off the sides of the towers, imbuing them with a golden hue. A shaft of reflected light broke the gathering shadows.

Atcho stood, his face frozen in dread. "That's it," he rasped, pointing. "That's the greatest, most visible symbol of US financial wealth and economic power. It's the next step in hitting larger and taller buildings and doing it in the US. That's the target."

42

"Now that we think we know where Klaus is going to strike," Burly said, "what do we do?"

"We go there," Atcho replied. "If Sofia's come to the same conclusion, that's where we'll find her, and if we're right, that's where we'll find Klaus. Can you check with Eitan and see if he's come up with anything?"

"I can try," Burly said. "We've been trading phone messages." He turned to Sam. "Can you get me on a secure line?"

Sam nodded. "And I'll talk to the security director at the towers, not that he'll take any action. He shares our bosses' view of O'Brian and sees me in the same light." He paused as another thought surfaced. "The fact is, when the towers were built and the architects, developers, and owners discussed security, they decided against passive measures that would inhibit entry. So, for instance, they chose not to include obstacles and barriers that would slow down traffic into the parking areas. But you're thinking that the threat comes from a guy carrying a suitcase, right?"

Atcho nodded absently. "I'm not saying no one is going to try conventional explosives, but if we're talking about Klaus, that's a nuclear threat."

"All right. Let me see if I can get someone from building security on the phone at the towers. They don't like to talk to me, but they'll take my call because I'm from the FBI."

Sam left the table and walked across the room to a phone booth.

"Good kid," Burly observed in his absence.

"I can see why O'Brian puts so much stock in him," Atcho replied.

"What are you going to do about Sofia?"

"I'll leave a message for her with Bob. She lives for Jameson and Kattrina and will call out there to see how they're doing. My message will say that we've reached the same conclusions she has regarding the Twin Towers, that security is informed, and that the FBI is cooperating. On that basis, I'll ask her to go back to Montana."

"Do you think she'll do that?"

Atcho sighed. "Only if she thinks the threat is neutralized."

"What do we do in the meantime?"

Atcho glanced at his watch. "She won't be there now. She has to sleep and she's smart enough to know it. We'll get there early in the morning and watch for her."

Sam returned to the table shaking his head. "I got the usual patronizing attitude from Twin Towers' security. They treat me like the boy who cried wolf." He rubbed his eyes tiredly. "They forget the end of that story —a real wolf showed up."

"Are they going to *do* anything?"

"They said they'll keep an eye out for Sofia and a guy with a briefcase —they were being sarcastic. Obviously, lots of guys with briefcases go there every day. I'll get photos of Klaus faxed over to them. I managed to set up a meeting for tomorrow morning. I figured if I bring you two along, they might take me more seriously. What do you think?"

"They should listen," Burly said. "We've had first-hand experience with Klaus and his bombs. Maybe that will make an impression. Meanwhile, get me to that secure line."

43

Early the next morning, Sofia sat up in bed, her eyes blurry from a restless night. Her head pounded, and her body ached. She sat contemplating a conversation she'd had with Bob and Isabel just before bed. Atcho had left a message for her, and she had understood it—he had reached the same conclusion on the probable target and wanted her to return to Montana to be with Jameson. Isabel had put Jameson on the phone for a few minutes, and his little voice begging Sofia to come and take him home had brought her near to tears.

"I'll be there soon," she had told him, her voice soothing. "Daddy too. We love you so much."

She analyzed the situation. *The Israelis tipped us that the financial area is the probable target, but they could be wrong. Even if we're right, that doesn't mean Klaus will hit the Twin Towers. But that is the tallest target with the greatest symbolic value. Regardless, Klaus must have at least considered it and probably has people scoping it out.* She took a deep breath, got out of bed, and crossed to the window.

Her room was on a low floor of a national chain, a good place to stay, but its view was limited to the buildings across the street. Already, people moved purposefully to work.

For a few moments, she thought of cancelling today's plan to roam the World Trade Center again. The pull to return to a safe place and be with her baby son was almost overpowering, but then the pragmatism of a seasoned intelligence operations officer set in. *Klaus won't present himself. He won't be readily visible. We're going to have to draw him out.*

With dread in the pit of her stomach and a lump in her throat, she dressed, pulled on her heavy coat and boots, and once more made her way into the streets of New York City. She hailed a cab and watched without seeing as the rush-hour view passed by. Soon, the towers loomed ahead of her, their lower parts visible through the windshield.

The taxi pulled to the curb. Sofia mustered a positive countenance and stepped out onto the sidewalk. Then she began her trek.

The forecast had called for temperatures diving below twenty degrees with wind gusts up to thirty-three miles per hour. The biting cold caused her to tuck her chin into her collar. She turned her head as she walked to allow her own vapor to pass by—it impeded her view. Her fur-lined gloves barely seemed to break the icy breeze, and she thrust her hands into her side pockets for added warmth, pushing them against the inner lining to hug the coat closer around her.

The usual horde of pedestrians hurried through the plaza into the soaring buildings. Sofia moved with them, deciding that a hot cup of coffee and a bagel might help make her rounds more tolerable and allow for the sun to rise higher and do its work of warming the day.

As she sat in the coffee shop people-watching, her mind wandered through the events that had brought her to this moment. Despite challenges, she thought most of it had been happy. Tragedy had befallen her when her first husband had been killed in the Middle East.

An image of him formed in her head, young, strong-minded, handsome. After losing him, she had thought she could never love again. And then, five years later, Atcho entered her life, a filthy, brutalized political prisoner just released to the United States Interests section of the Swiss Embassy in Havana. Despite the obvious ravages he had endured, he carried himself with such nobility. His fellow ex-prisoners had treated him with high regard, and yet his overriding concern was for his daughter, Isabel, whom he had not seen in nineteen years.

Sofia did not see Atcho again until early 1988, when she received an invitation to a reception at a prominent hotel in downtown Washington, DC. Her CIA cover at the time was that of a senior intelligence supervisor for the US State Department, stationed at its headquarters.

The reception was to celebrate Atcho's recognition by Ronald Reagan at the State of the Union Address earlier that same evening. The organizers had invited all those who had been with Atcho in captivity or assisted with his release. The party was a surprise for him. By then, he had reunited with his daughter and forged a successful career as a real estate investor in Washington, DC. The attraction she had felt in Havana resurfaced.

Something about Atcho in the days and months after their reacquaintance had been enigmatic. Sofia noticed that he held friends away, and he ended their romance just as it had begun. Convinced that Atcho carried a burden thrust on him by outside forces, she had sought Burly's help. Her instincts had been vindicated when she learned that Atcho had resisted coercive efforts by a foreign power to be their secret agent. That power had threatened Isabel.

Together, Atcho, Burly, and Sofia had defeated the threat and then participated in subsequent clandestine operations in Siberia, Berlin, and Kuwait. In between the first two missions, she and Atcho had married, and between the second two, she had born Jameson.

Atcho had soothed Sofia's pain over losing her first husband, and together they had begun to live fully. *And now that could end abruptly.*

Sofia doused the thought. *No time to be maudlin.*

She left the coffee shop, rode the escalator back up to the main floor, and exited on West Street.

―――――――――

Klaus decided to oversee Sofia's capture personally. He arrived at the World Trade Center early and walked around to examine the complex from the point of view of each man stationed to watch for her. Satisfied that she could be spotted regardless of rush-hour crowds, he loitered between street vendors to wait.

Shortly after eight o'clock, a runner came to let him know that she had been seen emerging from a taxi, wearing the same white coat as the previous two days, and heading toward the North Tower's main door.

"Olek will pick her up there," the runner told him. "He'll wait for you. Amir is with him and will follow her when she goes by. He has a cell phone and will call back to Olek about her movements."

"Let's go." Klaus set off at a fast pace, shouldering past people who slowed him down. His mind raced as he anticipated bringing the wife of his arch-nemesis under his control. The last time Sofia and Klaus had seen each other face to face was in Berlin just before the Wall fell. He recalled her initial look of shock and then resolve as he forced Atcho at gunpoint to accompany him.

The only other time Klaus had seen her was through the reticles of a sniper scope as he pulled the trigger. She had fled across his field of view, leaving him no time for careful aim. The bullet had gone through her leg.

"You won't be treated so well this time," he muttered under his breath as he approached the building's revolving door. "Where is she?" he demanded upon seeing Olek. They spoke in Arabic.

"They took a down escalator. Amir just reported that she entered a coffee shop."

"Stay here and keep watch for her. I'll go down. We'll let you know if she comes this way."

Olek gave him the name of the establishment, and Klaus hurried to the escalator, still jammed with people making their way to work. Amir met him outside the coffee shop.

"She's in line," Amir said. "She doesn't seem in a hurry."

"We'll wait for her."

Amir pointed her out and they watched from a distance as Sofia took a seat at a table and sipped her coffee. Forty minutes later, she left and rode the escalator back up to the ground floor.

Klaus and Amir followed. When Sofia turned toward the West Street exit, Klaus ordered, "Get the car and the pickup team over there."

His heart beating faster, his breaths becoming shorter, he closed the distance. At the big rotating doors, Klaus stood back and waited for the next set of people to exit. Once outside, he spotted Sofia and hurried to catch up.

She turned north toward Fulton Street, ambling along against the wind, oblivious to the danger that approached from behind.

Klaus closed in on her right side, put his arm across her back, and clamped his left hand onto her left shoulder. With his right hand, he shoved a pistol into her side.

"Keep walking, Ms. Xiquez," he snarled. "You found me."

Sofia remained silent and kept walking.

"Veer to your left toward the corner of West and Fulton. With any luck, our car will arrive at the same time we do."

Sofia complied. If she felt anxious, her expression failed to reveal it.

Her composure amused Klaus. "You think you're tough," he said in broken English. "Listen to me. When the car comes, I'll open the door. Then, I want you to scream for help. Be loud, and then get in the car. If you don't do those two things, I'll shoot you on the spot and leave your body lying in a heap. Do you understand?"

"How's your bomb?" Sofia responded without emotion. "Have you got one to work yet?"

"How's your son?" Klaus retorted, his voice thick with brutality. "This is no game. I hope you gave Jameson—"

"Leave my son out of this," Sofia snapped angrily. "You attack children? Coward."

"He's an infidel, a combatant against *jihad*. I hope you gave him many kisses before you abandoned him. You won't see him again."

"Then I have nothing to lose."

"But you do. Atcho is still alive and might be able to save your son and himself, and maybe even you. You came here to draw me out. Now I'll use you to expose him."

"Which is why you want the drama as we get in the car."

"Exactly. One of our men will videotape the event and release the clip to the news agencies. Atcho will see it and come for you, I'm sure of that."

"Why not just kill me now?"

Klaus smirked. "I'm tempted, but I want Atcho to think he has a chance of saving you." He laughed without mirth. "He doesn't, but he'll try."

"You've got it all figured out," Sofia mocked. "Atcho's smarter than you. He beat you in Berlin, Kuwait, and Austin, and he'll beat you here."

"But you'll be dead." Klaus smirked. "I'll wave at you both from Paradise."

"Ooh, a martyr," Sofia derided. "How noble."

"Shut up," Klaus hissed. "There's the car."

Atcho hurried with Burly and Sam through the main doors of Building 7 at the World Trade Center. An escort waiting for them in the lobby whisked them through check-in and took them upstairs to the security operations center for the complex.

The head of security met them in the foyer of the office suite. "Mr. Xiquez," the man said, "I'm George Luciano. Jim Dude called to let me know you were on your way." He looked at Burly and tossed Sam a patronizing look. "I assure you that all is being done to locate and recover your wife. The police were informed immediately after the attack, and the FBI is already cooperating."

"Let me see the video," Atcho said tersely.

Luciano led them down a wide corridor to a conference room. "In addition to the clip that showed up on the news," he explained as they walked, "we also have surveillance video. Our technicians pulled it together. I'll show you what we've got so far."

Atcho only nodded as they entered the conference room, where a young man and woman worked over a VCR. They glanced up with grim faces as the group entered.

"We're ready," the woman said. "We've spliced together several views. The first footage is the news clip." She pressed a button on a remote control, and a television screen hanging from a corner wall lit up.

An image of a reporter appeared. "I'm at the corner of West and Fulton," he said, "where just a little while ago, a woman was abducted in broad daylight." He pivoted and held his palm out to indicate the location. "Just after rush hour, witnesses say they saw a woman struggling against an assailant who pushed her into a car. She yelled for help, but before anyone could react, it sped away. Fifteen minutes later, the video footage you are about to see was delivered to our station with no attribution. Authorities are investigating."

As the group watched, the television screen flashed to a distant scene showing a man and woman walking closely together across the World Trade Center plaza. As they approached the street, the camera zoomed in and focused on the woman's face.

Atcho sucked in his breath. Burly grimaced. Sam stared.

Sofia's face filled the screen. The video showed the man next to her with one arm wrapped around her back, his hand clamping her shoulder. The camera shifted to show the man's face.

"Klaus," Atcho growled.

"You know him?" Luciano asked.

"I killed his brother in a firefight. This is his fourth attempt at revenge."

"So, this is personal," Luciano said flatly.

"This goes way beyond personal," Burly interjected. "That man is a known terrorist. He's a threat not just to Atcho and his wife, but also to the US, and specifically the World Trade Center. He intends to bomb it."

"Which explains why you're here," Luciano said, turning to Sam. "You called last night to set up this meeting, and after that, Ms. Xiquez was kidnapped. What did you want to see us about?"

Sam looked cornered. His eyes rounded. "To let you know what Burly just said—that we believe this building is about to get hit with a bomb."

As he spoke, the conference room door swung open and Jim Dude walked in. "That's a *personal* belief that my *very* young special agent carries," Dude said sternly, his voice raised. "It's *not* the official position of the FBI or the New York field office." He faced Sam. "It's a good thing one of your more senior colleagues saw your phone traffic and clued me in. You're walking on thin ice."

Atcho's eyes burned with anger. He stepped close to Dude. "Sam is the only official in New York who takes the threat seriously." He pointed at the television screen. "Look at the quality of that recording. Klaus pre-positioned his photographer. He wanted me to see this video."

"There's another thing," Burly interjected. He indicated for Dude to step away a few paces with him so they could confer in private. "I spoke with Mossad this morning. Their analysis also leads to the conclusion that the Twin Towers are targeted."

Dude regarded him sharply. "Is that a formal notice to our government?"

Burly shook his head. "It's wending its way through both bureaucracies. I got the information through backchannels."

Dude spun around and caught Atcho's furious gaze. "Does he know?"

"He does," Burly replied. "We think the attack is imminent. Like at any moment."

"Can you replay that recording?" Dude called to Luciano.

The security chief nodded to the female technician. She pointed the remote and started rewinding.

"Sir," she said as the VCR whirred, "while we compiled these recordings, we saw some things you should be aware of."

"What is being done to find my wife?" Atcho cut in, his attention directed pointedly at Dude.

The FBI agent exhaled. "The city police and our agents are combing the streets now." He turned to the young lady. "What did you see that was unusual?"

She glanced at Atcho worriedly and pressed the remote. The group watched again, mesmerized by the vivid details of Sofia's abduction. When it was finished, Dude turned to the technician. "Would you mind answering my question?"

She indicated the TV monitor. "We started looking for any footage that showed Mrs. Xiquez," she said. "We kept finding more and more of it. This is the third day in a row that she's been videoed all over the complex, always wearing that same overcoat, boots, and gloves." As she spoke, the technician let the video run. When the initial clip had finished, it continued on to other sequences of Sofia moving through the WTC complex. Footage toward the end showed Klaus in various places close to Sofia, apparently watching her. The technician stopped the machine, eyed Atcho, and said, "It was as if she was trying to be noticed."

"That's exactly what she was doing," Atcho responded. "She wanted Klaus to see her, to draw him out."

"Why would she do that?" Luciano asked.

"Because the FBI won't do its job, and neither will the CIA or the Department of Defense. They're more concerned with procedure than protection these days. That man planted a nuclear bomb outside our house, and they still don't take him seriously." He whirled on Dude. "We have a family to protect, and if you won't do your job, we'll do it for you. That's why she's sacrificing herself…"

He turned to Burly. "The president knows me. He backed our actions in Berlin and Kuwait. Why doesn't he back us now?"

Before Burly could answer, Atcho went on. "We know why—bad advice from his intelligence agencies and the Pentagon. And the FBI is cut off from information they need to make good decisions." His voice trailed away as he caught himself.

Then he poked a crooked finger at Luciano. "You're getting bad advice too. Klaus is part of an organization that's growing rapidly. It's got funding and technology, and it knows tactics. They've rehearsed in other countries." He faced Dude. "Have you bothered to connect the bombings in Buenos Aires and Lima? That man who kidnapped my wife is a recognized terrorist and was present at all three of those bombings."

Dude blanched, his eyes widening. He said nothing.

Atcho did not wait for a response. "They're coming for your Twin Towers," he told Luciano, "and the bureaucrats are wearing blinders."

The room descended into silence.

"I've reviewed Mr. Luciano's security arrangements," Dude said finally, almost apologetically. "They're robust and adequate. I can't second-guess our intelligence agencies. If the Pentagon and the CIA tell the president that our country is secure from a significant terror attack, I have to rely on that. My concentration at the moment is on finding your wife."

Atcho nodded, deadpan. "Find her, and you might find Klaus," he said. "But my best advice to Mr. Luciano is to start inspecting every briefcase, every purse, every bag that comes into this building." He leveled his gaze at the man. "If you had started yesterday, you might still be too late." His brow furrowed. "Would you mind if I stay in here for a while to review those tapes?"

Luciano assented with a nod. "Take your time. If you see something, let us know. Meanwhile, I'll do what I can to beef up security. How much time do we have?"

"I don't know, but I'd say an attack is imminent." Atcho sat down, leaned his elbows on the table, and buried his head in his hands. "Sofia deliberately baited Klaus. He knows it. He used her to lure me here. For all we know, the bomb is already somewhere in the complex. The stage is set."

"What's your plan?" Burly asked when everyone else had left the conference room.

Atcho shook his head. "I don't know. I'm going through the videos again. Maybe Sofia was able to leave a clue or a message. She'll try to learn Klaus' plan and communicate with us."

"Have you thought of what Klaus might do to her?"

Atcho closed his eyes and nodded. "I try not to think about it." He sniffed. "If she manages to free herself, I pity Klaus."

One particular detail in the video of Sofia's abduction haunted him. He re-ran the tape and watched again, his heart aching.

Just as Klaus had forced Sofia into the car, she struggled upright momentarily and faced back toward the building. As she did, she brought her right hand up, just for a second, to cover her heart.

Her gesture was one Atcho recognized, a message directly to him that said, "I love you. I always will."

On seeing the footage again, Atcho covered his face.

"Burly, please," he said in a broken voice. "I need to be alone for a few minutes."

44

Klaus studied his handiwork carefully, examining each connection and diode in minute detail. Yielding to impulse, he rubbed his hand over the lead sphere containing the plutonium. Satisfied, he rubbed his eyes and switched off the light over his workbench. He swung around on a swivel stool and observed Ramzi on the other side of the room, still bent over his own devices.

"I'm ready," Klaus called in Arabic. "We can go at any time."

Ramzi turned around and smiled. "I'll be finished in a few hours. We are already loading components onto the van. Is tomorrow soon enough?"

Klaus' eyes gleamed, and then he gave Ramzi a questioning look. "I'm curious about something. Why are we hitting the World Trade Center instead of the United Nations? The United States is not our only enemy, and we could hit several of them at one time if we bomb the UN head-quarters."

"You're not the only person to come up with that idea," Ramzi replied while turning back to his work, soldering gun in hand. "You know that no target is sanctioned in the US without Sheikh Omar's approval—well, he doesn't give approval, but we all know that if he thinks something is a bad idea, that's a path we will not pursue."

"Why would hitting the UN be a bad idea?"

"I had the same question, but I understand the reasoning. A Muslim striking the United Nations would be bad for Muslims. Not only would we hurt some of our own countries, but also other nations who either support or tolerate us. That could make things hard for Muslims living in those countries, but even more importantly, we could find ourselves actively opposed there.

"There's a stronger reason, though. The UN headquarters isn't the head of the snake. It's the anus. It's where all the smelly waste pours out onto the world. No one means anything they say in all their meetings. It's just a place for people to pretend that they get along while scheming behind each other's backs.

"The US is the head of the snake, and the brain cavity is right here in New York City. We'll kill the snake by killing the financial system. If either bomb works as planned..." He blew over his hands to simulate an explosion, arched his eyebrows, and laughed. "Bye-bye America. We'll rip open its belly, leaving it easy prey for jackals and other filthy beasts that feast on carrion."

Klaus nodded his understanding. Ramzi continued working, the rancid smell of solder and strong chemicals filling the air. At the opposite end of the workshop, a van was parked with its rear doors open. Blue plastic barrels had already been arranged in its dim interior.

"I've had some experience with explosives, but your design is beyond anything I've worked with," Klaus said. "Can you explain what you've done?"

Ramzi looked up at him and smiled patiently. "The difference is that you've mainly used explosives intended for routine military missions or converted from civilian use, like for mining or road construction. We can't get a big enough blast out of those to do the kind of damage we need to topple at least one tower, and hopefully both. But knocking the second one down relies on putting enough force at the precise point on the first one. To do that, we had to identify the exact location against a foundation wall and enhance the explosives' power sufficiently to penetrate completely through the outer wall. That's where my powdered metals come in to expand the blast. Then gravity takes over. It's a simple combination of civil and chemical engineering, and physics." He chuckled. "If you like, you can help us load the nitroglycerine. We have four sealed buckets of it."

Klaus shook his head, laughing. "Never mind that. I have to make it to the target in one piece."

"How are you getting in? They'll be looking for men with briefcases."

"You know how stupid the Americans are. They barely check the people who keep their businesses and lives running. I'll go in through the employees' entrance. A brother who works in security there will let me in, and I already have a work uniform with ID. I'll carry a toolbox in with me. I reconfigured the bomb so that it's long and fits under a false bottom.

"All the parts interact the same way as in the original bomb. It was a matter of extending the wires and making sure the current to each component was the same. I've run all the tests dozens of times, and they check out. I'm ready."

Ramzi nodded his approval. "We're planning on striking just after noon. People will be going to lunch, and the restaurants near the parking garage will be packed. We'll kill a lot of people then. Which one of us detonates first?"

Klaus pursed his lips. "I'd say we detonate at the same time."

Ramzi shook his head. "We can't guarantee that we can do that. On my bomb, we're using detonation cords. There are four of them, and they feed into the nitroglycerine. We only need one. The other three are back-ups, and they burn at a rate that gives us time to get out. What about you? Have you provided sufficient time to escape?"

Klaus' eyes became somber. "I won't be staying around this time, brother. I'll be spending tomorrow night in Paradise."

Ramzi looked at him in wonder. "A martyr? You're going to blow up with your bomb?"

Klaus dropped his head and nodded. "I'm tired of them not working, for whatever reason. They're ruining my reputation. I can blame Atcho for that, but the fact is, nothing gets blown up. This time, I'm going to make sure the damn thing goes. I'll go up high enough in the building so that I won't be affected by your initial blast, and I'll set the timer to go off five minutes after your expected detonation. If mine doesn't go off then, I'll click the remote, and if that still doesn't work, I'll open the bomb. I set a failsafe."

The wonder in Ramzi's eyes had not receded. He crossed the room to Klaus and embraced him. "You have truly earned your way into Paradise with all the rewards of a martyr. I will make sure that no one forgets your sacrifice."

They discussed other details while Ramzi resumed his work. As time proceeded past midnight into early morning, he jutted his jaw toward a small door near the van.

"What about the woman?"

Klaus followed his glance. "She's yours. Do what you want with her. Give her to your men for sport, if you like. Just promise me one thing." He reached across and grasped Ramzi's shoulder. "Make sure she's dead before the day is out."

Ramzi held Klaus' gaze for an extended time and then dropped his head. "It shall be done, my brother, as you wish."

45

Sofia's eyes opened slowly; her mind felt dull. She tried to turn on her side, but her arms were bound at the wrist behind her back. Her ankles were also tied together. Finding herself constrained shocked her to full consciousness, and she struggled against the ropes momentarily as memory of her capture flooded back.

Fully awake in a dark room, she remembered walking to the car with Klaus.

Klaus. Her blood ran cold at the thought of him. She had played through his charade of making a public spectacle of her abduction—doing so served her own purpose of providing a positive identification of the terrorist to Atcho and authorities via the expected video.

She remembered her small gesture. Just before ducking her head to enter the car, she had brought her right hand over her heart in a circular movement. The motion was slight and would not be noticed by most people, but Sofia was sure that Atcho would see the video and understand.

The tiny action was one of intimacy between Atcho and Sofia. It had sprung spontaneously, a cute way of expressing their affection in public places when they caught each other's eye. They had used the signal in

countless meetings, parties, even formal events, and it always served to
warm their hearts when they found themselves separated by distance.

In this instance, Sofia had sent her love to Atcho as a last farewell. She
did not expect to live through the events that were sure to follow. She
only hoped that pulling Klaus out of the shadows would provide Atcho
with an opportunity to trip him up, to save New York and the millions of
people squeezed into a single square mile, the size of the blast area. And
with Klaus eliminated, the direct threat against Jameson, Isabel, Kattrina,
and the rest of her extended family would disappear.

Another man had been waiting in the back seat when Sofia fell into
the car. He immediately clamped a wet cloth over her mouth and nose.
She remembered nothing else.

Now, lying in the dark, her mind quickly turned to survival. She had
no death wish. Having exposed Klaus and finding herself still alive with
her mental acuity intact, she assessed her situation.

She still wore her heavy coat and boots. The only light entering the
room came from under a door several feet away, and it was dim. Otherwise, she was in a pitch-black area of indeterminate size. The murmur of
voices floated from the other side.

The surface on which she lay was cold and hard, and she guessed it to
be the floor. She struggled onto her back, bent her knees, and shoved
with her feet until she bumped her head against an upright surface. A
wall.

She tilted her neck and shoved with her feet, repeating until the
backs of her shoulders pressed against the wall. Her breaths came in
short gasps as she watched the light for signs of approaching guards, but
none came. She continued the action until she had propped herself up in
a sitting position. Then, by rocking onto one side and then the other, she
inched her wrists past her buttocks and up under her knees. *Thank God
for all that ballet and martial arts training.*

Sofia's coat became an obstacle, its thick folds adding friction and
bulk to overcome. Her eyes watered and her breathing became
constricted as she curled her body into a tight knot and pushed her wrists
over her feet, struggling unmercifully to pull the rope and her palms over
the spike heels.

A sense of panic set in as she sensed that she had tied herself into a knot and could not slide the rope the remaining millimeters past the pointed toes of her boots. Then, holding back a scream, she scrunched her stomach, pushed her shoulders against her knees, and shoved her arms forward with her remaining strength. The rope slid forward, and her legs fell to the floor with a muffled thump.

Sofia stayed still and listened. The low murmur of voices beyond the door continued without interruption.

She rolled onto her stomach, pushed herself to a standing position, and hopped to the door. The voices on the other side continued in Arabic. Sofia distinguished two men, one of them Klaus.

She rotated her wrists by the faint light below the door as best she could until she could make out the ends of the rope and the shape of the knot. Then, using her teeth, she struggled with it until it came loose.

When her hands were finally free, she worked the cord around her feet until it fell loose. Then she felt her way around the bare room, judging it to be an empty storage room.

46

February 26, 1992

"It's time," Ramzi said. He shook Klaus for a second time. "If you're going in with the maintenance crew, you need to leave soon."

Klaus blinked. Ramzi had worked through the night, and Klaus had stayed with him until he fell asleep in a chair. As he woke up, he remembered the last thing Ramzi had told him.

"Don't detonate before noon," Ramzi had said, leering. "That's when we'll blow our bomb. Remember to get high enough that you won't be wiped out in the initial blast. When you feel the building rumble, you'll know my work is complete, and you can finish your task. If nothing has happened by twelve-fifteen, then, as the Americans say, bombs away."

"I'll go to the seventy-eighth floor," Klaus had replied, eyes gleaming with anticipation. "That's where the transfer lobby to reach the higher floors is located. It's low enough that, with the hole your bomb creates, we'll leave a massive crater in Manhattan, and it's high enough to generate a huge quantity of radioactive fallout. Mine will toss thirty-two floors full of infidels into the sky. With any luck, it'll shoot them into the jet streams and drop them in bloody clumps over the country all the way to California."

Klaus shook himself to wake up. "That's the wrong direction," he said flatly, almost in a growl. "The jet streams will blow everything out to sea."

Ramzi regarded him with a dreamy expression. "I know. I let my imagination run away with me for a moment." He scoffed. "Maybe some of it will land on Buckingham Palace in London."

Klaus stretched, yawned, and scratched the back of his neck. Then he went to the next room to clean up and dress.

"How will you get to the Trade Center?" Ramzi asked when Klaus emerged.

"I'll ride the bus. I scouted a stop used by a few of the center's employees, and I've ridden the line a few times, so I'll look familiar to them. I'll go in with them. Our brother on the inside will pass me through."

"He's doing a great service for our *jihad*. Do I know him?"

Klaus shrugged. "I don't know. My *hawaladar* in Tripoli directed him to me. He only knows to let me in, nothing more."

Ramzi nodded his approval and gestured to the small door of the storage room where Sofia was held. "Do you want to see the woman again?"

Klaus shook his head. "I don't want to be corrupted on this of all days. I'll just go. Be sure to deal with her as promised."

Ramzi gave him a somber look. "After the bombing, we'll celebrate with her, and then I'll take care of it. You can damn me to hell from Paradise if I fail. Do you want breakfast before you go?"

"I'll have several hours with nothing to do before you arrive. I'll put some fruit and bread in my toolbox to eat if I get hungry. That will make the contents look even more innocent."

They walked to the entrance of the workshop together, embraced, and kissed each other's cheeks.

"Live a long and happy life," Klaus said, "and then I'll see you in Paradise." He started to leave and then, on impulse, turned back. "Who's going to drive? Not Salameh, I hope."

Ramzi grunted. "Not Salameh. I have a friend who grew up in New York City. He was a limo driver here for many years and knows all the streets. He'll drive us to the target the smoothest way, without jarring the nitroglycerine."

Klaus stared, his doubt manifest in his expression. "Why have you tolerated Salameh?"

"He's my friend. He came here with me for *jihad*."

Klaus shook his head. Then he turned, waved over his shoulder, and started down the driveway carrying his toolbox.

After Klaus left, Ramzi went to the van and checked all the connections, then woke up Salameh and the limo driver.

"Time for final preparations," he said, his passive expression belying the tingling of excitement he felt.

Salameh turned over on his mattress on the floor, pulled his blanket back over his head, and groaned his objection to having his sleep interrupted. Then he yawned and reluctantly climbed out of bed.

Tariq, the limo driver, bounded to his feet. "Let's go." He prodded Salameh. "Who else will ever have an opportunity like this one?"

The two followed Ramzi back into the workshop. He opened a locker and gestured at four gray buckets made of heavy plastic with sealed lids. A very narrow tube protruded from the center of each one.

"These go in the van." He peered sternly at Salameh. "Do I need to remind you how carefully you have to carry them?"

Salameh regarded him with wild eyes and shook his head.

"If you drop them," Ramzi continued, "we'll leave a crater in New York City, but we won't hit our target and our rewards in Paradise will be greatly diminished. Do you understand?"

Salameh nodded and picked up one of the buckets.

"Arrange them in front of the blue plastic barrels," Yousef said.

Once the nitroglycerine was loaded, Ramzi demonstrated how to thread the detonation cords through the surgical tubing. "This will subdue the smoke, so people are less likely to notice it. In the parking garage, that probably won't be an issue, and we'll lock the van anyway. The tubing will also slow down the burning, giving us time to escape from the blast area."

"Do you mind telling me how it all works?" Tariq asked.

"Of course," Ramzi said with pride. "The blue plastic barrels are filled with several hundred pounds of urea nitrate crystals mixed with nitric acid. The yellow barrels behind them contain sulfuric acid. We'll insert the detonation cords through the tubes on top of the nitroglycerin in the gray buckets. They are the fuses that ignite the nitroglycerine. When it explodes, it will cause the other elements to explode. Above the barrels are pressurized canisters of compressed hydrogen. That's what will make the explosion reach high into the building."

"And above that will be Klaus and his bomb," Tariq breathed.

Ramzi nodded. "When we park in the garage, light the fuses—and run." He laughed.

They finished loading their cargo and inserting the fuses. Then Salameh glanced toward the storage room door.

"What about the woman?"

"She'll be here when we get back. Klaus gave her to me. You can have fun with her afterward."

Salameh looked at his watch. "We won't leave for another hour. Can't we play with her a little now?"

Ramzi glanced at the door and then back at Salameh's hopeful face. "All right, but just for a few minutes—if you can bring her here. She's tied up in there. Can you handle her by yourself?"

Salameh grinned, lascivious intent gleaming in his eyes. Without saying another word, he headed toward the room.

Sitting on the floor next to the door with one of the ropes in her hands, Sofia dozed intermittently. Not knowing when she might need agility more than warmth, she had taken off her heavy coat and draped it over her shoulders.

She heard the men in the other room moving about and talking, but she could make out none of the conversation. Then she heard approaching footsteps and the key turning in the door.

She leaped to her feet and crouched, the rope strung between both hands. Her coat fell to the floor.

The door opened. A man stepped in, silhouetted against the light.

Sofia sprang. Crossing her arms and tossing the rope around Salameh's neck, she yanked it tight.

Not being a true garrote, the rope tightened and pinched off Salameh's airway, but did not cut into his skin. He immediately tossed furiously from side to side, fighting to remove a demon from his back. As his breath constricted, he panicked and slammed Sofia back against a wall.

She held on, but Salameh slammed her again and again. The rope slipped through her hands, burning them.

In the other room, Ramzi and Tariq heard the commotion and came running. In the dim light that spilled into the closet, they saw that Salameh had fallen to his knees and was clutching at his neck while Sofia clung to his back, still holding the rope around his throat. They rushed to his side and beat their fists into Sofia's head and hands until she let go of the cord.

Salameh fell forward, supporting himself on his hands and catching his breath while Ramzi and Tariq pulled Sofia into the other room. Forced to the ground on her stomach, she was helpless to stave off the blows Tariq delivered to the back of her head while straddling her.

Moments later, Salameh reeled from the closet, lust for vengeance written on his face. He staggered toward Sofia and delivered a powerful kick to the side of her head.

Her mind reeled, her vision blurred, and she lost consciousness. Blood spilled to the floor from an open gash above her temple.

Salameh continued kicking until he had exhausted himself.

Panting and sweating, he looked up at Ramzi. "What should we do with her?"

"Throw her in the van. She'll be one more infidel the authorities will try to piece together in two hours."

47

"Atcho, get some rest," Burly urged. "Building management has a full staff and augmentation. If Klaus comes in, we'll get him."

Atcho shook his head. "He can set that bomb off any time. We have to get close to him before he knows we've spotted him. Let's hope he hasn't decided to go martyr on us. If he has, all bets are off. Have you distributed those NUKEXs?"

"We had some flown in last night, but we don't have enough for the entire staff. I gave them to Luciano and showed him how to use them. He'll distribute them as he sees fit. You got yours?"

Atcho patted his jacket and nodded wearily.

They were sitting at a desk in the middle of the World Trade Center security operations control room in Building 7 of the complex. From that vantage, they could see most of the plaza on the north side of both buildings. Arrayed on the walls around them were banks of monitors that officers were watching closely.

Atcho heaved a sigh. "Even with all these eyes looking for him, Klaus will be tough to spot. Is there any progress on setting up full inspections at the entries?"

Burly scoffed. "There are 'political considerations.'" He mimed quotation marks in the air, and his expression projected his disgust. "The building is governed by the port authority, which falls under city government, and the politicians don't want to upset the public." He shot Atcho a sympathetic glance. "Anything on Sofia?"

Atcho closed his eyes and shook his head. "The news stations broadcast the picture of her and Klaus everywhere, the police mounted a huge search, and the FBI is working with them. People are calling in by the hundreds, but no solid leads. The trouble is that law enforcement is viewing this as a vendetta kidnapping, and not what it really is—Klaus' deliberate diversion. He wanted me here in New York City for the big bang, and here I am."

"Then Sofia's effort was useless?"

Atcho pushed his chair back, dropped his hands between his knees, and lowered his head. "I don't want to think that. Her aim was to smoke Klaus out. She did that. We know for certain he's in the city, and he wouldn't have spotted her at the WTC if he wasn't scoping it out. She pinpointed the target. His freedom of movement will be restricted too, because more eyes will be searching for him."

He looked up suddenly and scanned the room. "We're looking at this the wrong way, Burly," he exclaimed. "He won't come in wearing a suit and carrying a briefcase. What time is it?"

"Nearly eleven o'clock. What are you thinking?"

"Remember in Berlin, Klaus and his brother came into the hotel dressed as maintenance men to kidnap me? They had inside help and breached State Department security."

He jumped to his feet and grabbed the nearest security officer, a shift supervisor, by the shoulder. "Do you monitor employees as they enter the building?"

The man nodded and pointed to a row of screens watched by only a light crew. "Over there. I can get them to pull up this morning's clips."

"Do it and have your crew check for anything irregular on employees coming in this morning." He handed the officer a photo of Klaus. "This is the face."

"We all have that, sir, but we've been focusing on the public entrances."

"Exactly. Get people to review videos of everyone coming in through the staff entries. Look for anybody carrying something, anything that appears bulky. Chances are, the guy we're looking for is already inside. If you spot him, track which building he goes to and let me know immediately." He paused a moment in thought. "Can you pull a one-hundred-percent accounting of where each employee is?"

The security officer nodded. "It'll take some time."

"How much?"

"Twenty, thirty minutes."

"Do it. Do you need to clear it with Luciano?"

"No. He told me to fully cooperate." The man hurried away to carry out Atcho's instructions.

Burly nudged him. "You really think he's here already?"

"He has Sofia, and he has me where he wants me. He's ready to pull the trigger."

Klaus remained in a men's restroom near the staff entrance for a time, and then moved to a coffee shop. He lingered there only long enough to appear to grab a cup of morning coffee before heading out to complete routine tasks. Then he went to another restroom, and finally made his way into a long underground tunnel that would take him to the North Tower. Arriving there, he looked at his watch with dismay. He still had three hours to kill.

Finding a broom closet, he deposited his toolbox in a dark corner and swept the floor outside, watching closely for anyone entering the storeroom.

Another hour passed. Retrieving his toolbox, he made his way to the Paths Concourse and sought out the coffee shop where he had observed Sofia yesterday, smiling at the memory of her forced composure when he had confronted her.

He looked at his watch again. Still two hours to go. *One hundred and twenty minutes—and then poof.* He smiled again, picturing flying, mutilated bodies disappearing in a cloud of smoke.

He sauntered back into the maintenance areas below ground and found a cargo elevator for the higher floors. His contact in WTC security had provided him with a pass, which he used with no difficulty. On arriving at the seventy-eighth floor, he took a few minutes to observe the breathtaking view of the city and the countryside beyond. He had read somewhere that, on a clear day, the Twin Towers were visible from Bear Mountain, a few miles south of West Point. He smirked at the thought. *We came so close to getting your family, Atcho, but we've got your wife, and we'll get you today.*

He made his way to the nearest maintenance room, found a dark corner to open his toolbox, and began munching on an apple.

Salameh held the garage doors to the workshop open while Tariq edged the van into the driveway, and then closed them. He hurried to enter the van through the rear, since the side doors were blocked by the collection of blue, gray, and yellow plastic barrels.

No one spoke. Ramzi sat in the front passenger seat. Sofia, bloodied, limp, and intermittently conscious, had been propped in the only unoccupied space on the floor. On entering and settling across from her, Salameh prodded her again with the bottom of his boot and then two more times for good measure. He grinned at Ramzi, who, eyes wide, signaled for him to stop and pointed at the nitroglycerine.

Salameh understood the message and fell into sullen silence.

Tariq guided the van with great care over the rough driveway and emerged onto Pamrapo Avenue, sliding into mid-morning traffic. He drove southeast and followed the main road, then turned north on Garfield Avenue. His route was carefully chosen for smooth driving with the fewest number of stops, the least traffic, and the best road surface. Tariq took care to keep a distance between the van and vehicles ahead, gliding to a halt when necessary, always mindful of the destructive cargo behind him.

Ramzi sat rigidly, allowing only his head and eyes to move, watching in all directions, including checking on Salameh to be sure he behaved himself.

Salameh continued to eye Sofia in sullen silence, nudging her with his boot whenever Ramzi was not looking.

They reached Interstate 78 and turned to traverse the Holland Tunnel. Tariq drove at a speed that kept traffic flowing past him on the left. On reaching the other side, they took the exit that wound around toward West Street and then turned south.

The tall spires of the Twin Towers loomed ahead of them. Ramzi viewed them with the detached attention of an engineer examining a project, reviewing in his mind the placement and magnitude of forces required to bring them down.

48

"There." Luciano pointed at the video screen in front of him. "Play that back," he instructed the officer working the controls.

As Atcho watched with Burly and Luciano, a man dressed in a maintenance uniform entered the field of view. He moved with a line of employees entering the World Trade Center through a staff portal.

"Look," Luciano exclaimed as the video rolled. "He has trouble with his ID card, then he's taken aside by a security guard, and watch this—he's allowed through." He turned to another officer. "Get that security guard and bring him to me."

"Have you tracked where the man went, the one who had trouble with the ID?" Atcho asked. "The video is too grainy to make him out. He looks like he's carrying something, a container of some sort."

"We're combing the files," Luciano said. "He went straight to a restroom and stayed there for an extended time, and then made his way to a coffee shop. We don't know yet where he went from there. We'll keep looking."

"I'll wait. Warn your people to look out for him, but if they see him, they need to keep a distance. That container could be the bomb."

"It's time to evacuate the building," Luciano said.

"If you do that, he'll know we're on to him, and he'll blow it," Burly interjected. "For whatever reason, he seems to be biding his time, like he's waiting for something. Instead of causing a panic that could alert him and trigger his action, let's use the time to get close to him."

Luciano hesitated, his face showing the weight of decision. He sighed. "All right."

An officer nudged his elbow and pointed to a screen. Luciano peered at it and turned to Atcho.

"We've got a clear shot of him. Is that your guy?"

Atcho moved closer to the screen and scrutinized the image in front of him. "That hat is hiding his full face, but the lower half of the face looks like him, and that's the right build. Where was that taken?"

"On the Paths Concourse. He appears to be headed to the North Tower."

A phone rang. The security officer at the control panel answered it. "Sir," he called to Luciano, "we've got him. He's on the seventy-eighth level Sky Lobby mopping the floor."

"Patch us in."

Atcho's heart thumped when the live image appeared on the screen. His face flushed red and sweat beaded on his forehead. His hands became clammy.

"That's him," he said, "and there's his bomb." He pointed to a toolbox sitting to one side of the screen, apparently against a wall. "Get me over there. Fast." He glanced at his watch. The digital readout blinked 11:50.

Luciano's face flushed with frustration. "I'm sending over a quick reaction force," he said. "We don't know when he'll blow that thing. I can get my men there faster than I can get you there."

"Fine." Atcho matched Luciano's tone. "But they have to keep control of Klaus' hands. I'm sure he has a remote, and he's willing to blow himself up. We've already seen that. Tell them to hold him until I get there. No one opens that container. And shut down those elevators."

"Agreed. I have some undercover men in suits I'll send up. They know what to do." He made the call.

Each of the passing minutes seemed like centuries to Atcho. He watched in fascination as Klaus mopped methodically back and forth.

The flow of people entering and exiting the elevators slowed visibly. If Klaus noticed, he showed no indication.

Soon, only four men other than Klaus remained on the floor. Three had meandered into Klaus' vicinity and one had moved toward the container, which now could be clearly identified as a toolbox.

In a sudden flurry of action, the three men near Klaus lunged. One tackled his feet and the other two grabbed his arms. In an instant, they had him on his back. The fourth man walked over to the toolbox and took up a position next to it.

Atcho turned toward Luciano, who had just hung up a phone. "The subject is subdued, and our guys have the remote," the security chief told him.

"Get me over there," Atcho growled.

On West Street, Tariq maneuvered the van to the parking garage entrance they had already scouted. He coaxed the vehicle over the hump that led into the dim interior and then eased it down the long ramp. Continuing past the rows of parked cars, they made their way to parking level B-2.

Tariq slowed to a halt.

Ramzi stared in consternation.

Ahead of them, a concrete beam suspended from the ceiling. A sign posted on it warned of the maximum height that a vehicle could pass beneath it without scraping the beam. The van was two inches too tall.

Ramzi whirled toward Salameh and fixed furious eyes on him. "Didn't you check the height when you rented this van?"

Salameh shrugged. "It looked like the right height."

Ramzi closed his eyes and faced the front, containing his anger.

"What do we do?" Tariq asked.

Ramzi's mind flipped rapidly through alternatives. If they tried to ram or scrape under the beam, they ran the risk of detonating the bomb while they were still in the van. If they let air out of the tires, they risked being spotted, and the uneven wobble of the van driving on flattened tires could set off the nitroglycerine.

"Park over there," he told Tariq, pointing to an area reserved for delivery vehicles. Anger sparked in his eyes. "We won't be able to get to the outer wall. Pray for as much destruction as possible."

Tariq did as instructed.

"Hand me the fuses and get out," Ramzi ordered Salameh.

Gingerly, Salameh crouched and picked up the four fuses tied together and resting on one of the four buckets of nitroglycerine. The opposite end of each fuse led into a corresponding tube in the cylinders.

Ramzi took the ends of the fuses. "Go," he told Salameh. "You too," he said to Tariq. "I'll meet you outside."

Salameh clambered over Sofia, taking one last opportunity to kick her as he opened the rear door and hopped out. He closed it and ran. Tariq followed, their footsteps barely echoing in the cavernous parking garage.

Ramzi moved rapidly, holding the fuses together in one hand while pulling a cigarette lighter from his pocket with the other. The flame leaped when he flipped the lid on the lighter, and he watched it with fascination as he held it to the fuses.

The smell of flame and acrid smoke reached his nostrils. He coughed, and his eyes watered. He stayed only long enough to see the flame traveling along the surgical tube-coated fuses. Then he jumped from the van, locked it, and ran after his comrades' receding footsteps.

As Atcho rode the elevator up to the seventy-eighth floor of the North Tower with Luciano, he fought down overwhelming emotion. Worry about Sofia overrode all others, and his mind replayed the sequence of his interactions with Klaus: waking up in the Berlin Mövenpick Hotel to find the terrorist pointing a gun at Sofia's head and then forcing Atcho to crawl through the dark, smelly tunnels under that city; the firefight during which Atcho had killed Klaus' brother on the east side of the Wall; their confrontation inside the Stasi headquarters as the Wall crumbled; Klaus' orchestrated assault on Sofia there; his terrorist attack in Kuwait; and then his foray against Atcho's home in Austin.

The elevator halted and the doors slid open. There, sitting cross-legged against the opposite wall with his hands interlocked behind his head, was Klaus. He grinned when he saw Atcho.

Atcho strode across the foyer, and before anyone grasped his impulse, he seized Klaus by the throat and landed a fist square in his face.

Klaus sprawled across the floor onto his back and lay there, stunned.

"Where's my wife?" Atcho snarled. He took two steps toward Klaus and was about to grab him again when Luciano intervened.

"The bomb first," Luciano said.

His lungs heaving, Atcho caught himself. Blood slid from Klaus' nose and he wiped it with a thumb. "You can't save her anyway. She'll watch you die on TV with thousands of infidels—maybe millions. The news channels will replay the scene over and over for years."

Atcho looked across to the toolbox sitting against the wall. Klaus followed his glance and chortled. "The timer. Do you remember that it has a timer?" He laughed. "You can't stop what will happen now, and this afternoon your wife will die, but not before she entertains many men."

Atcho glared at Klaus, then reached into his jacket and pulled out a small cloth bag. He extracted a silvery device that was rounded on one side and flat on the other. The NUKEX.

He approached the toolbox cautiously, examining it from each side. As he did, a high-pitched tone sounded from inside.

Klaus, now sitting back against the wall under the watchful eyes of the undercover security men, laughed. "It's over, Atcho," he called. "You have one minute to do whatever you think you can do. I set a short delay on the timer. I had no need of a long one."

The men looked at each other. Atcho froze momentarily and then squatted over the toolbox. Gingerly, he picked it up and turned it over.

Luciano ran to his side. "What are you doing?"

"The bomb has to be in a false bottom. Your people at the employee entrance would have done a physical inspection of the contents, right?"

Luciano nodded. "They didn't know to be on the lookout for a bomb when he entered, and they wouldn't be looking for a false bottom."

Atcho laid the NUKEX flat on one end of the bottom and pressed a button to activate it. "This thing takes thirty seconds to warm up," he yelled to Luciano, "and I don't know which end the bomb's trigger mechanism is on." Sweat already dripped from his brow and his heart beat rapidly. Gritting his teeth, he pressed the NUKEX to one end of the box and moved it along the center lengthwise. "If we have time, this should melt any electronic wires and components directly below it."

As seconds ticked away, Atcho knew he would fail. He should be feeling increasing heat from around the edge of the NUKEX. It was there, but not enough to accomplish its task. He needed at least another minute.

"Is anyone timing this?" he yelled.

"I am," Klaus called, indicating his watch with a mocking smile. "You have fifteen seconds."

Next to him, Luciano turned white and blew out his breath. He pulled up his wrist to see his own watch and inhaled sharply. "You're at five, four, three, two, one..."

49

Eighty floors below in the parking garage, the stench of burning plastic and det cord mixed with acid seeped out of the van. A pregnant woman walking by on her way to work noticed, but the smell was still only light, so she merely held her breath until she was past the unpleasantness and entered her place of work.

On the seventy-eighth floor, Atcho stared at the toolbox in disbelief. The timer had wound to zero, but he was still squatting over it. Nothing happened.

He stared over his shoulder at Klaus. "They won't be singing songs about you in Mecca." He coughed, surprised at the tautness of his voice. "Now we know. Your bombs don't work."

Klaus continued to grin, and Atcho stared at him in puzzlement.

"History is already written," the terrorist said. "You can't escape it."

Just then, a tremor vibrated through the floor and the huge plate-glass windows creaked. A roar sounded through the ventilation system. Moments later, smoke spilled through the air ducts.

Sitting against the wall, Klaus laughed uproariously. "You celebrated too soon."

Suddenly, he bounded to his feet. The security officers, distracted by the commotion, realized their immediate danger too late. Klaus connected a hard jab to the closest one's face and then, spinning around, brought his foot hard against the side of the second one's head. Both men went down.

Across the foyer, the third security officer reached for his gun. He was too late. In a flash, Klaus had crouched over his second victim, grabbed the man's pistol, and fired.

The security officer across the foyer dropped.

Klaus swung his weapon and fired again. Luciano fell to the floor.

"How things change," he called to Atcho. "I could have just let you die with me here, but I want to kill you myself. What a blessed day this is. Allah delivered you into my hands." Then, puzzled, he looked around for Atcho. "There's nowhere to hide," he said, and laughed.

Breathing heavily, Atcho crouched out of sight and considered his next move. When Klaus had turned to shoot Luciano, Atcho had scooped up the third security officer's weapon and dived behind a row of planters between the elevators and the Sky Lobby windows. He checked the magazine and then turned as the elevator doors from higher floors began to open, watching panicked people stream out and run to a second bank of elevators that would take them to lower levels. Many already held kerchiefs over their faces against increasing smoke. Atcho heard bits and pieces of their cries.

"An explosion in the basement..."

"They think a power junction blew..."

"Maybe a bomb?"

Then a cluster of people spotted the prone security officers and shouted for help to rescue them, then dragged them out of the crowd's path and tried to revive them. One of the rescuers screamed over the din upon discovering blood spilling from Luciano and the wounded security officer, adding to the pandemonium.

To Atcho's horror, there was a sharp *pop-pop-pop* as shots rang out.

Klaus fired indiscriminately into the crowd in Atcho's direction to clear the field.

Atcho raised his head over the planters. Not able to spot Klaus, but seeing the wounded dropping, he understood Klaus' tactic. He leaped to a low crouch, aimed his weapon in Klaus' direction, and yelled at the crowd, "Get down. Get down. Get down."

Amid more screaming, the path in front of Atcho cleared, and he ran toward Klaus. The terrorist had stopped firing and was crouched against a wall, out of bullets.

He scanned the scene, defiance still plastered on his face as a crowd of angry people formed around him and closed in. Before Atcho could reach him, they bore down on him, fists flying and legs kicking. Klaus' pistol clattered across the floor.

Atcho waded in. When he broke through the crowd, the terrorist was lying in a pool of blood, battered but still conscious.

Atcho crouched beside him, grasped the front of his shirt, and leaned into the man's mangled face. "Where's my wife?"

Klaus opened his eyes, then gave Atcho a mocking grin and chuckled through blood bubbling between his teeth. "As you Americans love to say, the fat lady didn't sing yet." He raised his head and clutched Atcho's arm. "By now, your Sofia is on her way to hell. I hope she enjoys her farewell party."

Atcho cocked his fist back and plowed it into the center of Klaus' face. The back of the terrorist's head bounced off the marble floor and he lay still.

50

The long line of tenants, their employees, and clients plodded down the emergency stairs, descending into smoke-filled darkness. Two of the security officers manhandled a handcuffed Klaus between them. Behind them, gun in hand, Atcho followed, keeping close watch on Klaus as they descended.

Luciano had regained consciousness. Despite a wound to his chest just below the shoulder, he had insisted on staying in the Sky Lobby to assist and instruct people heading to the emergency exits. One of his men had applied first aid and stopped his bleeding.

The other wounded security officer had been less lucky, having sustained a shot to the head that had knocked him unconscious. So far, he was still out. Luciano had called for an emergency medical team and ordered his recovered men to join Atcho in escorting Klaus down to waiting authorities.

After reawakening, Klaus had at first been gleeful at the sight of throngs of infidels clambering down the poorly lit steps. Then, as minutes proceeded into hours and he realized that the North Tower would not topple, much less fall into its twin, he became morose. He mocked the rescue teams that passed them going up, laden with equipment, and brightened when, after two hours of descending stairs that sent pain shooting through even his very toned physique, he emerged with his captors to see the devastation wrought by Ramzi's bomb.

A squad of policemen closed around Atcho, the security officers, and Klaus as they followed the line of survivors through the dark and smoldering lobby at ground level and escorted them to a cordoned-off area.

A sedan and a dark van, both with flashing strobes, waited there. The front doors of the sedan opened. Burly stepped out on one side, Jim Dude on the other, and they came forward with solemn faces to meet Atcho.

"No news?" Atcho asked, anticipating the answer. Burly shook his head and put a hand on Atcho's shoulder.

"I'm sorry."

Klaus and his escorts continued past them. "What? No wife?" Klaus mocked.

Atcho ignored him.

Klaus suddenly and deliberately stopped. He turned and looked up at the Twin Towers looming above them. "Next time, we'll take them both down."

Jim Dude regarded him in disgust. With a nod of his head, five armed men emerged from the van and surrounded Klaus and his entourage. They wore jackets marked with "FBI" in big yellow letters. The police escort fell away, and the FBI agents hustled Klaus toward the van.

"I want a lawyer," Klaus jeered as he entered the vehicle. "Atcho assaulted me, and I was unarmed." He leaned back and guffawed as he was thrust into the interior. "I know my rights."

"Put him in a deep, dark hole," Atcho muttered to Dude.

Suddenly, a gunshot pierced the air. All eyes shifted to the van. Three of the agents lifted their hands in the air and backed away as Klaus appeared, wielding a pistol. He glanced about wildly, and his eyes met Atcho's.

A grin started to form across his face but ended abruptly as three more shots rang out and he was blown backwards by the force of bullets.

Atcho continued firing until his clip was empty. Then he walked over and looked down at Klaus while one of the FBI agents checked for a pulse. The agent looked up at Atcho and shook his head. "Lights out," he said.

Dude appeared at his shoulder. "Every agent and officer not involved here is out looking for your wife." His face fell. "I am so sorry…"

Atcho waved him away. "No time for that now." He looked around at the lines of ambulances, police cars, and fire engines, and then at the blackened base of the tower. "How many casualties?"

"Twenty-three dead so far, and scores wounded. We'll be searching for people through the night, maybe for days."

Atcho stared around again and started walking back toward the building. Burly followed him.

Atcho waved him away. "I need a few minutes alone."

Burly dropped back, and Atcho walked on, conscious of the thick coat of dust that covered everything; of the intermittent dark streaks of blood where people had lain, perhaps gasping out their last breaths; of the lethal glass shards strewn about; and of the flashing blue strobe lights all around him.

A stench invaded his senses: smoke, mixed with a sharp acidic odor and the smell of death. He heard the screaming of sirens, some waxing, some waning, as ambulances arrived and carried victims away.

Close to the building, rescue workers hurried in all directions, some bearing stretchers, others applying emergency care on the ground. Citizens helped citizens as more people emerged from the lobby, having labored down the staircases from the highest reaches.

Atcho continued walking toward the building, his mind and body weary. He stopped near the back end of an ambulance to see what was being done. Rescue workers carried a stretcher across the street, aided by dust-covered civilians. They struggled over the road surface made slippery by the thick dust.

Atcho sought to help but saw that the situation was handled and knew he would be in the way. He sat against a concrete planter on the side of the street and leaned his head back into the hedge, his mind descending into blankness.

A few feet away, the rescue volunteers continued to load the victim into the ambulance.

"Watch her hand," a female volunteer called to the others in a hoarse voice. "It's bleeding badly."

The volunteer's voice caught Atcho's attention. He raised his head and looked toward the ambulance. She was coated in dust, the color of her hair indistinguishable. Her clothes, too, were colorless, her shoulders hunched, and she moved as though in pain. She helped load the stretcher into the ambulance and then stepped back. When she did, she turned, and Atcho saw her face, her features obscured by matted dust and streaks of blood.

"We're good," she called to the drivers. "You can take her away."

That voice. Atcho marveled that the voice he knew so well came from this ghostly creature standing hunched in the street only a few yards from him.

He pushed himself upright and started toward her. "Sofia?" he called.

The woman did not hear him.

He tried again, still stumbling to close the few remaining feet. "Sofia?"

She turned and stood still, eyeing him as he continued toward her, ragged and dirty. Her lower jaw dropped, and her tired eyes widened and then filled with tears that streaked down her dust-covered cheeks. Then she flung her arms up and, ignoring the pain, hobbled over to meet him in an embrace.

EPILOGUE

"I'll always be haunted by the notion that I could have stopped the explosion," Sofia said. "I was right there. I could have pulled the fuses."

"You couldn't have known," Atcho replied gently. "You were beat up, you didn't know where you were, and you couldn't see through the smoke. If you had tried, you might have jostled one of those buckets of nitro and blown yourself up along with everyone else. Best to get that notion out of your head."

Sofia nodded absently and sipped her coffee.

"I'm just glad you made it," Atcho said.

Sofia nodded again, her mind still grappling with the surreal moments before the blast, now remembered only in bits and pieces. The acrid smoke had stirred her awake, and she sensed danger more than understood what it was. She was on the floor at the back of the van. Her survival instinct had kicked in, and she found the inside latch and grappled with it until it opened before she slid out onto the garage floor. Seeing an exit sign, she hobbled past it and then increased her speed as she remembered the nature of the danger. Reaching the street, she had just ducked down between some bushes and the outside wall when the explosion blew.

"I'll have survivor's guilt for years to come," she murmured.

They sat next to each other in a swing on the Montana ranch house's front porch, taking in the view. Two weeks had passed since the attack on the World Trade Center. Bob, Isabel, and Kattrina had stayed in Montana to be with the family while Sofia recovered.

"It's good the investigators found the van wreckage that first day," Atcho mused. "They managed to lift the VIN, and that led to the rental agency, so they caught one of the terrorists right away—a guy called Salameh. They must have been rough on him—he gave up information fast. Can you believe that idiot tried to get his rental deposit back? He claimed that the van had been stolen." Atcho gave a small laugh. "He needed the money to fly out of the country. I'd love to have seen his face when he walked out of the rental office and found himself surrounded by the FBI."

"He's the one who came after me in the workshop," Sofia growled. "He should be put away forever. If I ever get a chance at him..." She left the sentence unfinished. "At least they got enough information from him to catch the limo driver and stop the release of the bomb technician who was already in jail."

"How about the way that technician was able to help Ramzi?" Atcho said. "He would call one of Ramzi's men, who would conference Ramzi in and hang up. Then Ramzi could ask him whatever questions he wanted with no phone records tracing to him." He shook his head. "Unreal."

"And Ramzi got away," Sofia said glumly. "He was on an airplane out of New York City within a couple of hours." She snuggled Atcho. "I still can't believe I'm alive."

"I can't either." Atcho kissed her on the forehead. "You were in as bad of shape as the people you helped," he said reprovingly. "You should have gone to the hospital yourself."

"I'm resilient," Sofia replied with a small smile. "I heal fast. They needed the help more than I did." She sighed. "Any news on the wounded FBI agent?"

"I heard from Dude this morning," Atcho said. "The agent is back on his feet and expected to make a full recovery."

"What about the bomb? Any word on why it didn't detonate?"

Atcho chuckled. "Klaus modified the bomb to fit in the toolbox in order to get it through security. It was longer and narrower than the suitcase." He shook his head. "To do that required that he move some components closer to each other and others farther away. What he didn't know, because he wasn't a technician, is that amps required at each component would change. He sent enough electricity through the system for the test diodes to indicate positively, but not enough to set the reaction in motion. He outsmarted himself."

Sofia considered Atcho's words. "So otherwise, it would have been a viable bomb."

Atcho nodded. "We think so."

Sofia remained silent a moment. "What did they do with him?"

Atcho shook his head and pursed his lips. "A good guess is that he was dropped into a very deep ocean."

"And what about the remaining bombs? Do we know where they are?"

"No," Atcho said grimly. "At least two of them are out there loose somewhere."

Sofia gazed out across the serene landscape, then rose stiffly and limped to the front of the porch. There she watched Kattrina and Jameson making snowballs in the front yard.

Isabel emerged from the house and climbed down the stairs to play with the children. Atcho moved next to Sofia and put an arm around her waist while they both watched the peaceful scene.

"Maybe it's time we stopped this," Sofia said after a while.

"Stop what?" Atcho asked, genuinely puzzled. He took in his daughter at the bottom of the stairs, his granddaughter and son playing in the snow, and the mountains on the horizon far across the prairie. "I like what I'm seeing."

"You know what I mean," Sofia said with a slight edge to her voice. "You can't keep going out to save humanity. I need you at home. Your daughter needs peace of mind. Your granddaughter needs her grandfather, and Jameson needs his father."

"We all need you, too," Atcho groused. "Time for you to get serious about your gardening club." He was quiet for a moment. "Our kids can't grow up always believing in tooth fairies, and the bad guys won't quit because you and I are growing gray hair. When we're threatened, I'll meet it."

Sofia leaned her head against Atcho's shoulder and squeezed his arm.

Behind them, the front door closed, and Bob came to stand beside them. "Good speech," he told Atcho. "You're my hero." He laughed good-naturedly, slapped Atcho on the back, and headed down the porch stairs.

Sofia struggled down the stairs behind him. "You're right," she called over her shoulder to Atcho. "I'm with you."

"What do you mean?" Atcho called after her, a look of concern crossing his face.

Sofia waved him off.

"Bob, what did she mean?" Atcho called again.

Bob stopped on the stairs and turned toward Atcho.

"Think about it," he said, and chuckled. "She's your wife."

AFTER DUNKIRK
Book #1 in the After Dunkirk series

From the beaches of Dunkirk to the codebreakers of Bletchley Park, from Resistance bombings in the south of France to the machinations in the basements of MI-6.

Winston Churchill called it Britain's finest hour. The Royal Navy evacuated 330,000 soldiers from Dunkirk. But more than 200,000 were left behind.

On the beaches, Jeremy Littlefield hides for his life. His path home will draw him through the iron will and the unbreakable heart of the French Resistance.

Only a few miles away, his brother, Lance, rallies fellow soldiers to start a trek that will take them across Europe, sabotaging the Germans in a mission tantamount to suicide.

Back in England, their sister Claire works at Bletchley Park, cracking the codes that could save the lives of her brothers, and thousands of their comrades.

Finally, there is Paul, the cerebral eldest son, working for MI-6, who always knows more than he is able to tell his beloved siblings.

Get your copy today at
severnriverbooks.com/series/after-dunkirk

JOIN THE READER LIST

Never miss a new release! Sign up to receive exclusive updates from author Lee Jackson.

Join today at
severnriverbooks.com/authors/lee-jackson

ACKNOWLEDGMENTS

I owe thanks to so many people who helped frame my books. In particular for this one, I must specifically express my gratitude to my stalwarts, John Shephard for keeping me on track, my sister Anita for reminding me to be sensitive, and my necessarily unnamed friend for paying attention to procedural and tactical detail. Beyond them are a host of people who contributed their insights. I am grateful to all of them.

ABOUT THE AUTHOR

Lee Jackson is the Wall Street Journal bestselling author of The Reluctant Assassin series and the After Dunkirk series. He graduated from West Point and is a former Infantry Officer of the US Army. Lee deployed to Iraq and Afghanistan, splitting 38 months between them as a senior intelligence supervisor for the Department of the Army. Lee lives and works with his wife in Texas, and his novels are enjoyed by readers around the world.

Sign up for Lee Jackson's newsletter at
severnriverbooks.com/authors/lee-jackson
LeeJackson@SevernRiverBooks.com

Made in the USA
Coppell, TX
07 October 2022